THE HAMMER OF GAUL

JAY ROBISON

THE HAMMER OF GAUL

Histria SciFi & Fantasy

Las Vegas ◇ Chicago ◇ Palm Beach

Published in the United States of America by
Histria Books
7181 N. Hualapai Way, Ste. 130-86
Las Vegas, NV 89166 USA
HistriaBooks.com

Histria SciFi & Fantasy is an imprint of Histria Books encompassing outstanding, innovative works in the genres of science fiction and fantasy. Titles published under the imprints of Histria Books are distributed worldwide.

This is a work of fiction. Names, characters, places, and incidents either are the product of the author's imagination or are used fictitiously, and any resemblance to actual persons, living or dead, business establishments, events, or locales is entirely coincidental.

ISBN 979-8-88860-181-5 (softbound)
ISBN 979-8-88860-180-8 (eBook)

CONTENTS

Pars Prima   vii

1. (56 Bce, Luca, Gallia Cisalpina)   1
2. (Ten Years From Now, Central Atlantic Ocean)   4
3. (Eastern Atlantic Ocean, June 2022)   13
4. (Pagus Mardani, Northern Gaul, 53 Bce)   19
5. (Central Gaul, 53 Bce)   32
6. (Northern Gallic Coast, 53 Bce)   38
7. (Pagus Mardani, Northern Gaul, 53 Bce)   44
8. (Pagus Mardani, Northern Gaul, 53 Bc)   55
9. (Pagus Mardani, Central Gaul, 53 Bce)   65
10. (Carrhae, Southeastern Asia Minor, 53 Bce)   73
11. (Pagus Mardani, Northern Gaul, 53 Bce)   77
12. (Morgennus, Northern Gaul, 53 Bce)   83
13. (Torbay, Cornwall, England, 1688 Ce)   94
    Pars Secunda   99
14. (Alesia, Central Gaul, 52 Bce)   100
15. (Pagus Mardani, 52 Bce)   109
16. (Seine River, Northern Gaul, 52 Bce)   122
17. (Alesia, Central Gaul, 52 Bce)   126
18. (Rome, Province Of Italia, 52 Bce)   137
19. (Alesia, Central Gaul, 52 Bce)   154
20. (Alesia, Central Gaul, 52 Bce)   167
21. (Alesia, Central Gaul, 52 Bce)   180
22. (Alesia, Central Gaul, 52 Bce)   194
    Pars Tertia   203
23. (Rome, Italia, 52 Bce)   204
24. (Bibracte, Central Gaul, Late 52 Bce)   218
25. (Bibracte, Central Gaul, 51 Bce)   232
26. (Bibracte, Central Gaul, 51 Bce)   243
27. (Aedui Territory, Eastern Gaul, 51 Bce)   250
28. (Bibracte, Central Gaul, 51 Bce)   260
29. (Bibracte, Central Gaul, 51 Bce)   269
30. (Bibracte, Central Gaul, 51 Bce)   276

31. (Bibracte, Central Gaul, 51 Bce)   286
   Epilogue   297

   Character List   301
   Glossary   305

PARS PRIMA

Omne initium novie ab alio principio
—Lucius Annaeus Seneca

1

(56 BCE, LUCA, GALLIA CISALPINA)

He watched as the three most powerful men in the world dined on course after course of the finest food in the world, chatting among themselves and occasionally deigning to notice the handful of people they'd allowed to come. The point of this meeting was for Gnaeus Pompey Magnus, Marcus Licinius Crassus and Gaius Julius Caesar to divvy up the Roman Republic among them, not to be flattered. But just a little flattery made them feel needed. They were the tripod upon which the Roman Republic rested, but tripods could be tricky things. Very stable...unless and until one leg was knocked out of alignment.

The man watching this triumvirate hold court was not a slave, but he faded into the background as well as any slave born. In looks, in social station, in almost any sense, the man known as Arminius Comedentis was utterly average. A gray man. The one area where he was not average, where he was decidedly above average, was brains. He was smart, and he knew it. For many invisible but smart people, particularly men, unrecognized genius caused rage. While this Gray Man had had his moments of that when he was younger, he'd found that embracing his averageness to be the key to satisfaction. It was an advantage.

Because he was so average, and could make himself so invisible, no one thought twice about speaking their most intimate secrets in his presence. And that suited Comedentis just fine. He collected secrets the way Crassus, it was said, collected gold. Working his way into Pompey's inner circle and gaining his ear had taken years and patience. A patient man, this bothered Comedentis not at all.

He felt someone brush his back. He didn't have to look to know who it was. Delfina was one of Pompey's household slaves, working mostly in the kitchen but adept enough to fill any role needed. Of late, she'd been filling the empty spot in Comedentis's bed. For all his grayness, people found Comedentis rather charming one on one. Especially women. Delfina had been a little girl when Pompey and his men routed the pirate base where she'd grown up. She tried swimming away, much to the Romans' amusement, and had been known as Delfina—the she-dolphin—ever since. Romans loved their clever nicknames. Comedentis's own name meant "eater" in Latin. Which suited him just fine. He was an eater—of secrets, of rumor and gossip. It also allowed him not to have to explain his birth name. Delfina was an inch or two shorter than himself, with skin the color of finely aged leather and just as supple. More importantly, she was not shy about sharing all the gossip and secrets she herself learned or heard from Pompey's other slaves. Comedentis kept promising to buy Delfina's freedom. She'd been such a valuable little spy he might even keep that promise. Someday.

"Who is the second-richest man in Rome?"

"I don't know," Delfina said. "But I'm sure you'll tell me."

"It's not difficult, dear Delfina. It's Crassus's latrine cleaner of course," said Comedentis, his face and tone completely serious.

Delfina wasn't stupid by any means, but Comedentis felt her intelligence was more of a base cunning than a strategic nature. Besides, deadpan humor was a yet to be discovered art. Turning to look at her, her face showed her effort to work out his logic. Her eyes widened and she grinned when she figured it out.

"Of course!" she said, trying to keep quiet. "It's because Crassus sh—"

"Indeed." Comedentis allowed himself a smirk.

"How long?" asked Delfina.

"How long till what?"

"How long till they turn on each other?"

Comedentis considered this. It was a remarkably shrewd question. He shrugged his shoulders. "Who knows? As long as all three live, I believe things will stay as they are. Should one die…"

"Then what?"

"Then, my little dolphin, a Rome big enough for three will suddenly become too small for two. Which one goes first, only Fortuna can say. Any of a hundred small things can end a man's life on any given day. We will need to do our best to ensure that Pompey ends up as the last man standing."

"Why?" Delfina all but spit on the floor. Obedient she may be, but Delfina had no love for her owner. "What's he done for us?"

"Why, nothing. Not really. But where I come from, there's a saying you might appreciate: 'The rising tide lifts all boats.' Like it or not our fortunes are linked to Pompey's. If he rises, so do we."

Delfina watched the triumvirs laughing over some no doubt inane joke. Catching a subtle signal from the head of the kitchens, Delfina sighed. "I will see you later," she said and gave him a quick but sensual kiss.

Comedentis edged a little closer, being careful to hear and observe. Who knew what valuable secrets would be his before the night was over?

2

(TEN YEARS FROM NOW, CENTRAL ATLANTIC OCEAN)

Wyatt Carver stood, waiting. He did not like to wait. He was not used to having to do it. Being one of the richest and most influential men in the world meant that others had to wait on him. That was how it worked. Wyatt Carver regularly made lists of the world's wealthiest people. The exact position depended on where the stock market was, and what the parameters the list-makers were using, but he was always in the top five, usually the top three.

Behind people like Wyatt Carver and the other flamboyant billionaires who regularly made "world's wealthiest" lists, there were others, families usually, whose wealth and influence were so great they were essentially invisible unless they chose not to be. The Schmitz family was one of those. Those few who'd heard about them whispered stories about how their wealth went back centuries, maybe millennia. One rather infamous conspiracy theorist claimed that the source of the Schmitz family fortune was the fabled lost treasure of the Knights Templar. Carver didn't know if that was true, nor did he really care. All he knew was that the Schmitz family was paying him a lot of money to amuse one of the few members of their clan with any kind of a public profile.

Taggart "Tagg" Schmitz was one of those people who fancied himself a deep thinker and great intellectual, though Carver hadn't been impressed when they'd met in person a few times previously. The man's mind was a mile wide and an inch deep. Apparently, the Schmitzes thought Tagg would be the perfect family candidate for a political career. Mile wide and inch deep Tagg's intellect might be, but that width—combined with a certain charisma—made him a favorite on the cable news circuit. Rumor had him up for Secretary of Commerce when the current secretary left, and no doubt things would take off from there. Tagg Schmitz fancied himself a man's man, in the mold of Teddy Roosevelt, so when word of Wyatt Carver's latest breakthrough got to the Schmitz powers-that-be, Tagg saw an opportunity to one-up his idol.

Carver tried, and failed, to keep his feet from tapping impatiently. Dr. Nicole Kapoor joined him, looking out at the vast and empty ocean.

"I've just gotten word. He's on his way. We should be getting a visual any time."

Carver sighed grumpily. "I don't recall you being demoted to message carrier. Where's Grayson?" Herman Grayson was Carver's right hand, his organizer. Some even called him the neck that moved the head—Carver—around.

"Grayson is making sure all the *t*'s are crossed and *i*'s dotted. He knows how important this is. I was coming here anyway; if this little stunt works and ends up with the Schmitzes owing us a favor, I'm hoping it will end up helping my own research."

"He should have been here an hour ago."

"Stop being such a grouch, Wyatt. The rich are different from you and me."

Carver couldn't help himself and barked with short, abrupt laughter. Kapoor's ironic quoting of Fitzgerald had its intended effect. After more waiting, they could finally make out Tagg Schmitz's superyacht on the horizon.

Wyatt Carver had made his fortune in batteries. As the demand for electric cars and other green energy solutions grew, so too did the need for more efficient and cheaper energy storage. Carver had finally cracked that nut and it had made him rich beyond the dreams of avarice, allowing him to turn his engineering and design genius to other problems that piqued his interest. His ongoing pet project was boreholes. He hoped to be the first person to drill all the way through the Earth's crust and into the mantle. He hadn't managed it yet but was getting close, and the project had produced numerous profitable spinoff technologies in drilling. It also was acting as proof of concept for less ambitious boreholes that would tap Earth's abundant geothermal energy, adding another arrow to the green energy quiver.

There was one spinoff Carver had kept a close secret. The Mohole 2 project had uncovered a few shards of highly exotic matter, stuff that had been theoretical and was thought to exist only in equally theoretical strange matter stars. Even now, after all that Carver had seen in the experiments he'd been quietly carrying out, he couldn't quite believe it. It was like being in a *Doctor Who* episode and he half expected a blue box to appear at any moment. Beyond a handful of physicists and Nicole Kapoor, who specialized in molecular genetics, no one knew. Not even the engineers working on the borehole. How the Schmitz clan had gotten word Carver didn't know. They were hundreds of miles from anywhere, and communications were closely monitored. He couldn't be too upset though, this little venture was burning through cash in amounts that even someone as wealthy as Carver found alarming. He was running out of funds he could spend without answering to his board of directors. If things worked maybe the bottomless well of money the Schmitzes controlled would solve that little problem. As Tagg Schmitz's football field–sized yacht docked with the platform, Wyatt Carver straightened his tie.

"Showtime."

Tagg Schmitz sipped appreciatively at his Scotch and looked around. "Nice setup you have here, Carver."

Wyatt put on his most sincere fake smile. "If I have to spend most of my time on this drilling rig, I might as well make it comfortable. Am I right?"

Schmitz laughed. "I suppose you are."

Carver and Schmitz made small talk about business and politics as aides flitted about, making sure all needs were being anticipated and met. Finally, Tagg got around to the point.

"I hear you can make my impossible dream come true," Schmitz said. "TR—Teddy Roosevelt," the man explained unnecessarily, "bagged himself some good trophies after he left the White House. But there was one animal even he could not possibly have gotten. Ever since I was a kid and watched *Jurassic Park* for the first time, I've wanted to hunt a tyrannosaurus. I hear tell you are the man to make it happen." He wasn't exaggerating when he talked of impossible dreams.

"If everything goes to plan I can at least set you on your way."

"Good, good. What should I know?"

Carver paused, then decided to be straightforward. "In some ways, your guess will be as good as mine. I'm assuming you've brought suitable equipment for your hunt?" Schmitz nodded. Carver continued. "We're in uncharted territory here. We're going to load you and your party up with wide-spectrum antibiotics and a new wide-spectrum antiviral that we developed, but beyond that, you're going to be our eyes and ears."

"I'd like to know how you can pull this off. Not that I doubt you believe you can do it. Gramma is tighter than a nervous virgin when it comes to spending her own money and I know what she's paid you. But I'll be taking the actual risk."

"It's complicated. Beyond the leading edge of theoretical physics. Essentially, we'll be creating a wormhole to the Triassic era and send you and your team through it."

Schmitz frowned. "I won't, like, change history, will I? What if I accidentally step on a bug or something and come back to find apes or birds or killer crabs ruling Earth?"

Carver smiled, a little indulgently. "As I mentioned in the packet I sent to you and your grandmother, you *will* be going back in time. But not in our universe. Any changes you make won't affect your personal past, or the past of anyone here."

"So...I'll be going back in time, but to a parallel universe?"

Carver was impressed. Maybe the man wasn't as dumb as he looked.

"Yes, that's pretty much it. We've been able to investigate, even access, what most people would call parallel universes. We've even found one that's virtually identical to our own and had success looking at different time periods. Effectively, we can send you back in time, just not in our own reality."

Tagg Schmitz nodded and looked like he truly understood what Carver was saying. Maybe he did. Looking shrewd, he asked Carver, "As our great President Reagan was fond of saying, 'Trust but verify.' I trust you, but can you verify?"

Carver smiled. Verify? I'll show you verify, he thought to himself. "Mr. Schmitz, if you'll follow me, I'll be happy to show you something you'll never forget."

NICOLE KAPOOR LOOKED up when Carver entered what she thought of as "the aviary," a converted lab. The male bird not only noticed but was vocal in his displeasure that his peace had been disturbed. From the smug look on Wyatt's face Tagg Schmitz's reaction was exactly what he'd been hoping for.

"Are those..." Schmitz was so slack jawed he could hardly speak.

"They are," Carver said. "The only living dodo birds seen in about 500 years. Proof that we can not only look at parallel universes but interact with them. We accidentally opened a passage, and this pair came through."

Schmitz tried to recover and look shrewd. He didn't entirely succeed.

"How do I know they aren't clones? I've heard about that stuff. There's a lab in China trying to clone mammoths."

"That's a good question, Mr. Schmitz," Nicole said.

"Ah, Dr. Kapoor. I was hoping to get to see you again." Schmitz smiled at her. Nicole was a little impressed he remembered her. No wonder his family had picked him for a career in politics.

"Yes, I apologize. My presence was required here. As I said, you ask a good question. There have been attempts to clone dodo birds. I even worked briefly on one attempt. However, no complete preserved specimen exists and the little bit of soft tissue from the birds that are still available have DNA that's too degraded to be viable for cloning. We've been able to tell dodos were members of the pigeon family and a few other things but that's about it. I have some friends from that old cloning project, and I'd be happy to refer you to them if you wish to verify this."

Schmitz held up his hands in a gesture of mock surrender. "No, that will not be necessary. I believe you." He took a couple of steps toward the dodos' enclosure but stopped when the male started squawking and puffing himself up.

"You'll have to forgive Maurice here," Carver said. "His mate is sitting on a clutch of eggs and he's quite protective. Perhaps we should leave them in peace."

"Of course. Maybe when I come back from my hunt, we can talk price. Wouldn't mind having one of these in my collection either."

"We can talk of course," Carver said, before Nicole could voice any objection. "For now, we'll get you and your people settled in and make sure everything's in place for your...safari."

THE PREPARATIONS WYATT CARVER spoke of took a couple of weeks. Tagg Schmitz alternately fished and made a nuisance of himself, while his team—mostly burly South Africans along with a Vietnamese jungle guide—kept to themselves. At last, though, everything was in place. Schmitz and his team stepped into the room. Schmitz looked around. He seemed a little disappointed. It was a nondescript room with a clear area in front of two rows of long desks and a handful of computer terminals.

"I thought it would be more...exciting," he said.

"I thought about adding some Van de Graaf generators to add atmosphere but was talked out of it," said Carver with his most sincere fake laugh. "Seriously though, I know it always looks more thrilling in the movies but all we need are a few desks and workstations. The hardware that will open the wormhole is built into the structure of the room. Now, if you'll just step this way..." Carver ushered the men to one side.

"What do we do now?" Schmitz asked.

"You wait," Carver said.

"Wait for what?"

"You'll know."

Two of his staff physicists were already at their stations. Carver sat down at his own terminal. He would be monitoring readings and energy levels and knew enough about how everything worked to be able to help if needed. Nicole sat next him, finger pressing on the earpiece she wore. It would be her job to alert them if anything outside the lab threatened the operation.

For the first few minutes, nothing much happened. Nothing visible anyway. A hum, barely audible at first, began to fill the room. Then the air at the front of the lab, a few steps from where Schmitz and his team stood, began to shimmer. Except it wasn't the air. The fabric of reality itself was shimmering. Warping. Unraveling, ever so slowly and ever so gently.

Nicole pressed the earpiece into her ear harder, as if she was trying to hear something that wasn't quite coming through. An image was beginning to form in the widening hole between universes, like an old-style scrambled cable TV channel.

"Wyatt, I'm getting reports of a power surge. Should we abort?"

"We're almost there. Almost..."

There was a soundless flash. The Mohole 2 platforms were engulfed by a purple-black cloud. The duty officer on a US Navy destroyer in the area described it as looking like a tumor. What they did not know, would not ever know, was that the power surge resulted in a hole being punched in space-time itself by excited fragments of exotic matter and setting off a storm—a time storm. The mysterious cloud lingered over the site for months. Several reconnaissance drones were sent in and were lost as soon as they crossed into the cloud bank. When the cloud finally dissipated there was no trace of Mohole 2 or any of its personnel. At least, no trace that any authorities on the planet would ever be able to find.

This "time storm" was not limited to the middle of the Atlantic Ocean. Space-time fractures opened throughout the continuum, much as a bullet hole in glass will cause a spiderweb of fractures away from the hole itself.

In July 1937, aviator Amelia Earhart and her navigator Fred Noonan, on course for a refueling stop on tiny Howland Island in the South Pacific, encountered an unexplained front of purple-black clouds extending all the way down to the ocean's surface. Low on fuel, they could not fly over or around it. Bracing herself, Earhart flew through it. Her last contact was a few garbled radio transmissions. The *USS Itasca*, on station at Howland to assist Earhart, wrongly assumed that she and Noonan had had to ditch their aircraft on a nearby atoll. No conclusive trace of Earhart, Noonan, or their Lockheed Electra airplane was ever found.

In May 2024, an unexplained and highly localized weather event appeared over southeastern Turkey during a NATO military exercise code-named "Crimson Sword." A US Marines FA-18 fighter-bomber narrowly avoided the phenomenon; two French aircraft—a reconnaissance plane and a Mirage 2000D fighter jet—were reported lost, as were a small number of personnel playing as part of the opposition force in the exercise.

Nor were these fissures confined to Earth's present or recent past. A test of an experimental unmanned vehicle in 2103 failed when the craft mysteriously disappeared. Unbeknownst to the operators, the craft crashed near Roswell, New Mexico, in 1947. In the fall of 1688, a country vicar near the Cornish port town of Torbay took a walk with his baby daughter, his mind troubled by rumors of a coming uprising against King James II as well as grief over the recent loss of his wife. An exhaustive search of the surrounding area the next day turned up no traces, and the disappearance of Rev. Steadfast Cooper became a local legend. Roughly a century before that, the pitiful survivors of the Roanoke Colony in North America left to hopefully find shelter with the nearby Croatoan natives. The English colonists never made it. Later accounts from a handful of Croatoans of a strange purple fog were dismissed as superstitious nonsense.

And then, there was Dr. David Castellanos and his nephew Kevin Rhee-Castellanos. They were sailing from New York City to Cherbourg, France. The winds had been excellent and from what David could tell, they would arrive in Cherbourg ahead of schedule.

When the *Stork* was reported three days late in Cherbourg, the Castellanos family and the group of doctor's charities coordinating medical aid for the current refugee crisis used all their resources to start a massive search. It turned up nothing. Dr. David Castellanos and Kevin Rhee-Castellanos were declared missing, but their family adamantly refused to believe they were dead.

3

(EASTERN ATLANTIC OCEAN, JUNE 2022)

The sailing ship *Stork* had had favorable winds and smooth seas for three weeks. Dr. David Castellanos finished his calculations, then checked them against his GPS. They were right on course. He glanced back at his nephew Kevin, hunched over some diagrams. He was trying to restore an old Victrola he'd picked up at a flea market before they left. The Atlantic had been calm so far, but it was still the Atlantic. It was probably never going to be smooth enough for him to put the old record player back together and get it working.

David was a physician, an obstetrician-gynecologist. His plan was to sail to Cherbourg, France, where he would meet up with friends who would be donating their medical talents to aid refugees from the latest crisis. The European Union, with agreement from Britain, was setting up temporary camps on a few small islands just outside the Straits of Gibraltar. The islands themselves were little more than rocky outcroppings in the middle of the ocean. Airstrips were being set up but for now they were most accessible by sea. A flotilla was being organized that would sail from Cherbourg down the French and Spanish coasts that would deliver food, shelter, and medical supplies and staff. In addition to English, David was fluent in Spanish and Arabic—thanks to being the son of a Cuban chef and an Egyptian musician. He could get by in French as long as things didn't get too technical. His language skills were almost as attractive as his medical credentials.

David had always wanted to make a sailing trip like this, and a recent bad breakup had only increased that desire. David's parents had instilled a strong sense of public service in him and his brother and sister. He did free clinic work but the pictures and news coverage of starving and battered men, women and children being pulled from the sea had pulled at him. He needed to get away, and this would allow him to do that while serving a worthy cause.

David's nephew Kevin Rhee-Castellanos was a late addition to the trip, but David was glad for the company. Kevin and his mother Anne were defectors, escaping North Korea and finding asylum in the United States. Kevin was only about six at the time. After being settled in the US, David's father had given Anne a job as a line cook at his restaurant. Anne and David's sister Samara had fallen in love and married, and Samara had adopted Kevin. David loved being a "cool uncle" and Kevin was a good kid, but he had a lack of focus that worried David. Kevin was almost 20, and a post-high school gap year was now gap *years*, plural. Kevin was good with computer systems and an inveterate tinkerer. He could make old things work like new. David hoped the experience would help Kevin find some direction. He heard a frustrated sigh.

"You'll get it working. Be grateful that the seas have been smooth enough to let you work on it as much as you have. That's pretty unusual for the Atlantic," David said.

"I know," Kevin said. "I'm so close I can taste it. There's something wrong with the speed governor. Cab Calloway sounds like Alvin and the Chipmunks doing jazz."

"I'm surprised you're this close, given the state it was in. What'd it set you back, 20 bucks?"

"Thirty-five," Kevin said. "And I only paid that much because the body and the horn were still in good shape. Found a tone arm in good condition and figured I could machine the guts. Which I did. But something's off with the mechanism that governs how fast the turntable moves. And what do you mean, you're surprised I'm this close? The car was a lot tougher, and I got it running better than new."

Kevin had saved up money for a car and settled on a '62 Studebaker GT Hawk. That had been his first big "fixer upper" project. Much like the Victrola, the body had been in great shape, the engine and transmission not so much, though the engine had been salvageable at least and Kevin had gotten a good deal on a rebuilt transmission. His classmates had teased him quite a bit over buying a 50-year-old car...until its V8 engine outclassed a brand-new Dodge Avenger in a drag race. David knew his nephew had gotten into some hot water over that little stunt, but he'd made his point.

Kevin rolled up the Victrola diagrams and stared into the middle distance. "What's that?"

"What's what?" David asked.

"That." Kevin pointed.

David followed where his nephew pointed. It took him a moment, but then he could see it too. Strange wisps of what seemed to be fog, about one or two nautical miles straight ahead of them. It was hard to tell from this distance, but David could swear the fog had an almost lavender color to it.

"What is it, you think?" Kevin asked.

"Probably just regular fog—maybe there's something on the water giving it that weird color. Still, it's not the right time of day or conditions for fog." If it was early morning, or if the temperature was rising or falling rapidly, that would be one thing. But none of those conditions applied just now. David said nothing to Kevin but there was something about this that just didn't feel right. "Tell you what," he said, "let me get on the horn and see if there's anyone else in the area and what they think."

Selecting a band reserved for non-emergency but potentially urgent communications, David keyed his mic and spoke.

"This is *SV Stork* enroute to Cherbourg," David said, adding his current location. "I have eyes on a weather phenomenon I'm not familiar with. If there are other ships in the area that are seeing this and are familiar, please advise."

After a moment David got a response. "Stork this is the *USNS Barton*. We're about 50 nautical miles south southeast of your reported position. Can you describe what you're seeing?"

The *USNS Clara Barton* was a United States Navy hospital ship, a new one. If he had to guess, the vessel was doing the same thing he was—assisting the burgeoning refugee crisis. David described the rapidly expanding fog bank, which had turned from lavender to purple black. David had had Kevin cut the sails and he was trying to run parallel, but the prevailing winds were pushing the water—and the *Stork*—right toward whatever this was.

"*Stork*, *Barton*. We have no visual in your area, but our radar is showing fair skies and smooth sailing in your area. Suggest you try to avoid...-nomena..." Suddenly there was a lot of static on the line as the leading edge of the fog bank was almost to the *Stork*'s bow.

"*Barton*, *Stork*. Please repeat. You're breaking up."

Any response from the *Barton* was too garbled for David to understand. Kevin stood behind him, looking terrified as the fog began sweeping lengthwise across the sailboat. He saw his nephew grip the edge of the navigation station.

What happened next would be forever hard for David to describe. The nearest thing he could compare it to would be the sensation he felt once watching a 3-D screening of an action movie when there was a scene showing the pilot's view of a diving airplane. David's stomach had lurched as if he too were diving. He felt something like that now. He looked up at his nephew. Kevin looked ghostly pale, as if he were going to be sick.

And then...it was over. The fog lifted and once again the sky was clear and moderate steady winds out of the west picked back up. Kevin still looked unsettled, but he was getting his color back.

"Uhhh...that was weird."

"Let's furl the sails. I'll try to raise the *Barton* or maybe the French Coast Guard and figure out what just happened."

Kevin nodded, looking calmer now that he had something else to focus on. The two of them furled the sails. The ship would still drift eastward, there was no help for it. The ocean was far too deep here for them to anchor. But until David knew what they'd just sailed through he was going to play it safe. "It's probably nothing" were the last words of more boat skippers than anyone could count. David cycled through several bands used for general marine communication but got nothing but static. GPS was down as well, and the satellite phone was showing no signal.

David grumbled. "What the actual hell?"

"What?" Kevin asked.

"I'm not getting anything. No radio, no GPS, no satphone. Bupkis. Thoughts?"

Aside from tinkering on old machinery, Kevin had a great interest —if not an obsession—with internet rabbit holes. Nothing harmful like violent conspiracy theories. His current fixation was time slips as an explanation for a whole host of unsolved mysteries, disappearances mostly. Before that it had been doomsday scenarios.

"Hmm. The communications and GPS going down suddenly might suggest an EMP," Kevin said.

"EMP?"

"Eee em pee," Kevin said. "Electromagnetic pulse? Geez, Unc, read some science besides medicine sometime. It's a pulse that overloads and fries anything with electronics beyond vacuum tubes."

David thought for a moment. "Like that thing they used in *Ocean's Eleven*?"

"The original with the Rat Pack is better. But yes, more or less. Except we're talking about something a lot stronger. Could come from a big solar flare, or God forbid, a big nuke in the upper atmosphere."

"Sounds grim. I'm sensing a 'but.'"

"Well...if it was an EMP our electronics would be dead. Like, scrap. They're not though. They're working, still drawing power from the solar cells. It's just as if they're not receiving anything. I'll run a diagnostic, see if it's some fault in the electronics or maybe a software bug or something."

"Sounds good. I'll figure out our coordinates. The old-fashioned way." Kevin wasn't the only person in the family with a fascination for old technology and methods. David had a replica sextant and an antique British Navy marine chronometer his own uncle Daoud had given him before Daoud had traveled to Antarctica to climb Vinson Massif. He hadn't returned from the trip.

"I've never understood why you calculate position the old-fashioned way, Uncle David."

"Says the man who is resurrecting a century-old record player. Look, electronics can fail, but the sun and stars are forever. And that chronometer is even older than your victrola and will go another two hundred years as long as nothing happens to it."

David took the measurements and calculated the coordinates. While not as pinpoint accurate as GPS, the sextant and chronometer had been correct to within a mile or less of his GPS coordinates. David had made something of a game of deriving their position on their trip, so he was confident their latitude and longitude would be spot on now. From what he could tell, they hadn't moved appreciably. Kevin reported that his diagnostic hadn't found anything either. As far as their radio and satellite receivers were concerned, everything was working perfectly. David kept trying to raise the French Coast Guard, the *Barton* or any other nearby vessel but had no success.

"What do we do, Uncle David?"

"Unfurl the sails and keep heading for Cherbourg. Maybe even Brest; it's closer. It's the only thing we can do. We're too far from New York to sail back there, assuming we could even make headway against the prevailing winds. Let's get to a safe port. We'll figure out what happened soon enough." Kevin nodded his agreement. What other choice did they have?

4

(PAGUS MARDANI, NORTHERN GAUL, 53 BCE)

It was a bright and pleasant early summer day. Livilla worked in companionable silence with Matwyn nearby. "Mother" Matwyn as most called her. She was the wise woman healer of their little village, so little it didn't really have its own name. The Romans called it *Pagus Mardani*, literally "the hamlet of the Mardani." Livilla's own people just called it "home," or "the village" in their own language. Of course, the Mardani themselves weren't a numerous or powerful people. For most of Livilla's life they'd been living a precarious existence on a small slice of territory near the sea between the far more powerful Veneti and Lexovii tribes. They had one fortified town, Mortorgenn, which the Romans called Morgennus and referred to as an *oppidum*. Livilla was wary of the Romans despite being half-Roman herself. Her father, Gaius Ferrarius, had fled during Cornelius Sulla's dictatorship and the constant proscriptions of so-called enemies. Ferrarius himself was too minor a figure to merit attention from the powerful, but all it really took to be punished or killed as an enemy of the Roman Republic was a jealous rival. Ferrarius had plenty of those and had made armor and swords for the forces of Sulla's opponent, Gaius Marius, making him a tempting target for someone with a grudge.

So Ferrarius ran away and settled among the Mardani, who welcomed his skills. This little unnamed village had attracted numerous strays, including Livilla's own mother Livia, and Livia's father Sevel, the village mystic. According to stories Livilla heard growing up, Sevel and young Livia were found wandering the coast of Britannia by Mardani traders, out of his head and ranting in a strange language none of them could understand. Somewhat to the surprise of the trading party he could speak Latin after a fashion and Sevel was persuaded to return with the traders where he learned Mardani and adjusted to life among them. He became a spiritual guide, a seer of sorts. It had been Sevel who'd convinced their chief, Borodur, to ally with the Romans when their Veneti cousins rose against the expanding Republic. Livilla wasn't naïve enough to believe their small body of slingers had tipped the war in the Romans' favor, but Sevel had said that the Romans—especially their leader Gaius Julius Caesar—would have long memories as to who their friends were and who kept their word when they sued for peace. This Caesar person seemed inclined to be merciful, but only once. More than one story of a tribe that had broken a peace treaty with Caesar and his legions had circulated to their remote territory. Even if the rebel tribes won an initial victory, rebellion inevitably ended the same for them all: in slavery and execution. Usually on the crosses the Romans seemed to favor for executing traitors. Caesar may be willing to show mercy once, but twice? Never.

Livilla looked up from the herbs she'd been busily grinding into a powder. She would make the mixture into a soothing, warming poultice for her father's arms and shoulders. Ferrarius was one of the strongest men in Mardani territory and still vigorous in his middle age, but Livilla knew that years of beating iron into swords and tools for his adopted people was taking its toll. Though he rarely complained, Livilla knew her father was feeling aches in his muscles and bones much more these days.

Matwyn showed her how to mix a poultice that sent heat into sore muscles, promoting healing and lessening the minor aches and pains of age. Matwyn would know all about the aches and pains of age. It was said that not only was Matwyn the oldest person of the Mardani, but that even the Veneti and Lexovii had no one older among them. Matwyn herself couldn't count her years, only saying that when Ramira and Bennozha gave birth it would be her fifth generation. The wise woman was sure Ramira would deliver her child before the next full moon, though given the size of her belly Livilla wouldn't be surprised if it was sooner than that. Bennozha still had a month or two before her time came. Bennozha was another adopted stray. She'd been found as a young girl in a strange boat with a woman presumed to be her mother. The woman was near death and never recovered, and the girl was too young to be able to say her name so when she was adopted into the tribe, she was given the name "Bennozha," meaning gift. Bennozha's raven-black hair and copper-colored skin made her stand out among the pale Mardani.

"Grind those any finer and they'll be dust, girl," said Matwyn.

Livilla smiled at the old woman. "You're right. That's what I get for being lost in my thoughts."

"Oh? Thinking of Kellax? He's feasting with the gods, dearie, though I'm sure he's pleased if you're sending him fond thoughts."

Kellax was her husband, late-husband rather. He'd been a sweet young man, eager to please but lacking in ambition. When he did get a burst of motivation it was impulsive and not well thought out. His last such impulse was his decision to volunteer as an auxiliary for Caesar's expedition to Britannia last year. He would, he promised, earn his fortune in spoils, and give Livilla the life he said she deserved. In the end he hadn't even died in battle; a minor wound festered and Kellax had succumbed to the infection.

"No, I wasn't thinking of him, not really," Livilla said. "I was thinking about Ramira and Bennozha. What it must be like for them, knowing they will soon be mothers."

"Ah," said Matwyn. "A little jealous, perhaps?"

Livilla smiled again, this time a little sadly. "A little. I'd hoped Kellax would leave me with a child before he left, but it seems his seed was as ambitious as he was."

Matwyn cackled like a mad hen, something she only did when

she was truly amused. "There's ways around that, daughter. I know how many invitations you've turned down since learning of Kellax's death. Though if you could get pregnant from your own fingers, you'd have a whole brood."

Livilla blushed. She had not been entirely celibate in the last year but the encounters she'd chosen to have had been few and far between. It wasn't from a lack of desire. Her body certainly wanted her to sleep with someone and finger work was only satisfying to a point. Something held her back that she could not quite define beyond a vague sense that there was something—someone—else for her, someone yet to come.

"True, Mother Matwyn, true. It's just never seemed quite right. It's not even grief for Kellax. I did feel great affection for him, even convinced myself I loved him, but I don't know. I miss him but I don't feel as sad as I should."

"Hmm," the old woman said, as if something she'd long suspected had been confirmed. "Livilla, you feel what you feel. There is no 'right' or 'wrong.' I'd had my reservations about your match with Kellax, but he was a good man and treated you well, so I kept those reservations to myself. I will only say what I told you when you first came into your womanhood: You will know your husband when you meet him."

"But when will that be?"

"The gods alone know. Perhaps at an auspicious time I'll lead you in beseeching the Benevolent Mother for an answer. I only know what I feel—he will come to you, and you will know. Until then, I will continue to train you. I've trained a fair few people in healing arts and you're one of the most promising students I've ever had. Come, let's get this poultice mixed for your father. I've a feeling there's some cold and damp weather coming, and it'll make his aches worse."

KEVIN RHEE-CASTELLANOS SAT ALONE on the deck of the *Stork* in the twilight. He'd been trying to read but found he couldn't concentrate.

That was okay. It's not like he hadn't read the pamphlet in his hands a dozen times already. The weather had gone from pleasant to chilly and misty in the last day or so and Kevin breathed into his hands to warm them. He needed the fresh air. He pulled the wool cardigan Uncle David had knitted for him a little tighter and hoped that by the time the chill drove him back below deck his uncle would either be asleep or in a better mood. His Uncle David was one of the most mild-mannered, even-tempered people he knew. They still had heat and light thanks to the solar cells on the roof of the boat, but after a week of no functioning communications or electronic navigation aids, with only David's sextant and chronometer to give them their latitude and longitude, they were both getting jumpy. For Uncle David, that meant getting unusually short-tempered and irritable.

Kevin had his own theory of the case, as it were. Ever since he'd been old enough to start exploring the internet, not long after his mother's marriage to Samara Castellanos and his adoption by her at age nine, he'd been fascinated by stories of unsolved mysteries and unexplained phenomena. He stayed away from the truly toxic and violent conspiracy theories, but anything that seemed to defy explanation was catnip to Kevin. The spookier the better. His latest obsession was time slips. He'd started exploring that particular rabbit hole after reading a slender book—pamphlet really—that his moms had brought back from a trip to England about a year ago. They'd tacked on a vacation in Cornwall to a restaurant business conference in London, staying in the seaside town of Torbay. They'd found the book, formidably titled "Thee Mysterious Dis-Appearance of One Reverend Steadfaste Cooper, Vicar" in a tiny used book shop housed in a cottage on the seaside near their bed and breakfast. The pamphlet dated from the late 19th century but was itself apparently a reproduction of a pamphlet that had been circulating in the area since the early 1700s. According to the pamphlet, a country vicar by the name of Steadfast Cooper had taken his young daughter Bess on an evening walk in the fall of 1688. Rev. Cooper was not only troubled by rumors that forces would land nearby with the object of over-throwing King James II and VII Stuart of England and Scotland but also the recent loss of his wife to a mysterious fever. According to locals at the time, it had been a misty evening but not so much so that someone familiar with the area—as Rev. Cooper was, according to everyone in the village—would have lost their way. An extensive search turned up no traces or remains. One of the local nobles had even offered a notorious poacher amnesty if he would assist the search; alas, even the man who "knew if a Ghoste had wiped his arse six months prior in the Woode" was unable to find any signs of the vicar anywhere.

Kevin had been intrigued enough to start researching and see if there were any similar accounts anywhere. That's when he found out about time slips. There were some that were obvious hoaxes or delusions, but one early discussion board he found on an obscure corner of the web asserted that the craft that crashed at Roswell in 1947 was neither an alien spacecraft nor the advanced weather balloon that the Army claimed it was in official stories of the day. No, this person, who went by the *nom de net* Aria51Baritone, asserted that the conflicting stories amounted to a double-fake on the part of the American government, to draw attention away from the fact that craft was human, but from the future. To bolster their case, Aria51Baritone pointed to some documents they'd obtained containing eyewitness accounts of the Roswell UFO tumbling out of a purplish cloud bank before crashing, and that upon investigation the strange script described by the first people on the scene were an odd dialect of English. One that had been simplified and had strong influence from Spanish and Mandarin Chinese. Kevin had his doubts as to the authenticity of Aria51Baritone's documents but thought they made a compelling case.

He'd investigated other supposed cases as well, especially the disappearance of Amelia Earhart and the famous Flight 19, lost in the Bermuda Triangle. He wasn't sure about those. There'd been a few others, though, local legends mostly, that had the appearance of purple-black fog in common. As he reviewed his own circumstances, Kevin was convinced that he and his uncle had moved in time if not space. Uncle David was having none of it. Ever the man of science,

David insisted there was a rational explanation for everything and that they'd figure it all out and have a good laugh over drinks at a wine bar in Cherbourg. Kevin had stuck to his guns, and they'd had a pretty serious argument over it. The breaking point was over the pole star. Uncle David was the astronomy nerd in the family. He often said that astronomy and sailing went hand in hand and even Kevin knew that Polaris, within a degree of the celestial north pole, would mark latitude between the Earth's north pole and equator. Except that Polaris didn't seem to be the pole star. According to Uncle David's own observations a dimmer star in Ursa Major, called Kochab, appeared closer to the celestial north pole than Polaris. David had been irritated; sure he'd made some sort of mistake in his observations, and had lost his temper when Kevin argued that they'd been displaced in time. David had ended the fight by saying he didn't want to hear the phrase "time slip" again and stomped off to his cabin. Kevin retreated to the deck to collect his thoughts and calm down in the cool night air.

It was all so obvious, he thought. Here they were, anchored in a cove on what the sun, moon and stars all asserted was the northwest coast of France. But there was no evidence of civilization, no electric lights and all the radio bands had been dead silent. Kevin had thought he saw something that looked like a square-sailed longboat in the far distance. His uncle had dismissed that as a *fata morgana*, a mirage or reflection of something on the ocean beyond the visible horizon. A trick of the light essentially. Kevin wasn't so sure. His uncle had been making noises about electromagnetic pulses, something Kevin had dismissed almost immediately. An EMP would have fried their electronics, all of which were still functioning. And they would have seen signs of civilization this close to the French coast, which they had not so far. Kevin thought of the famous dictum of Sherlock Holmes: When everything has been eliminated what remains, however improbable, is the truth.

Eventually Kevin did go back below deck, but he didn't feel sleepy, so he sat in a chair in the "living room" (he wasn't sure what the correct nautical term was) and alternated between reading and quietly strumming on his guitar. He didn't remember falling asleep during one of his reading stretches but awoke to his uncle gently shaking his shoulder. Kevin felt stiff and grimy.

"Hey. Good morning," David said. "Sorry about last night. I absolutely hate it when things don't work for no reason. I hate things I can't explain in general. When a doctor can't explain something it's usually bad for everyone. None of this is your fault and I shouldn't be taking it out on you."

"That's OK," Kevin said.

"No, it's not, and I will try to do better. Now, let's get some coffee and set our sails to run north." Uncle David looked at the dreary weather outside. It seemed closer to early spring weather than early summer weather to Kevin, but for all that didn't look especially threatening. Though with the radio not receiving anything they couldn't get a weather forecast. That worried Kevin and Kevin knew it worried Uncle David even more. When Kevin had asked to come with him on this trip, David had been very clear to him, and to his mothers. While modern technology made this kind of voyage a lot safer than it would have been even just a few years ago, it wasn't without risk. Even with radio, GPS and satellite phones, the unknown always lurked. The problem was that on this side of the mysterious fog bank the universe of unknowns seemed a hell of a lot bigger.

The skies stayed sullen gray but otherwise the weather held. They made good speed and toward the end of the day reached the tip of the Cotenin Peninsula that jutted into the English Channel, where Cherbourg Harbor should be. Should be but wasn't. David stared blankly; incomprehension clear on his face. What the hell were they going to do now?

Mother Matwyn had been correct about the coming weather. That surprised Livilla not at all, for Mother Matwyn was correct about most things most of the time. Most of the Mardani and their non-Mardani near-neighbors attributed this to mystical powers. Matwyn didn't exactly discourage these rumors, but to Livilla at least the old wise woman never claimed any special powers. She remembered something she'd told her early on when she was just starting to learn healing traditions.

"As life goes on, you start to learn what clues and signs can mean —if you pay attention to what the world is telling you. It's experience, that's all. Now, if you're going to say that my long life and ability to pay attention are gifts from the gods, I won't argue. But all I can say is more people have those gifts than they realize. They just choose not to use them."

What Matwyn had said made a lot of sense to Livilla. It's not that Livilla didn't believe in the gods, but she'd long felt people were all too willing to ascribe events to divine judgement or action when they were too lazy to just think. Most phenomena had understandable explanations, if you just paid attention and used your brains, Livilla thought. Still, she'd seen a few things from the old woman—and her grandfather Sevel as well—that made her think they both had at least a touch of the divine. Not that Sevel had been giving anyone demonstrations of his divine power or anything else the last few days. He'd been refusing to leave his small hut. Livilla had been worried that her grandfather was sick, until Matwyn told her that he was physically healthy but just "in a mood." Occasionally he got that way, usually when he sensed a big event was coming. She was sure Matwyn had things in hand and would ask for her help if needed.

It was chilly, almost cold even, for early summer. Livilla had been able to see her breath when she'd woken up just before sunrise. Now that the sun was finally peeking over the horizon, the rest of the village was starting to stir.

She was surprised to hear hoofbeats. Livilla turned to see Borodur, Mardani chief and war leader, riding toward her. "War leader" was a bit grandiose but it was one of the tribal leader's traditional titles. The Mardani weren't powerful enough to seek war; at most they engaged in raids that their neighbors more or less chose to ignore as long as there were no serious injuries or damage. Livilla never really understood the point of raiding. Her father said that men needed an outlet sometimes but that didn't change her opinion that raids, even sanctioned ones, were risky and ridiculous and not worth it.

"Ah, Livilla. You're a welcome sight this morning. Everyone else are being lazy layabouts I see." Borodur said this with a grin. He was serious when he had to be but was otherwise easygoing and good-humored. He ruled by charisma and persuasion rather than bullying and force, though it helped that Borodur was bigger than anyone else, even Ferrarius. He was still handsome too, though some gray was starting to show through his chestnut-colored hair and beard. Livilla supposed that if she were ten years older she'd be one of the women panting after the chief. Though his devotion to his wife was well known, Borodur had several concubines as befit a man of his stature. As it was, Livilla viewed the chief as a favorite uncle and not an object of attraction. She wondered why he was here so early. He must have left Mortorgenn when it was just light enough to ride safely. Not that the chief was a stranger to his people, but he'd been spending a lot more time in the oppidum of late. Between the Romans' more aggressive expansion and the increasing restlessness of their more powerful neighbors, most of Borodur's time was taken up with affairs of leadership.

"Just because you're up early doesn't mean everyone else is lazy, Borodur. Besides, you can't fool me, this is no social call. Nothing serious, I hope? Should I get Father or Matwyn?"

"I will want to talk to them, but no it's not serious. Not in the way you're probably thinking anyway. A whale, a huge one, has beached itself and it will take all hands to butcher and process the meat once it dies. I've even sent out runners to some of the Veneti clans nearby. I'd invite the Romans' area garrison but they're at least a day away."

"What about the ones in Mortorgenn?" There was a tiny, token garrison of ten men staying in the hill fort, under the command of a very young junior *quaestor*, not even as old as Livilla herself. Her father taught her about Roman society to the extent he was able. A quaestor dealt with matters of money and financing and a certain number of them were elected yearly for the Republic. In the army, they would oversee a legion's finances. Normally, such a junior officer would assist a legion's paymaster, but Caesar had left a token force after subduing the Veneti and the general left in charge when the proconsul had departed on yet another campaign decided to parcel out his men in small packets throughout the region. Ferrarius had explained that the general assumed, probably correctly, that if the Veneti or anyone else in the area decided on another rebellion that less than a legion of Romans wouldn't stand a real chance. This way, if things went badly, at least a small body could escape and bring more substantial reinforcements. If things went well, there would be a constant reminder that the Romans were watching. Given that the harvests were shaping up to be very poor this summer the scattered Roman legionaries would be easier to feed. The Romans staying at Mortorgenn seemed friendly at least. The assistant quaestor nominally in charge, Chlorus, had taken a very willing Bennozha as a lover and was the presumed father of her unborn child.

Borodur shrugged his shoulders. "Chlorus is from a noble family, the Romans' version of it anyway, so he probably considers such work beneath him and not worth trying to force his men into doing. I'm sure the only reason he's in charge is to give him an easy accomplishment. It's not like I plan to cause trouble."

"You could always tell him Bennozha will be there. If it helps, tell him she'll be there naked."

Borodur snorted. "No, though it's for the girl's sake, sweet young thing. I'm surprised he got her pregnant. If it weren't for the fact I knew Chlorus was Bennozha's first and only I'd never believe it. The kid probably just got his first hairs the day before yesterday."

Livilla laughed, knowing exactly which hairs Borodur meant, then nodded toward Matwyn, hobbling out of her hut. "Matwyn's up. I'll go wake father and we'll have everyone meet you." After Borodur told her where the beached whale was, she went off to wake her father and then rouse the rest of the village. This was good news. Their village did little more than subsistence farming; they raised sheep for wool and meat and did some fishing. But it was clear the weather would be cool and damp and the harvest would be poor. The

Mardani didn't hunt whales, it was considered far too dangerous, but they took full advantage when one of the mighty beasts beached themselves. Just one of the creatures would feed them and keep them in oil for years. Hope the Romans liked whale meat, Livilla thought, because that was going to be their food supply from the Mardani.

She went to her and her father's hut and found him already awake and getting dressed. She told him about the whale, and he grunted in answer before going outside to use the latrine shared with their neighbors. Livilla knew that he usually had to get at least one cup of her morning tea in him before he started using actual words. The tea blend had been her first successful experiment after learning herb lore from Matwyn. That learning would be ongoing, but she'd come up with a blend that tasted good and was a mild stimulant. Perfect for those who weren't morning people. People like Gaius Ferrarius.

Ferrarius already had a pot of water heating over their brazier and Livilla was able to have a steaming cup of tea waiting when he came back from attending to business. He sniffed and sipped experimentally. Satisfied, he took a longer drink.

"Ahhh. That'll do. Thank you, as always," Ferrarius told her daughter. "You were up early this morning."

Livilla shrugged. "I woke up not long before sunrise and couldn't get back to sleep. I was enjoying the quiet. I was just about to wake you anyway when Borodur rode up."

"That whale will be good luck for us. I haven't told you, but there's rumblings of trouble, especially east and south. Caesar still expects all of Gaul to feed his troops but if the harvests go as badly as our farmers think it will there will be more uprisings. Nothing like being hungry to make you fight. You're not to say anything about this, understand. Sevel and Matwyn know but Borodur wants this kept close."

Livilla nodded. Her father was a close advisor to the chief. She was used to keeping his secrets. She set about changing her clothes to something more suitable for the messy job ahead. Her father finished his tea and gathered up axes and other cutting tools and sharpened the ones that needed it. By the time Livilla and Ferrarius were ready most of the village was too. Even Sevel was coming with them; Matwyn, apparently, had persuaded him to come out of his hut. Livilla smiled to herself. She knew how persuasive Matwyn could be.

The village set out for the beach. Livilla walked near the head of the procession. Her village didn't have an official headman, but most deferred to Ferrarius. He set a pace that would have them at the beach by about mid-morning. Everyone was in high spirits; only a few of the elders had ever seen a whale but everyone had heard stories. Elephants were almost mythical creatures to most of them, but they'd all heard stories of Hannibal's campaigns in the distant past and how he'd used elephants as beasts of war. No one quite believed the stories that whales were far bigger.

As they crested a ridge of dunes above the beach, Livilla gasped. Below her was the biggest creature she had ever seen or would ever see. A few of the elders had said a whale was as big as a whole herd of elephants. Never having seen an elephant, Livilla had no frame of reference. It seemed that if the stories of a whale's size were exaggerated, they weren't exaggerated much. No wonder Borodur had summoned all the Mardani and some of their neighbors. Even divided up this beast would feed everyone in the area for a long time.

A few people had arrived and stood near the whale, seeming tiny in comparison. There was no activity yet and Livilla was puzzled until she saw the animal exhale out of a hole on the top of its head. It was still alive.

"We won't kill it. We'll wait till it breathes its last and then we'll harvest. This is a gift from the sea gods and we must show the proper respect," Matwyn said. "Until then, we will wait and give what comfort we can."

5

(CENTRAL GAUL, 53 BCE)

Gaius Julius Caesar sat in his tent, alone, contemplating his next move. The previous year had been disastrous, despite the positive face he put on it for the sake of his generals and men. In the end, his relief of Quintus Cicero helped them ignore the defeats leading up to that signal victory. He must, it was clear, make another expedition into Germania and punish the tribes that had aided Ambiorix but he could not afford any major defeats. The easiest thing to do would be to just conquer the German tribes outright and annex their territories into the Republic. That, however, would be a logistical nightmare and would require a lot more men. The discipline of the legions and his own leadership would almost certainly win out in the end, but at what cost? Besides, the situation in Gaul was far from settled with Ambiorix himself still free and stirring up trouble. He couldn't risk a rebellion in his rear and being caught between hostile forces. Especially with the political situation in Rome itself being what it was.

Caesar stood up and stretched. He was not quite 50, still in full vigor, but old enough that the small aches and pains of life on campaign were starting to creep in. At least he hadn't had a seizure in some time. Having the falling sickness was an open secret, but it was one Caesar didn't go out of his way to acknowledge. He couldn't afford any appearance of weakness. Hipparchus, the Greek physician who had come with Publius Cornelius Aquila and his young nephew Gaius Cornelius Chlorus, attributed Caesar's run of good health solely to his own ministrations. Caesar thought the man a blowhard if not entirely without skill; he was prepared to indulge the man's ego as Aquila had essentially volunteered the Greek *medicus* to Caesar's personal service. It was a goodwill gesture that was easy enough for Caesar to accept. The Cornelii were an old and powerful Roman family that were not necessarily his friends, so having a few of them on his side was a good thing. Besides, he liked Aquila on a personal level. It was said he received his *cognomen* from a young eagle perched outside his family home as his mother gave birth to him.

As if thought were enough to summon the man himself, Publius Cornelius Aquila entered the tent, ushered by one of Caesar's body slaves. Officially, Aquila was one of his *lictors*, a group of men who were a combination of bodyguards and personal aides. Aquila was about ten years older than Caesar himself. As a proconsul invested with *imperium*—which gave him absolute authority in Gaul—Caesar was entitled to eleven lictors, all of whom were retired centurions chosen by himself personally. They all could and did serve admirably as official bodyguards when protocol demanded it, such as when Caesar was present in a Roman city or wished to overawe a barbarian leader. That wasn't needed in a legionary camp, however, so Caesar's lictors had secondary skills he could call upon when needed. In Aquila's case that secondary job was overseeing sacrifices and reading entrails for omens, auspicious or otherwise.

Theoretically that should have been Caesar's job as he held the office of *Pontifex Maximus*, chief priest of the Roman state, and he made sure he presided over particularly important ceremonies. The rest he tended to delegate to Aquila who, as a member of the Roman college of priests, was more than qualified. Probably more qualified than Caesar himself. The office of Pontifex Maximus was far more political than religious and even admission into the lesser priesthood was seen by most as a first step in a larger public career. Indeed,

Caesar himself had his eye on membership for his great-nephew Octavius, who had already impressed with his sharp mind. Aquila was a bit different. He was a true believer. Not that Caesar didn't believe in the gods, but Aquila had a spiritual bent that was unusual. That spiritual belief was tempered with just enough worldliness to make him a good ally. That and the fact that while Aquila might like to be Pontifex Maximus himself one day, his ambitions did not seem to extend further.

"Aquila. It is good to see you as always. Please sit. Here to report the auspices I assume?"

"Indeed Caesar," Aquila said. "The Remi priests were a little put out that you did not oversee the sacrifice personally but were soothed by my gifting them the horns, skin and wool from the ram they provided. In your name of course. I'd heard they were planning to formally request such in any event, so I took the ram by the horns, as it were."

Caesar inclined his head in approval. In a way, he was a little regretful. The ram had been a magnificent beast, with an unusual chestnut-colored coat, but he couldn't fault Aquila's reasoning nor the fact that Aquila had credited Caesar with the gift. That would not go unrewarded.

"Well done, Aquila. You acted properly of course. I'm guessing that was not all," Caesar said.

"No. I wanted to discuss my interpretation of the auspices with you first before the omens are announced publicly. The Remi priests do not speak Latin. I, however, speak Remi. At least well enough to get by without an interpreter most of the time," Aquila said with a self-satisfied grin.

Caesar sighed. "It's good to know I can still be surprised. I only wish you didn't enjoy it so much, Aquila."

Aquila laughed. "There are men who would consider getting one over on Gaius Julius Caesar the greatest achievement of their life. In all seriousness, however, I find it useful to understand speech others might not realize I understand and to be able to speak it myself without relying on an interpreter. In this case I was able to emphasize that the results of the sacrifice must not be shared until you announce it publicly."

"Yes. I would be lying if I said having to trust interpreters is something I enjoy. Why did you learn Remi particularly?"

Aquila shrugged. "Convenience. I had a Remi slave when I lived in Narbo. Most of the Gauls speak similar languages so I can usually make myself understood with almost any of them."

Caesar motioned his own slave to bring them some wine. "Now, the auspices?" Caesar knew, better than almost anyone, how subjective reading auspices was and how susceptible to manipulation it could be. He himself had done some...creative interpretation...of sacrifices in his day.

"Yes, Caesar. Most was standard, easy to sell as a sign of the gods' continuing favor. I did notice a prominent—and most unusual—formation of veins near the liver that had a clear trident-like shape. My own opinion, if I may share it, is that it shows favor from Neptune. Perhaps you will receive a gift from the sea."

Caesar rubbed his jaw, feeling a little stubble. He'd have to summon his barber when this meeting with Aquila was done. "I can't dispute your interpretation. Though perhaps we should emphasize Neptune's favor and leave off talk of gifts from the sea."

"Hmm. Yes. Yes, I think you are right. Especially in light of the other thing I have to show you. You know I said I gifted the ram's skin and wool to the Remi druids? Well, as the coat was being shaved, I noticed a mark on the skin. A birthmark."

"Oh?" Caesar was intrigued. Birthmarks, whether on a person or a sacrificial animal, were always significant.

"Oh yes. I have one myself. You know the story of how I got my *cognomen* of course."

Caesar cracked a rare smile and nodded. "It is rather famous after all."

"It's not quite true. I was actually born with an eagle-shaped birthmark. You know better than most how stories grow in the telling, Caesar, so I am happy to let the perched eagle story be retold. Better than having to bare my backside every time the story's repeated."

Caesar laughed this time but sobered quickly when Aquila brought out a small package from under his cloak and unwrapped it. Caesar's eyes widened. Interpreting the shape of a birthmark or blemish was often as subjective as reading entrails or the flight of birds but this one was unambiguous. It was shaped like a *caduceus*, the winged staff with twined snakes symbolizing Mercury, wing-footed messenger of the gods.

"What could it mean?" Caesar asked.

"You tell me. You're Pontifex Maximus after all."

Caesar considered. Mercury was the messenger of the gods, so perhaps there would be a message coming? But what kind of message? And when? Caesar said as much to Aquila.

"I don't disagree. I do have to wonder...the Gauls have a special reverence for Mercury. Their version of Mercury anyway. Lugus, I think they call him, if I am remembering correctly. Perhaps this sign has to do with either the Gauls as a whole, or one particular Gallic tribe."

"Hmm. Something to think upon, in any event. See if you can preserve that skin so that the mark is left intact. Have a faithful rendering drawn in case you cannot. Is there anything else, Aquila?"

"Only this," Aquila said, handing Caesar a small scroll case. "My nephew wrote from Morgennus. Most of his letter concerned personal matters surely of no interest to you but I copied some passages reporting current conditions for your review. Pullo also dictated a report, which is included."

"Very good. I shall be along before midday to announce the auspices and I will personally thank our Remi allies for their generosity. Again, you did well, Aquila. Fortuna blesses me by having one so reliable nearby."

Caesar took a moment to scan the sheets Aquila had given him after the man left. He hadn't been sure about giving Aquila's young nephew Chlorus his first taste of command but then decided that the Mardani had proven their loyalty and if they did have a mind to rebel, they were too insignificant to cause trouble. It also gave him a means to reward Vibius Pullo for his valor in the recent battles. It was a promotion of sorts and gave Pullo a well-deserved rest. Besides, the veteran was the perfect person to teach and guide a young man like Chlorus at the beginning of his career and if worse came to worse could rein him in if needed. Judging from both reports no reining in had been necessary. The Mardani continued to be friendly and loyal. According to Pullo, young Chlorus was even dallying with a young Mardani woman. That could be a good thing so long as the young man didn't have any foolish notions of making a wife out of a barbarian Gaul.

The rest of Caesar's day was uneventful. He announced the auspices, solemnly thanked the Remi druids, then had a light lunch and a shave before meeting with Marcus Antonius to discuss legionary matters. Perhaps Antonius had some ideas on how the rest of the campaign should go. Caesar was starting to plan things out in his head but if nothing else it would be an interesting test of how much Antonius had learned on this venture. The man had a good mind when he chose to use it and not be impulsive.

Caesar's dreams that night were jumbled and troubled. He kept seeing a caduceus and wondering what the message would be and if he would recognize it in time.

6

(NORTHERN GALLIC COAST, 53 BCE)

The walk along the beach was more of a struggle than David had thought it would be. Kevin had suggested that they explore the shore, and he'd agreed, more as a peace offering to his nephew than anything else. David had found a small, sheltered inlet where he anchored the *Stork* and they set out. Kevin carried a backpack with food, water, and fire materials; David carried some extra water and what he called "a basic medical kit." His nephew begged to differ.

"You're carrying an urgent care center on your back," Kevin said. "Is it worth it? I mean, we'll be back before nightfall."

"I've carried this type of kit with me for years. Ever since I delivered a baby on a highway. You never know what's going to happen. Besides, what has gone to plan or been normal since we sailed through that fog bank?"

"You delivered a baby on a highway? I think you kind of buried the lede on that one," Kevin said.

David sighed. "I'm surprised your mom or your Uncle Gabe never told you the story. Happened the summer between the end of med school and the start of residency. I was volunteering at a free clinic, did a supply run, and drove back on the interstate. There was a big accident that shut down traffic for hours. Someone came running down the line of cars looking for a doctor—there was a woman in labor about half a dozen cars ahead of me. Anyway, that was the day I really learned that you never know what will happen."

"What about the baby?"

David laughed. "Not the moral of the story, but the baby was fine. Luckily the woman was in a van, so we had some privacy. Everything was routine and healthy."

David doubted he'd have to deliver a baby while they were out and about, but you never knew. At this point he'd be happy to see anyone at all. He still wasn't entirely sure he believed Kevin's theory, but he knew his arguments against it seemed increasingly weak. Cities were gone. Not destroyed; it was as if all signs of civilization on the western and northern coasts of France never existed. Or—if Kevin was right—didn't exist *yet*.

After getting their land legs back, David and Kevin settled into a rhythm. They saw signs of life, but no actual people. They were about ready to stop and eat lunch, and David was going to suggest they head back, when Kevin thought he heard something in the distance. Cautiously, David crept up to the top of a small dune. There were people! The first he'd seen in over a week. Quite a group of them. They were gathered around a beached whale with what seemed like reverence. Like they were keeping vigil with the mighty beast. David thought it was a North Atlantic right whale, but he wasn't sure. His whale watching guide was back aboard his boat.

Then he saw the bird. That was when David's increasingly elaborate stories of why everything was off collapsed. It was when he had to admit his nephew was right. That they'd been, somehow, displaced in time and were now in the deep past with no hope of returning to their present.

David was no master of "useless" facts like his nephew, but thanks to one of his oldest friends he knew a fair bit about recently extinct animals. Particularly the bird exploring the area near the dune where he and Kevin were resting. David had known Paisley Goodwin since they'd been in the first grade. When she was a bit older, she was diagnosed as being on the autism spectrum—Asperger's Syndrome as they called it then—but in first grade she was the weird kid that didn't quite fit in. When David had been paired with her to do a presentation on an extinct species, they clicked. The assignment fit Paisley's obsession with the great auk, northern hemisphere birds that filled a similar niche to penguins in the southern hemisphere. In fact, penguins owed their name to the great auk. The northern birds were called "pinguins" and according to Paisley it was the southern birds' resemblance to the auk that gave rise to their designation as "penguins." Auks went extinct in the 19th century, due to reckless hunting and habitat loss. David's ability to channel Paisley's knowledge led to an A+ on the project and a lifelong friendship. Thanks to their success David had never forgotten what he learned about the great auk. And he had no doubt he was looking at a live one. The last credited sighting of a live great auk was in Canada in 1852, but here one was, on a beach in France, three feet tall and calmly going about its business without a care in the world.

A wave of nausea struck David and he ejected his breakfast. Feeling faint, he sat down. Kevin looked at him, concerned.

"Uncle David, are you alright?"

Dr. David Castellanos was far from "alright." How could he be? He looked at his nephew and tried to reply, but no words would come out.

KEVIN TRIED NOT to panic as he saw his uncle spew his breakfast and half-faint, his mouth working but no sound coming out. Finally, he started muttering something about "that bird" before hunching up and saying nothing more. It was like David was catatonic. What bird was his uncle talking about? What was it that caused this reaction?

Kevin looked cautiously out over the top of the sand dune. In the distance he saw the people still gathered around the beached whale. Occasional gouts of mist from the animal's blowhole were the only sign that it still lived. Closer, Kevin did see a bird. It looked like a large penguin but wasn't one. There were definitely differences and besides, penguins only lived south of the equator. What kind of bird it was Kevin couldn't say; he was no birder. He knew a few distinct birds, like the puffin or the albatross but that was as far as his avian knowledge went. He checked on his uncle again. David's eyes were open, his stare vacant. Was he having some kind of breakdown? What would Kevin do?

From the direction of the beached whale, Kevin heard a low moan. He chanced another look. For a moment, the people were silent as if acknowledging the passing of the huge creature. Then dozens of them started swarming all around the whale and began butchering it. Kevin was repulsed at first, then thought about his reaction. If he and David were truly in the past, why shouldn't people harvest a beached whale? Why let all that meat, fat, oil, even the bones go to waste? For a while, Kevin contented himself with watching. Hopefully his uncle would snap out of whatever was possessing him and they would figure out what to do. In the meantime, Kevin would see what he might be able to learn about the beach people. He and David would have to approach them at some point and Kevin thought perhaps there would be clues as to *when* they were.

Kevin lost track of time, fascinated by what he was watching. The Beach People, as he thought of them, used iron tools, axes and machete-like knives to strip the skin and fat from the whale and cut away the meat underneath. Mostly it was the men who did the cutting, though Kevin saw a few muscular women helping with this bloody task. The rest of the women, and a few men, began smoking and salting the meat, and rendering the fat. Kevin knew from his study of history that whale oil was a valuable commodity even into the 20th century, until cheap petroleum and growing scarcity of whales due to excess hunting made it commercially unviable. Kevin crept up to the crest of the dune to get a better view. Perhaps it was his fascination or maybe he was counting on the Beach People being too focused on their task to notice him, but the longer Kevin watched, the less careful he was to stay hidden. One of the Beach People, a big man by the looks of him, climbed on top of the beached giant. The

Dude, as Kevin mentally named him, paused a moment, taking in the view, then pointed straight at Kevin. That's when it happened.

Kevin couldn't see what caused the whale to shudder. Maybe it was a post-death spasm; maybe someone out of view accidentally caused the beast to shift. Whatever it was, it caused The Dude to fall, and the fall looked bad. Kevin dashed down to his uncle, still out of it behind the dune.

"Uncle David! Uncle David! Someone's hurt. I need you to focus and follow me. Quick!"

Everyone paused a few moments after the beached whale breathed its last, then got to work. Livilla joined in, helping strip layers of skin and blubber and then carrying them off to be processed. The fat would be rendered in giant iron pots over small bonfires. The skins would be tanned like any other hides; the giant sheets would be perfect for tents and ground covers, even roofs. The bounty would be shared by the Mardani and everyone else who came to help. No doubt a large portion of the meat would go to help feed the Roman army when their quartermasters made the rounds in the fall after the harvest, but that was not a problem. There would be tons of it, more than enough to give the Romans their due and ensure no one starved. Livilla knew from what her father had said that the Mardani and their Veneti and Lexovii neighbors were not optimistic about the fall harvest. Livilla had a feeling she and everyone else would be trying to find new ways to cook whale meat. It was better than starving to death.

Everyone worked hard. The older children and young men occasionally broke to horse around and throw bits of blubber and guts at each other until one of the elders scolded them to get back to work. It was exhausting but fun. Livilla watched Borodur climb to the top of the whale, like he was king of a mountain. She chuckled to herself and went back to her task of cutting thick layers of blubber from pieces of whale skin. While he was beginning to butcher meat from the great beast's back, Livilla had no doubt the headman was showing his younger followers he was still as fit as any of them. She didn't see Borodur lose his balance and fall but snapped to attention as soon as she heard the shouting. Livilla immediately dropped what she was doing and rushed to the gathered group. The headman was down; there weren't any obvious broken bones, but he'd managed to cut his leg very badly. Livilla took charge. Her first priority was to put pressure on the big gash before Borodur bled his life away. Someone, she didn't know who, pressed a certain variety of moss into her hand, one she knew helped absorb blood and promoted clotting. Without a second thought she stripped off her skirt and used it to help put pressure on the wound. Once again focused, Livilla didn't notice the two strangers who'd joined them. One was young, around her age, with golden skin, a smooth face, and eyes with peculiar folds that made them seem slanted. The other was older, though if Livilla was any judge not much. He was bearded and his skin was olive-hued, different from his companion's. Maybe he was Roman, or part Roman like her? He had very kind-looking, deep brown eyes, but there was also a haunted look. A look that she'd seen before but couldn't place in the moment. There was something about him that made Livilla tingle. This is not the time for that, she scolded herself. The man said something in a strange language that she couldn't understand, and yet—like the haunted look in his eyes—seemed somehow familiar. Both tickled a memory that seemed just out of reach.

7

———

(PAGUS MARDANI, NORTHERN GAUL, 53 BCE)

David wasn't sure how much time had passed while he'd shut the world out. He had a watch, an old faithful his parents had given him when he passed his boards and embarked on private practice. If he wore it, the simple motion of walking around and exposing the face to light would keep it powered. He hadn't reset it since they'd passed through The Fog, as he was beginning to think of it. The easiest thing to do would be to set it according to the sun. When the sun reached its peak, set the watch at noon. David pulled his awareness back to the moment. If he was going to help an injured person, he had to be present. Focused. With Kevin leading the way David's feet carried him to the scene much quicker than he would have thought possible. He was already shrugging off his pack with his first aid kit as he reached the scene. David was so focused he didn't notice or question the fact that these strangers parted to let him through.

"Don't worry miss. I can help."

The young woman looked up at him, a flicker of understanding crossing her face. She was amazingly beautiful. She reminded him, in general, of the office manager at the practice he'd left. Aoife—who accepted "Eva" from people who didn't speak Irish—was black haired and had a complexion somewhere halfway between her father's Italian olive skin and her mother's apple-cheeked Irish fairness. This woman had a face that belonged to the British Isles with some Mediterranean mixed in. David put that aside, along with the fact this beautiful woman was naked from the waist down. She was using her skirt on the wound the man on top of the whale had suffered in his fall. Her uncomprehending look told him he had, without thinking, spoken English.

The young woman had the look of someone who knew she *should* understand something, but it was just out of her reach. Out of the corner of his eye he saw an elder give him a sharp look. Maybe "don't worry miss. I can help" was like Arthur Dent's "I seem to be having tremendous difficulty with my lifestyle" in *Hitchhiker's Guide to the Galaxy*, which was a deadly insult for a race of aliens and sparked an interstellar war. No one else looked angry though. Get out of your head, Castellanos, David scolded himself.

A man helping the young woman, who bore a strong resemblance and was no doubt a close relative, asked a question. It took a moment, but something finally clicked.

By the time David reached high school, he knew his future lay in the life sciences. Maybe as a doctor, maybe as a researcher, but it would be something along those lines. When picking classes for his freshman year, he decided to take Latin. If he was going to be a scientist, or a doctor maybe, having some knowledge of Latin would be a big plus. If nothing else, it would give him a leg up on the language half of the SAT. His Latin teacher was a colorful, irascible man named Ralph Chaplin who was the kind of teacher students either really loved or really hated. David fell into the former category. Mr. Chaplin emphasized knowledge of Latin as a written language. He didn't really care about pronunciation. "Go to an immersion camp if you want to talk like you think Cicero did," he'd say. "Fact is, we don't know how the Romans spoke it and there's none around now to care." That would invariably be followed by Mr. Chaplin taking his

dowel rod pointer and smacking charts of declensions and conjuga-
tions with increasing irritation until he inevitably broke it. There
were always running bets on how many of the rods he'd break in a
semester. The over-under was never less than three.

So it took a moment for the words of the tree-armed man to register. But finally, they did.

Quis es?" Who are you? This man was speaking Latin! David dug
deep, trying to remember the vocabulary Ralph Chaplin had drilled
into his brain twenty years ago.

"*Ego sum David. Ego sum medicus,*" David said haltingly. He was
trying to tell them his name, and that he was able to help. Thinking
he should introduce his nephew, David added, "*Ipse est Kevin.*"

The young woman made a smile that lit up her face. "Ego sum
Livilla. Potesne me iuvare?"

David's ear was starting to adjust, and his fluency in Spanish
helped. "Iuvare" sounded like it was related to "ayudar"—the
Spanish verb for help. He decided it was worth the risk to guess she
was asking for help.

"Sic," David said, answering yes.

Nodding to indicate the man on the ground, Livilla said "Ipse est
Borodur." This man—Borodur—looked to be middle-aged but in
good health aside from the gaping gash in his leg. It was clear he'd
led a hard life—the man had more scars than David could possibly
count.

Communication after that was a sort of pidgin of Latin and
pantomime. Livilla had done an admirable job. David noticed a very
old woman watching every move she, and now he, made. He had no
doubt this old woman was the healer for these people. She watched
with the same expression every med school teacher David had ever
had had worn. Her face was neutral, and she mostly said nothing,
occasionally offering brief comments in a language that was not
Latin. David looked at the wound. Amazingly, Borodur didn't seem to
have suffered any broken bones in his fall. Even more incredibly, the
cut had been on the front of his leg. Had the man's femoral artery
running along the inner thigh been severed, he'd have bled out in

seconds. Livilla had done very well. A strip of cloth, presumably part of the skirt she'd been wearing, was being used as a tourniquet. The rest was being used to keep pressure on the wound and slow Borodur's bleeding. At David's direction, Livilla carefully lifted the cloth. The bleeding hadn't completely stopped but had slowed to a slow seep. Between the tourniquet and what looked like plant spores packed into wound, Livilla had kept her patient from bleeding to death.

David quickly washed his hands and put on a pair of gloves. Working quickly but confidently, he flushed the wound with sterile saline and then, with Livilla's help, David stitched Borodur's leg muscle together. Using a disposable cauterizer, he then touched the remaining bleeders before installing a drainage tube and stitching the skin. God willing and the crick don't rise, as a West Virginia colleague was fond of saying, everything would heal cleanly. He'd help keep an eye on things, though something told him Livilla would have her patient well in hand. Brief though their acquaintance was, he was struck by her intelligence and competence. Hopefully his Latin would improve quickly and he could actually have a conversation with her. He watched as Livilla and the old woman made a poultice to put on the wound site. Other than make clear they should keep the area around the drainage tube clear, David said nothing, and watched. Pharmaco-botany wasn't exactly his wheelhouse, but David knew a few honest herbal healers and respected their skill. Plus, he'd learned a few things. He recognized one of the plants being used as having antibiotic properties, and the others seemed harmless enough. David hoped to learn more. He had what seemed like a lot of antibiotics when he considered what was boxed up back on the *Stork* but if he and Kevin were stuck back in Roman times forever eventually David's modern medicines would run out and his modern equipment would fail no matter how carefully he shepherded both. A group of muscular young men carefully placed Borodur on a litter and carried him away from the whale. Livilla indicated David and Kevin should follow, and they did.

"Who are they? Where could they have come from?" Ramira asked. Ramira had spent a little time as Matwyn's apprentice until they both decided Ramira didn't have the mind or temperament to be a healer. The young woman was good at following directions and was a big help mixing a painkilling poultice for Borodur while Livilla and Matwyn mixed a relaxing tea for the headman. Bennozha was with them as well, helping wherever she could. She had reported a little spotting after arriving at the beach, so Matwyn ordered her to rest and avoid anything strenuous. Conversation passed the time, and it was inevitable conversation would revolve around the two mysterious strangers.

"The older man looks like he could be Roman. Or maybe a Jew. The younger man with him...I've never seen skin the color of his before!" Bennozha said.

"And how would you know what a Jew looks like? Have you ever met one?" Ramira asked.

Bennozha bristled. "No. But Chlorus says he has. He's told me all about them!"

"No need to get testy, Bennozha. You too Ramira." Livilla didn't even bother looking up as she dipped a finger into the brewing tea, then tasting a drop. She crumbled a little more of a certain herb into the mixture and kept stirring. Livilla looked at Matwyn, expecting her to say something about the squabble, but the old woman was staying tight-lipped.

"I suppose he could be Jewish," said a low, rumbling voice. Gaius Ferrarius ducked into the shelter where the women worked. "I doubt it though. I knew a few Jews when I lived in Narbo. He has their look but doesn't observe any of the rituals. Jews live by their rituals." Livilla's father had been conferring with Borodur's senior lieutenants. For now, it didn't seem as if their chief was in danger of dying but he wasn't going to be up to making any leadership decisions for a few days at least.

Bennozha gave Ramira a triumphant "I told you so" look. "Chlorus says they're always stirring up trouble and don't believe in the gods."

"They don't believe in *our* gods. They believe in a single, all-powerful god who forbids them to worship any other god," Gaius said. Livilla paused to look at her father. She hoped he would continue. He rarely talked about his life before settling with the Mardani. She was in luck. Warming to the topic, Ferrarius continued, "the men I had dealings with were men like most other, though they had rules about eating or drinking with people who didn't share their faith. Philo and Saul were both honest men, at least in their dealings with me. Never caused any trouble that I knew about."

"Where do you think our new guests came from, Father?" Livilla asked.

"I don't know. If the quality of their clothes is anything to judge by, they are wealthy. And it's obvious that the one who calls himself 'David' is a competent doctor. Though Matwyn is a better judge of that than I am."

The old woman finally broke her silence. "Yes. Very competent. Very confident. He also seemed very respectful. He definitely knew what he was doing—I've never seen anyone stitch a wound that well or cleanly. He's better at that than I ever was. At least, when I could still hold a needle." She held up her arthritic hands. "It's too bad he and I couldn't talk more."

"He was a lot better than that Greek doctor Chlorus had with him for a while," said Ramira.

Bennozha laughed. Normally she was quick to defend her lover, but she hadn't been fond of the physician who'd come with Chlorus, a pompous Greek dandy named Hipparchus. "Yes. Hipparchus is a bit full of himself."

"That's something that's been, not bugging me exactly but nagging at me," Ferrarius said. "Both David and the young man Keffin seem very educated but their Latin is barbarous, and neither seem to speak Greek. How can you be an educated man and not speak Greek or Latin?" Livilla knew her father didn't speak any Greek aside from a few dirty words but then Gaius Ferrarius never claimed to be an educated man.

Livilla paused to sniff the vapor coming off the tea. Almost ready, she thought, but not quite. To her father, she said, "I heard the two of them speak a different language. It wasn't like any languages of the people around us, but I felt like I *should* be able to understand it. It sounded almost familiar somehow."

Matwyn changed the subject. "Ferrarius, have you seen Sevel? He was there when Borodur got hurt but I haven't seen him since."

Ferrarius rubbed his stubbled jaw. "No, now that you mention it, Mother Matwyn. Maybe he's gone back to the village. He's been acting odd for a couple of weeks now." Livilla looked sidewise at her mentor. She knew her father well enough to know he was fishing for information. Livilla also knew very well that Matwyn would reveal nothing until she felt she had to. In some cases that meant never but Livilla didn't think that would be the case here. Matwyn had told her that illnesses of the mind were the most difficult to treat because they depended on the patient themselves to overcome. Most of the time, Matwyn said, giving someone the time and personal space they needed would suffice. It was clear she felt that way about whatever had Sevel in his mood.

Livilla gave the sedative tea one last tiny taste and judged it ready. Using thick hide mitts, she lifted the pot off the fire. Matwyn nodded at her.

"You should take that in. Perhaps you should help our visiting medicus keep an eye on Borodur for a while," Matwyn said. There was something about Matwyn's look that said the old woman had ulterior motives.

"You sly old she-wolf. Are you trying to pair me up with someone I can barely talk to?"

"I'm not trying to do anything, Livilla. He may not even like women. The golden-skinned man with him could be his lover, though I don't think so. I believe they are close relatives, probably by adoption given there is no physical resemblance between them."

"You learned all this by observing?"

Matwyn's face split with a proud smile. "You are learning, daughter. Now go. You can at least speak with our new friends, after a fashion. And if you are steel and he is flint and you make sparks when you come together, then that will happen. I've said what I've said about your future husband, and I will say no more. Now go. I believe our guests might respond better to a beautiful face than your father's hard one."

KEVIN WATCHED as his uncle checked his patient's pulse, respiration and blood pressure. Much like his method of calculating latitude and longitude the old-fashioned way, David used an old-school sphygmomanometer, complete with squeeze bulb and analog dial, to check the big man's blood pressure. David must have sensed Kevin looking at him.

"Yeah, yeah, I know. But learning this taught me two things."

"What are those?" Kevin asked.

"It's always good to be prepared. This isn't the first time I've had to take blood pressure myself and an electronic machine wasn't available. It's not all fun and catching babies in vans." Kevin chuckled, remembering the story from earlier.

"What's the other thing?"

"Nurses love it when a doctor can do what most docs consider 'scut work.' As long as you're not obnoxious about it and act like you can do it better. I've had more than one nurse be my friend for life because I took vitals and let them have 5 minutes for a coffee or even just getting off their feet. And believe me, you want the nurses to be your friend. Most of them have seen more than any five doctors and they know all the juiciest gossip."

Kevin's jaw dropped a little. "I never figured you for a gossip hound, Uncle David."

"Knowledge is power, Kev. Never forget it." David wrote down the man's vitals in a notebook he had handy. Kevin could swear that his uncle's first aid backpack was like Mary Poppins' carpet bag: bottomless and stocked with anything one could possibly need. The burly patient, pumped full of painkillers, was resting comfortably.

"How is The Dude?"

"Abiding," David said with a grin. "I realize there's nothing you can't tie to a movie you've seen, but his name is Borodur and if I'm understanding things correctly he's the leader here." David sighed. "This has taken my mind off of things, but I wish we could figure out *when* we were."

"Yeah. About that..." Kevin said. His uncle looked at him expectantly.

"Are you going to continue or are you going to make me pull your teeth? I should remind you I'm a doctor, not a dentist," David said.

"Okay, *Dr. McCoy*. Anyway, I've been thinking about that. That other big guy, your new girlfriend's dad. Or uncle maybe—"

"Wait a minute. She's not my girlfriend, we just met. If she's not half my age she's not much more than that."

"I saw how she was looking at you when you were stitching up The Dude—uh, Borodur—here. And don't tell me you weren't appreciating more than her medical skill." David's blush told Kevin his aim had been true. "Now, can I continue?" David nodded.

"The real big guy, the one I'm assuming is Livilla's dad, spoke Latin but the Romans don't seem to have established a presence here. I'm guessing we're in the 50s BC. Definitely during or before Caesar's campaigns," Kevin said.

David was impressed. "Since when did you learn so much about Roman history? I thought you hated Latin? As I recall, you barely toughed out a year with old Mr. Chaplin."

"Yeah, he was nuts. And while the Latin language drove me crazy, I liked a lot of the history. Especially getting to watch *I, Claudius* on Fridays if we got through our work for the week," Kevin said.

"Well, you're going to have to work on your language skills. It shouldn't be too bad with your grasp of Spanish," David said. "If you're correct about the time period, Livilla and her people speak a

Celtic dialect and some Latin. If her father or uncle are more fluent, I hope they'll help us learn enough of both to get by."

Kevin frowned. "Are you that sure they'll let us stay?"

"Why wouldn't they?"

"Your new female admirer seems to be a fan but I'm not sure about the rest. There was one old geezer who was really giving us the stink eye," Kevin said. "And we will have to figure out what we're going to do with the boat."

"As to the old man...hopefully he won't be a problem. There's something going on there, but I don't know what. If there's enough good will from seeing to Borodur here maybe his suspicions won't matter." His uncle looked Kevin in the eyes, very serious. "We've got to assume we're stuck here. That as far as our family and friends are concerned, we mysteriously disappeared at sea. If that assumption is correct, we will have to figure out how to make some kind of life for ourselves. If these people, or anywhere else, needs a doctor, then that's what I'll do. And I'm sure your gift of tinkering with old machinery will come in handy."

"You know, for someone who was really skeptical about this theory, you've really come around," Kevin said.

"It was that bird we saw on the beach. The great auk. I happen to know it's been extinct since before the Civil War. It was the final piece of the puzzle, the thing that I finally couldn't explain away," David said,

Kevin nodded. "What about the *Stork*? We won't want to leave that unattended for long," Kevin said.

"I agree," David said. "We should figure out a place to anchor her nearby and soon. I'm thinking tomorrow, or the day after tomorrow at the latest. Here's the question though: could you hike back and sail her on your own? I'm not sure I should leave Borodur here. Not that I'm not sure Livilla and the old woman couldn't handle things but on the off chance he took a turn and I was gone...it probably wouldn't be good."

"No, you're right," Kevin said. "It's not ideal, but I can get *Stork* here on my own assuming we can find a spot. It's not like I didn't sail her on my own plenty of times while you were sleeping."

"True. We—"

Whatever his uncle was going to say was lost as Livilla entered with a pot of a fragrant warm drink. She acknowledged Kevin with a polite smile but lit up when she saw David. Yep, she's got it bad. So does my uncle, even if he won't admit it, Kevin thought.

8

(PAGUS MARDANI, NORTHERN GAUL, 53 BC)

Livilla had been feeling an increasing attraction to the strange but kind healer who had fallen into village's midst, but it was Bennozha—or rather, Bennozha's clumsiness—that finally made her see it. When the man, who was already being referred to as David Medicus, arrived it was about halfway between full moons. Those first few days were a blur. As Borodur began his recovery his sons constructed a rough palanquin to carry him. Livilla, Matwyn, and Ferrarius convinced Borodur's family and his chief lieutenants that the headman should recover at their village. It was closer to the beach and David Medicus would have access to his wonder medicines and tools, stored in his equally wondrous boat, which could be anchored near the village in a small, sheltered river—the oppidum was further inland. The village was a manageable distance from Mortorgenn, especially on horseback, should any urgent leadership matters arise.

David Medicus and his nephew, Keffin Flavens (so-called for his golden skin), were true enigmas. David's Latin improved rapidly in the days after his arrival. He explained that he'd studied Latin in his youth under a strict but entertaining tutor, but that he'd learned

Latin as a written language. Not a spoken one. So Livilla's father had been correct. David was educated just as her father had guessed on that first day. The tongue David and Keffin spoke when by themselves still nagged at Livilla. She still felt that she *should* understand the language, but it was more than that. She wondered if that was the reason for her grandfather's reluctance to have anything to do with the newcomers. Keffin was convinced Sevel didn't like them; David was unfailingly polite but had largely given up trying to make friends after Sevel had rebuffed him numerous times. Livilla didn't think it was hostility. She could swear it was fear. It didn't make sense to her, but she knew Sevel better than anyone except her father or Matwyn. He looked like he was seeing the spirits of people long departed. She'd said as much to Matwyn, who continued to stay mostly silent on the matter.

Old Mother Matwyn was more forthcoming about David's medical skill. Borodur was up and walking, if gingerly, within a few days and the stitched wound was healing clean and would leave only a thin scar. The tube David had left in when he initially sewed up the leg had drained infection out and kept it from festering. Even Matwyn hadn't seen such a thing before. As his ability to communicate improved he explained his medical training centered on treating women, especially during pregnancy and childbirth, but that all medical students where he was trained were expected to have some general knowledge. Matwyn had been skeptical. Male healers weren't common but not unheard of. Pregnancy and childbirth were firmly in the sphere of women. Matwyn had had David examine Ramira as a test of sorts. He performed a thorough examination with the same quiet confidence he'd had when treating Borodur and—without knowing it—agreed with Matwyn's assertion that Ramira would deliver her baby before the coming full moon. David was very good at not giving away much by his facial expression but Livilla was sure she saw a smile flash across his face. He knew he was being tested and knew he'd just passed. Outside of Ramira's hearing, David expressed concern that her baby had not yet turned.

After Ramira left Bennozha came in for her examination,

bringing a refreshing tea that was a specialty of Bennozha's adopted mother. Not looking where she was going, Bennozha ran into David, spilling the tea all over him and staining his tunic top. David's and Keffin's clothes had been the subject of much speculation in the village. Even Chlorus, who came from one of Rome's oldest and wealthiest families, did not have clothes so well made. Yet while both men weren't careless they also didn't act as if their clothing was as precious and expensive as the quality of the workmanship suggested. Livilla didn't know any rich people aside from Chlorus, and didn't claim to know him particularly well, but she guessed he'd have been livid to have his finest clothes stained with tea. Livilla knew she would have been. But David acted as if it was nothing, waving off Bennozha's apologies. With Livilla's help to translate, David assured the young woman it was fine, and he was not angry. All that, though, was just a prelude.

David took off his shirt, and she saw it. A tattoo that looked like a painting on his skin and yet was clearly permanent. David's shoulder blade was adorned with the staff of Mercury, its wings rendered in exquisite detail and snakes so realistic they looked as if they might slither away. She'd seen tattoos before. The Mardani didn't use them, but some neighboring tribes did. They were geometric designs in black. Beautiful in their way but not terribly complex.

This was no simple, monochrome tattoo. This was an artistic masterwork full of color. More proof that David Medicus was a very wealthy man even if he didn't act like it. Livilla couldn't help herself. She reached out, tentatively, and touched the wings of the tattoo. She half-expected to feel feathers despite knowing better, and yet she did feel something unexpected. The closest thing she could compare it to was the spark that sometimes leapt from one's fingertips on cold, dry days. Except this spark didn't hurt. It sent tingles all through her. David tensed as if he felt something unexpected. Did he like it too? Did he feel a wave of warmth and pleasure sweep through him, as she did? There was no way for Livilla to know, but he didn't shy away as if he disliked what he was feeling at least.

"That's my..." and said a word she did not recognize, presumably in his native language. It sounded like "dadoo." David fumbled, not knowing the word's Latin equivalent. Livilla guessed the word from the context.

"*Stigmata*," Livilla said.

David laughed, then must have seen Livilla's questioning look.

"Didn't mean to offend," he said, sounding a bit worried.

"You didn't offend me. I'm just wondering why you find that word funny."

After a moment David's face lit up with understanding. "My birth language borrow some words from Latin. Words sometimes same or close but mean different. *Stigmata* to me mean markings some religious people have."

"Your tattoo isn't religious? You're not a priest of Mercury?"

David laughed again. "No. Definitely not. Was gift I gave myself. When I finish medical studies. Where I come from, that is a sign for doctors."

"Strange. You're not angry? At Bennozha?" Livilla asked.

"No. It's just clothes and I have more. I'll use for dirty jobs after it dries."

They stood there a few long moments, looking at each other. David was a puzzle and Livilla loved solving puzzles. That would have to wait; Bennozha's examination came first. Matwyn again mostly supervised but now more convinced of David's skill took a more active role. The three of them agreed that the young copper-skinned woman still had a couple of months to go before delivery but that overall she was healthy. David expressed some concern over Bennozha's spotting but it was light and there were no other concerning signs that Bennozha might go into labor early. He merely repeated Matwyn's order to avoid strenuous work and—much to Bennozha's disappointment—advised her to avoid sex.

"Most of the time it's healthy for a pregnant woman," David said. "I even encourage. With your light bleeding, though, better to be safe."

After a nice chat and some more consulting, David walked back to the boat he and Keffin lived on. Jobix, Ramira's husband, had gone with Keffin to retrieve it. Jobix was a stolid if reliable man who simply said that there were things inside the boat that defied description. Some thought Jobix was being coy on purpose but after seeing the vessel for herself Livilla wasn't so sure. The only boats she'd ever seen were the biremes and triremes that occasionally plied the waters between Gaul and Britannia. There were worn-out with ragged sails and either two or three banks of oars. Livilla's father said that the good ships sailed the Middle Sea at the heart of the Roman Republic's growing territory and network of client states. Ferrarius said he'd even once seen a quiquireme, a ship with five banks of oars and had heard stories of even larger vessels used by the rulers of Aegyptus or other eastern kingdoms. The way he told the story made it clear he wasn't sure that they weren't exaggerated.

David and Keffin's boat wasn't anything like a giant pleasure barge or king or queen's flagship. The boat, which David said was named for a bird said to bring babies in children's stories, wasn't tiny, but it wasn't even as large as the few trading vessels Livilla herself had seen. It was much sleeker and with a triangular rather than a square sail. The hull was white and completely smooth, looking as if it had been made of a single piece of...something. She was pretty sure the boat wasn't built from wood but what it was made from Livilla couldn't even begin to guess.

It was a puzzle. And Livilla loved puzzles.

David looked at Livilla. Those eyes, so blue and intelligent. Curious. Beautiful. That hair, black as a raven's feather and falling in waves to her lushly rounded hips and firm backside. Those full lips, begging to be kissed. He leaned closer and Livilla leaned toward him closing her eyes, mouth opened slightly. It felt so right. It felt...

"Uncle David."

David startled awake to Kevin shaking him lightly.

"Huh? What?"

"Livilla's outside. She says Ramira's in labor and that she and Matwyn would like your help."

"Hm. Yes. Tell her I'll be out in a few moments."

Kevin snickered and left. It was a warm night and David was sure the main reason he needed a few minutes was obvious under the thin sheet. Once that was under control David dressed and quickly packed his tools. Some necessities were always packed, such as latex gloves, a scalpel and his combination stethoscope and fetoscope. He hesitated a moment before packing his ultrasound wand and tablet. He wasn't worried about changing history. Kevin had asserted that they were either in an alternate past or had created one just by their presence. He was firm in his belief that it was impossible to change one's personal past timeline. Kevin called it "The Stan Lee Theory" because according to his nephew this principle was the rule that governed time travel in the Marvel Comics universe. There was no way to know for sure; David just told himself that Kevin had been right about everything so far and he was probably right about this. No, his reluctance had everything to do with setting expectations among the people he was likely going to be living with for the foreseeable future. No matter how careful he was, David's electronic equipment would wear out and fail. The supply of antibiotics and painkillers he'd brought—meant as a symbolic contribution for a refugee crisis—would inevitably be exhausted no matter how carefully he used them. After that, all he would have would be his personal knowledge and the tools and drugs available to the people here and now.

David had great respect for traditional healers, especially midwives. He'd spent time in Alexandria, where his mother grew up and where most of that side of his family still lived, working in clinics in the poorest areas of that ancient city. He'd seen first hand the good these people—mostly women—did relying on knowledge handed down mother to daughter for thousands of years. When doctors like himself respected that knowledge and worked as true partners, folk medicine and modern knowledge could make a true difference. He felt like a resident again and considered himself more of a student to Matwyn, and Livilla's equal. Not that David would hold back sharing his own knowledge.

Backpack with his medical kit slung over one shoulder, he clambered down the rope ladder from the *Stork*'s deck to the dock where his sailboat was anchored. The Mardani mostly herded sheep and traded wool with neighboring tribes and even the Romans, but they did some fishing also. Occasionally they would even send trading expeditions across the British Channel to the English coast for lead, tin and other things that were scarce in France. Or Gaul, as David reminded himself. David was glad it was dark and Livilla couldn't see him blush.

"I understand Ramira's in labor?"

"Yes, though Matwyn says her baby won't be born until midday tomorrow. She was hoping you'd attend with me while she and Galwyn got some sleep," Livilla said. Galwyn was Ramira's mother.

They walked toward the hut where Ramira and her husband Jobix lived. Jobix had been firmly ejected. David aside, the birth would be a woman-only affair. David asked where Jobix would be—if things went badly, he wanted to be able to get the man quickly.

"He's with father, Borodur and some of the other men. I'm sure there will be some drinking and storytelling. Throwing dice or bones. Anything to keep Jobix's mind occupied. What do men do where you come from? When their women are birthing?"

"Often they will be present," David said. He was amused at Livilla's shocked expression. "It didn't use to be that way. My sister and I were born five years apart. My father wasn't allowed in the delivery room when my sister was born. By the time I came along he was. That's how fast it changed."

"Change comes slowly here but it seems like there's been a lot of it the last year or two. Mostly thanks to the Romans," Livilla said.

"Aren't you Roman?" David asked her. "Or at least part Roman?"

"I am by blood I guess," she said. "But I've never *felt* Roman. Not like my father does. He's lived with the Mardani a long time but in his heart, he'll always be a Roman citizen. But no, the Romans and this Caesar person have upended everything. My husband was killed because of them."

"I'm sorry," David said. "I never knew you were married. Was he killed fighting—" David's voice caught as he couldn't quite believe what he was about to say, "—Caesar and his legions?"

"Not fighting against them, rather fighting with them. Caesar's generals were recruiting men for his expedition to Britannia, and Kellax thought he'd make his fortune. According to one of our men who came back he cut himself in a fall, the wound festered and Kellax died."

"I'm sorry," David said again, mostly because he didn't know what else he *could* say.

Livilla shrugged. "Such things happen. That's why we're so grateful to you. Everyone was afraid the same thing would happen to Borodur."

It was David's turn to shrug. "I was in the right place at the right time. I was happy to be able to help."

Livilla looked like she wanted to ask more but they had come to Ramira's house. Livilla opened the leather-hinged door and they both stepped inside. Jobix and Ramira's home was small but tidy, with only two rooms. The first room was for dining and receiving guests; the back room was the bedroom. A high-pitched groan told David that Ramira must have just had another contraction.

David was starting to learn some Mardani and recognized Matwyn's greeting. He returned it. He could see why she was so beloved. David was surprised at how much affection he felt for the old woman in the short time he'd known her. Livilla still translated, but David was understanding more, even if Mardani pronunciation gave him fits.

Matwyn and Ramira's mother, Galwyn, had been keeping an eye on things and the old healer reported that things seemed to be going well. "You," she said, pointing to David, "listen to baby's heart. Then we will speak. Privately."

David nodded. Taking his fetoscope, he pressed one end on Ramira's swollen midsection and moved it around, searching for her baby's heartbeat. He found it and keeping mental track of the time judged the baby's heart rate to be perfectly normal and the heart itself strong. David nodded to Matwyn, and the old woman began shuffling out of the room. David and Livilla followed her. As soon as the three of them were in the front room and out of earshot of Ramira and Galwyn, Matwyn turned. Keeping her voice low, she said "The baby is breech. I'm concerned. I examined her before you came. The boy's rear end is down when his head should be."

David did not comment on Matwyn's assertion that Ramira's baby was a boy. He wouldn't be surprised if it were true. Livilla had told him some of the wise woman's story. Matwyn herself claimed no mystical powers, but many others credited her with them. David wasn't so sure there wasn't something to those stories. Mother Matwyn seemed to have a connection with her people and the world around her that went beyond keen observation and many years of learning to read people. Regardless, Matwyn was seeking his counsel. It was time for David to share some of his own wisdom.

"It's early. I think we can turn the baby and hopefully avoid complications. Matwyn, I would suggest you listen to the baby's heartbeat and make sure nothing seems to be going wrong. Livilla, Galwyn and I will turn the baby."

Matwyn nodded her agreement and the three of them trooped back into the bedroom. Matwyn explained the situation in rapid Mardani. David could see the fear on Galwyn's face and on Ramira's, but also a trust in Matwyn, and by extension in David and Livilla. David handed Matwyn his fetoscope. He'd shown the wise woman how to use it soon after he'd arrived, and it hadn't taken long for the old woman to become a pro. David guessed her age had to be close to a hundred and didn't doubt her hearing was still more sensitive than his.

Working together, David, Livilla and Galwyn pushed and shoved on Ramira's middle, manipulating the baby. Finally, he believed they'd succeeded. Taking his ultrasound wand and tablet out of his backpack, David moved it over Ramira's belly, checking the baby. Only Livilla could really see what David was doing--looking at the moving image of Ramira's soon to be born baby (indeed, a boy) still in the womb. And now pointed head-down. All that remained was to keep the young woman comfortable until it was time for the real work to begin.

9

(PAGUS MARDANI, CENTRAL GAUL, 53 BCE)

Kevin trudged toward Jobix and Ramira's modest hut, carrying his uncle's French press and a bag of ground coffee under one arm, and his guitar in the other. Uncle David had enough coffee to last him for quite a while, but the bag Kevin carried was the last of his uncle's beloved Blue Mountain, undoubtedly the last of its kind on Earth. At least for a couple millennia, until coffee was transplanted from eastern Africa to Jamaica. Had coffee even been discovered? Even with his mind for random facts, Kevin couldn't remember when a lucky herdsman in Ethiopia would notice how hyper his goats acted after eating cherries from a nondescript bush.

Kevin thought the stuff was vile. He'd given it another try a few days ago after exhausting his supply of energy drinks. Even sweetened with maple sugar—a coveted luxury item the Mardani collected every spring from the maple stands in the surrounding woods—Kevin just couldn't stand it. Even Gaius Ferrarius, who had to have a potent morning tea brewed by his daughter to truly wake up, couldn't stand it and wondered if David were brave or mad for enjoying such a drink. Kevin's uncle had only laughed and said something about there being more for him. Kevin was picking up the Mardani language faster than his uncle and he knew enough to catch whispers that this mysterious black drink was the source of his miraculous powers. There were rumors that David was a new incarnation of Asclepius, a famous doctor of ancient Greece who became a god after his death and that Kevin—"Keffin," as the Mardani pronounced it— was a golden-skinned agent of Mercury sent to guide and guard him. The rumors were dying down a bit as they both became more famil- iar, but there would always be that small seed of wonder.

"Flavens!" Borodur's voice brought him out of his reverie. The tribe's leader and made the trip from the oppidum called either Mortorgenn or Morgennus, depending on whether one was Mardani or Roman. It was Borodur's custom, apparently, to be personally present when a child was born to the tribe if he possibly could. "Flavens," the yellow or golden one, according to his uncle, was Kevin's new nickname. Borodur sat with a group of men keeping Jobix company while his wife labored and beckoned Kevin to join them. Kevin held up the French press and coffee.

"Must give to my uncle. Join you after," Kevin said. Borodur nodded. The men's idea of keeping Jobix company apparently consisted of friendly wrestling matches which to Kevin resembled mixed martial arts rather than classic wrestling. Actually, Kevin thought, it's kind of like professional wrestling, except the power moves are real and they are not choreographed.

Kevin knocked on the door of Jobix and Ramira's small home. Ramira's younger sister, Chloe, answered the door. If he understood things correctly, Chloe had come into her womanhood and was now eligible to be married. The way she had been looking at him made Kevin uncomfortable. She was about the age of a high school fresh- man, and she'd been eying him like he was her first meal after a weeklong fast. This time, though, she just glared. From the room at the back he could hear Ramira scream. It probably wouldn't be long before Jobix was a dad.

"No more men allowed," Chloe said.

Kevin held out the press and coffee. "Bring for uncle. You give?"

Chloe nodded and took them. Kevin turned to leave and when he gave a last look at the doorway he could swear the look on Chloe's face went from irritated to sultry. Kevin gulped and hurried to join the men. One of Borodur's sons was wrestling a man Kevin didn't recognize. Jobix seemed to be acting as a referee. Though as Kevin watched a moment longer, "referee" was the wrong word; referees enforced rules and there didn't seem to be any rules that he could tell. Maybe Jobix was just making sure the contestants didn't cripple or kill each other. Borodur sat presiding over it all, cheering on his son. Next to him were Ferrarius and a soldier, the first actual Roman Kevin had seen since his arrival. Not counting to Ferrarius, who Kevin thought of as more Mardani than Roman.

"Keffin, welcome!" Borodur said. Kevin had gotten used to the way the Mardani pronounced his name. The hard "vee" sound seemed impossible for them. Borodur said nothing further; his son had his opponent in a submission hold. The man tried to slip out, but his struggles grew weaker and weaker until finally he tapped his opponent's shoulder in surrender.

"Ha ha, well done Allodur!" Borodur said. Jobix clapped the Allodur's back. Turning to Kevin and nodding at the Roman, Borodur switched to heavily accented Latin. "Keffin Flavens, this is legionary Vibius Pullo, down from Morgennus with his commander Gaius Cornelius Chlorus."

Kevin's mouth went a little dry. Pullo was built like a football player. In fact, Kevin thought ruefully, the New York Jets' prospects would probably be a little better if Pullo was in their offensive line. Not that he'd ever know how good or bad the Jets would be this season or ever. Pullo was hard-faced and solid muscle. When he spoke, it was in a rumbling, gravelly bass that seemed to come from the middle of his barrel chest.

"You do a good job making your woods and paths safe, Borodur, but bandits are like mice. They can hide anywhere and make you think they're gone."

Borodur grunted his agreement. Jobix turned to Kevin. "Do you have news?"

"No news. Chloe not let me in door. Ramira still in labor."

Jobix sighed. Allodur wiped himself off with a scrap of cloth. "There's probably time for at least one more match," he said. "We have to decide who will face me to be champion!"

"Yes, there are a whole herd of ewes who can't wait to serve as your harem," said the man Allodur had just beaten. The man's good-natured grin showed he was teasing and Allodur laughed louder than anyone else. Kevin had spent a decent amount of time with the Mardani men and had come to like most of them. As Kevin restored his old Studebaker he'd made friends with some of the students of his high school's "Auto Jammers" club—they were the auto shop kids who liked to show off their work. Any outsider listening in would be convinced a bloody fight would start any second given all the insults flying around, but it was all "busting balls," and if your balls were getting busted you were one of the gang.

"Ah, but Allodur raises a good point. Who should be next?" Jobix asked.

Borodur rather theatrically pretended to think about it. "I think Pullo should go into the ring. For the Senate and the People of Rome!" Pullo grinned and gave the Mardani chief a mock salute. "Now the question is…who should his opponent be?"

Ferrarius cleared his throat. "If Legionary Pullo fights for the glory of Rome, perhaps our new friend Keffin Flavens should fight for the glory of his people. The 'Koy-ree' is it?" Kevin gulped. He couldn't exactly say no and besides, he could tell from the shit-eating grin on Ferrarius's face that this was grade-A ball busting. They were saying he was one of the gang. If only there wasn't such a good chance his actual balls would actually be busted. Pullo reminded Kevin of nothing so much as the side of beef Sylvester Stallone used as a body bag in the first *Rocky*. Except Pullo would punch back. Oh well. Kevin felt committed.

Following Pullo's lead Kevin stripped off his shirt and stepped into the rough circle. When he was young, no more than two or three years after he and his mother had escaped North Korea and after they'd been settled in New York, Anne Rhee decided her son should take tae kwan do lessons. Though Anne had no fondness for the

DPRK she wanted her son to stay connected to his Korean roots. If nothing else, it would give him some exercise. For a time, Kevin enjoyed it but after barely passing his blue belt test both his skill and enthusiasm plateaued. Finally, he convinced his mother to let him quit the lessons.

Kevin's teacher agreed he'd gone about as far as he probably could but was still sorry to see him go. "Keep up with your forms and practice. You're always welcome to come back anytime, even if it's just for a little sparring or a refresher."

As he squared off against Pullo—who looked like he was made of granite rather than flesh—he remembered something else Master had told him: "If you *look* like you can fight you will probably scare off 99% of anyone looking to start trouble. Most of the time you're dealing with bullies, and bullies are almost always cowards."

A Roman legionary, who'd fought alongside Julius freakin' Caesar for Pete's sake, was unlikely to be intimidated by a fighting stance learned in a strip mall dojo. But it might make Kevin himself look slightly less ridiculous. Pullo's brows arched and his mouth quirked into an almost-grin that quickly disappeared. The legionary circled, arms out in a classic wrestling pose, as Kevin pivoted on his back foot to keep himself side-on to his opponent. Pullo made a few feints and Kevin made a few jabs of his own. The voice of Kevin's old tae kwan do master echoed in his head: "Patience is your best friend. Let your opponent make the first move." Problem was, Pullo seemed to follow the same philosophy.

Kevin didn't know how long they circled. Time seemed to slow down. Stretch out. Finally, Pullo went in for a grapple. Kevin blocked him, then danced back. There was a hint of amusement in the Roman's eyes and Pullo gave a small nod of approval that only Kevin could see. For a time that was how things went. Kevin was able to keep Pullo at bay more by virtue of using tactics the legionary had never seen than by any superior skill. Kevin was even able to score a hit with a spinning sidekick that got a barely audible grunt from Pullo. It probably hurt my ankle worse than him, Kevin thought. In the end, it was the soldier's greater stamina that won out. After putting up what he hoped was a respectable struggle, Kevin tapped Pullo's arm three times to signal his surrender. Kevin slumped to the ground and turned over to find Pullo holding out his hand to help him up.

"I didn't expect such a good match Flavens. You did well."

"You barely sweat," Kevin said, miming wiping his forehead because he didn't actually know the word in Latin or Mardani.

"*Sudor*," Pullo said, supplying the word. "You scored a hit. I wasn't expecting it." Kevin grinned. The other men crowded around, slapping his back and complimenting him as if he had won the match. It was an unfamiliar feeling. He'd had friends in high school but few close ones and none that he really kept in touch with after graduation. There were times when he felt like he was floating through life, accepted by many different groups but truly belonging to none. There were many times, deep down, when Kevin Rhee-Castellanos still felt like the weird kid whose mom packed him "stinky cabbage" for lunch and who couldn't speak English. Kevin's attempt to give up his mother's kimchi failed miserably and while the teasing faded as he adjusted to life in America he always felt like an outsider. Now, for the first time in his life, Kevin felt like he belonged. It was a good feeling.

Vibius Pullo eyed his commanding officer as they rode side by side toward Morgennus. Pullo hummed the tune his new friend Kevin Flavens had played on his strange lyre. Pullo hadn't understood a word of the song, but Kevin explained it was about a man who lived on the beach, using a flavorful and strong type of alcoholic drink to dull the pain of his regrets.

Chlorus could use some of this "mark-a-reeta," which seemed to be not wine but rather a mix of fruit juice and a particularly strong alcohol made of the roots of a desert-dwelling plant which grew very far away. The young officer was in a mean mood. Caesar himself had given Pullo this posting after last year's campaigns and though nothing concrete was said, Pullo understood it was a reward for his bravery in combat. Basically, Pullo was to help season Chlorus for his further military career which would undoubtedly in turn groom him for his political career a few years in the future. A few of Pullo's brother legionaries had busted his chops about a cushy assignment. Pullo didn't care. It *was* a cushy assignment, and he deserved it. The scars on his body and the increasing ache of his knees and hips on cool damp days were constant reminders of how faithfully he'd served Rome year after year. Once this campaign was over, Pullo would retire and be given an estate that the slaves he planned to buy with his war spoils would labor on, on his behalf. He would never be rich like Caesar, or his former commander Quintus Tullius Cicero, but it would be a comfortable life. Gods willing, he might even be able to find a woman young enough to bear him children. He always wanted to be the head of his own little clan.

"...that quack," Chlorus said. Pullo brought his attention back to the moment. He'd been so lost in his retirement daydream he'd completely tuned the young officer out. Chlorus, his pale face mottled red with fury, clearly expected him to respond. Pullo halted his horse, pretending to scan the area for bandits to buy himself some time. The name David Medicus popped into his head. Of course, Pullo thought. He's mad about Bennozha not welcoming him into her bed or at least her body.

"This David Medicus seems pretty knowledgeable," Pullo said. He was trying to be neutral. Not getting laid could make anyone grumpy but all men had to deal with it from time to time. There was no use throwing a tantrum like a child deprived of its favorite toy. Pullo wasn't worried that Chlorus would make life hard for him. For all that the kid was from the Cornelii, Pullo himself felt he could count on Quintus Tullius to protect him, maybe Caesar as well. But Chlorus *would* hold a grudge and generally be a bigger pain in the ass than a thistle lodged in a riding blanket. Being noncommittal seemed the best course.

"Knowledgeable," Chlorus sniffed. "Everyone knows sex is good for women with child. It makes for a healthy baby. That's what my nursemaid always said anyway. Who does that man think he is, putting such ideas in people's heads? Who did he study under? For that matter, where did he and that...companion...of his even come from? It all seems pretty suspicious to me."

Pullo grunted, hoping Chlorus would take the sound for agreement. Chlorus was a decent soldier and had potential to be a good officer. Pullo had seen a lot of young men with wealth and connections come and go in his own Thirteenth Legion and others; Chlorus was better than most. But he had the cluelessness and prejudices of his station and it showed here. Physicians weren't held in terribly high esteem, it was true. But one could gain fame and money as a successful doctor, even if they came from nothing. Celer, the chief surgeon for the Thirteenth Legion, was one such. Wealthy families like Chlorus's could afford expensive Greek, Egyptian or Jewish doctors; ordinary Romans had to make do with whoever they could afford. Anyone could set themselves up as physician; you hoped you got one who knew what they were doing. David Medicus knew what he was doing. Pullo had seen Borodur's healed leg wound and had marveled. Something like that almost always festered, leading to amputation and often death. Borodur had a thin pink scar already starting to fade to white, its length the only testimony to its severity.

"Let's stop," Chlorus said. "I have to piss."

Pullo kept watch while Chlorus relieved himself. He heard a yelp followed by a string of oaths. The old veteran smiled to himself. Patrician or not, the kid was learning to swear like a good soldier at least. He'd better see what's wrong though.

It turned out to be a cut finger, and Pullo helped Chlorus bind it with a strip of cloth. The veteran thought about suggesting they turn back and let David, Livilla or Matwyn treat the cut. He decided against it. The suggestion would not be well received and besides, it was just a small cut. It wasn't that serious.

10

(CARRHAE, SOUTHEASTERN ASIA MINOR, 53 BCE)

The Parthian *Spahbod*—Great General—Surena watched the vultures and other carrion birds feasting in the distance. His camp was far enough away from the battlefield—called Carrhae by the Romans for a small nearby town—that he could not smell the stench of death. Mostly. So long as the wind blew the toward the battlefield and away from the Parthian camp that is.

Sipping sweet wine from a small chalice, Surena shifted his gaze to his army. Most of his men were celebrating Parthia's great victory, as well they should. The Romans had not been merely defeated; they'd been all but completely wiped out. Utterly humiliated. Surena would let his men celebrate and rest a few days before returning home in triumph. He himself was relishing the moment when he would present his great king, Orodes, the legionary standards taken in this battle. Surena respected Roman soldiers and knew they would rather die than surrender their legion's standard. And so they had, aside from a few dozen sullen survivors.

Surena saw his bodyguards tense and readied himself for visitors. There were three. The first was Surena's aide-de-camp, a young noble who was proving himself quite capable indeed. The other two were a large man, almost as large as the men guarding the entrance to Surena's tent, and a nervous-looking Armenian Surena's army had swept up on its march, who claimed to be a silver and gold smith. The large man held a burlap bag that looked strained by its contents. Surena's aide bowed and handed him a scroll.

"The latest reports, *Spahbod*," the aide said. Surena said nothing as he took the scroll, then unrolled and skimmed it.

"I see four of the prisoners escaped in the night," Surena said.

"Yes, *Spahbod*," the aide said. The young man seemed so resolute in not saying anything further that Surena would have bet his best charger that he had strong feelings on the matter. Later, when the two of them had some privacy, Surena would seek his opinions. The general himself was not unduly upset. Assuming the escapees even got back to friendly territory, having them tell a tale of defeat no doubt magnified by their ordeal could be a good thing. Maybe—just maybe—the Romans would think twice before crossing swords with Parthia again. Surena made sure his face betrayed none of this. Judging from stories Surena's eyes and ears in camp had relayed back to him, this guard captain was getting ambitions above his station. The fact that prisoners had escaped under his watch might be useful leverage someday. Surena dismissed his young aide with a wave.

"Go. Join the celebrations. We will speak further later." The aide bowed again, then scurried away. Surena turned his attention to the Armenian goldsmith. Once again, Surena had to keep his face from betraying his amusement. The Armenian looked ready to piss himself.

"Show me," Surena said.

"Y-yes *Spahbod*," the goldsmith stuttered. The giant said nothing as he reached inside the sack and brought out a human head coated in electrum, an alloy of silver and gold. This time, Surena did not hide a smile of satisfaction. The gold and silver used to coat this very special head had cost Surena a fair piece of his personal spoils from the Roman baggage train, but it was worth it. Sometimes, short-term gains must be bypassed for even greater benefits farther in the future. More for effect than anything else, Surena made a show of looking the work over.

"Yes," he said. "Yes. Well done." Looking again at the goldsmith, Surena said "I have heard you have your eye on one of the Roman camp followers, yes?"

"I am humbled that you would learn such a thing about someone such as myself, *Spahbod*," the goldsmith said.

"You did not answer my question."

"Y-yes, *S-spahbod*," the Armenian stuttered. "A young thing, still fresh and healthy looking."

"Excellent. I set her aside so she would not be claimed by another, as I was sure that you would not have spoken falsely of your skill to impress me. Because I was confident a man such as yourself would know the consequences of falling short of my expectations."

"Y-yes, *Spahbod*. I am grateful, *Spahbod*."

"As you should be. Now go. Enjoy your prize."

"Yes, *Spahbod*." The goldsmith left, bowing and scraping and no doubt glad of leaving with his head attached and positively overjoyed at the prospect of the sweet thing soon to warm his bed. Surena had seen the girl. Were the great general younger and still hot blooded, he might have sampled her himself. As would have been his right. He'd chosen not to, however. He'd brought two of his favorite concubines, both well-trained in the arts of love.

To his bodyguards, Surena said, "See that I am not further disturbed until I send for dinner. At that time, I will wish my aide to dine with me."

"Yes, *Spahbod*. It shall be done," the senior bodyguard said.

Alone again, Surena truly studied the head. The Armenian had done well; King Orodes would be very pleased. He planned to mention the goldsmith should his king deign to ask. Yes, Surena murmured to himself. Very good. The usually arrogant face, frozen in shock that death should come even for one such as him, had been very well preserved indeed. What King Orodes would do with the gilded head of Marcus Licinius Crassus, reputed to be the wealthiest of all men, was anyone's guess. Even someone as exalted as Surena would not presume to know the mind of his monarch. Not if they had a particle of sense at least. King Orodes was said to be fond of Greek tragedies. Perhaps he would direct the head to be used as a prop for a performance of one of them. Surena did not know and, truly, did not really care. So long as the Great King remembered just *who* gifted it to him. That was all a *spahbod* already wealthy beyond the dreams of most could really ask for.

Judging from the sounds of revelry drifting into his tent, his aide would be occupied for some time, and Surena was not yet hungry. Not for food at least. He summoned his concubines. He would have his own celebration. It was only right that he, too, enjoy the great victory.

11

(PAGUS MARDANI, NORTHERN GAUL, 53 BCE)

David carefully placed his violin in its case. It wasn't his "good" one. That one was in his apartment in New York, the home he would never return to. The loss of that instrument hurt; his mother had gotten it for him from a luthier in Italy who claimed to be able to trace his teaching back to the Stradivari family itself. Whether or not that was true he'd made a fine instrument. David had opted to bring a violin made of composite carbon fiber on this trip. Less sweet sounding perhaps but able to withstand a bit more punishment. Though none of her children followed in Sarai Castellanos' footsteps as a professional musician, David and his siblings had taken lessons and were able to play at least one instrument. His brother Gabriel played flute and his sister Samara played piano. David was a good enough violinist to have gone to music school if he'd chosen but the pull of science and medicine had been stronger. David did not regret the choice. Music became his retreat, something that helped him relax. He looked at Kevin, who was finishing tuning his guitar.

"From the way our new friends reacted to my guitar I can only imagine what they'll think of your violin," Kevin said.

"You'd better hope we're in an alternate universe," David said.

"Otherwise it'll be hard to explain how 'Margaritaville' became a beloved and ancient folk song."

Kevin laughed. "I wasn't expecting that to catch on, but I guess a sweet hook and a story of regrets in love is universal."

David was looking forward to this evening and he knew his nephew was as well. It was the fourteenth day after Ramira gave birth, and her and Jobix's son still lived. According to Livilla, it was Mardani custom that newborn babies were not acknowledged for fourteen days. The child and its mother stayed in seclusion during that time. Of course, everyone in the village found an excuse to visit and see the new arrival, but childbirth was dangerous. If the baby could survive its first two weeks, it was thought that it showed the strength and favor to live. If it did not, the Mardani believed the baby's spirit returned to the gods to come back to the world at a different time.

Ramira was recovering well, and her son was not only surviving but thriving. Ramira was producing plenty of milk and the boy was drinking every drop and gaining weight nicely. Tonight the boy—to be named Auldur, after Ramira's father—would be acknowledged by Jobix as his son and by Borodur as a member of the Mardani. Feasting, music and dancing would follow.

Kevin shut the clasps on his guitar case. It had straps that allowed it to be carried like a backpack—very useful considering they had to climb up and down a rope ladder. "I'm ready if you are, Unc."

David shouldered the backpack that held his emergency medical kit. "Let's go."

They climbed down and found Livilla, Ferrarius and Ramira's sister Chloe waiting for them. Chloe gave Kevin a smile David could only describe as predatory. He was about to tease his nephew when he caught sight of Livilla. She wore a tight-fitting two-piece outfit made of white leather that accentuated her curves. The top was closed by an obsidian toggle that gave enticing peeks of her cleavage while not showing too much. Similar toggles kept the skirt fastened. David had thought Livilla attractive from the first but tonight she took his breath away. He knew he was being rude, but he couldn't help staring at her. Livilla stared at him too. Hopefully she liked what she saw.

"Uh, Uncle? Earth to Uncle David?" Kevin asked.

"Hm? What?" Shaking his head slightly and switching languages he said, "Kevin—speak Latin or Mardani. It's the only way we're going to learn!"

Kevin rolled his eyes. Livilla pointed to the violin case. "Do you play the lute like Kevin does? I'm guessing it's not the same kind since it's smaller."

David smiled at Livilla. She was so beautiful. She smiled back, eyes sparkling. "You'll have to wait and see."

"I can't wait."

The four of them walked to the village center. A bonfire was already burning and most of the village was already there. Matwyn was notably absent, as were Bennozha and her adoptive mother. It was probably nothing, David thought, but worry nagged at him. They were just running late. If it was something more serious, Matwyn would send word. The healer had given him a corner of her house, the largest in the village. He'd packed a couple crates with medicines, tests and basic equipment and left them there. Matwyn's house was the closest thing to a clinic they had.

David saw Kevin talking with Borodur's son Allodur and some of the other men. Kevin's Mardani and Latin had improved very quickly; total immersion was a great way to learn a new language. David knew his nephew often felt like an outsider and was glad he was making friends. He was trying to mingle, too, but couldn't keep his eyes off Livilla. David hadn't thought much of relationships, or sex, since before he'd left New York. The spectacularly awful end to his relationship with Sandy had left him numb. As he spent more time with Livilla, learning about traditional healing methods both with her and from her, his attraction grew. She was smart, capable and steady. Exactly the type of person David always thought he'd want by his side in any situation. And...

And she was beautiful. Particularly tonight.

With impeccable timing, as daylight faded, Borodur stepped to the front of the crowd and raised his hands for attention. Everyone fell silent, and he began the naming and acceptance ceremony for Auldur. Sevel stepped forward and performed blessing that seemed very familiar to David—not all that far from the anointing with oil that was part of an Episcopal baptism he'd gone to once as a guest. It was probably just a coincidence. The assembled village roared their approval, startling little Auldur, who made his displeasure very loudly known. After that was feasting, then music and dancing. Boro-dur's daughter Boryllis led a quartet that performed a number of traditional Mardani favorites.

Livilla came to him, holding out her hand.

"I'm not a great dancer," David protested.

"It doesn't matter. You're the only one I want to dance with."

David did his best to match her steps. Livilla merely smiled at him, her moves becoming more provocative. She seemed to be purposefully giving him glimpses down her top. If Fruit of the Loom existed, they might have found Pagus Mardani an untapped market. He was hypnotized. And then, the music stopped.

"Come on," Livilla said. "It's time to eat."

There were whale steaks, of course, and a huge cut of wild beef that had been slow roasting since before dawn. Plant dishes were scarcer; Livilla had told him, confidentially, that the summer had been cool and damp and the harvests poorer than expected. The Mardani, who were small enough to do more foraging than farming, were in better shape than many of their Veneti and Lexovii neighbors but it was going to be a lean winter. No one was thinking about that right now. Tonight was a night for joy and for showering the newest Mardani child with gifts.

People started shouting for Kevin to perform "Margaritaville," which he obliged and followed up with a medley of pop music from the Beatles to the present. Their old present anyway. Livilla led David someone a little more private, where they could hear the music while being alone. This time her face and shining blue eyes were no dream. They moved towards each other and their lips touched. Tentatively, at first, and then the kiss became more intense. Their hands began to roam around each other's bodies and they broke off. For a moment, neither David nor Livilla said anything.

"Do you want—"

"There you are!" Kevin said. "Sorry to interrupt, uncle, but my hands are starting to cramp and I need a break. It's your turn to entertain."

David sighed and Livilla laughed. "There'll be time later. I've been wanting to see you perform with your strange lute," she said.

"Very well. As the hero of a famous romantic tale of my birth country said, 'As you wish.'" Kevin snorted. David side-eyed him.

LIVILLA AND KEVIN found a spot near the front that her father and grandfather had saved. She watched, fascinated, as David opened the case he carried his lute in. He took an odd-looking bow out first; Livilla couldn't guess what it was for. It could not shoot arrows, that much was obvious; it looked more like a fire bow that was sometimes used to start a fire if flint and a piece of iron or steel weren't handy. He rubbed a block of something on the bow. Then, with a care that bordered on reverence, David lifted his lute from the case. It had the same general shape as Keffin's but was much smaller and had four strings rather than six. And instead of the lute being laid on its side and plucked with either fingers or what Keffin called a "pick," David lifted this lute to his chin with one hand and laid the bow on the string. David paused; was he nervous? Livilla knew she would be. Pagus Mardani didn't often attract traveling musicians or poets, but a few had passed through over the years. David did not have the inflated bravado those men had had. But then, Livilla thought, David never felt the need to brag about himself. It was one of the things she liked most about him.

David drew the bow across the strings, making his lute cry. Livilla had never heard anything like it, and neither had any other Mardani. Before anyone had time to react, David began playing in earnest. None of the music he played was familiar, of course, and yet Livilla could tell he was playing a series of different songs, one blending into the other and yet sounding distinct. David's slender fingers flew up and down the neck of the instrument in a way she found hypnotic and—considering those hands and been exploring her curves just a few moments ago—arousing. David himself was transported. His eyes were closed as he played song after song from memory.

"How does he do it?" Livilla asked. She was talking to herself, but Keffin heard her and answered.

"Lots of practice. Memory. Uncle David almost never forgets something he takes the time to learn. My grandmother has said more than once he could have done this for a living, if he hadn't wanted to be a doctor."

Livilla fell silent, wanting to be lost again. Time seemed to stop and nothing else seemed to exist. After some time, David launched into another song, and his nephew joined him on stage, singing. Once that song ended, Keffin took his guitar. They played several songs together; one was about a trading ship that tragically sank in a storm; another was about a warrior who returns from the grave to gain revenge on the warriors who betrayed him. When they were done, there was a few moments of silence, then applause and shouting. Except for one person. Sevel had tears streaming down his face. But before Livilla could say anything to her grandfather, Bennozha's mother Aethelwyn burst in, running toward David. Livilla knew enough to know she'd be needed too and joined them. The woman was beside herself.

"Good, Livilla, you're here too. Both of you need to come right away. It's Bennozha. Matwyn needs your help with her."

12

(MORGENNUS, NORTHERN GAUL, 53 BCE)

Pullo paced while the healer woman examined Chlorus. The young man, delirious, moaned and mumbled things that only occasionally made sense. She directed the two apprentices with her to bathe Chlorus in cool water in hopes of bringing his fever down. The wise woman motioned for Pullo.

"That hand is going to have to come off. The flesh is dead," she said.

"And the flesh being dead, it's starting to poison his body?" Pullo asked.

"You've seen this before, have you?" The woman looked Pullo up and down. "I'd wager you have at that."

"I'm no *medicus* but the first time I held a fellow-soldier down while his dead leg was taken off, I was not much older than this one. Is there nothing that can be done?"

"If you've seen wounds like this, you know the answer to your own question. Not even that new man Matwyn's taken under her wing would say different, though it's said he sewed Borodur's leg back on after a shark bit it off."

Pullo laughed, the absurdity of the rumor being a welcome relief from the grim situation. "No, his leg wasn't bitten off. It did get badly sliced open and David Medicus was instrumental in treating it. Though David Medicus himself gives Livilla equal credit."

"Humble and talented. You've met him?"

"Briefly. I know his nephew a little better."

The wise woman's eyes narrowed. "That being so, why did you not send for him?"

"The wound was healing clean till Chlorus re-opened it, then it festered very quickly. And Chlorus took a dislike to the man. His pride wouldn't let him seek help."

"As I see it, Roman, your officer has a choice: die horribly of blood poisoning with his pride intact or get help from the one person that might—just might—have a chance of saving his life."

Pullo nodded. The woman had the right of it. He would ride to Pagus Mardani himself and bring David back.

DAVID AND LIVILLA rushed into Matwyn's hut to Bennozha's bedside. David could see at a look that the situation was grim. He knew at once what was going on.

"It's an abruption," he said, mixing in the English term. Seeing Livilla and Matwyn's puzzled looks, he explained further: "The placenta, the organ that becomes the afterbirth, is tearing away from the wall of her womb."

Matwyn nodded. "Yes, I've seen this before. She will bleed to death. Her and the baby both."

"I should have suspected something was going on when she started spotting. Light spotting is not usually serious, but—"

Livilla laid her hand on his shoulder. "You couldn't have known, David."

"Not even I suspected it," Matwyn said. "Wishing we could change the past won't change it. We need to act, quickly." Turning to Aethelwynn, busy holding a cloth to her daughter's birth canal, Matwyn asked "Is it slowing down at all?"

Aethelwynn stifled a sob. "I don't think so."

David rooted through one of the crates he'd stored in the corner Matwyn had given him. He'd half-forgotten the almost random assortment of things he'd brought from New York. Most of it, like the antibiotics, painkillers and prenatal vitamins, made sense. There was also equipment like tubing, needles, and IV bags, not to mention pregnancy tests. There were other things like the multiple boxes of reading glasses in a range of prescriptions that had made him scratch his head. Among those were close to a thousand blood typing tests. About the same size and modeled after a home pregnancy test, a drop of blood on one end was all that was needed. After about a minute a small liquid crystal display showed the blood and Rh types. According to the person who'd donated them, they were highly accurate and were awaiting approval from the FDA. He'd already tested them on Kevin and himself. He knew Kevin was type O-, a type called "the universal donor" because it could be received by all other blood types. David heard a rustle at the entrance to Matwyn's treatment room and saw Chloe.

"Chloe. Get Kevin. Right now, tell him to hurry." Chloe nodded and ran off. Taking one of the blood typing tests, he held the testing end against one of the blood-soaked rags Aethelwynn had discarded. The display showed "AB+."

"Thank God," David breathed.

"Are you praying?" asked Livilla.

"After a fashion. You might say that Fortuna is smiling on us. This is going to sound insane, but there's a chance we can save Bennozha."

"And what is this insanity?" asked Matwyn.

"I can take a little blood from anyone who's healthy and give it in turn to Bennozha to replace the blood she's losing. I can't guarantee it will save her life but it's our only chance."

"You're right," Matwyn said. "It is insane. But I can see that you speak truly. And I know you would never willingly let someone under your care suffer needlessly. I saw that even before we could understand each other. What of the baby? She's in labor and it won't be long."

"We'll have to hope. It's a longshot but if the child survives the birth we might be able to save it, too. But our priority should be Bennozha. I'll be honest; this is something I'd never do unless there was no other choice."

"I trust you, David," Livilla said.

"Let us do this," Matwyn said. "I will give blood first."

"I appreciate that, Matwyn, but you, me and Livilla should not donate unless there's no other choice. The amount of blood I would need to take won't be harmful but it will be enough to make a person light headed for a time, almost as if they've had a little too much wine. The three of us will need to have clear heads."

"Then I will go first," Aethelwynn said. "It's only right. Livilla, Matwyn, can you help stop her bleeding? I think it's slowed a little."

There was a second bed and David directed Aethelwynn to lie down. Saying a silent prayer of thanks that he had practiced at "nurse work" David was able to quickly find a good vein and soon Aethelwynn's blood was flowing into a one-pint IV bag.

"That barely hurt at all," Aethelwynn said. "It felt like a pinch."

"You're doing very well, Aethelwynn. It won't take long."

Just then, Chloe led Kevin into the room. Seeing all the blood, he paled. Looking up from tending Bennozha, Matwyn told Chloe to get every healthy adult who wasn't pregnant or nursing to line up outside and await further instructions.

"You needed me, Uncle David?"

"Yes," David said, not looking up from his own work. "I do. Or your blood at least. Just a moment." David disconnected the needle leading from Aethelwynn's arm to the IV bag. Grabbing an unused plant drying rack, he improvised a hanger and connected the bag. He made sure it was dripping its contents into Bennozha's arm, replacing the precious blood she was losing. By the time he was done, Kevin was ready to make his donation. Over the next few hours, David took a pint of blood from almost every adult in the village; at first, Bennozha was needing the blood as fast as he could get it, but she then slowed as her labor deepened. She drifted in and out of consciousness, sometimes speaking in a language David did not understand. Neither did anyone else.

"That was the language she spoke when we found her with her dying birth mother on the beach," Matwyn said.

Things calmed enough that the three healers were able to catch their breath. It was only then that David realized there was one person he hadn't seen show up to donate blood. Allodur. When he mentioned it, Chloe piped up. She'd stayed to help fetch things and people so no one else had to.

"Borodur sent him to fetch Chlorus. He thought Chlorus would probably want to be here and Allodur could make the trip the fastest," the young woman said.

David nodded. Bennozha was clinging to life for the moment, but David knew better than anyone how quickly that could change. Hopefully Chlorus would hurry.

PULLO WASN'T FAR outside Morgennus when he heard hoofbeats. He halted his own horse and tensed as he saw a silhouette. It looked familiar but Pullo eased his hand toward the hilt of his sword just in case.

"Hail! Pullo...is that you?"

Pullo squinted—not that that would help him see better in the dark. Then he placed the voice.

"Allodur? What are you doing here?"

Allodur brought his horse next to Pullo's.

"I might ask the same thing. Father sent me to fetch Chlorus. Bennozha went into labor early."

"Great gods. How is she?"

"Not good, but I don't know the details. I'd rather not. It's healer and women's business."

"We're on similar missions, then," Pullo said. "I was going to fetch David Medicus, for Chlorus. He has a festering wound and it's poisoning his blood."

Allodur muttered something in Mardani under his breath. Pullo could guess its meaning. "Father often tells me I need to be decisive. I can't give you orders, Pullo, but we should get a litter and get Chlorus to the village as quickly as we can. David Medicus spent every moment by Father's side until he was sure of recovery. If Bennozha is as bad as I fear she is he will not leave. We're better off taking Chlorus to him."

"Let's go, then."

By the time the wise woman and her apprentices had Chlorus ready for travel, Pullo and Allodur had built a travois that would be sturdy enough to hold the young man. Only two points of the travois would touch the ground, making it easier for Pullo's horse to pull and hopefully keeping painful bounces to a minimum. It would have to work; if they walked they would never get Chlorus to David in time.

Matwyn covered the tiny body. Livilla struggled to stay focused on Bennozha, who was mercifully unconscious. She was clinging fiercely to life. David sat slumped, looking utterly defeated. He had tried, so hard, to save Bennozha's baby. She'd never seen someone try to pump and breathe life into a stillborn before. Making sure that Bennozha was comfortable, she went to him. Before she could get to where David sat, Vibius Pullo walked in. David looked up.

"Pullo? Is Chlorus here?" David asked.

"That is why I'm here, *medicus*," Pullo said. The legionary looked to where Bennozha lay.

"She's alive, for the moment," Livilla said.

"The child?" asked Pullo.

Livilla said nothing, merely shaking her head. The tough Roman soldier softened a little, showing his grief.

"What is happening with Chlorus?" David asked.

"He cut his hand on our way back to the oppidum when we were here last time. It healed cleanly at first, but then he re-opened the wound and it festered."

"How bad is it?"

"Bad," Pullo said. "I've seen wounds like it before. To me, his hand looks dead."

Suddenly, David looked very tired. But before he could ask Pullo any other questions, Allodur and another Roman soldier came in, carrying Chlorus on a stretcher between them. Matwyn, who had been observing but saying nothing, directed them to put Chlorus on the empty bed. Livilla didn't even have to see the young man's wounded hand to know how bad it was; the smell of it made her nauseous. Even so, she wasn't quite prepared for what she saw. Even Matwyn, so stoic in situations like these, winced. David muttered an oath that Livilla had come to understand was something from his own language often said in dire situations.

"That hand will have to come off," Matwyn said. Livilla nodded. She was amazed that Chlorus was still alive. She remembered one patient she'd helped Matwyn with not long after Livilla began her apprenticeship. The man, known for his stubbornness, had gotten frostbite but hadn't wanted to have any of his toes cut off. By the time he was brought to Matwyn it was too late. The gangrenous toes spread their poison throughout his body. He died not long after. Chlorus's hand looked even worse.

Looking at the delirious Chlorus, David asked Pullo, "Matwyn is right. That hand will have to come off. Had he come earlier we might have saved it."

Pullo only nodded. "You must do what you must do."

"First, we have to get his fever down. I have something for that, but it will probably take a few hours to work."

"What will you do in the meantime?" Livilla asked.

"Study how to amputate a hand. I've never done it before."

Livilla watched as David stripped off the tight-fitting gloves he wore when treating someone, at least when blood or open wounds were involved. He then removed the mask he wore. Chlorus was mercifully unconscious; David checked his pulse and breathing and seemed satisfied. Still, he looked like a beaten man and Livilla couldn't understand why. Bennozha's life hung in the balance but the fact she still lived was a victory. Even Matwyn couldn't have kept the young woman from bleeding to death and the fact that David knew how to replace that blood had everyone in awe. Livilla had heard the whispers that the strange man was Asclepius reborn and after this those whispers would only get louder.

Livilla put her hands on David's shoulders and looked into those brown eyes she was growing to love. They had all the kindness and compassion she'd become very attracted to, mingled with grief and a sense of failure. Before she could speak up, Pullo voiced her thoughts. Pullo and Ferrarius had helped hold Chlorus still. He'd been semiconscious during the operation as David had amputated Chlorus's left hand with a saw Ferrarius had originally made for Jobix and Ramira as a gift. Even Sevel had come to observe the desperate emergency surgery.

"You look like a defeated centurion, David Medicus. Why?"

"It shouldn't have come to this. Bennozha's baby shouldn't have died. She shouldn't be fighting for her life. And Chlorus shouldn't have had to lose his hand. If I'd had more, if I'd been where I should have been…"

"You are where you needed to be," Sevel said. Livilla looked at her grandfather in shock. He'd said little the last month or so, and he'd gone out of his way to avoid any interaction with David or his nephew. "If you weren't here, we would be mourning the end of three lives, not just one. It is sad that Bennozha and Chlorus's daughter died before she had a chance to live. But Bennozha is young, and thanks to you she may yet have a chance to bear children."

"That's very kind of you, Sevel. Very kind. But her survival isn't certain. Neither is Chlorus's, really. I'm hopeful. But I've never done an amputation before today. What if I did something wrong?" David sighed, pressing his fingers into his eyes. Livilla hoped this self-doubt was due to exhaustion. He hadn't slept in a day and had barely eaten.

David sighed as if he were Atlas bearing the weight of the world. "I just need to be alone." He walked away, out of the house and almost certainly toward the boat that doubled as his and Keffin's house. Livilla was torn. Her heart told her she needed to follow, no matter what David just said. She was torn.

"We have to go to him," her grandfather said.

"What?" Livilla couldn't quite believe what she was hearing.

"We have to go to him. You and I both."

Livilla frowned, fighting an impulse to be angry at the grandfather she loved above everyone but her own father.

"Why? Why now? You've said almost nothing to anyone since before the whale butchering. You've avoided David and Keffin to the point where they're sure you hate them. And now you're saying you and I have to go to him?"

Sevel sighed. "I understand why you'd be angry at me, Livilla. All I can say is that I'm sorry about the way I've handled things. We will go to David, and hopefully things will be clearer to you after."

Livilla watched, as her grandfather shuffled away. She followed and they made their way slowly to where David and Keffin's boat was docked. Keffin greeted them as they climbed aboard.

"He's in his room," Keffin said. "I'm worried. He's shutting down. He did this right before we met all of you. It took Borodur getting hurt and me telling him he had to help to snap him out of it. What if I can't bring him out of it this time?"

"Grandfather and I want to talk to him," Livilla said.

"Why does he want to help?" Kevin asked, with an edge in his voice. "He's barely said a word to us."

"I can only tell you what I've told Livilla," Sevel said. "That I am sorry, and I hope things will be clearer soon."

Kevin led them below decks. Livilla had never been invited inside the boat itself and was not prepared for what she saw. She now realized why Jobix refused to describe what he'd seen when he'd helped Kevin bring the boat to the sheltered river inlet. She was in another world. There were things writing on their outside edge lined up on shelves. They weren't scrolls. She'd never seen anything like them.

"They're *codices*," her grandfather said. His eyes were wide too but there was something about his reaction that said he'd seen some of these things before. "They have writing in them, like scrolls, but they are kept differently."

"You've seen them before?" Livilla asked.

"Yes. Never that small though."

She wanted to ask her grandfather if she'd ever seen furnishings as fine as they were seeing. The shelves, chairs, were made with a precision that she could not comprehend. And then there was the lighting. There were no torches, but an almost-natural yellow light filled the room. Keffin didn't slow down, however, and there was no time to ask Sevel anything else. He'd clearly seen at least some things like this before. His face had an expression of wonder, but not shock. Keffin opened a closed door into what was clearly a bedroom. As with the furniture in the outer room, she'd never seen a bed so big or soft-looking. David was in the middle of it, curled into a tight ball. Walking around Keffin and her grandfather, she held him. It was as if they were two soup spoons, nested together.

"I said I want to be alone," David said, his voice muffled.

"No. You need to be with people," Livilla said.

"She is right," Sevel said. Then, he said something she didn't understand. It sounded like the language David and his nephew spoke between themselves, though they'd been doing that less and less. David clearly did understand, and he sat bolt upright, a shocked expression on his face.

"What year was it, when you came through the fog?" It took a moment for David to register that Sevel was speaking in English.

"Two thousand and twenty-two," David finally said.

"Tell me, did King James keep his throne? Were rumors of invasion true?"

"Which King James?" Kevin asked, once he got over his own shock.

"James II."

David shrugged. History facts weren't his strength. Kevin thought a moment.

"He was driven off the throne by William and Mary. Uh, William III and Mary II if I'm remembering right."

"So. The rumors *were* true. I've always wondered. Let me tell you a story…"

13

(TORBAY, CORNWALL, ENGLAND, 1688 CE)

The gloomy weather outside matched Rev. Steadfast Cooper's mood. He'd agreed to hold this secret meeting at his house, though why he needed including at all was beyond him. He had tried begging off, telling the man known only as "The Archdeacon" and the local Anglican priests and vicars with him that he was still in mourning and needed to tend to his young daughter who was still upset at the loss of her mother. The truth was, Steadfast was more bereft than Livia seemed to be, but it was hard to tell. She was just four and Steadfast knew little of the mind of young children.

He tried to stay focused as The Archdeacon—the irony of the man taking a popish rank as his *nom de guerre* was no doubt intentional—ranted against King James II and his intentions, and the duplicity of the male Stuarts.

"Mary can be trusted, without question," The Archdeacon said. "She's never wavered in her loyalty to Protestantism. The Dutch would not have tolerated her as William's wife were it not so."

"Our king is no more reliable than his father and his promises no more trustworthy," one of Steadfast's fellow vicars grumbled. "And what did Charles I and his dithering get us? Twenty years under that tight-arse Cromwell. The British Isles need a monarch. Just not one with loyalties to Rome."

The Archdeacon turned to Steadfast, his eyes boring into him like a woodworker's drill. "Your thoughts, Rev. Cooper? You've said little."

Steadfast sighed. "Yes. This is a hard thing. King Henry's separation from Rome was a good and necessary thing, and yet...James is our lawful sovereign. We should trust him." He held up his hands, forestalling the objections he knew would come to that last point. "I agree, the Stuart kings have not exactly been, you shall pardon the word, steadfast, in their commitment to the path King Henry set us upon so long ago and that we might be better served with a Stuart queen in James's stead. And even if James II proves faithful to his promise not to interfere in religious matters, what a King James III might do once he gains the throne—or what an ambitious regent might do should he gain the throne before he gains his manhood— are open questions. I—"

Just then, Steadfast heard his daughter cry out. "I apologize, gentlemen. I must attend young Livia. Her sleep has been unsettled since her mother's passing."

One of his fellow vicars, the one who'd grumbled about Cromwell's Puritan prudishness, glared at Steadfast, clearly annoyed. "Do you not have a governess man?"

Steadfast fought his own irritation down. As if he could afford a governess on a vicar's pay. "A widow-matron of the village helps me see to Livia's needs. I felt it better she not be here while we discussed matters."

"Your discretion and judgement are most appreciated," said The Archdeacon. "Go to your little girl. But please, give me your answer by morning."

"How?"

The Archdeacon handed Steadfast a silver penny coin. The operative pressed on the profile of the king, causing a tiny compartment to pop out from the edge.

"I trust you can write legibly and small, Reverend Cooper," he said. "A man will be in the village selling hot meat pies. Tell him you've heard he sells haggis pies and that you wish to try one. He will, sadly, not have any such pies but will offer you six lamb pies for a penny. Pay him with this penny and not trouble yourself with the rest."

With that The Archdeacon and his friends took their leave. Steadfast decided to dress Livia and take a walk. It was dark, but he'd grown up in this village and knew its paths as well as he knew the Sermon on the Mount. A walk would help clear his head and hopefully tire Livia out so she would sleep once more.

The night was indeed comforting as he walked a familiar loop of trails that would lead back to the vicarage after about an hour or so. The weather was crisp and dry, not yet cold but holding promise of the coming fall. As Steadfast and Livia Cooper turned back toward their modest home, a fog arose. Steadfast thought it a bit unusual but gave it no further thought. Fog was common near the coast; how or why it occurred or did not was a mystery to him, a mystery he never gave much thought to. Natural science had never held much interest.

Had Steadfast Cooper known what the fog was, what it would do, he might have tried—likely in vain—to flee it. Instead, he and his young daughter walked through it, and he found himself in a world he could scarcely imagine.

"We hadn't moved from where we went through the fog," Sevel said, "though I didn't realize that until later. I was able to pick out a distinct landmark I knew. But all I knew then was that suddenly the woods had become wilder, and a charcoaler's cottage I knew of nearby was nowhere to be found. I had my daughter to protect, and it felt like we were the only two people in the world. We wandered for days and I was on the verge of giving up when people finally found us."

"The trade delegation?" Livilla asked.

"Yes, led by Borodur's great-uncle. We couldn't understand each other, but they seemed to know we were in trouble and wanted to help us. Gradually, as I learned the Mardani language, I came to understand more of what happened." Looking at David, Sevel said, "You had an advantage, knowing Latin."

"As a written language," David said. "Even in your day—your day as an Englishman at least—some people spoke Latin."

"Why did you learn it, if I may ask? Are you a papist?"

David laughed. "No. Well, that's not quite true. My father is Catholic. My mother is a Coptic Christian, from Egypt. I'm both and neither. I've never been especially religious."

"And what of you, young man?" Sevel asked Kevin. Kevin shrugged.

"That's a bit of a long story, but the place my mother and I lived in till I was about six discouraged any sort of religious worship."

"Hmm." Sevel would have liked to have pursued that. Perhaps he would, later, but now was not the time.

Livilla looked at David. "Where did you come from? You and Keffin? I know you've said you come from far away, but I've always sensed that wasn't the truth. Not the whole truth anyway."

"No, you're correct," David said. "It was the truth but it left out a lot of detail. I suppose, Sevel, you know of England's colonies in the New World?"

"Know or knew?" Sevel, David and Kevin all laughed. Verb tenses had become much more complicated. "Yes. Before I was appointed to my vicarage I used to minister to the sailors of Torbay before they set sail across the Atlantic."

"That's where Kevin and I come from. New York City. Though it might still have been New Amsterdam when you disappeared, I don't know," David said.

"No, it was under English rule. I daresay it must be still?" Sevel said.

Kevin spoke up. "No, not quite. But that's another long story."

David yawned. Livilla looked at him with a frown of concern.

"I have a feeling there will be many long stories to share," she said. "But our medicus needs sleep, rather badly. Grandfather, send someone when Bennozha or Chlorus wake up."

Sevel looked from David to Livilla and smiled faintly. "Yes, granddaughter. I would ask one last question."

"Yes?" David asked.

"Does England still have a king in the year 2022?"

"It does. A queen, actually. Elizabeth II."

Sevel laughed. "How about that? A queen! A second Elizabeth no less!" Allowing Kevin to lead the way, with that he took his leave.

DAVID LAY BACK DOWN and Livilla held him as before. For a time he said nothing; she wondered if he'd fallen asleep. Then, the turned over to face her. "Did you ever know that? About Sevel?" he asked.

"No. Though a lot of things make sense now that never quite had. Like when I hear you speak your native language. I always thought I *should* understand it. When Grandfather told his story, I suddenly had a memory. When I was a little girl, Mother always sung me a lullaby but I could never quite understand the words. Could she have been singing me a song in this 'English' tongue?"

David considered for a moment. "Maybe. Very possibly." He kissed her then, and neither of them spoke further for a while. She thought David wanted to do more than kiss, and she would have been more than willing, but then he stopped.

"What's wrong?" Livilla tried to keep the frustration out of her voice and wasn't sure she entirely succeeded.

"I'm sorry. I'm just so damn tired Livilla. Physically and spiritually. I don't want to promise certain things I won't be able to follow through on right now."

Livilla sighed. She was beyond exhausted too, but also very aroused. She flipped over and nestled against David, making him be the big spoon this time.

"It's fine, David Medicus. We have plenty of time." With that, they both fell sound asleep.

PARS SECUNDA

Audi, vide, tace, si tu vis vivere in pace
—Marcus Aurelius Antoninus

14

(ALESIA, CENTRAL GAUL, 52 BCE)

It comes down to this, thought Caesar two days after the Kalends of September. A whole summer's campaigning hung on a siege. As the chiefs of his Gallic allies had warned him, the previous fall's harvest had been poor, but the Roman demands for food for its legions were no less because of it. Perhaps, Caesar had reflected on more than one occasion, his quartermasters and officers had been more heavy-handed than strictly necessary in collecting the meat and grain they'd promised. In the end, he needed to feed his troops. Hungry soldiers were ineffective soldiers, and far too often they were mutinous soldiers.

And so it came down to a siege. Caesar hated siege warfare. Not for the usual reason that a siege left no room for valor. It was true, pitched battle or storming an enemy stronghold brought glory. But even more frequently, they brought death. Far better the grind of a siege that ultimately brought victory than the glorious charge that ended in defeat. Caesar had sipped that bitter wine at Gergovia earlier in the summer and he couldn't afford to do so here. No, thought Caesar, the worst thing about a siege is that it's so damn boring. And the problem is that if soldiers get too bored they won't stay alert. Discipline goes to hell and the enemy breaches the gates.

Here at Alesia, storming Gallic war chief Vercingetorix's stronghold wasn't even an option. The oppidum sat atop a hill and was protected by six-foot-tall walls, and on three sides by river or unfavorable ground. There was only one option—frontal assault. Julius Caesar was not afraid to fight an enemy who outnumbered him; that had been the rule rather than the exception throughout his military career. His own superior strategy and the discipline of his legions allowed him to fight as if he commanded a force two, even three times as large as his actual numbers. But in a direct assault of the kind he'd need to take Alesia by force all the discipline in the world wouldn't count for much, and there would be no room for fancy tricks and superior strategy. Caesar believed he was outnumbered at least three to one. So, a siege it would have to be.

Caesar's solution was to set his men to building earthworks the likes of which had never been seen. If anyone could have seen the siege works from above, they would have seen the oppidum at Alesia surrounded by two concentric rings. The inner ring would prevent any attempt by Vercingetorix and his army to break out of the hill fort. The Gallic king had already attempted that once, just before the earthworks were finished, and his men had barely turned the attack back. This inner ring had a system of forts, ramparts, walls and ditches that stretched nearly 12 *miles*, standard Roman miles, with a height of over 12 *pedes*, standard Roman feet. Moats in front of the walls and ditches filled with sharpened stakes had already proved their worth in making any attack costly and futile. The outer layer, set up nearly identically to the inner ring, stretched nearly 14 *miles*. It had been a massive undertaking, completed in less than a month. There had been no time for boredom. Caesar was proud of his men and had told them so.

Caesar looked up as Aquila entered his tent.

"Yes?"

"Legate Antony and *Evocatus* Postumus Agnus were hoping to speak with you."

"Did they say what it was concerning?"

"No, Caesar."

Caesar finished the sentence he'd been writing. His account of these Gallic campaigns would certainly shore up his support in Rome but putting a good face on the defeat at Gergovia would take some doing. He'd think further on it later. Caesar was fairly certain this had to be important. Antony might seek his company out of boredom if he weren't carousing with his men but Agnus—one of the elite *evocati*—would not ask to speak to him without very good reason.

"Show them in, then stay with us, Aquila. I sense you wish to speak as well."

"You are right as usual, Caesar," Aquila said.

The lictor ushered Mark Antony and Postumus Agnus into the tent. They couldn't have been more different. Antony had a physique to please any sculptor. Well-formed, muscular, with a broad, handsome face and prominent nose. Agnus, on the other hand, was every inch the hardened legionary. The evocatus had a weathered face with a hard body. He looked like a human battering ram.

"What is it?

"Agnus insisted we come see you. After hearing him out, I agreed," Antony said.

Caesar wasn't trying to intimidate, but it was clear even this hardened veteran was more than a little afraid of him. That was fine. Soldiers should be a little afraid of their commander.

"*Medicus* Celer, sir. He wishes to speak with you. He needs more help in the infirmary tents, he says. He and Corvus are overwhelmed."

"Why didn't he come to me directly?" Caesar asked.

"Too busy, he says. I've known him since he joined up. He wouldn't complain without having his reasons."

Caesar considered for a moment and then stood up. "I'll speak with Celer. I agree with you, *Evocatus* Agnus. He is not given to complain without reason."

If he'd had other matters or plans for the day, Caesar would not have concerned himself with this. But it was good to be seen in the camp and seen to be concerned with day-to-day affairs. A commander who was out of touch lost loyalty, and a commander who lost loyalty lost wars.

They walked out of the tent toward the infirmary. Lucius Celer was a Romanized Remi who'd joined the legions at the beginning of Caesar's campaigns in Gaul four years ago. Celer had suffered a knee injury that first summer which made soldiering impossible, but he showed he had some talent as a medicus. In the years since he'd risen to be one of the chief surgeons in Caesar's legions. The Remi were one of the few tribes who'd stayed loyal in the face of Vercingetorix's rebellion, and Celer's prominence was a point of pride for them.

"I'm not sure there's much I can do for him in the short term but if nothing else I can show the Remi I value their loyalty by supporting one of their favorites—when every other tribe in Gaul has deserted."

"The Mardani have stayed loyal," Antony said.

"Words, so far, though they haven't sent men to Vercingetorix as far as I know. Hopefully Pullo's trip to them will bear fruit. But even if they do come, they are too few to make a difference. Still, I suppose I will have to reward them suitably."

"Yes," said Antony. "And their slingers are the best I've seen. Those lead sling bullets are devastating. I wish we had thousands of them, raining sling shot down from the ramparts."

"That's just the problem," Caesar said. "We need thousands when they can only send a hundred at best."

"Every little bit helps, said the old woman as she pissed into the sea," said Antony.

Aquila rolled his eyes. Caesar merely grunted. "As you say."

The three men came to the main infirmary tent. There were four altogether; the main one was for the most serious cases, surgeries, and personal workspace for Celer, his chief assistant Corvus, and their assistants. At the moment, the tents were mostly empty aside from the usual injuries from work details and a few cases of the flux. Nothing out of the ordinary for a siege. As Agnus had explained to Antony, Celer's worry about handling the workload had as much to do with what he anticipated as the actual workload of the present.

He was stripping off a tunic with some blood stains as Caesar,

Antony and Agnus entered. Celer's hair was starting to go gray but retained the toughness he'd developed as a solider before his knee injury. Corvus couldn't have been any different physically. Corvus's name meant "crow," a name he'd picked up in his life among the Romans. Corvus didn't seem to mind and insisted that his true name was quite unpronounceable to anyone but his own people. He was from a tribe who lived in the south of Numidia, on the fringes of the great desert there. Corvus's father was their chief, and he sent Corvus to live among the Romans, learn their ways, and hopefully be a bridge; when his people were wiped out in the innumerable inter-tribal wars of their home, Corvus's time among the Romans became permanent exile. He discovered he had a talent for medicine, and life as a legionary doctor suited both his talent and his warrior spirit. With his tall, gaunt build and dark skin, he soon became known as Corvus.

"Caesar," he said in his low, pleasant voice. "This is an unexpected if welcome surprise."

"I was told Celer wished to speak to me?" Caesar said.

"I do!" Celer said, shrugging on a clean tunic. "I know it doesn't look like it, but we're understaffed. Things are quiet now, but tell me, as one soldier to another—you expect a major battle. Maybe more than one. Corvus and I are doing our best to train the doctors we have, and maybe one or two of them will be decent by the time we need them, but a lot of men are going to die that could be saved. I didn't really like that idiot Hipparchus but at least he had training and ability. Normally I'd count on having help from some of the healer-druids but..." Celer said no more, instead spreading his hands.

Caesar sighed. "I will do what I can, Celer. I've sent Vibius Pullo to the Mardani to bring some of their slingers and a medicus of great skill who is said to have settled among them." With a nod to Antony, Caesar added, "I'm assured of Mardani loyalty and confident that Pullo will be successful."

Aquila fidgeted. Caesar looked sharply at him. "You wish to say something. Aquila?"

"I'm not so sure of his skill, Caesar. You saw what happened to poor Chlorus's hand."

"So glad you've agreed to share your medical expertise, Aquila," Celer said. The sarcasm in his voice was almost physical. "Explain to me how you would have sewed the stump better? Prevented it from festering?"

"Hipparchus said--"

Celer cut Aquila off. "Hipparchus may believe that his skills are near divine, but he wipes his ass just like the rest of us. Pullo's account of events was quite detailed. Chlorus refused treatment until the flesh of his hand died and was starting to spew poison into his blood. Forget the amputation, just the fact he was able to save Chlorus's life tells me all I need to know about his skill." Antony snickered. Like many military doctors, Celer's education had been experience rather than texts and lectures. Celer still had a common soldier's way of speech. Even Caesar found himself having to suppress a grin.

Aquila opened his mouth to respond but Caesar cut him off. "Enough! Assuming this Davidius Medicus is real, and the stories of his abilities are not exaggerated—and I believe they are not, Pullo not being given to flights of fancy--I will accept his help and assign him to you, Celer. And I will send messages to what allies we still have for men of healing skill. That is all I can do."

"We are most grateful for your efforts, Caesar. We can only do what we are able to do. The rest is in the hands of the gods."

"As you say," Caesar said. "I must take my leave. I am able to provide supplies more readily than trained healers, so provide Tribune Antony with a list of any supplies or equipment you may need for all the infirmaries. You have served me and your fellow soldiers well, Celer. I will see to it you have the tools to succeed."

"Gratitude, Caesar," Celer said. "If nothing else for being willing to listen. As you say, Vibius Pullo is an honest man not given to exaggeration. I've heard a few of the rumors as well, from some of the other men that helped bring Chlorus here. I am curious as to whether this Davidius person is marked by Mercury as they say."

"What did you say?" asked Caesar.

"I've heard rumors that he is marked with the staff of Mercury on his back. A *stigmata* that is like a fresco on skin," Celer said.

Without saying a word Caesar left, hurrying back to his tent. Antony and Pullo scrambled in his wake, but he waved off every attempt to talk to him. This would be important, but he didn't know when. I must have it at hand, Caesar thought. I must be prepared.

Antony and Agnus watched Caesar disappear into his tent.

"I should not have disturbed him," Agnus said.

Antony considered the veteran. Agnus meant "little lamb," and whether by accident or design the name was quite ironic—as Roman names often were. Caesar himself was a perfect example; there were varying stories about how the *cognomen* "Caesar" came to be used in the general's branch of the Julii family, but one of the origins was in the word for "hairy." This, for a man who tried to conceal his growing baldness by combing his thinning hair over the bare spot on his head. Antony couldn't think of someone less like a lamb of any size than Postumus Agnus. In body and temperament, the *evocatus* resembled one of the fierce, muscular Molossian dogs that fought with the legions. Relentless, savage in battle and utterly loyal. In any physical contest, Gaius Julius Caesar wouldn't stand a chance against Postumus Agnus. The soldier could break him in half. And yet this man, whom Antony had seen throw himself into battle with no care for himself, was terrified he offended his commander. That was the secret of Caesar's greatness, thought Antony. Agnus's fear wasn't a fear of Caesar's cruelty; it was the fear of losing the esteem of a general the elite legionary would gladly follow to the gates of Dis itself.

"I know that look, Agnus. I wouldn't be surprised if Caesar's in his tent now writing down whatever it was that struck him about that rumor."

Agnus relaxed. Antony clapped the veteran on the shoulder.

"Now," said the legate, "I feel the need to get drunk and play dice. Let's go find a game."

Antony could have found his way through this camp, or the three others arrayed inside the massive earthworks, blindfolded. In fact, he'd had to find his way through a legionary camp blind drunk more than a few times. All Roman military camps were laid out exactly the same way: like a small city. Each legion of 6,000 men, plus orderlies and auxiliaries and followers, had their own camp. Blocks of tents were separated by streets, with the main street, the *Via Principalis*, running down the center of the camp between the two main gates. Just as they were at the center of battle on the field, the legionaries occupied the heart of the camp. The tents of allied forces ringed them, and auxiliaries and camp followers were housed below the Via Principalis, near the small camp forum. The officers' tents lined the main street, flanking the altar dedicated to Mars and Jupiter Optimus Maximus.

The officers' tents wouldn't be where the action was. Antony thought about stopping by the forum, seeing if any of the whores there looked worthwhile, but decided against it. Caesar would be victorious and when he was, Antony would have his pick of slaves as part of the spoils. He didn't need a raging case of pox in the meantime.

Mark Antony found his dice game, and the men were only too happy to have him join. Agnus declined Antony's offer to stake him, preferring to watch. Antony knew that many of the officers looked down on him for mixing with the common soldiers. He'd been told all his life that carousing with plebeians didn't befit his station. That he should act like a dignified patrician. The only reason the other legates didn't say the same thing openly here is that Caesar didn't care, and Antony clearly had Caesar's favor.

They're probably still clucking like fat hens, and that prig Trebonius is the worst of them, worse even than Cornelius Aquila. At least he respected Aquila. Trebonius, in Antony's eyes, was all pride and no ability.

He slammed the dice down, acknowledging the cheer as he won

the toss. Someday, Trebonius and the officers like him will be surprised when their own troops mutiny. I never will be, because I'm not too good to move among the ordinary soldiers, and most of all not too good to listen to what they're saying with my own ears.

Antony didn't hear anything out of the ordinary on this night. Despite the tedium of the siege, morale was good. A few raids had kept them on their toes, and the breakout attempt that Antony and his cavalry narrowly defeated built confidence while at the same time providing a warning against complacency.

Mostly, though, Antony came back to the rumor Celer had repeated, about this mysterious new healer with a *caduceus* marked on his skin. Why would a medicus bear the symbol of the messenger of the gods? It was a riddle, as rumors tended to be. But like his commander, Antony couldn't help but feel that it was important. Rumor, after all, tended to have at least a kernel of truth at their heart. Caesar knew it, and Antony knew it as well.

15

(PAGUS MARDANI, 52 BCE)

"Call," David said, throwing a batch of colored, wafer-sized tokens into the middle of the table. Over the winter, Kevin had introduced Texas Hold 'Em to the Mardani, who took to it with gusto. New pastimes were rare enough and the Mardani, especially the men, loved any kind of gambling. Even a few of the women had learned, with Livilla and Matwyn being the best. Matwyn was the best poker player overall, even exceeding her two teachers. She rarely played because she almost always won—her ability to tell whether or not someone was bluffing was beyond belief. Livilla was almost as good. She was not much of a gambler but enjoyed the psychology and strategy of poker. As Kenny Rogers would have said, Livilla knew when to hold 'em and when to fold 'em.

David locked eyes with his nephew. Borodur, Ferrarius, Allodur and Livilla had all folded. David looked at his hole cards—a pair of aces. An ace and pair of eights in the flop—the first three of five community cards—had given him a full house, and the last two community cards—the "turn" and the "river"—hadn't improved his fortunes. Still, aces over eights was a solid hand and David had a feeling Kevin was bluffing.

A little sheepishly, Kevin showed his cards, revealing a pair of threes. David revealed his. "Dead Man's Hand," he said, and raked in the tokens.

"Why do you call it that?" asked Ferrarius.

David chuckled. "There was a famous gambler, known for playing this type of card game." David was speaking Mardani, and the word he used for "card" meant something closer to "painted tile." In fact, he'd heard that at least one enterprising wood worker in Mortorgenn was attempting to recreate playing cards using thin tiles of painted wood. Paper was a rare and precious commodity, made either of papyrus and imported from Egypt or—more commonly here in rural Gaul—made from sheep skin. David had had numerous decks and was happy to give one away. He'd been going to an annual obstetrics conference in Las Vegas for years and always picked up a couple souvenir decks of cards from one of the famous casinos. He'd then bring them on the *Stork* to help pass time during one of his solo trips up the Hudson River or along the coast to Massachusetts or Maine. He unfailingly forgot where he put the cards in between trips. He, Kevin and Livilla had gone over the *Stork* from stem to stern and took a complete inventory. Among other things, he'd found about half a dozen decks of cards stashed in various places. Kevin thought it would be hilarious to teach the Mardani Texas Hold 'Em but was surprised at how quickly it became popular.

"Anyway," David continuing his explanation to Ferrarius, "this gambler, called Wild Bill, was playing a game of poker when someone attacked him from behind without warning, killing him. He was holding three aces and two eights, so forever after it has been called 'the dead man's hand.'"

Ferrarius grunted. "That's a good story. A cowardly way to kill someone though."

"Yes," David said as he began to gather up the cards and chips, "people have always believed that." They'd been playing for pride today. The Mardani bartered more than they used money; David had been surprised at how little actual money he'd seen, a handful of silver *solidi* minted by the Romans at the open market in Mortorgenn. Most of the time, if there were stakes involved, whoever won the most chips won the stakes. Livestock, a skill or a desirable item were the most common things. Or, whoever lost had to perform some kind of dare or prank. That had become less common after a dare where the losers had to run naked in a raging blizzard nearly caused serious frostbite. David had chewed Kevin out for that one.

Livilla was helping David pick up. Suddenly, she stopped. "Oooh!" she said.

David looked at her, trying not to be alarmed. "Are you okay?" "Okay," along with "poker," "flop," "turn," "call" and "river" had jumped from English to Mardani.

Livilla put a hand on her middle. "The baby. He's kicking."

It had been nearly a year since David and Kevin had improbably found themselves in northern Gaul in the 50's BCE. It had been a year of changes. Livilla had moved onto the boat with David and more or less changed places with Kevin, who was spending a great deal of time with Ferrarius. About a month before the Mardani summer solstice celebrations, called *Pelldeiz*—"long day"—Livilla told David she was pretty sure she was pregnant. David used one of his tests to confirm it, though it took some persuading to get Livilla to pee on a stick. Matwyn found the whole thing hilarious. She claimed to know for a while that Livilla was pregnant with a baby conceived around the Ides of March. Over the winter Sevel and Ferrarius had taught David the Roman method for keeping dates. The Kalends of any given month was the first day; the Ides fell mid-month, either on the 13th or 15th day depending on the month in question. The Nones fell in between the Kalends and the Ides, on the 9th. All other days were calculated in relation to these fixed monthly points. Instead of saying "March 3rd," a Roman or Romanized person would say "two days after the Kalends of March."

A discreet ultrasound confirmed that Matwyn was pretty much correct in dating the baby's conception and that if all went well, Livilla would deliver their child not long after the winter solstice

—*Berrdeiz* in Mardani, perhaps between the Kalends and Ides of January. He was overjoyed, as was Livilla, but when he'd asked Matwyn about some kind of formal ceremony the old wise woman let out one of her mad hen cackles.

"You've been together since well before last *Berrdeiz* and no one doubts your devotion." Taking pity on David's confusion, Matwyn explained, "There are formal ceremonies, and you and Livilla can have one if you truly wish it. Most of the time a union between two people is understood and if there are children born of the union, or other stated or implied promises the community will enforce the customary responsibilities. Something more formal is usually reserved for the leadership, to officially cement alliances before the gods as well as the people."

David nodded. "That makes sense," he'd said. In the end, he traded one of the odds and ends from his boat—a souvenir shot glass of all things—for a pair of matching silver rings, which he and Livilla exchanged on *Pelldeiz*. Despite some rough spots, life was good.

David moved his hand to the baby bump that was now just becoming visible under the loose clothing Livilla preferred for day-to-day life. The child—a boy, David had seen during one of his exams—decided he'd done enough kicking for the moment.

"Of course he stopped!" David said, laughing.

"Don't worry. You'll feel him one of these times. I think he's teasing you."

David moved to kiss the woman he thought of as his wife when he heard a noise. It was some distance away and he couldn't quite make it out.

"Did you hear that?" David asked Livilla.

She frowned. They then heard the noise again. It sounded slightly closer.

"I think that's a *cornicens*," she said. Livilla had developed a fascination with 21st century music, even if it was not always to her taste. One evening, she'd described some of the different instruments she knew of to David. The *cornicens* was a tuba-like brass instrument that snaked around the player, much as a marching tuba or sousaphone would. The *cornicens* didn't sound much like either of those instruments. David thought it sounded like a bass vuvuzela.

"We should see what's going on," Livilla said. "It sounds like some sort of messenger or embassy is getting close and wants us to be ready to receive them. Borodur will want us with him, especially if it's the Romans."

KEVIN HEARD THE HORNS TOO. He was outside, visiting the latrine behind Ferrarius's house alongside Borodur when they heard the first horn blast. Tying the leather belt that held up his pants, Borodur looked in the direction the sound seemed to be coming from.

"Romans. Army unless I miss my guess," Borodur said. "Coming to officially ask for auxiliaries I'm sure. They did the same when Caesar was recruiting for his little venture in Britannia."

Kevin felt a little bit of worry. He'd grown to have a lot of respect for the Mardani chief and considered him a friend. He also felt a lot of gratitude toward the big man. Kevin understood that even though he and his uncle had quickly earned a lot of good will here in the village, the decision on allowing them to stay permanently had been Borodur's alone.

"What will you do?" Kevin asked.

"I'll send a body of slingers to show Caesar I keep my promises and value the alliance. Along with most of the rest of the whale meat." Kevin couldn't help but make a face. The preserved meat from the beached whale the Mardani had been butchering on the day Kevin and David had met them had helped them survive what would have been a lean winter but everyone was thoroughly sick of it.

Borodur locked eyes with Kevin, an uncharacteristically stern look on his face. "I feel in my bones he'll want Davidius to go with them. Probably you, too—the Roman army values its engineers, and you are a very skilled one." Kevin blushed. He felt like he hadn't done much, merely suggesting a few improvements to common tools and structures to Ferrarius over the winter. He certainly didn't consider himself a civil engineer. Getting his Victrola to spin at 78 rpm still eluded him for a start.

"I'll admit, it would be exciting to maybe meet Julius Caesar," Kevin said. "I'd miss living here though. It's become my home."

"We would miss you as well," Borodur said. "But you're a young man, and young men should have adventures."

Uncle David and Livilla—Kevin couldn't think of her as "Aunt" Livilla though she technically was now—joined them. David had been hesitant about his relationship with her at first, worried about the age difference.

"Unc, a lot of the women here and now expect to be paired with an older man. Maybe a much older one if they're a daughter of a chief or important man who needs to seal an alliance. Besides, no one believes you're as old as you say you are. Same for me," Kevin said.

"Who told you that?" David asked.

Kevin had blushed then and blushed now with the memory. "Chloe told me."

"Been spending some time with her, have you?"

"Um, yes. She's been very...persistent."

"Just remember, there's several boxes of condoms in the hold. Use whatever you need."

Kevin brought his mind back to the present. After several more horn blasts, each becoming clearer and louder, they caught sight of the party. As Borodur had guessed, it was a party of Romans. Kevin smiled as he recognized the figure on horseback, leading the delegation.

"Pullo!"

After a few more minutes, the party came into the village and halted. Pullo slid off his horse and exchanged formal greetings with Borodur, then clasped forearms with Kevin and then David in the traditional Roman way.

"Borodur, I wasn't expecting to find you here. It's a welcome surprise."

"I came down from the oppidum for the day. Flavens here has taught us a wonderful gambling game. It's called *poker*." The Mardani chief stumbled a little over the English word. A look of anticipation crossed Pullo and his fellow soldiers' faces. If the Mardani loved to gamble, the Romans were fanatics.

"I'll teach you," Kevin said.

"Good," Pullo said. "Back to business. I'm sure you've been expecting this, but Caesar is requested a body of slingers to join him at Alesia."

Borodur turned to Allodur, who'd joined them by now. "Allodur, leave now for Mortorgenn. Most of the men we'll need will be there; send runners for the rest. Then, tell the people building the rafts to hurry and finish, and begin loading them." To Pullo he said, "I'll accompany you to the oppidum; the levy will muster there."

"That will be good, Borodur, but I must speak with Davidius first."

Kevin looked at his uncle. That sounded ominous.

"It's out of the question. There is no way you're coming with me. Especially being pregnant."

Livilla was shocked at her husband's reaction. He hadn't put his foot down on something before; she was used to him encouraging her outspokenness and independence. And up to now he'd encouraged her to be active during her pregnancy and not treated her as a fragile thing, the way so many men did, especially with a first child. She said as much.

"Darling," David said, using a pet name she liked from his native language, "you are correct. I haven't treated you as fragile these last five months. Being active is good for you, and our son. But being pregnant also lowers your body's defenses against disease. And an army camp is a breeding ground for diseases of all kinds. Not to mention you'll be a beautiful young woman surrounded by a lot of soldiers who won't take 'no' for an answer."

Livilla wasn't sure, deep down, she believed David when he said diseases were caused by tiny, unseen creatures. Even after she'd seen one such thing on one of the wondrous tools he had on his boat. Their boat, now. But he'd said it with the confidence of someone who knew something as a simple fact he didn't question. In the end, Livilla believed that if David said something related to healing, odds were it was true. And his concern about soldiers' behavior was valid. Still, she would go with him. Livilla felt very strongly that she had to.

"You would leave me behind so easily? Not be here when our son is born? What if something goes wrong, like it did with Bennozha?"

"Matwyn would be here."

"Matwyn is wise beyond understanding. But she's not you," Livilla crossed her arms and fought the tears that threatened. Of all the side effects of pregnancy, Livilla hated the easy tears most. Some days it felt like anything could make her cry.

David sighed. "The truth? I'd feel like I was dying a little every day we were apart. And if something did go wrong? I'd never forgive myself. I still have a hard time when I think of Bennozha. If it had happened back home, I might well have saved her daughter as well."

Livlla hugged David. "No one blames you. Even Bennozha, in her sadness, has never blamed you. The fact you were able to save her is a miracle. Chlorus too, even though he *does* blame you for losing his hand. Even though I know better, I can see why some people say you are Asclepius in mortal guise."

David looked at her. She loved those kind, brown eyes, and they were shining with love. He kissed her.

"I don't know how I can be apart from you," David said.

They kissed again, more passionately.

"I'm not going to win this argument, am I?" he asked.

"No. You are not," Livilla said.

After ending their disagreement in the most pleasurable of all ways, Livilla and David sought out Pullo. He and his men were resting and eating before heading out to Mortorgen. They found him, deep in conversation with Ferrarius.

"...we could use a seasoned blacksmith. You'd certainly be welcome," Pullo was saying.

"And what's this, father? You're coming too?" Livilla asked.

"Too? You're coming as well? Davidius, you would allow this?" Livilla's father had approved of her relationship with David but he sounded angry at him now.

"First, Ferrarius, you of all people should know how hard it is to change your daughter's mind on anything once she's made it up. She knows the risks, and she's agreed to listen to me when it comes to limiting them. Besides, Pullo says Caesar is desperate for good doctors. Livilla's knowledge of plants and their medicinal uses is a lot better than mine. She will be a great help."

Ferrarius frowned but said nothing. Pullo nodded towards his men. "I'm giving them the rest of the day, and the night, to rest, and we'll go to Morgennus in the morning. Keffin Flavens has already said he'd like to join us as well."

"I'm not surprised. I'm sure his tinkering skill will come in handy."

"Yes. He was telling me about a device he and Ferrarius were working on over the winter for striking coins and medallions. And the talking plate machine. Though that still doesn't work quite right, he said."

Livilla laughed. "Yes, it's true. He says it still spins too fast."

"He should bring it with him," Pullo said. "Lot of quiet time on a siege."

They spent the rest of the evening talking over a variety of topics. Invariably, though, the subject always came back to Vercingetorix and his rebellion.

"We got bloodied at Gergovia, and no one can say different. Caesar's put as good a face on it as possible to keep our spirits up, but it was a defeat. We've got 'em bottled up good at Alesia though. Vercingetorix is done. He isn't getting out and none of his friends are getting in. Still, it's good you and the Mardani slingers will be coming with us. It'll show Borodur keeps his word, and Caesar respects that. A lot. And you, Davidius, will help him keep a promise to his chief medicus. He'll reward you for that, mark my words."

They went to bed after that and Livilla felt like the next morning came far too soon. They hadn't stayed up that late, but Livilla felt like she needed to sleep all the time. That was a pregnancy side effect she didn't mind. Especially if it meant sleeping in the wonderful big bed she and David shared on the *Stork*. Had any woman, anywhere, ever slept in such comfort? She'd wager not even the highest patrician matron in Rome had such a bed. Maybe not even the queen of Egypt. She woke slowly. David was already up and heating water for the vile morning drink he called "coffee." The smell was nice at least. He'd also been drinking the same morning tea Livilla made for her father and seemed to enjoy it. Insurance, he said, for when his coffee was gone.

"I thought you said you were running out of that stuff." Her voice was fuzzy and she felt more asleep than awake.

"I have some left. A few pounds." David used the Roman term, *libra*, though his pound wasn't quite the same as a true Roman pound, Livilla had learned. "I need it bad this morning. Once it's gone, it's gone. Although…" David snapped his fingers, something he often did when he got a sudden idea. It was one of his many strange habits, one Livilla happened to love. He walked into their room from the small kitchen and stood at the side of their bed. "…maybe I could have Caesar ask Cleopatra. It grows in Africa after all. I can see it now: 'Dear Cleo,' he could say. 'Have you heard any stories about goats acting weird after eating cherries from a certain bush that grows to the south? Let me know. A friend of mine says they're valuable and he's desperate for some. Yours truly, Caesar.'"

Livilla pulled David down into bed with her. "You're ridiculous. But I love you and want to spend all day lounging in bed with you. Preferably with no clothes."

David sighed. "That does sound good. Unfortunately, not an option…but there might be time for a quickie while the water heats up," he said, a hopeful look on his face. "Quickie" was another word from English, that so far had stayed between the two of them. And though she would have rather spent more time, it ended up being fun and exciting. And it would be exciting to think about the rest of the day. Maybe they could have more time tonight—if she could stay awake!

David left her some hot water to make her tea, pouring the rest into a small jug he called a "French press." Livilla's grandfather had explained in one of their conversations over the winter, the area they now lived in would one day be called France. David explained that, at the peak of its power, France would rule an empire of its own vaster than that of the Romans. Livilla still couldn't believe that her grandfather came from 1600 years in the future, that her husband had lived in a day that was four hundred years beyond even that. And yet, as she lived on the *Stork*, saw the wonders like the flameless torches they used for light, or the sheets and bed more comfortable than many kings or queens probably enjoyed, the idea became less strange. And her grandfather finally solved the mystery that had been bothering her since David and Keffin's arrival: why their birth language, English, sounded familiar. Sevel said his daughter Livia—Livilla's mother—used to sing Livilla a lullaby she remembered from her girlhood. One of the few things she had remembered from the world where her grandfather Sevel was a pontiff named "Steadfast Cooper" and Livia had been called "Bess"—a nickname that came from Livia's middle name, Elizabeth.

After hot tea and a quick wash, Livilla felt ready to face the day. David poured the rest of his coffee into a steel flagon whose top was sealed and yet he could drink from. Another wonder. Even better, it would keep his hot drink hot for hours. He also selected a map that he packed carefully in his shoulder bag with the medical kit he always kept in there. Paper was something that had convinced Livilla that her now-husband was a very rich man indeed. He had so much of it, bound up in so many codices—books, David called them. Livilla had gotten to see and feel a sheet of papyrus once, when Julius Caesar's herald had come to Mardani territory seeking men for the expedition to Britannia. The paper David had bound in more codices than she could count, along with an unbelievable number of loose sheets, seemed thinner. Cheaper. It was a contradiction she was still trying to understand.

To Livilla's surprise she and David weren't even the last ones at the meeting point in the center of the village. Her father had a pair of horses with riding blankets ready for them. Keffin kept mumbling about inventing something called a "stirrup," which had yet to materialize. They were waiting on the Romans. Finally, they appeared, Pullo's loud haranguing adding to their hungover misery. Jobix and a couple of the other men had shared a batch of *ouisghia*, a potent alcoholic drink the Mardani brewed, with the legionaries and they had clearly overdone it.

The ride to Mortorgenn was pleasant for everyone except the hungover soldiers, but once they arrived it was all business. Most of Mardani territory was less than a day's ride from the oppidum so most of slingers were already there. They would be commanded by Bordur's younger son Dolovix, who was running them through their paces while waiting for the last few stragglers to arrive from the Mardani border areas. Borodur seemed scandalized at the thought of Livilla joining David on the trek but stayed as neutral as he could. It was none of his business after all.

David unfolded a map that showed the hills, valleys, rivers and plains of Gaul. Borodur had seen David's incredible maps and still seemed amazed by them. Pullo was utterly in awe. They couldn't read the words in small print on the map, but they knew the land and couldn't believe how realistic the map was. The large cargo rafts were being loaded with supplies at a dock at the mouth of the Seine River. Alesia sat at a point where two rivers met but by following first the Seine and then a number of other rivers they would arrive at a point near Caesar's earthworks. In Borodur's judgement it would be quicker and safer than marching through territories belonging to tribes allied or sympathetic to Vercingetorix and not likely to be friendly to a party still allied with the Romans. David would take the *Stork* down river and then a short distance up the coast to the mouth of the Seine. It was decided Dolovix and the men he had would begin marching overland in the morning. David, Livilla, Kevin and Ferrarius would take the Stork to the meeting point, and they would all get underway.

Alas, there was no time to return to the village, their boat, and its luxurious bed. Not that she wasn't ungrateful for Borodur's hospitality and his giving them a private area. They made love, knowing that privacy would be hard to come by in the coming weeks. Afterwards, the baby started kicking and David was able to feel him move. His hand stayed over Livilla's midsection as they slept.

16

(SEINE RIVER, NORTHERN GAUL, 52 BCE)

They were being seen off in true Mardani fashion: with a feast. David was touched by the generosity of the people of Pagus Mardani. When Ferrarius had told him how well-loved Livilla was in the village, he hadn't been exaggerating. They received cups and plates and many winter clothes. David was particularly grateful of the latter. Nights were already starting to get cool. He'd brought some warm clothes, but the refugee camps he and Kevin had been sailing towards had been in the tropics so he hadn't expected to need too many. David stood up and stretched and Kevin, sitting with him, did too. The women were preparing food for the evening feast. David had offered to help but had been politely turned down. He sensed Livilla wanted to spend time with her friends alone.

David, Kevin, Livilla and Ferrarius had sailed the *Stork* to the meeting area near the mouth of the River Sequana—the river David knew as the Seine. He hoped that she wouldn't run aground but they'd find out the hard way.

He'd brought a few blank journals with him and turned one of them into a ledger book detailing everything he had on the boat. Everything David had brought with him from 2022. He'd even forgotten some of it. Most of it made sense: antibiotics, painkillers, prenatal vitamins and other drugs, including emergency contraception and chemical abortion pills. There were also plenty of latex gloves, tubing, IV bags, blood typing tests and several boxes of pregnancy tests. From there, things got a little random, stuff donated by family friends and colleagues who wanted to feel they'd done something. There were, for example, two boxes of reading glasses in a range of prescriptions. Finally, there were the two kevlar vests, designed to stop blades. His mother and his sister had both insisted. Even Philippe, his contact with the medical aid group coordinating the response to the refugee crisis, had agreed it would be a good idea.

"Get one designed for knives. They'll be searching everyone for guns, and knives and machetes will be a lot easier to smuggle in. If someone starts shooting, odds are a ballistic vest won't stop the bullets anyway," Philippe had said. David had wanted to at least leave some of the medication with Matwyn but the old woman declined with thanks.

"I'm grateful to you. For many things," the old wise woman said. "More than you'll know. But I will use the tools I know. You will need your own more than I will."

The feast was one to remember. There were songs and stories, lots of alcohol and above all food. Pullo knew all about Mardani hospitality but they were a proud people and they wanted to make sure Pullo's fellow soldiers spread the word as well. The next day was a day of recovery and the day after that, at high tide, they set out, down the Sequani and towards area where the future of their world would be decided.

Their days settled into a rhythm. David enjoyed this time with his family, the people who were closer to him than anyone else. One evening after dinner, once they were safely anchored for the night, the four of them began talking. "Tell me about your family," Ferrarius said to David.

"My father Ricardo is a master cook," David said. "My mother Sarai was a musician. Both of them moved to New York, where I was born, from other places."

"Where?" Asked Livilla.

"My father is from Cuba. It's an island far across the ocean. It's warm all the time there. He says it's full of fruit and flowers."

"You've never been?"

"No. It was ruled by a man I suppose you would call a dictator or tyrant. My father's story is a lot like your parents in a way; this dictator, Castro, was not afraid to imprison or murder his enemies, and he decided my father and his family were enemies."

"So they fled," Livilla said, understanding.

"Just like I fled from Sulla," Ferrarius said.

"My mother was born in Alexandria. Egypt in her time was also ruled by a dictator. My mother's family wasn't directly persecuted but they didn't trust the dictator, a man named Nasser. So they saved money and sent some people abroad. Mom's family thought that if things got really bad, they could help get the others out of Egypt."

"Have you been to Egypt?"

"Yes. I spent some time in Alexandria with my relatives."

Alexandria, at least, Livilla had heard of. Egypt's capital rivaled Rome itself as a center of power and, some said, exceeded it in splendor.

"I would like to visit there," she said.

"I would too. I think it is very different from the city I know."

Livilla turned to Kevin and asked him, "How did you come to meet David?"

Kevin was silent for a moment before he replied. David knew he was gathering his thoughts.

"I'm too young to remember a lot of it," he said. "In a weird way me and my mom's story is a lot like Uncle David's parents'. My grandparents. I was born far to the east."

"So it's true? You come from Serica?" Ferrarius asked. Serica was the Roman name for China. There was little, almost no contact, between the two civilizations, but they were aware of each other.

"Not quite," Kevin said, "but from near there. Korea, it's called. Before I was born, there was a war that divided our homeland. One half came to be ruled by a tyrant, much like the tyrant that ruled Cuba only far more brutal. This rule was perpetuated by the tyrant's son and later his grandson. My mother is a cook, and she came to be the personal cook for a relative of the grandson. Mother never said, but I think he is my father. Anyway, this man, the one my mother worked for, enjoyed gambling."

"A fine pastime," Ferrarius said, and they all chuckled.

Continuing his story, Kevin said, "This man—and I don't know his name because my mother has never said it—was one of the few people in North Korea allowed to travel abroad. He went to a city known for its gambling houses and he was allowed to take mother with him. She insisted on taking me. She saw her chance for us to escape, and we did. I don't remember much. Flashes of running through the streets. She was given a job at Grandpa Ricardo's restaurant, fell in love with Uncle David's, uh, sibling and I got adopted into the family." Not knowing what anyone would think of two women marrying, Kevin was cautious with that piece of information.

Their voyage downriver was blessedly uneventful. About three weeks into it, Pullo, David and Dolovix consulted one of David's maps.

"At this rate, we'll reach Lutetia by midday tomorrow," Pullo said. Lutetia, David had figured out, was the main oppidum of the Parisii, the tribe who would give their name to the great city that would arise in Lutetia's place—Paris.

"I'm guessing it'd be better to try and slip past at night?" Kevin asked.

Dolovix nodded. "We could try and bluff our way past but I'd only want to do that as a last resort. Vercingetorix never sent an envoy to us. Either he just assumed we'd follow him or figured we were too small to bother with. At least the Romans paid us respect by asking us for men."

Pullo grunted. "We don't know what news or rumors are running around the country. Dolovix is right. We're better off sneaking past unseen. But if we're spotted, we bluff our way past."

17

─────────

(ALESIA, CENTRAL GAUL, 52 BCE)

Caesar stood on the ramparts of his inner wall, the circumvellation wall. It was the Ides of September. The cries of the starving women and children in the area between the circumvellation and the walls of Alesia were piteous to anyone capable of pity. Caesar was capable of pity, but he'd learned at a young age that pity, like anything else, was a tool. A tool to be used when needed. A tool to be all but forgotten when it was not needed.

"The siege must be working," Gaius Trebonius said. The legate was, along with Antony, Caesar's most capable officer. If only the man didn't have a *pilum* up his rear end.

"As you say, Trebonius," said Antony, who stood opposite his rival, flanking Caesar. "Still, it's hard to listen to. Some of the women are even offering their bodies. We could use some fresh women in the camps."

"You and your whores, Antony. Do you ever not think with your prick?" Trebonius's disgust was obvious.

Caesar held up his hand to forestall the inevitable sniping.

"They stay where they are. Vercingetorix is counting on my mercy. And if I were him, I'd be waiting to charge out of his gates through the opening we make, breach our lines, and make us chase him all over Gaul. The gods may curse my cruelty, but the Senate and people will praise it."

Antony looked like he was going to respond, but at that moment Vorenus, one of his centurions, came up to them, escorting a travel-stained Pullo. Vorenus's tall lean build belied his powerful strength. He was one of his bravest, most able veterans in the Gallic legions. Vorenus saluted smartly.

"Vibius Pullo has returned and wishes to speak to you, Imperator," said Vorenus.

"What news do you have, Pullo?" Caesar hoped it was good.

"The Mardani are camped a few hours away, awaiting your pleasure, Caesar. They bring around a hundred men and tons of food," Pullo said. "Their new medicus is with them."

"That is good news," Caesar said.

"We also learned a relief army is on the way."

"That is no less than we expected. How did you gain this intelligence?"

"We came by river. We paused so we would pass by Lutetia in the dark and one of our foraging parties had the chance to spy on a Parisii camp. Our men were quiet as ghosts. Theirs were drunk and loud."

"Very clever. You shall be rewarded, Pullo." Caesar turned to Antony. "Organize an escort. We're having enough problems foraging as it is. I don't want that supply train to fall into enemy hands right when we're on the verge of starving them out."

Antony in his turn ordered Vorenus to pick an escort of foot soldiers while he himself selected a cavalry escort. The company, once assembled, was small enough to march quickly, even with empty horse carts. Assuming Pullo's report of the distance to the Mardani camp was accurate—and Antony had no reason to assume it wasn't—they would load the wagons and camp tonight and be back before midday tomorrow.

Antony frowned as the orderly brought his horse. He'd lost his reliable stallion at Gergovia. He'd been one horse in a thousand, even-tempered and fazed by nothing. This mare was skittish. He'd have asked for another one if Caesar hadn't wanted him to set out immediately.

Vorenus had the foot assembled in short order. While it helped that the men were eager to get outside the walls of the siege works, it helped even more that Vorenus was one of those officers the men did not question. It was Trebonius who'd seen the man's potential and gotten him the promotion first to decurion, and then to centurion. The prig had an eye for soldiers, that was certain, Antony had to grudgingly admit. If only he wasn't so unpleasant.

IT WAS past midday when their escort arrived, their trumpets waking Livilla up from her nap. Most of the camp was relaxing, except those on watch. David, as was his usual custom, was making notes in the blank codex he wrote in. He explained to her that he was keeping a diary along with a guide to medicinal plants and their best uses. "Maybe I'll write a book of my own someday," David said. "If nothing else I'll be preserving valuable knowledge."

Out of habit, David wrote in his native language. He was teaching her some English along with how to read Latin, and she'd learned to recognize a few words. The English alphabet was the same as Latin, with two extra letters. However, Livilla could not recognize any words in the looping scrawl David wrote with the self-inking stylus he called a "ballpoint pen." She doubted she'd ever be able to, despite David's assurances that it was just English written in a style called "cursive" that was faster to write. That may be, but it was no easier to read. Livilla wondered how David himself could read his own writing, but he never seemed to have any difficulty. She was helping him experiment with making ink against the day when those styluses ran dry and he didn't have any more.

Livilla went with David to greet the Romans. Their leader was a handsome man mounted on horseback, looking every inch the Roman officer. A tall centurion stepped forward.

"I present Marcus of the Antonii, legate of Gaius Julius Caesar, proconsul of Cisalpine and Transalpine Gaul and Illyricum."

David had an unreadable expression on his face. It seemed to Livilla he knew this Marcus Antonius, by reputation if not personally. How was that possible? Was this man as famous as Caesar, that his name came down through the ages to come?

Marcus Antonius dismounted; David, Kevin, Dolovix and Ferrarius strode forward to meet him, with Livilla about half a step behind David.

"We greet you, Legate Marcus Antonius. I am Dolovix of the Mardani, son of Borodur, headman and war leader of our people. I bring one hundred slingers to help Caesar bring peace to Gaul. Our new medicus David, his nephew Keffin Flavens, and our master smith Gaius Ferrarius are here as well." Dolovix gestured toward the two other men in turn.

"It is good to meet you, and even better to see all the food you bring with you," Antony said. "Caesar wishes me to convey his greetings and gratitude," Antony said. "But I have to say, David Medicus and Keffin Flavens, you do not look Mardani. Nor does the beautiful woman behind you. To say nothing of your boat. Does it even have oars?"

"No, it moves by sail only," David said. "Kevin and I were blown off-course while sailing."

"From Egypt? You, Davidius, have that look if I'm any judge, even if your nephew does not. And your accent is...strange to say the least."

"My mother was Egyptian," David said. Moving on before the legate could probe further, David turned to Livilla. She bowed slightly. "This is my wife, Livilla Ferraria."

"Ah, a Roman?"

"Half-Roman, Legatus," Livilla said. "My mother was born in Britannia."

"I'm assuming your father is your master smith?" Antony asked. Livilla nodded. "And how did you come to live with the Mardani?" Antony asked Ferrarius.

"I was a weaponsmith for Gaius Marius, and had to flee Rome after Sulla's victory," Ferrarius said. "The Mardani took me in."

Dolovix then outlined what they had brought with them and an exact count of their fighters. Antony was pleased. He directed his foot soldiers to begin transferring supplies and sat down to supervise.

Livilla sat with Antony, exchanging pleasantries. She sensed Antony would gladly bed her, but he remained respectful. Most of the rest of the camp worked side by side with the Roman legionaries to load the barrels of whale meat and boxes of lead sling shot onto the wagons; David and Kevin unloaded the medicine and equipment from the *Stork*. Everyone wanted to be underway as early as possible the next day. Formidable as the combined Roman and Mardani forces were, no one wanted to risk a raid by the enemy, or even having the enemy discover them by accident. It ended up being a pleasant evening, and they threw a small feast for their Roman guests. The night passed uneventfully.

They were underway soon after dawn. They were maybe halfway to the Roman lines when something startled Antony's already skittish horse. Whether it was an animal or just a trick of the light they never did see; suddenly the horse reared, and Antony was thrown off.

DAVID SPRINTED TOWARD ANTONY, who was not getting up. Livilla watched as her husband examined the legate. David's hand came away bloody.

"Get me some gauze, quickly," David shouted. "He's bleeding. Badly."

David removed Antony's armor. An exposed tree root had gone in between the leather breast plate and back plate of the legate's armor and left a long, deep gash. The tall centurion, Vorenus his name was, loomed over him.

"How serious is it?" he asked.

"Not fatal. But we should get him back to camp. Move him onto the cart my wife and I were riding on. We'll need to move quickly."

"The army surgeons can help him?"

"I can help him, Centurion Vorenus, but I'll look forward to working with them. It will be best if we get back to camp as fast as this wagon can carry us."

They got Antony into the wagon. He revived a little and was clearly in great pain. David dug into his first aid kit and brought out two hydrocodone pills.

"Swallow these," David said.

"What are they?" Antony asked, his voice thick.

"They'll help with the pain. Swallow them."

Antony took the pills. David didn't know if the man trusted him or just responded to his authority. He didn't care. The wagon took off as the pills took effect, and Antony fell mercifully asleep.

The teamster drove hell-bent for leather back into the Roman camp. Whatever the old record might have been, David was sure they broke it. He was sore and Livilla was looking a little nauseous. Once they arrived the soldiers who'd rode with them carried Antony to his tent on a makeshift litter.

"I'm going to need light," David said. "As many lamps as you can get."

Almost immediately, the tent was ablaze with oil lamps. David would have preferred electric light, but he wanted to save that for an emergency. He wanted to do without if he could, all the better to avoid awkward questions. A muscular man a few inches shorter than David and a tall, gaunt man who would not have looked out of place on a basketball team materialized beside him.

"Celer," the shorter man said, "I'm chief surgeon of the camps here."

"I am Corvus," said the tall man in a deep, pleasing voice that reminded David of Morgan Freeman. "Tell us what you would like us to do, Davidius Medicus."

"We'll need clean water that's been boiled to start," David said.

David carefully scrubbed up and put on latex gloves, indicating to Celer and Corvus that they should do the same. They looked at him as if he was mad but complied. Carefully, David peeled the bandage off and took a good look at the wound. Antony had been both the victim of very bad luck and the beneficiary of very good luck. If it hadn't been for a sharp tree root sticking out of the ground, he'd have probably escaped with bruises and maybe a cracked rib. As it was, the root slid along the ribcage rather than penetrating between them and causing far more serious injury.

Carefully, David cleansed the wound with saline and then numbed the area with a few quick shots of lidocaine. He then stitched the wound up. As he was finishing, Alexander came back with the water. Carefully cleaning Antony up, he looked at Livilla.

"I think he should heal up nicely. He'll have a spectacular scar, though. And he'll have to rest awhile; he lost a lot of blood."

"Speaking of blood, love, you're covered in it."

David looked down. She was right. Mark Antony had bled like a stuck pig.

"I suppose I should change."

David stripped out of his bloody scrubs, which Livilla took to wash, and put on clean ones. Neither of them saw Julius Caesar lingering at the entrance to Antony's tent, watching.

Caesar had been meeting with his staff when he received word of Antony's injury. He resisted the urge to see him right away and instead finished the meeting. According to the soldier who brought the report, one of the spokesmen for the Mardani was a supremely skilled physician, and this man was treating his legate. It must be the mysterious doctor who had amputated Chlorus's hand, Caesar thought. He dismissed the thought and the messenger. He decided to watch, quietly, so as not to get in the way. Caesar dismissed his officers and they left when he made it clear he would not be meeting with any of them privately.

Caesar watched as this surgeon worked with confidence and skill. He did not hesitate to give orders to Celer or Corvus. This medicus was respectful, and Caesar saw that he listened to what both the legionary surgeons had to say. Caesar was no physician, but he recognized the way of command. It was a skill that was not only used on the battlefield.

They finished and then a woman—obviously the foreign doctor's lover—said something and pointed to the bloodstains. He stripped off the bloody shirt. Caesar gasped when he saw the tattoo. This was no simple native work. Most of the frescoes Caesar had seen in some of Rome's finest houses were not half so exquisitely painted. He thought of the birthmark on the sacred ram that had been sacrificed last summer.

Pullo walked up, stopping short at the entrance to the surgeon's tent when he saw his leader.

"Tell me, Pullo," Caesar said softly so as not to draw attention to them. "Where did you say this mysterious man came from?"

"He said he and his nephew were sailing on the *Mare Atlanticus* and were blown off-course. They encountered the Mardani on a beach about a day's ride from their oppidum."

Caesar felt his blood go cold. "A gift from the sea," he murmured.

"I guess you could say so," Pullo said.

Before he got too lost in thought, "Report to me once there's word on the legate's condition, Pullo. I shall be in my tent. The lictors on duty will be instructed to admit you."

DAVID HEARD someone enter the tent.

"He's comfortable, but will need to rest a while," he said without looking up. "He lost quite a bit of blood and I don't want him popping any of these stitches."

"That's good to know. But I think you and I need to talk about other things."

David looked up then. When he saw who it was, he got goosebumps. The man standing at the door to Antony's tent could only be Gaius Julius Caesar. One of the most famous men in history. If the busts David had seen of him were idealized, they weren't far from the truth.

Caesar was tall, at least by the standards of his day. David estimated he was probably a match for David's own 5'10.". He definitely looked Italian, but had a somewhat lighter complexion than many, and slightly florid. He had a prominent nose, high forehead and cheekbones, a bald spot he tried to cover with a combover, and a wide mouth and strong chin.

"My apologies. I am David Castellanos. I am a doctor who came with the Mardani. This is my wife, Livilla Ferraria."

"Yes. I have heard of you. I'm told you have a rather impressive tattoo. I'd like to see it." Caesar didn't make that sound like a request.

As Livilla looked on nervously, David removed his shirt. He could feel Caesar's eyes burning into his back. He could swear his shoulder blade felt hotter, but that had to have been his imagination.

"What do you know about prophecy, medicus? Signs and portents?"

"That it's cryptic, often misinterpreted, and very frequently complete nonsense," said David.

"You do not believe in the gods?"

David considered his answer. Caesar's face was unreadable, and David couldn't tell if he was being tested or if he truly was treading on dangerous ground. "I...am open to the idea there is something beyond the physical world. But as a famous man of science where I'm from once said: 'Extraordinary claims require extraordinary evidence.'"

Caesar actually laughed at that. "You are a man after my own heart, it seems, David of the Castellanii. A most unusual name. Of course, that's not surprising. You speak Latin well, but with an accent I've never heard before."

That's because my native language hasn't even been born yet, David thought, though he said only, "I come from very far away."

"Yes, I suspect you do. I am Gaius of the Julii, called Caesar."

"I know who you are. You are very famous where I'm from."

"And where is that, exactly? You have something of the look of

Egypt or Numidia about you, yet it is clear you are not from there by your speech."

Livilla stirred. David knew what that meant. But he wouldn't have held her back even had he been capable.

"Forgive me, Imperator," she said. "I would ask what my husband will not—that you speak plainly. You clearly know things about him and have him at a disadvantage."

Caesar looked amused rather than offended.

"Is she always so outspoken?"

"Yes. That's why I married her," David said.

He laughed. "Good man. Far be it for me to refuse such a request. Very well, I'll speak plainly. About a year ago, I took the auspices from a sacred ram, donated by my Gallic allies. One of my lictors, Cornelius Aquila, is also a priest and skilled at reading livers and entrails. They told him I would receive a gift or blessing from the sea. On top of it all, the ram bore a birthmark that resembled the caduceus. And here you come, treating my wounded legate and friend. In all likelihood saving his life if I am any judge. I have never seen a wound so finely stitched. If it doesn't fester, I don't doubt Antony will recover fully."

"It won't fester," David said. "I will ensure that."

"Very well. I take you at your word. In any event, here you appear, with a tattoo of the caduceus. You speak with an accent like no other, and you bring equipment and medicine like none ever seen before. The needle you used to stitch Antony's wound was of a quality the finest smiths could not hope to match, Celer and Corvus say. And finally, you arrive in a personal sailing boat that looks like none other. Tell me, Davidius Castellanus Medicus, what am I to make of all this? Am I to be forgiven if I see this as, you might say, extraordinary evidence?"

David sighed. "I suppose, put that way, I can see why you think so. All I can say is, where I come from such tools are plentiful, and while I'm proud of my medical education and training—it's extensive, and very good—it is training, not divine. I also realize you don't know me, and as yet you have no reason to trust me. I came with Dolovix and his slingers because I hoped to be a help. Livilla, too, has knowledge and skill that will help Celer, Corvus and their people."

He tried not to fidget as Caesar stared at him. Into his soul, David felt like. As if he were being weighed on an existential level. "What is your medical training?" he asked David at last.

"Two years of specialized theoretical training and anatomy and two years of practical clinical training. That was followed by seven years of training specializing in pregnancy and childbirth. All of that on a foundation of 20 years' general education and pre-medical studies."

Caesar looked like he had a million more questions but said nothing, merely nodding. "That explains much." Looking at the sleeping Antony, he said, "please let me know if anything changes."

"Of course. Celer and Corvus looked like they needed a break. Even if nothing changes when they come back, I will bring word then."

"Very well." Caesar left, nearly running into Kevin at the entrance to the tent. "Ah. You must be the one they call Flavens. I can see why. They tell me you actually gave Pullo a challenge in a wrestling match?"

Kevin could only stutter a reply. "Yuh-y-yes."

"An accomplishment to be proud of."

And with that, Gaius Julius Caesar took his leave. David looked up at his nephew.

"Close your mouth. Unless you want to catch some flies."

18

(ROME, PROVINCE OF ITALIA, 52 BCE)

Comedentis unrolled the papyrus scroll. While he had a vague title as one of Pompey's personal secretaries, his true job was to filter reports from Pompey's vast network of clients, the great man's eyes and ears all over the Roman Republic and beyond. Most were mundane reports on shipping and harvests, or titillating gossip that had little real value. Comedentis's duty was primarily to sift through these reports to find grains of fact, much as one might sift through silt in a river to find gold or silver.

Some letters, though, would always have news of value—much as a rich mine has its veins of precious metals. The one he'd just unrolled was one such. It read:

To Gnaeus Pompey Magnus, it said. *The siege continues. There is not much of military importance to report. Our morale remains high, and Caesar is confident of victory. That is no less than you would expect. By the time this dispatch reaches you, this great rebellion will most likely be crushed. I must, however, report something strange of great importance. Seven days after the Ides of September, a body of slingers belonging to a small Gallic tribe, the Mardani, arrived at the camp. With them they brought much food, and a strange foreign medicus. He is no ordinary doctor. He wears clothes of the finest quality, uses tools no one has ever seen, and arrived on a sailing vessel the likes of which I have never seen. His skill in medicine, I must say, surpasses even the best doctors of Greece or Egypt. No one really knows who he is or where he came from. The Mardani will only say that he came to live with them after being shipwrecked and taking the daughter of a Roman exile to wife. What is most noteworthy is that this doctor bears a tattoo of the caduceus of Mercury on his shoulder. Caesar is convinced this medicus fulfills auspices taken at a sacrifice last summer. Whether that is, of course, I cannot say; I do not claim to know the thinking of the gods. I will endeavor to keep you informed, as always, for the sake of the Senate and the People of Rome.*

Comedentis re-rolled the scroll and put it aside with a few other letters that merited further study and mention to Pompey. This could be very significant indeed.

～

"Can't we do something for them?" Kevin asked, looking at the starving people from the ramparts.

"It's monstrous," Livilla said.

They both looked at David who was frowning. He'd been having problems sleeping these last two nights, Kevin knew, because of the plight of these poor people. They'd talked about it.

"Life is hard," Mark Antony said. He was giving them a tour of the ramparts along the inner wall of the siege works. "Will the child Livilla carries survive? Many infants do not. Is that cruel, or is that just life?" Livilla's hand went to her middle, to the life growing inside her.

"Being realistic about life isn't being cruel, I agree," Kevin said. "But this is cruelty, plain and simple. Cruelty by Vercingetorix to callously use his own women and children as part of a military strategy, and cruelty by Caesar to not let them in."

"Sometimes you have to be cruel to be kind," said Mark Antony. "Our men have been in the field for eight consecutive campaign seasons. They are loyal to Caesar, yes, but there are limits to even the greatest loyalty. If we can crush this rebellion here and now, we will pacify Gaul, Caesar can disband his legions and we can all live a happy, peaceful life." Antony stopped and winced, holding his still-bandaged wound.

"You should be in bed," David told Antony for perhaps the hundredth time.

"Yes, mommy," Antony said, and ignored David for perhaps the hundredth time.

"Do you honestly believe that?" Livilla asked Antony. "I've been to the camp forum. All the talk there is of discord between Caesar and Pompey, especially since Crassus was killed. Do you honestly believe that this war will end here? Or that Caesar will disband his battle-hardened troops without hard assurances of his future? We may be barbarians to you, but no chief would be so stupid. And Caesar is not stupid."

Antony clapped David on the back. "Hold on to this one, physician." Turning to Livilla, Antony said, "If you were a man, you'd go far in politics. You see to the heart of it. I honestly think that Caesar would rather continue a peaceful alliance with Pompey and find another to take Crassus's place, but I don't believe it's possible. There are too many winds against him. However, if Caesar can sail before the storm, who knows what may happen?"

"That's all well and good," David said. "But my concern is for those people. It's for people like them that I became a doctor in the first place. Now I get to watch them die a slow death. This is a war crime, pure and simple."

"War crime?" Antony asked. "How can you commit a crime against your enemy in the course of war? You do what you have to do to win. That's it. That is what we are doing here. If your soft sentiment reigned, physician, we'd be chasing these vermin around Gaul till Apollo's chariot fell from the sky."

"What if we can be both merciful and use that mercy to trap Vercingetorix?" Kevin asked.

Antony frowned. "Go on."

"A book I've read says that if you can get the enemy to fight on your terms, at a place and time of your choosing, your battle is almost always won before it is fought. We know that Vercingetorix will try to break through any opening in the wall we make for these wretches. I say let them through—at a place and time of our choosing. We can set up an ambush, and if Vercingetorix sends a sortie to break out, spring the trap."

Both his uncle and Livilla looked at Kevin like he was suddenly a stranger. Antony's frown deepened, and he rubbed his face, considering what he'd just had said.

"Yes. Yes, that might work. I don't know if Caesar will agree, but I will put it to him. He'll at least listen to me."

When they finished their tour, Kevin watched Mark Antony walk off, a little gingerly. He made his way back towards the tent they shared in the area of camp given to the Mardani. Livilla always seemed to need a nap these days, something his uncle said was common for a pregnant woman, and David himself looked exhausted. Kevin would probably find something else to do while they rested. The three of them let their thoughts wander on the walk back.

When they were back at their tent, Kevin asked the question that had been bothering him. One he'd held back on asking until now.

"Do you think Antony really will ask Caesar?"

David sighed. "I don't know. I had to read *The Gallic Wars* in Mr. Chaplin's class. But that was years ago, and I don't really remember anything besides 'I came, I saw, I conquered.'"

Livilla frowned. "What are you talking about?"

"Caesar wrote—will write?—an account of his campaigns in Gaul," David said. "It's pretty famous. I'd wager your grandfather might well have read it when he was studying Latin. That's when I read it, but that was a long time ago."

"Let me think," Kevin said. He'd re-read *The Gallic Wars* after he graduated from high school. In English, this time. What was it about the siege of Alesia? Something that horrified him. Then he remembered, and he had a sick feeling. "If I'm remembering right, all those people will die. But hey, haven't you and I already changed history just by being here, Uncle?" Kevin very much hoped he was right.

That they could make history go a different direction in this timeline.

"And what if you can't convince Caesar? What if he says no? What will you do?" Livilla sounded worried. Kevin was worried too. Uncle David was very laid back and easygoing, but he didn't compromise when it came to his morals. Why else would David have done something as crazy as sail a small boat across the ocean to help refugees? David couldn't imagine his uncle just swallowing his anger, but would he walk away? Make an enemy of Julius Caesar? Leave people behind that might need his help?

"I don't know, dear. Maybe I'm being soft-hearted, as Antony says. But no matter how much I'll seem like I'm fitting in, I'll always be a 21st century person. With 21st century morality."

"People aren't so cruel then? They don't kill women and children in war?"

"I wish I could say no, Livilla. Ask Kevin. He can tell you more of what he remembers of North Korea, and of what his mother has told him. People do act cruelly, especially in war. But it is condemned, not celebrated. And occasionally leaders who do things like what Vercingetorix is doing face justice. Not often enough, but it does happen. I'm willing to compromise a lot, but not that last little piece of me. Hopefully Caesar will see reason."

ANTONY PROPOSED the idea to Caesar.

"It's not the worst idea I've heard," Caesar said, considering the possibilities.

"I find myself agreeing with Antony," said Gaius Trebonius, sounding surprised to hear himself say so. "We can send a message of mercy while at the same time dealing the enemy a demoralizing defeat."

"What would the plan be?" Caesar asked.

Kevin had sketched out his idea with Antony after their tour of the inner wall, and Antony had spent time refining it before bringing it to Caesar, going so far as to talk to Dolovix, who was with him now. Tomorrow night, or the night after at the latest, they would direct the refugees toward the weakest part of the wall, where the inner and outer walls of the siege works nearly met along the River Ose. There would be a half-moon, with some light to see but plenty of shadows. Vercingetorix had attacked that point in a breakout attempt already, and few troops had gotten through, though as of today—two days before the Kalends of October—the relief army still had not showed and there had been no further attacks from Alesia itself.

Dolovix, remembering an ambush of his father's, suggested that his Mardani slingers and a select group of legionaries darken themselves with river mud and hide in the shadows. If any of Vercingetorix's warriors attempted to follow, they'd spring the trap.

"And what do we do with the Alesians themselves?" Caesar asked.

"Davidius has made some plans for a camp behind the contravellation wall, subject to your approval," Antony said. "He requested that some of the surplus food brought by the Mardani be used to feed them. Antony handed Caesar the plans David had drawn up.

Caesar looked them over carefully. Antony knew they were well-organized and thought out, down to a very exact daily ration for each camp resident. The physician, it seemed, had a gift for administration. He would make a great quaestor, Antony thought.

"Our mysterious doctor has put a great deal of thought into this, so it seems," Caesar said.

"Yes. He says he has some small experience in running what he calls 'refugee camps.'" Antony stumbled over the foreign words. Davidius had thrown a lot of words out, regarding the food and medical needs of the Alesians caught between the walls.

At first, Antony thought Davidius was an ordinary physician, with extraordinary skills. He'd known of a few master doctors during his youthful sojourn in Greece. Most doctors were barely trained at best and if you were lucky they didn't kill you. They prescribed powders, tonics and poultices that, Antony felt, was like throwing dice—their effectiveness was entirely random. There were a few, though, of unquestioned skill. Men who served the powerful and were revered. Asclepius had been one such. He'd been so good he became a god.

Davidius was a different breed altogether. He had a natural authority that even Caesar responded to in the right circumstances. He made no fantastic claims about the medicines he gave. If anything, the opposite was true. Before giving Antony pills Davidius said would prevent his wound from festering, the doctor spent a long time going over possible negative effects and was adamant that Antony tell him immediately if anything felt wrong.

"Are you going to prescribe any prayers? Sacrifices?" Antony asked at the time.

"No," David said.

"Should I do so anyway?" Antony asked.

"If you like," Davidius said. "It certainly won't hurt. But that's up to you."

Unconsciously, Antony rubbed the stitched wound on his side. Three days after his fall, it looked spectacularly ugly and ached but even Antony could tell it was healing well. And this, from a doctor who claimed to be basically a midwife.

"Yes, he is certainly most extraordinary," Antony said, bringing his mind back to the present. "Do you think it's true…"

"What?" Caesar said.

"Do you think it's true that he's Asclepius come back to the mortal life? That's what some are saying."

"Let them talk," Caesar said, a little too sharply, Antony thought. "I know what I need to know about Davidius.

"And what should I tell him?"

"Tell him that I haven't decided anything final, but to make his preparations anyway. If I agree to this mad scheme, I'll want him and his men to be ready. Assign Pullo to work with Dolovix. If nothing else, they can get comfortable working together, since I plan to pair the Mardani slingers with that cohort anyway. Pullo knows them well and they respect him."

"Yes, Caesar." Antony knew Caesar would be as good as his word, but he hated not being there. He set off for his tent, knowing David would be checking in on him. Maybe he would bring those things he called 'playing cards' and they could practice the game known as poker. Antony would have to try and make his own decks. Poker was a game for a true gambler, he thought happily. Dice got boring after a while.

As he waited for his other generals to attend him, Caesar looked over Davidius's proposal. It certainly was well set out. He'd seen much worse from experienced quaestors and aediles when it came for laying out needs and expenses for things like buildings or public games. Davidius's written Latin, like his spoken Latin, had an odd, foreign flavor to it. But it was perfectly understandable and clearly the product of a well-ordered, educated mind. One of the strangest things on the sheets Antony had given to him were the strange, sinuous symbols for many of the entries. They seemed to be numbers, because next to them he'd written in proper Roman numerals. It was almost as if he forgot himself. Were those strange symbols numbers in Davidius's language? They had to be and yet they looked so different. Regardless, Caesar knew instinctually these figures were correct. They were too precise not to be. With the surplus food the Mardani had brought with them, they could feed the Alesians without cutting into their own supplies. The only real question was if this barbarian Dolovix's ambush plan would work.

David was getting more nervous as the sun sank below the horizon. He'd spent most of the day organizing the building of rough shelters for the refugees. He'd been shocked that Caesar had approved the plan, if grudgingly. Apparently Mark Antony had been convinced and argued strongly on his and Dolovix's behalf. Most of Caesar's officers had been convinced including, surprisingly, Gaius Trebonius. David understood that Trebonius and Antony were often at each other's throats, and it was easy to see why. In the relatively short time David had known him, he'd seen that Antony possessed a first-class mind. When Antony dedicated himself to something he wanted to learn, whether it was Texas Hold 'em or cavalry strategy, he mastered it thoroughly and quickly. He simply did not bother himself with tasks that did not interest him. Antony also liked to have fun and made no secret of it. That made him the opposite of Trebonius, a stolid man, dedicated to detail to the point of tedium, and in David's view, obsessed with proper behavior for its own sake. Maybe that's what convinced Caesar in the end, David thought, over the objection of a group of officers led by another legate, Labienus.

Caesar however made it clear David owed him a favor. "I am impressed by your plans. I will give you this much food and not a barrel more. But remember—after this, you belong to me."

The field between the walls of Alesia and the inner wall of the Roman siege works was a desolate no-man's-land. Except for the lack of barbed wire and gunpowder artillery it would not have looked out of place in World War I. To even get to the Roman walls, any attack would have to traverse two deep trenches and a moat filled with water diverted from the Ose and Oserain Rivers. The open fields were strewn with what the Romans called *stimuli*, that David thought of as caltrops: wooden boards with iron hooks embedded that would pierce hoof or boot with equal ease. Then at last there was what the Romans euphemistically called the "field of lilies:" pits with sharpened stakes at the bottom of them, and not all of them obvious.

It would be hard enough to charge through these deadly obstacles in daytime. To try it at night, David thought, would be suicidal, though who knew what the Gauls might do if desperate enough? Heartless as the expulsion of the civilians from the fortress was, David had to agree with the assessments of everyone from Caesar and Antony down to the lowest private soldier: the siege was working and conditions inside the fortress had to be getting grim. The Gallic relief army was late, but everyone felt it was only a matter of when it would arrive, not if. David wondered how much, if anything, would change simply because of his and Kevin's presence. Would the

Mardani even be here if not for him? Kevin's memory, though good, was imperfect but he was pretty sure Caesar had made no mention of ever receiving tons of whale meat.

The sun sank below the horizon. Twilight faded into dark. Dolovix, Pullo and their men would be getting into position before the half-moon rose and the refugees were escorted in. All David could do now was finish getting things ready and wait.

PULLO WAITED in the shadows along the banks of the river, his legionaries interspersed with Dolovix and his slingers. The civilians expelled from Alesia, mainly women and children along with the lame, sick and elderly, paraded by on the narrow path the Roman soldiers had cleared through their siege lines. His heart was racing at the thought of battle. He was scared, but not ashamed of it. His first commander, a hard old Sabine decurion with skin like leather armor, had told him to embrace his fear.

"It sharpens your senses," he'd said, "and makes you more aware of everything around you. Otherwise it paralyzes you, and you're dead."

Pullo didn't feel paralyzed. He felt alive. He felt a little like he'd had a good drink of *gwersugan*, the greenish liquor made from the wormwood plant that a handful of elders at Morgennus liked to brew. Everything seemed sharper, brighter. Thankfully, his head wasn't spinning.

The grim procession seemed to go on forever. The light of the half-moon gave these people a solemn dignity. Pullo didn't know if it was his imagination, but there seemed to be a mix of fear, resignation and anger on their faces. Who were they angry at? The Romans, for their war of conquest? Vercingetorix and the other chiefs who expelled them from the fortress where they'd been safe? The gods, for bringing this calamity upon them?

Pullo remembered something else the old decurion had told him. "We celebrate warriors," he'd said. "And warrior virtues should be celebrated. Strength, leadership, courage, these are all good things. But never forget that most people aren't warriors. They just want to get along. Raise crops, eat, drink, hump and do what they do in peace. So, if you go to war, make sure it is worth it. And if you go to war as someone's ally, make damn sure you're on the winning side."

Pullo thought his arguments were compelling and had never forgotten them. In the end, though, Rome would prevail. The nations rising in revolt now might be successful, even for a season or two. But Caesar would not give up and Rome would not forget. Even if Caesar fell in battle, another would come and take his place, perhaps Pompey or some younger general of ambition. Rome would grind Gaul down relentlessly and take it.

The veteran watched as the last of the refugees went through the opening in the line. Legionaries immediately began securing the area, the weakest point in the siege lines, as the slingers covered them. Pullo waited for the enemy to try to break out behind the civilians. He waited. And waited.

He waited all night. The attack never came.

David was finding out again why he hated the administrative side of medicine. At least if he'd made it to the island refugee camp and not the first century BCE, everything would have been set up. Volunteers would be keeping track of the incomers and what they needed; David would have been concentrating on what he loved—treating patients who needed him.

Livilla had helped a great deal, but she had dropped exhausted into the bed at the back of the tent before the first Alesians had arrived. Now they were thronging in. Caesar had given him Celer and Corvus, along with the camp orderlies and surgeons to use as he saw fit until there was a greater need for them but aside from Corvus none of them could read or write. That left just the two of them to record the names of everyone coming into the camp, along with their daily food ration.

The Romans were proving a mixed blessing. On the plus side, no one could set up a camp like a group of legionaries. It had been one thing for David to learn about the system the Romans had for their military camps in Polybius as a high school Latin student. It was quite another for him to see the orderly precision first hand. The office manager at the first practice he worked in had always said that the first rule of running anything was to not re-invent the wheel when you didn't have to. And when it came to camps, the Romans had a finely tuned wheel. So, the refugees were organized exactly the way the military camps inside the siege lines were--in a grid pattern with streets. The main difference was that this camp was not fortified. The healthiest individuals and families were housed in the middle of the camp, sicker patients quarantined in tents on below the *Via Principalis*. They'd made room for a forum; David figured that even if there was nothing to buy or sell it would make a convenient assembly point for the residents to get their food rations in an orderly way. Space was made for an altar, should anyone want to enshrine any gods there. Finally, a commander's tent was set up for he and Livilla to stay in, with the military doctors and orderlies staying in other shelters along the camp's main street.

On the other hand, the Roman doctors were being less than cooperative when it came to following his direct commands on things like sanitary procedures. What was so bad about washing your hands with soap in between seeing patients? I'm going to have to be Semmelweis, Lister and Jenner all rolled into one, David thought.

But that probably wasn't even the main problem. He noticed that Celer and Corvus had no problems following orders once David explained the logic behind them. They found many of them odd, but they responded to David's confidence and authority, although if he had to justify every order they'd never accomplish anything. The real problem, David realized, was that he was a man of no standing to these people. He'd arrived with a small body of barbarian troops. True, he'd stitched up one of their generals and gained some favor from Caesar because of it, but David was not an officer, or even a Roman.

"Look," David said to a particularly stubborn doctor, a Greek named Hipparchus, "I will be happy to explain why this soap is so important. Later. For now, you have to accept my word that it is, whether you want to or not. If these people have a disease or an infection you can spread it to others. You can get sick yourself. Do you want that?"

"So you say," said Hipparchus, stroking his impeccably oiled and styled beard. "I happen to know my humors are perfectly in balance and I have been in good health all my life. This...stuff...won't make a difference. In fact, how do I know they won't throw my humors out of balance?"

"Is there a problem here?"

David and Hipparchus both turned to see Mark Antony.

"This man is my personal physician, Hipparchus," said Antony to the obviously shocked Greek doctor. "I haven't forgotten you are a favorite of Cornelius Aquila. I have also not forgotten you owe me ten sestertii from that dice game on the Nones of Sexitilis either. Now do as he says," Antony pointed to David, "or be prepared to suffer consequences."

Everyone was now looking at them.

"That goes for all of you," said Antony raising his voice. He lifted his shirt to reveal the still ugly, but obviously well-healing gash in his side. "Can any of you sew up a wound this well? Or provide medicines to prevent festering? No? Then shut up and do as you're told." After that, there was a flurry of careful hand washing. They may not believe David about the benefits, but it wasn't worth punishment from a Legionary tribune answerable only to Caesar himself.

"Thank you for that," David said. "I wished it weren't necessary."

Antony made a dismissive gesture. "If it weren't for you, I'd gushing pus from my side and trying to make my peace with the gods. And how are the wretches your soft heart rescued? What do you call them?"

"Refugees," David said. "Better than I expected, really. Weak of course and half-starved. Some of them have the flux but that's what the salt water is for. Food, rest and security will be the best thing for them."

"You know, I wasn't sure about this mad plan of yours. But I think it might just work to our advantage after all. Vercingetorix didn't have the balls to follow his own plan after all, and here the civilians of Alesia sit, eating better than the soldiers inside the fortress. That will destroy their morale."

"That's not why I did it," David said, "but I suppose you're right."

"Well, good night, physician. You look like you need sleep."

David finally got some after the last of the refugees trudged in. Livilla didn't even stir as he dropped into the bed without even undressing or getting under the covers. He was asleep before his head hit the pillow.

IN THE WHIRLWIND days that followed, Livilla realized she'd married a chief, not just a healer. Despite David's protests, he had the camp up and running smoothly within a day. He quickly found the most capable and honest orderlies and put them in charge of food distribution, rotating them so the burden did not fall too heavily on any one person. He also worked out a schedule with Celer and Corvus so that a senior doctor was always on duty. David shared treatments for common illnesses like diarrhea—the flux--and told them to come to the senior doctor on duty with anything more serious.

David himself took charge of examining and treating the pregnant women as well as the ones who had recently given birth. Livilla was at his side, helping with examinations and generally acting as his ambassador not only with the refugee women, but the midwives. They didn't know what to make of David but in Livilla they recognized, if not one of their own, someone they could related to. Celer seemed surprised that David was so committed. "Why not let their own midwives do it?"

"This is what I trained to do," he'd said after examining a young woman who looked to be about halfway along with a routine pregnancy. "It's what I love to do. And I want to keep learning what midwives here do, so I will know what to do when my medicines run out. And I want to teach them things that will help more women and infants survive childbirth."

"Like your hand washing?" Livilla asked.

"Well, yes. The doctor who first discovered the link between washing hands and childbed fever found that you could prevent fever almost entirely if you just washed your hands thoroughly. He used something stronger, but soap is what I have so soap is what I'll use. Plus, it's fairly easy to make and the ingredients are widely available. Just soak wood ash and strain the liquid, then add anything with a lot of fat. Even olive oil would work, I'm pretty sure I've seen soap made with it. Heaven knows the Romans have olive oil. I'd like to teach some of the women here how to make soap so they can make some money. But my other medicines, the pills, everything—once they're gone, they're gone."

"Why can't you make more?" Livilla was curious. David knew so much that was beyond her, even beyond educated Roman aristocrats like Caesar or Antony knew, it was hard for her to imagine what he couldn't do.

"Imagine if Borodur was stranded somewhere and lost his sword. The people he found didn't know anything about iron. How would he replace his sword?"

"I don't think he could," Livilla said. "He's not a smith or a smith's apprentice."

"Well, I can't make medicines. Even if I had the ingredients that went into them, I wouldn't know what to do."

"What will you do when you run out?"

"The best I can. Kevin is clever and can help me design versions of tools that a good metal-worker—like your father—could make. But that will only take me so far, so I need to learn as much as I need to teach."

A very pregnant young woman walked in. "Greetings, medicus," she said with a thick accent. Livilla understood it well enough. The Mardani language had its quirks but most of the tribes in Gaul could more or less understand each other. The young woman then began speaking angrily and so fast even Livilla had a hard time keeping up. David's Mardani had become nearly fluent over the winter but it was clear he was lost.

"She says she wants to know if you need a woman. Or a servant. She's not going back to her husband," Livilla said.

"What's her name?"

"Theda."

Livilla translated as her husband spoke to Theda. "I'm married to this woman. And I don't need servants. Let's just examine you and make sure you and that baby are healthy."

Theda spoke again, then turned to the side and spit.

"She said that she's sure the baby is strong," Livilla said. "Her man is a warrior of the Mandubii—they live at Alesia—and his seed is strong. But she curses her husband for turning her out."

"Theda, try not to be upset. It's not good for you or the baby. Now, let's make sure everything's going well."

Livilla watched as he went through the examination, another routine one. He listened to the baby's heartbeat with a strange instrument he called a "fetoscope." He felt Flora's abdomen and took measurements.

"Everything seems well, and I don't think it will be much longer until you deliver. Come back and see me in seven days. You can come before then if you start labor or if something doesn't feel right to you."

"Yes, medicus," Theda said.

"She's a pistol," David said after Theda was gone.

"Pistol?" Livilla asked.

"It's a kind of weapon. But it's also come to mean someone with a temper or even a strong, exciting personality."

Livilla put her arms around her husband, drawing him into a kiss. "Am I a pistol?"

"I think so."

They kissed again, and Livilla would have liked to have done more, but they heard someone come into the tent.

"How can I help you?" David asked, before looking to see who'd come in. He was surprised to see that it was Vibius Pullo.

"Centurion Pullo! A pleasant surprise. What do you need?"

"Legate Trebonius wanted me to come get you. One of his men is ill and he's afraid it's contagious."

"Has he been at the camp?" David asked.

"No," Pullo said.

"Hmm. Tell Trebonius I'll be there shortly. I'll need to pack my tools."

Livilla smiled as David looked at her with love and regret.

"Later darling. It's our lot in life as healers."

19

____

(ALESIA, CENTRAL GAUL, 52 BCE)

Kevin, too, had had a busy few days. Mark Antony had pushed Caesar for permission to move the *Stork* off the river and bring it inside the outer wall of the siegeworks. Everything of value that could be moved off the boat had been, but who knew what a raiding party might find that would be useful? Raiders might also simply destroy the vessel because they could. Kevin knew his uncle was pleased. For his part, Kevin had a feeling Mark Antony felt he was in David's debt, though Kevin knew that his uncle would never use medical treatment as leverage over a patient. David had no problem taking fair payment from those who had money to pay him, but he was also a "treat now, worry about payment later" type of doctor.

Kevin watched as the sailboat crept closer to the gate to the camp. The gate would stay closed as long as possible. The *Stork* was valuable, but not valuable enough to risk a Gallic relief army running off the Romans and breaking the siege. All was quiet so far.

"It's going well, don't you think?" said the young man standing beside Kevin. Kevin looked at him. Cleon was roughly Kevin's own age, though it was hard to tell. Life in this time was hard and aged people quickly. Kevin—and David as well—were both assumed to be younger than they were. There was also the problem of calculating years. Kevin might say, for example, that his birthday was January 13, 2001, but the Romans didn't number their years for the most part. They did have a calendar with a "year one" marking the founding of the city of Rome. Kevin remembered from Latin class and other history that date was 753 BCE by the reckoning Kevin was used to. However, the Romans only used the date they called *Ad Urbe Conditum*—"from the founding of the city"—to keep track of certain festivals and observances that only happened once a generation, sometimes less. Otherwise, the Romans marked their years with the names of the two men elected consuls of the republic, whose terms were one year. The current year was the year of the consulship of Gnaeus Pompey and Quintus Caecilius Metellus.

Less cultured people, like the Mardani, counted seasons to keep track of age. If one were a slave, even a valued one like Kevin's new friend Cleon, no one bothered keeping track of birthdays.

"I still can't believe we pulled it off," Kevin said. "How did you think of it?"

"My tutor, who was also probably my father though my mother never said one way or the other," Cleon said. "He was a dreamer, and he had big dreams. None of which came to anything, but he had some interesting ideas. He told me once how the Greeks move their ships across Corinth so they won't have to sail all the way around the Peloponnese. They're pulled across on rollers. Arkadios thought that could be done to move ships between the Middle Sea and the Red Sea, where they almost touch. I don't know about that, but it seemed like it would work for a shorter distance."

Kevin thought idly about the Suez Canal, whether it would be possible to create such a feat of engineering in this time. He didn't know. If it was as challenging as the Panama Canal had been, even the formidable Romans couldn't hope to copy it.

"Cleon, can I ask you a question? A personal one?" Kevin asked.

Cleon looked at him. He was a handsome young man. Kevin thought that if Cleon had been one of his classmates in high school, he would have been very popular with the girls. He had curly hair and a complexion that reminded Kevin strongly of his Grandma Sarai's. He had other features, particularly his nose, that seemed distinctly Roman.

"I'm a slave. You're a free man. You can do what you want." Cleon shrugged. There was no bitterness in the statement, not resentment or jealousy that Kevin could tell. His new friend seemed to be stating a simple fact.

"Yes, well," said Kevin. Cleon's response had thrown him off-stride. "That's kind of what I wanted to ask. What's it like being a slave?"

"Huh," said Cleon, as if he hadn't expected that question. "I don't know how to answer that. If you'll pardon me, Keffin Flavens, it would be like me asking you what it's like to be free. I was born a slave to a slave. I've never known anything different. My mother was a pirate's woman. They had a base on Rhodes. One of Pompey's fleets came, killed most of the men and took everyone else as slaves. Mother always told me that her life got better that day."

"Better?" Kevin was shocked and a little scandalized.

"We're well-fed and well-housed. We have a firm but kind master who doesn't abuse us. I know not everyone like me is so lucky, but my life isn't bad. Even here," Cleon gestured to the camp below the ramparts, "I'm being well-treated. Antony leased me."

"Leased you?" This was something new. You could lease slaves? Like a car? Or a condo? He was quickly realizing that the Roman version of slavery was different than that of the American south before the Civil War. It could be brutal, yes, and was for many. But for slaves like Cleon, who were smart and could learn valuable skills—like military engineering—life could be comfortable.

"Sure. I've even been able to make some extra money. If it keeps up I might even make enough to buy my freedom."

Kevin shook his head and returned to watching the sailboat's progress. It edged forward with agonizing slowness until finally the gates opened and it was safe inside. Kevin was about to suggest to Cleon they find something to eat when another slave, little more than a child, ran up to them. Kevin couldn't remember the kid's name but knew he was one of Caesar's junior body slaves. A gofer for the senior body slave, who was essentially Caesar's valet.

"Flavens," he said. "Your uncle sent me. He wants you to come right away."

"Come with me, Cleon," Kevin said. "Unless Antony needs you to do something else?"

"I'll come. If it's important enough for Manlius here to fetch you my *dominus* will probably be there too."

DAVID FINISHED his examination of the soldier. He was running a fever and had tenderness in his lower-left abdomen, so the diagnosis was straightforward. Quintus Claudius was the soldier's name, son of a minor branch of the powerful Claudii family and one of Trebonius's more promising young officers. It was a measure of concern that any unknown, sudden illness caused in an army camp that Caesar and Antony, along with another legate named Labienus, had come to watch. David took them all outside.

"It's not contagious," David said straight away. "It's his appendix."

"Appendix?"

"Alexander, if I may?"

Caesar's slave handed David the wax tablet he carried with him at all times. Paper was too expensive to waste, so the Romans used wax-coated tablets for any writing that David would have used scrap paper for. David took the stylus and sketched out the intestinal tract, with a larger-than-scale-sized appendix.

"I've made it bigger, but there is a small organ called the vermi-form appendix. No one really knows what its purpose was, but whatever it was it no longer serves that purpose. It's a leftover, a vestige. Sometimes, it can become inflamed and fester. If it bursts, it causes a far more serious infection that can be fatal."

"Can you keep it from bursting?" asked Trebonius.

"Yes. I will remove the appendix."

"You'll cut into him?" Caesar asked, surprised. "That's rather drastic."

"Not really. It's a simple surgery. Surgery always has risks, but if I thought it was riskier to operate than do nothing, I'd do nothing," David said.

"But it's not contagious?" asked Labienus.

"No, Legate Labienus, it is not. It could have happened to anyone."

"When do you wish to operate?" asked Caesar.

"As soon as Kevin can get here and help me set up the oil lamps so we'll have enough light. I'd rather not do this by lamplight. But an orderly or someone"—David couldn't make himself say "slave"—"should stay with him while I get things ready. If his pain gets worse, they will need to get me right away."

"Will you need help?" Caesar asked.

"Livilla will help. Corvus will observe but he's skilled enough to help if needed also. It's a simple surgery and young Quintus Claudius is healthy. Nothing is guaranteed but it should be routine. You may observe, Caesar, if you agree to take the necessary precautions and do what I say."

"I am not accustomed to taking orders in my own camp, physician."

"With all due respect, Caesar, on this battlefield I am the general and I give orders." David thought he saw the faintest smile play across Caesar's lips.

"Very well. I shall observe and let you be my surgeon-general. For this battle at least."

Caesar and his legates left. David groaned as he packed up his tools, and then they walked back to their tent together.

"What's wrong?" asked Livilla. She'd been observing quietly the whole time. I must have "That Look" on my face, David thought. "I'm just worried," he said. "I've done this operation enough that I'm not concerned about being able to do it, but I'm not used to working with an audience. Other than the father of any babies I'm delivering."

"I still can't believe men want to be with their women giving birth.

In any event, it will be fine," said Livilla reassuringly. "What will you need me to do?"

"What about me?" David saw Kevin come in, with another young man. Another slave, David thought. That's another thing I'll have to think about. When I have time to think.

"Kevin and..." David couldn't place the young man's name and was embarrassed.

"Cleon," Kevin said.

"Cleon, thank you. Welcome. Please forgive me. You two can start lighting the lamps and setting them up. I want the operating table to be as well lit as possible." David gestured to the bier-like table being used for surgeries. "Kevin, when you're done, please gown and mask up and scrub your hands. You're going to be my 'circulating nurse.' Whatever we need, even if it's just wiping our foreheads, you do it. I want Corvus to watch and learn and do as little as possible so he can concentrate."

"What about me?" Livilla asked.

"I'll need you to shave the area where I will cut in and wash it with soap. I'll need you to hand me things. You know the names of all the instruments I'll be using so you can give them to me when I ask, along with holding skin and muscle aside."

Livilla nodded and began gowning and scrubbing up alongside Corvus. Caesar returned, wearing a light tunic and after donning a gown and mask watched Kevin scrub his hands and forearms, then did the same. Two orderlies carried in a naked and unconscious Quintus Claudius and laid him on the operating table, where Livilla prepped him. David stepped up, made sure the lighting was bright enough, then asked Livilla for his scalpel. It was time.

CAESAR WATCHED as Davidius set up a table and cordoned off an area with rope. He rather enjoyed watching the strange doctor work, though the elaborate washing of the hands and lower arms he insisted on made Caesar wonder if there was truth to the rumor

Davidius was Jewish. Whether or not that was the case, Caesar thought about men and their qualities. He felt there were two kinds of people in the world: those born to lead and those born to follow. Of those born to lead, often the most effective were those who led only reluctantly, but then quietly took charge when they had to. As the legendary Cincinnatus had. Caesar was no reluctant leader but, he reflected, appearing to be one had served him well. With Davidius, however, there was no feigning. Outside his area of expertise, he was respectful, even deferential. But when it came to questions of medical care, he did not shrink from taking charge and issuing orders. Even to me, Caesar thought. What was that he'd said? "This is my battlefield and I am the general."

Antony walked up to Caesar, taking care to stay outside the area forbidden to everyone not involved in the coming surgery, or closely observing it as Caesar and Corvus were. Davidius had agreed to let Antony, Trebonius and Labienus to stay in the tent so long as they kept their distance. "Has he started yet?" Antony asked.

"No," said Caesar. "But he is well along in his preparations. It should not be long."

"Are you sure you are going to watch?"

"I thought I would. It would be silly not to after dressing in this special mask and gown and performing the handwashing ritual. Besides, it's not as if I've never seen a belly sliced open."

"A cousin of mine said the same thing after he'd been on a campaign," Antony said. "Poor bastard still fainted dead away every time he saw a hog or sheep butchered."

Caesar chuckled. "I take it you plan to watch?"

"I wouldn't miss it, though I doubt I'll see much. Davidius claims it is to minimize the risk of the surgical cut festering. Whether that's true or not I can say it worked for my little cut. Results are hard to argue with."

It wasn't long before David beckoned Caesar closer to the table. Pullo and Aquila stood guard at the surgical tent's entrance. No one else would be allowed in. Davidius's woman then shaved a patch of hair off the young Quintus Claudius's belly. She then dabbed a clear, astringent-smelling liquid on a square of cloth and wiped over the are she'd shaved.

"Will shaving his hair prevent infection?" Corvus asked.

"It will greatly lower the risk, as will cleansing the incision site with alcohol. This type of alcohol is poisonous to drink but if you have very strong liquor you can use that—provided you boil it first," Davidius said.

"Now, once again for you non-doctors observing this--you are here to watch. I will explain what I am doing as I do it, but you are not to get in my way. My highest priority is to help Quintus. My next-highest is to teach Corvus so he in his turn can teach others. The rest of you are here out of curiosity or a need to see your man is properly cared for. I understand. I mean no disrespect, but I will tolerate nothing that might endanger Quintus's life. Understood?"

Yes, thought Caesar, Davidius certainly had the way of command, though he seemed not to realize it. Give him a sick person to minister to and he became fierce as a veteran cutting his way through the enemy to win glory.

Davidius's instruments were laid out for him. He took one, a bell-like device suspended from a pair of tubes. David inserted the other end of the tubes into his ears.

"This is a stethoscope," Davidius explained. "I'm listening to his heart, lungs and bowels to make sure everything is good."

Apparently, it was. Satisfied, Davidius picked up an instrument made from the finest steel Caesar had ever seen. Caesar was a good judge of blades could see that though it was meant for cutting, this small knife looked far sharper even a shaving knife. The flesh parted under the knife, called a "scalpel," with ease as David carefully cut through skin, membrane and muscle. With his woman's help, Davidius held everything open with another instrument, which the doctor called a retractor.

Every so often, Davidius would direct his woman to mop up blood so he could see or direct his golden-skinned nephew to wipe his brow or assist in some other way. Caesar craned forward to get a better look. Caesar had seen guts spilled in any number of battles, and in his position as Pontifex Maximus, Caesar was used to examining animal entrails read for omens and hints of the future. But he'd never seen a man's insides like this before. And Davidius worked quickly and confidently, just as Caesar would if he were planning a campaign or directing his men on a battlefield. The man hadn't exaggerated when he'd named himself a general at all. Davidius would no doubt be mentioned in the same breath as Hippocrates and other legendary physicians before long. Caesar couldn't help but respect the man, even be a little in awe of him.

Davidius then came to the appendix. It was hard for Caesar to see much in the way of detail but could tell the doctor was sewing off something inside Quintus Claudius. Taking his scalpel again, Davidius made a quick cut and lifted the troublesome organ out of the young officer's body. Even with no medical training at all, Caesar could tell the thing was poisoned, inflamed. In fact, it burst when David put it down in a bowl on his table, issuing foul-smelling pus.

"It would have done that inside Quintus?" asked Corvus, a little repulsed.

"Almost certainly," David said. "And he would have died, or at the very least been severely ill."

They both watched as this strange physician then sewed up each layer of flesh he'd cut through. Quintus Claudius had slept through it all and did not seem to be in much pain.

The top of the table Quintus lay on was designed to turn into a litter when the surgery was done. Once bandages were secure over the incision, David stepped away, stripping the strange, tight-fitting gloves off his hand and untying the mask on his face. Kevin, Corvus and Livilla did the same. Caesar, not needing to touch the patient or any instruments, wore no gloves but he was glad to take the mask off.

"I'll move him to his own quarters once I'm sure he's recovering well, but for now I want to keep an eye on him," David said as he stripped off the robe, tossing it aside as if it were trash. "He can stay here and rest for a while and once he's more alert we can move him."

"That was extraordinary," Caesar said.

"He should recover fully," Davidius said.

"Do you need anything?" Antony asked.

"Dinner. And Quintus will need a bowl of warm broth when he wakes up."

"I will put Alexander at your disposal," said Caesar. "You spoke true, and you fight this battle well. I salute you, my medical imperator."

Caesar smiled to himself as he saw the bewildered expression on David's face.

DAVID HOPED the whale fajitas turned out well. His experiments while living with the Mardani had been edible, but not entirely satisfactory. Now, though, he thought he had the blend of spices just right. The tortillas he wasn't worried about. He could make Tia Nina's flour tortillas in his sleep and substituting in olive oil for vegetable or corn oil had been easy. It probably made the tortillas healthier, in fact. There were no peppers, of course, but there were plenty of onions.

It had been a long day. David hadn't realized how draining a simple appendectomy could be. Of course, it was the audience and not the procedure that had left him feeling wiped out. How sanguine would any of his colleagues have been about doing any simple operation—with, say, the President and Chairman of the Joint Chiefs of Staff looking on? And now here he was, cooking for Caesar and Antony when he'd been looking forward to a quiet evening with his wife. He'd already planned to make whale fajitas, so whale fajitas would be what they would get.

Quintus Claudius was recovering well just a short distance away. It was clear that however David felt about slavery, Quintus's slave, a Greek about Quintus's own age that had grown up with him, was devoted. And very competent. David was confident his care instructions would be followed to the letter, and that slave would come immediately if anything seemed wrong.

Caesar and Antony seemed fascinated that David not only could cook, but that he enjoyed doing so.

"Why not just have a slave do it?" Caesar asked.

"A slave wouldn't know the recipe for starters," David said, loading more scorn into the word "slave" than he'd really meant to.

"You seem to have a problem with slaves," Caesar said.

"It's slavery I have a problem with, Caesar. My country fought a terrible civil war over the issue. Over 600,000 men were killed, and the country was devastated. Even after 150 years the scars hadn't completely healed. I'm starting to realize that Rome's version of slavery is different but in the end you're still owning another human being as property."

Caesar did not look terribly impressed by David's argument but wasn't interested in pursuing it. David decided to move on to safer topics.

"My father is what I guess you'd call a master cook. He owns two restaurants—" his guests' puzzled looks brought David up short.

Livilla chucked affectionately. "You used English again, dear."

David found himself accidentally using English words less and less, but it still happened.

"Apologies. I don't know the Latin word for a place where people will pay to eat prepared meals," he said.

"*Popina,*" Antony offered.

"Thank you. Yes, he owns two *popinae.* My sister and brother followed his footsteps as professional chefs, but I know my way around a kitchen."

"He cooks at both of his eating houses?" Antony sounded surprised.

"Well no. At least not all the time," David said. "He owns them. He employs his cooks and chefs, to work for him and run things day-to-day. But Dad trains his chefs, comes up with recipes, and his name is on both businesses."

When the fajitas were done, David set them aside to cool, then shredded some cheese.

"Now," said David, demonstrating as he spoke, "you take a tortilla, this flatbread here, load meat and onions on it, and cheese if you like, then roll it up and take a bite."

Livilla went first. She was already familiar with how to make and eat fajitas from David's earlier experiments. Caesar and Antony followed, a little more hesitantly. David and Livilla waited until their guests took a bite before they ate.

"It's very unusual. Very distinctive," said Caesar.

"I do have to say that beef or chicken are more normal meats to use for this dish. As far as I know, no one's ever made it with whale meat."

"Yes," Antony said. "Chicken would taste good. Or duck. Or dormice. And I like the flatbread. It's like a plate you can eat."

"Dormice?"

"Physician, you haven't lived until you've had honeyed dormice fresh out of the oven." Antony motioned his slave to make him another fajita. Changing subjects, he said, "You really should at least hire a servant, if you won't buy a slave. That Gaulish woman, the one with the big bellyful, would serve you any way you liked."

David coughed. Livilla blushed but he was sure she was hiding a smile. All she said was, "It might not be a bad idea to have some help. When the baby comes."

"You're going to have a baby?" Caesar said. He raised his goblet. "May it be a son and the first of many." There was just a hint of sadness there, David thought. Then he remembered one of his conversations with Antony while the legate had still been on bed rest. Caesar had lost his only legitimate child, his daughter Julia, to complications of childbirth about two years ago. She'd been married to Pompey. With that tie gone, and Crassus dead in the east at the hands of the Parthians, David's understanding was that many people in the Roman world were holding their breaths. The tripartite alliance that had brought stability to the Republic was, as Miracle Max of *The Princess Bride* might have it, mostly dead. David brought his thoughts back to the present. Livilla had given her approval but it was his decision.

"Theda will be busy enough very soon. Her baby will arrive any day. But even so, you have to pay servants and I have no money."

"Nonsense," said Antony. "You're my personal physician. I'll pay you."

This was news to David. Livilla too, judging by his wife's shocked face. "Are you serious?" David asked.

"I joke about many things, so I will forgive you for thinking so, Davidius. But not about this. I need you around in case any more horses throw me onto something sharp. What are you accustomed to getting paid?"

That was a good question. David recalled, vaguely, that a *denarius* —in this period was worth about $10. "About 20,000 denarii," said David.

Antony nearly choked on his wine, Livilla gasped and even Caesar looked shocked.

"Your services are expensive," Antony said once he recovered.

"Well, I had extensive training, as Caesar already knows, and went into considerable debt to pay for it. I was still paying off that debt when I arrived here. Plus, I had to live in a large and very expensive city. But rest assured that where I come from that is average pay for a doctor."

"Yes. I'll admit I hadn't given thought to how much you would have paid your tutors for your training." Caesar said.

"Still," David said, "I imagine my creditors can't follow me here. I could probably make do with less."

"Hm. Yes. Perhaps 500 denarii a month. We will see if that is sufficient to your needs. An *as* per day should be sufficient for a servant."

They exchanged pleasantries as the evening wound down, Livilla talking about life among the Mardani and Caesar and Antony talking about prior campaigns. As the sun went down and his dinner guests prepared to leave, they heard a horn sounding in the distance. A horn that could mean one only thing.

The Gallic relief army had arrived at last.

20

(ALESIA, CENTRAL GAUL, 52 BCE)

Caesar seems more confident than usual, Antony thought. Of course, Caesar was always confident on the eve of battle. But the facts his commander laid out seemed awfully grim to Antony. Counting those inside the fortress and the scouts' estimates on the size of the relief army camped across the river, the Romans were outnumbered at least five to one, maybe more. Most Romans—especially those who had never seen battle—would argue that one Roman legionary was worth ten barbarian soldiers. It was true, Antony mused, that Roman discipline counted for much. It was —what was the term Flavens had used?—a *vis multiplicator.* A "force multiplier." Antony liked that, and it made a lot of sense. A well-trained, well-drilled, battle-hardened legion could take on an army several times its own size. But it was also a truth that in war, quantity could become its own quality. Not to mention that Fortuna was a most capricious and fickle goddess.

Caesar and his commanders looked over the map of the siege works.

"They're going to concentrate here," Caesar said, pointing to an area in the northwest where the inner and outer walls of the Roman lines nearly met at the river the locals called the Ose. Vercingetorix himself had tried to break out there at several points, with very limited success. A few of his cavalry had broken through to summon the relief army.

"The besiegers are now the besieged," Trebonius said. Gods, what a gift for the obvious the man had, thought Antony.

"Thanks to the Mardani and their food our situation in that regard isn't as grim as it might have been," said Caesar. "Even with the rations we're giving to the Mandubii...refugees, as our new physician friend calls them, we have plenty of meat and grain for the men."

"I don't trust that doctor," said Trebonius. "A soft-hearted barbarian stranger with radical ideas. He's not right."

"You say that even after he saved Quintus Claudius?" Antony asked. "You are full of gratitude, Trebonius. Or are you jealous this 'barbarian' will earn the friendship of the Claudii for saving one of their more promising young men?"

"But even he doesn't seem certain of Quintus's recovery! He kept talking about all the things that could go wrong even after the surgery was over."

"In my experience, Trebonius, most doctors make extravagant claims that never come to pass. Would you rather he failed to live up to vain boasting, or live up to cautious promises? I find his insistence on the latter quite refreshing," Antony said.

"I just don't like him," Trebonius repeated, a petulant tone creeping into his voice. "What kind of doctor doesn't prescribe prayers or sacrifices? It's as if he doesn't believe in the gods. Such behavior is hubris and will be punished."

Antony couldn't let Trebonius have the last word. "He never said not to pray. He just said prayers should be offered according to the customs and conscience of his patients. That's what he told me when I asked the same question. That doesn't sound like hubris to me. Quite the opposite."

Trebonius looked to respond but Caesar held up his hand. "Enough bickering you two. This avails us nothing. Can we return to the matter at hand?"

"The problem as I see it," said Labienus, "is that even if we know where the enemy is most likely to attack, they have so many men that they can attack us everywhere at once. If we concentrate our forces at the weak point in our walls, it will leave us vulnerable to attack even in our more strongly fortified areas."

"You are correct of course, Labienus," Caesar said. "We'll make sure the whole of our works is as well-defended as possible, but I intend to set aside a reserve. Thirteen cavalry cohorts, led by me, will be ready to reinforce any force along the outer walls that seems as if it will be overwhelmed. It will give us the element of surprise."

"That's nearly a legion's worth of horse, Caesar!" Trebonius said. "Are you sure that will not weaken us unduly?"

"It will not," Caesar said. Antony hoped Trebonius recognized that tone. Caesar used it when he'd made up his mind. There would be no debate on this issue.

Antony wondered again at his commander's confidence. Certainly, Caesar's military record would make any predictions of victory more than empty boasting. But even Caesar had known defeat. The battle at Gergovia had been, if not exactly a defeat, at the very least a setback that had prolonged the Gauls' rebellion. Confidence was one thing, but it seemed to Antony that Caesar was behaving as if the outcome were foretold. It couldn't be the Mardani reinforcements, even if their food stores gave them more security against a siege. The Gauls had neither the numbers nor the discipline for a prolonged siege of their own. Was it Davidius?

The strange medicus was more than he seemed. That much was obvious. Most doctors were out-and-out quacks. Anyone could call themselves a physician and hawk dubious cures and perform surgeries that often did far more harm than good. Such men—unless they harmed someone with influence—simply found another line of work once their reputations caught up with them. The best doctors, those that served the wealthy and powerful, were equally immodest, in Antony's experience. They were just better at making good on their extraordinary promises. Hipparchus was a perfect example.

That was what made Davidius such an enigma. Antony knew all too well his amazing skill. The only evidence of his fall two weeks ago was a long, thin cut, now fading to a scar. The stitches had come out and the wound had stayed closed. It was healing completely cleanly. Even more amazing had been the quiet confidence during the "appendectomy" surgery Davidius had performed on Quintus Claudius. One of the camp doctors might have sewn up Antony's wound almost as well. But as experienced and accomplished as the military doctors were—and they were almost always much more competent than those in the civilian world due to much more practical experience—none of them could have cut into a man's bowels as confidently or as well as Davidius had done.

Even considering that, though, Davidius was clearly more than he seemed. But what was he? His story of being shipwrecked and finding the Mardani was almost too simple, but then its very simplicity spoke to its truth. Aside from the fact that Ferrarius, as sober and stolid a Roman as Antony had ever met, verified the story. As did the Mardani, to a man. But was it the whole truth? Where did this man come from? Where had he gotten all these extraordinary things? There was the boat, safely inside the outer walls, made of some alien material that was certainly not wood. His medical tools were familiar and yet of unbelievable quality. The same was true of his clothes. And it was clear he and his nephew knew things beyond mere medical procedures that Caesar found valuable. Antony's commander was not a man who tolerated mere hangers-on. If Davidius had Caesar's ear, then his words must have merit.

When it came down to it, Antony admired Davidius. And was more than a little frightened of him.

As David went over preparations with Celer and Corvus, his opinion of Roman medicine and medical practice went up considerably. The more time he spent with the senior doctors, the more David liked and respected both men.

Celer, it turned out, was the son of a Remi butcher, the third of four boys in a rather large family. He was always more interested in studying the innards of the animals the men of the family slaughtered rather than butchering them for sale.

"My mother thought I was going to be an augur, the way I used to study livers and entrails and the like. Then she saw me sewing them back together," Celer laughed. "They weren't happy about me wanting to become a surgeon, but it wasn't as if I would stand to inherit my father's butcher shop. My oldest brother was far better suited anyway. Father encouraged me to join the Tenth Legion as an auxiliary and try to catch on with one of the legionary surgeons. 'Army doctors are the best, and I won't stand for you being less than the best.' Then I hurt my knee and made myself useful around the infirmary tent."

"We're not so different, though my father didn't object to my wanting to study medicine," David said. "He's a cook, a master cook. A 'chef,' my people call him. My brother and sister followed him into the family business, so he was happy to let me do what I wanted."

"I'd heard rumors you can cook. You cooked a meal for Caesar himself, without even a slave to help you," Corvus said. The African had shared his own story earlier. He'd already been an acolyte to his tribe's healer-shaman before becoming a hostage in all but name and coming to live among the Romans and continuing his medical studies under a Jewish physician serving the Roman propraetor of the region.

"Oh, I can cook, Corvus. Dad made sure of that. It's just that he and my brother and sister are good enough to make a living doing it. For me, it's a useful skill."

Celer and Corvus both showed David surgical instruments and other supplies. Most of the instruments were quite familiar: scalpels, forceps, probes. The Roman doctors even had a supply of brass catheters, though David wanted to cross his legs at the very thought of using one or having one used on him. Flexible plastic catheters were bad enough but brass? He wondered what his fellow doctors back in New York would think of that.

David did see one instrument he did not have, that he should have thought of.

"A bone saw," said Celer, handing one to David. "We're going to be taking a lot of arms and legs I fear, but that's always the way of it in a big battle like the one we're going to be having."

"I'll need one of those," David mused. "I don't have much experience with amputations. Not much call for it for a doctor that does childbirth. The one I performed on Cornelius Chlorus was my first."

"Really?" Celer was shocked. "I've never seen one so cleanly done. Hipparchus and Aquila have been using that against you but Corvus and I, and anyone with eyes, know different."

"Hipparchus I can understand. I've had to deal with his type before. But Aquila? We've barely even spoken."

"Publius Cornelius Aquila," said Celer, emphasizing the *nomen*, "is Chlorus's uncle. Even for someone from a family like the Cornelii losing a hand can make for a hard life."

"And if he'd let Pullo bring him to me right away, he'd be healthy and not missing four fingers and a thumb," David said.

"Facts are stubborn things, as my own medical tutor was fond of saying," Corvus said. "The story of your surgery on Quintus Claudius, not to mention your stitching up Antony, has gotten around. I imagine all of the men would rather you take off their arm or leg than anyone else, if it came to that."

"You and Celer are fine doctors, Corvus. I look forward to working with you," David said.

"And I look forward to working with you. And yes, I'm good," said Celer bluntly. The Romans didn't think much of empty boasts, but neither did they go in for false modesty. "But I know how good you are. I couldn't have done that surgery on young Quintus, not with your skill and confidence. There are many great things ahead for you, don't think otherwise. I never would have thought to use soap for hand washing, but it seems to work."

"Your *acetum* is quite effective as well, especially as a wound wash," David said. Acetum was concentrated vinegar, acetic acid. It was the Romans' disinfectant of choice and a very effective one. If David had realized that when setting up protocols for the refugee camp, he would have let the Roman medics choose between soap and acetum for washing their hands. Of course, they didn't know about germ theory and didn't realize that either vinegar or soap killed microbes that caused disease. They could recognize the results, though. For now, that was all that concerned David.

He was even more interested in their herbal remedies. Opium was used as a painkiller, as was a plant David recognized as "angel's trumpet." He added to the extensive notes he'd started taking over the winter in long talks with Livilla and Matwyn. His narcotics wouldn't last forever, and he needed to be prepared.

Neither would his antibiotics. That was what worried him most. There was no way he could manufacture penicillin or sulfa drugs. He looked at Celer's silver bracelets, bands really, that the doctor wore on his forearms. They beautiful and intricate linear abstract designs that were the forerunners of the beautiful Celtic art still alive in Ireland and Scotland in the 21st century. Silver. What a beautiful, useful metal. Then a light went off in David's brain.

"That's it, Celer!"

"What?"

"Silver! I can use silver to fight wound infections."

"I've never heard of such a thing," Corvus said.

"It's true. Silver can keep a wound from festering, but isn't harmful to people," said David.

"A rather expensive treatment."

"Good thing Caesar is rich."

Celer roared with laughter and slapped David on the back. "I knew I liked you. Now tell me about this system...you call it 'triage,' I believe."

Livilla stirred as David came into their tent. He didn't so much sit down as slump, as if his backbone had turned soft. She was worried. He was pushing himself too hard. Her husband wasn't sleeping enough and was getting dark rings around his eyes. Without bothering to undress, he collapsed into bed beside her.

"What's wrong?" she asked.

"Nothing. Go back to sleep. I spent longer with Celer and Corvus going over triage than I'd planned."

"Triage?" Livilla stumbled over the unfamiliar word.

"It's a system of classifying wounded or sick people, especially when you're going to be dealing with large numbers of them. When you can't save everyone, you can make sure that those with light wounds get care last, those beyond help are made comfortable, and those more seriously wounded but who can be saved get care first. The junior doctors and orderlies will classify soldiers coming in and treat the least serious cases. You, Celer, Corvus and I, and the more experienced doctors, will try to help the most serious cases."

And if Livilla knew her husband, he would be taking the worst of the worst on himself.

"You won't be able to save them all, my love."

"I know," David said, patting her thigh. "I'm lucky that I haven't lost many patients. That's why losing Bennozha's baby hurt so much. But I know one doctor who was in Rwanda. That's a place deep in Africa, far south of Egypt. Years in my past, some members of one Rwandan tribe, called the Hutus, decided to wipe out another tribe, called the Tutsi. The Tutsi, you see, had been placed in power over them, though their numbers were fewer."

"The way Rome puts client kings and chiefs in place on its borders," said Livilla, understanding immediately. David kissed her, the way he often did when she surprised and delighted him. She felt a stirring, wanting that kiss to lead to more kisses and other things, but she knew she had to listen. This story was important to David.

"That's exactly right, more or less," David said. "You have to understand that Rwanda was a poor country, so they fought with inexpensive weapons. They used machetes, which are somewhat like the *spatha* swords the legionaries carry. They have one edge and are intended to cut through dense plant growth and even butcher large animals. You can imagine what they do to human flesh.

"Anyway, I knew a surgeon who went to help people caught in this war. He saw bodies that had been cut to pieces. In the end, his dreams were so horrible he quit treating patients altogether. Last I heard he'd moved into research. Which is a shame because he was a gifted surgeon."

"That won't happen to you," Livilla said. "You have me to help you carry those burdens, and I will make sure your dreams are untroubled. And there's no time like now to start."

She kissed him deeply, passionately. She began undressing him.

"What are you doing?" David asked.

"Making sure you sleep soundly tonight."

Not all of David was tired, Livilla quickly realized. He moved to roll her on her back, but she stopped him.

"This is my night," she said.

Pleasure was a fire that streaked through Livilla's body as she explored her husband. Leisurely and thoroughly. At last, she was ready, and she gave her husband pleasure while taking her own. Sighing, she lay down beside him.

"Do you need me to finish you?" David asked. That was one of the things she loved about him. He was always concerned with her pleasure.

"Not tonight, love," she said. "You needed it. And I enjoyed myself, don't worry."

David laughed. "Well, I do feel more relaxed."

They held each other and soon David was sleeping soundly. That was good. He hadn't slept well in days. Now Livilla needed to fall asleep, but sleep proved elusive. It's the coming battle, she thought. So many life and death decisions coming. It was then that she truly understood what David was thinking because at that moment, Livilla too wished she could save them all.

BATTLE WILL COME TODAY, Caesar thought as he looked at the enemy's vast camp, less than a mile away from the Roman lines. He was confident of victory, despite the enemy numbers. He couldn't say why, but the strange foreign doctor and his even stranger nephew buoyed his spirits. Caesar had never been particularly religious, despite being Pontifex Maximus, but Davidius and Flavens were an emphatic answer to the omens in last summer's ram sacrifice. They were a gift from the sea, blown off-course to Gallic shores, with Davidius bearing Mercury's mark.

The relief army was trying to bridge the ditches in front of his outer lines, to make assaulting the contravellation wall easier. Caesar responded by drawing his own troops into two lines: one to hold the outer wall, commanded by Labienus, and one to hold the inner wall, commanded by Quintus Tullius Cicero. Perhaps if his younger brother won glory today, Caesar thought, Marcus Tullius Cicero—one of his most persistent critics in the Senate—might be more favorably disposed towards him. Caesar doubted it though; Marcus Tullius Cicero, *the* Cicero, was too much of an idealist. Be that as it may, Quintus was an officer of proven ability and would discharge his duties well. In spite of what his family might think of Caesar personally.

The task of engaging the enemy would fall to his cavalry, commanded by Antony and Gaius Trebonius. They would sortie outside the walls at just the right moment and take them by surprise. The Gauls' archers would exact a toll, but Caesar did not think it would be heavy enough to make a difference and Vercingetorix's allies would never be disciplined enough to hold off a Roman cavalry charge, superior numbers or no.

Facing his men, Caesar held up his arms. Every soldier's eyes were fixed on him. The gaze of Jupiter himself could not have been more exhilarating or daunting.

"My men! The enemy has superior numbers, but we have the superior strength. One Roman soldier is worth ten of them! So I say to you: it is not we who are outnumbered, but the Gauls. The gods have foretold our victory, but we must still win it. Stand with me!"

A great roar went up. One man stood up. Caesar recognized Pullo,

"Whether I live or die, you will praise me today, Caesar!"

"Of that I am certain, Vibius Pullo. For the Senate and the People of Rome!"

"For the Senate and the People of Rome!" cried the soldiers in response.

"Sound the charge!"

A soldier sounded his trumpet, and the cavalry surged forth. With a cry, the Gauls charged to meet them, both from outside the siege lines and within them.

ARROWS FELL on all sides of them. Caesar had predicted, correctly, that there were archers and skirmishers placed among the ranks of the Gauls assaulting the outer walls of the Roman siege works, but the knowledge only did so much good. Knowing they were there didn't make the arrows suddenly vanish. They were losing men and horses fast, despite their best efforts, and fighting these Gauls was like fighting the legendary hydra, only worse. Every Gaul killed seemed to be replaced by a dozen more. Each Roman soldier was worth ten Gallic warriors, Caesar had said. Antony figured he'd killed at least twice that number. And still, they kept coming.

"Fall back and reform, we'll charge again!" Antony shouted to his men. "If we're not careful, they'll surround us."

His cavalry did so. Far off on the other wing, he could see that Trebonius had given a similar order. Once his men had reformed, Antony sounded the charge again.

"How many times do we keep doing this?" asked a soldier at his side.

"As many times as we must."

"But they just keep coming!"

"And that is why we keep charging," said Antony. "The sea is much vaster than the sea wall, and yet the wall holds it back. We are the sea wall. The enemy is the sea. We hold them back from our lines so Caesar and the men on the ramparts can fight off those trying to break out from Alesia. We must win or die!"

"Victory or death!" the soldier cried as he charged through a knot of the enemy, cutting through at least a dozen before he was wounded by an arrow and unhorsed. The doomed man was quickly overwhelmed by Gauls. There wouldn't be much left of him.

After what seemed like hours but was nowhere near that based on how little the sun had moved, the Gauls at last fell back to regroup. Antony reformed his men to get ready for the next charge. We must be reducing their numbers, he thought, but you'd never know it from the endless stream of men coming forth. How long can we last?

THE BATTLE DRAGGED ON. Dolovix sent bullet after bullet from his sling, buckets of shot being replaced beside him so he could keep firing. Vercingetorix and his men were assaulting the inner walls in earnest now, counting on the distraction of his allies' assault from outside to divide the Romans' forces and weaken them. Word had come down the line that the Roman cavalry, led by Antony and Trebonius, was holding them off for now, inflicting heavy losses.

He loosed another shot at a warrior trying to climb the wall, hitting him on the forehead between the eyes. The enemy warrior was dead before he hit the ground, not uttering a sound. A second bullet followed, hitting a shoulder with bone-shattering force. Dolovix didn't stop. He couldn't. He felt like a human ballista, launching missile after missile, and he didn't miss many targets. None of his Mardani did. They were the best slingers in Gaul, and he intended to prove it today. David said Caesar recorded his battles in detail.

Well, thought Dolovix as he fired yet another shot, let him write about the bravery of the Mardani today, for all the world to know.

THE WALLS WERE HOLDING, but barely. The sun was beginning to dip below the horizon, but still the battle raged. Caesar had never been prouder of his men, but they were only human. Antony and Trebonius's cavalry formations were growing more ragged with each charge. They were inflicting tremendous losses on the relief army, but they had far less men and horses to begin with. Caesar thought his men could hold both the outer and inner walls if they must, but he wanted to avoid anything that might give Vercingetorix heart. Remove the hope of victory from your enemy and your own victory was all but assured.

It was time to make a dramatic move. He motioned to Labienus.

"What forces do you have in reserve?" Caesar asked him.

"I have several squadrons of Germans. They're itching to get into the fight and I'm increasingly hard-pressed to restrain them," Labienus said.

"Unleash them. Our cavalry is too hard-pressed. A surprise attack may be what we need to turn the tide."

"At once, Caesar."

He watched as Labienus set the Germans to their task. Four squadrons charged from the contravellation wall, hot for blood and battle. Antony and Trebonius were quick to seize the opportunity and charged with the Germans.

Finally, the Gauls broke. Their morale had to be sinking already as Antony and Trebonius turned back charge after charge. The Germans quickly overwhelmed the Gallic archers and skirmishers, all that had been keeping Caesar's cavalry at bay. As Antony and Trebonius charged in behind them, retreat became a rout. They left a trail of dead from the walls to the relief army's camp, giving them no time to reform and counterattack.

From the hill where Alesia stood, a horn sounded a mournful note. In response, closer, another horn sounded a retreat. As the sun set, Caesar had his own man sound the withdrawal. They had won a great victory today. But the battle was far from over.

21

(ALESIA, CENTRAL GAUL, 52 BCE)

It was near sunset when Caesar's battle was done. David's continued far into the night. He knew about when the battle was over. The flood of wounded coming in slowed from a flood to a trickle, then stopped.

"Jupiter bless those Germans," Celer said. "They're tough bastards; don't let anyone tell you differently. I'm glad they're on our side for now."

David had only done a single amputation before today. By the time he finished up his last patient, he'd probably taken more limbs than 90% of the surgeons in New York City combined. He'd had to make a conscious effort not to despair at that, try not to think about how many of those arms and legs piled up outside the tents, waiting to be burned, could have remained attached to their owners, if only.

If only. If only he'd had access to surgeons with the tools and skills to perform the necessary microsurgery. If only he'd had a specialty in orthopedics to go along with his specialty and obstetrics, with a ready supply of titanium pins and plates to hold together arm and leg bones shattered in more places than he could count. If only he had the special splints and casts that could hold them in place while the bones knit together properly. "If only" was his greatest enemy. He had none of these things. He would not have any of them, ever. Before long, what medicines he did have would be gone, and he'd have to make do with whatever 21st century knowledge combined with supplies from the first century BCE could accomplish. Whatever that was would never be enough for him, but David knew he would have to make peace with it. It was either that or go crazy. And going crazy wasn't an option. He had responsibilities, to Livilla, to their unborn child. Even to Caesar and this army, God help him.

David watched as Corvus gave a soldier wine spiked with opium juice, instructing a group of orderlies how to do it and how much to give. That, at least, would help him shepherd his own supply of narcotic painkillers and save them for only the most serious cases. The antibiotics were another story. Even saving the penicillins and sulfa drugs he had on hand for when he could confirm fever from wound infection and using *acetum* for everything else, his supply would be greatly diminished.

What had he gotten himself into? He knew, somehow, that there was no going back. To be certain, he would be faced with a choice after this battle was done and Caesar sent his armies to their winter quarters. At least, he would be faced with the illusion of a choice. He could no more go back to Pagus Mardani than he could go back to his Manhattan condo. His fate—and Livilla's, and their child's, since Livilla would never leave him—was irrevocably tied to Caesar's fate.

David had not shared with Caesar what awaited him on the Ides of March, 44 BCE. Kevin had argued persuasively that they should hold on to that secret like grim death. What would I do, if someone appeared, claimed to be from the future, and told me with great certainty when the date of my death would be, David wondered? He thought of a classic Robert Heinlein short story, the very first that great author published, a story called "Life-Line." In it, a professor builds a machine that can detect how long people will live. The world, of course, is turned upside down. In the real world, thought David, the professor probably would have been lynched.

As if thought of the man was enough to summon him, Caesar

entered the tent. David rose with the rest of the doctors to greet him, though all were swaying on their feet. Caesar himself looked so exhausted that any resentment David might have felt at his presence vanished instantly.

"How are things here?" Caesar asked.

"Celer and Corvus were wonders," David said. "I learned a great deal."

Corvus, hearing his name, turned around and inclined his head, a small smile on his lips. Celer let out one of his loud, booming laughs. "As ever, Davidius, you are too modest. Caesar, this man saved at least a dozen I would have given up for dead. And look," Celer pointed to the neatly sutured stump on one soldier's arm. "Have you ever seen an amputation done so neatly? It won't even need to be cauterized. His job on Chlorus wasn't a fluke." Celer made sure he said the last loud enough for Hipparchus to hear. The Greek doctor merely sniffed.

"I'm sure he'd rather have his arm," said David. "Still, I'm glad I could at least save their lives." Turning to Caesar he said, "We managed surprisingly well today."

"I hope you can keep managing well. I know the Gauls will be attacking again, and soon. If not tomorrow, then the day after." David nodded imperceptibly.

"We should be getting our rest, in that case," Celer said.

"Yes, I agree," David said. "Starting with our commander."

"I require little sleep," Caesar said.

"Far be it for me, as Mark Antony's personal physician, to give you orders on your own health. But I would prescribe a good night's sleep."

"Even if I wanted to sleep, I doubt I could," Caesar grumbled.

David went to his crate with all his medicines, looking through them carefully until he found what he was looking for.

"Take these two pills," he said to Caesar. "Don't call me until morning."

Caesar looked at the white pills skeptically. "What are these supposed to do?"

"Help you sleep. It's called valium. It would be best to swallow them with water, but a little wine with them probably wouldn't harm you, if you prefer to drink wine. Too much alcohol with pills like these can kill you."

"Is it like opium?" Caesar asked, still doubtful.

"Somewhat. Just not as strong. They're strong enough to relax you, and in this case give you a good night's sleep. I can't guarantee you will be good as new, but you will be rested."

"Very well," Caesar said. "And I think you should take your own advice, doctor. And that goes for Celer, Corvus, and the rest of you."

"We plan to sleep very soon, Caesar," Celer said.

"Good. And Davidius...I think at 5000 denarii a year, Antony's getting a great bargain for your services."

"Five thousand denarii, huh?" said Celer. "Jupiter's balls, maybe I should go into private practice!"

LIVILLA WAS ALARMED at how exhausted David looked when he stumbled into their tent.

"Sorry. I didn't mean to wake you." He was slurring his words as badly as if he'd had too much to drink, but there was no wine on his breath. Just the remnants of that horrible black brew he claimed to like, that he said made him more alert and awake when he was tired.

"You need rest," Livilla said.

"I doubt I can sleep," David said.

"Was it really that bad?"

"Worse. I knew doctors who served in war zones, but I wonder if they ever saw anything like this. I felt like I was surrounded by death."

Livilla's arms encircled her weary husband. She began kneading the knots in his shoulders and arms.

"Thank you. That feels wonderful."

"Good." Livilla said nothing as she continued massaging the tension out of him. Or at least as much as she could.

"They say you saved many lives today," she said as she continued to work. "Many men owe you a great debt."

"Not enough. I didn't save enough."

"And what would have been enough?"

"All of them."

Livilla stopped massaging David and looked him in the eye. Her expression was serious, even a little angry.

"Only a god could have saved all those men," she said. "And as you are fond of reminding everyone, you are not a god. You are a man. A wonderful, good, gifted man. You saved many soldiers today. Thousands of defenseless Mandubii owe you their lives because you —and you alone—were willing to speak for them."

"I only did what anyone would do," David said.

Livilla laughed, incredulous. He actually believed that!

"My love, 'everyone' would not have stood up to Gaius Julius Caesar. I think that's why he likes you."

"He likes me because I'm useful to him," David said.

"No doubt that is true," conceded Livilla. "But he respects you. And I don't think Caesar truly respects many."

David embraced her, his hands dropping to her midsection. Her waist was getting thicker, but it would be a little while before her pregnancy really showed, especially in the looser-fitting clothes she preferred. There were times when she wasn't sure about having her husband so involved in her pregnancy, for all that he was more skilled and knowledgeable than the most experienced midwife. But it was times like this, when his joy at the life growing inside her was so transparent, that Livilla realized Fortuna had been generous in her blessings. The blessings of the gods were not always unmixed, but this was one she would accept without reservation.

"Do you want to see it?" David asked.

"See what?"

"Our baby."

"How? Goddess willing it won't be born for another few months."

"I have a device that will let me see inside you. I used it when we turned Ramira's baby."

"I remember. How does it work?"

"It uses sound," David said.

"Sound? You hear sound, you don't see it." Livilla usually believed David's stories of his wondrous, magic-seeming devices. But sound you could see?

"Have you ever heard an echo?" David asked.

"Of course."

"An echo is just sound that bounces off something, usually a wall, and comes back to your ears. If you had the right kind of sound and the right kind of device, you could make a picture of the wall even if you couldn't see it. My machine uses sound too high to hear. But it can use the echoes to make pictures of the inside of a human body. I use it often to make sure a baby is healthy before it's born."

"And if it isn't healthy?"

"Well, most of the time that isn't an issue."

David clearly did not want to consider that possibility. Livilla had to, but she chose not to press. After being dealing with blood and death this day, let him see life. The life they had made together.

"Lie down," David said. She did.

He turned on the device David called a "laptop" and attached a strange wand to it. He then spread a strange jelly on her stomach and moved the wand back and forth, looking at the laptop.

A picture appeared, instantly. She'd been expecting that, though it still surprised her. He'd shown her pictures on his laptop before. Wonderful pictures that were far truer to life than any painter or sculptor could render. And wonderful didn't even describe the pictures that moved and talked, like a theater you could hold in your hand. It didn't matter that she couldn't understand the language; most of the time, she could follow the story.

This picture made from sound was different. Instead of color it was in black and white, rather grainy. She could see arms and legs. A head with the nose in profile. David smiled.

"That's it. That's our baby."

"So that's who's kicking me," Livilla said.

David maneuvered the wand around her belly. She was awestruck as her husband pointed out the brain, the heart. The spine. "Do you want to hear the heartbeat?" He asked.

Livilla was overwhelmed and couldn't speak. She nodded. David pressed a button and suddenly a rapid "whoosh whoosh whoosh" sound filled the quiet tent.

"That doesn't sound like a heartbeat," Livilla said. "And it sounds very fast."

David looked at something on the screen and nodded to himself. "Yes. Perfectly normal. And our baby is developing normally." He wiped the jelly off of Livilla's stomach and began putting his equipment away. Once again, he lay down beside her, one hand caressing the place where he knew the baby was growing inside her.

"Thank you, Livilla. I needed that," David said. They kissed.

"I should thank you. That was...I don't have words. I've attended enough births with Matwyn to know how women worry about bearing a healthy child. To know that I will..."

"Well, we'll check again in a few weeks to make sure." David yawned, his jaws cracking. "But I think I'm ready to sleep at last."

He set his head down. Livilla wasn't quite ready to go to sleep yet.

"Do you want a boy or a girl?" she asked.

David did not hear her. He'd fallen asleep before his head hit the pillow.

THE EXPECTED attack did not come that day, and Kevin found himself also playing surgeon. Just not on human patients. The Roman artillery commander had a dim memory of Ferrarius from the old days and asked the ironsmith to inspect the *ballistae* stationed on both walls. Ferrarius, in turn, vouched for Kevin. Cleon accompanied them also.

One thing that had surprised Kevin was learning that the Romans, for all their engineering prowess, lacked interest in complex mechanical devices. He and Cleon had had a long conversation during the battle while they helped in the infirmary. According to

Cleon, Greek and Greco-Egyptian natural philosophers, especially those based in Alexandria, loved to tinker with mechanical devices. The young slave spoke of a device at an Egyptian temple that would dispense a cupful of holy water at the drop of a coin.

"Have you heard of such a thing?" Cleon had asked, voice full of wonder. Kevin had had to suppress a laugh, not wanting his new friend to misunderstand and think Kevin was making fun of him. Kevin only allowed that yes, in fact, he *had* heard of such things though he had only a vague idea of how the devices worked. Which happened to be true and satisfied Cleon.

While not coin-operated, the *ballista* was about as complex as machine as the Romans produced. While not as powerful as the catapults and trebuchets that would succeed it in a few centuries, it was more flexible in that it could hurl either long, deadly iron-tipped spears or stone balls. There was a smaller version, called an *arcubalista* or a *carroballista*, depending on whether or not it was mounted on a cart or a fixed position like a wall. Finally, there was the *manuballista*, a hand-held version that was seldom used due to its limited range and slow reload time. With Ferrarius and Cleon to help guide him, he was soon almost expert at triaging the large machines. Most were functioning just fine, needing a slight adjustment here, or some grease there. The one the four of them were looking at now, on a wooden tower along the circumvallation wall and meant to cover an expected attack route from Alesia itself, had kept jamming during last night's attack.

"My own men are good at fixing these things in the heat of battle, but they just couldn't figure this one out," the artillery commander said. "Thankfully, Ferrarius, them slingers as what came with you covered us here and damn well. Still, it's hard to fix something when you're worried you'll get Gaul iron through your guts."

Kevin interpreted Ferrarius's grunt as "been there, done that." Livilla had said her father was reluctant to talk about his past, but he'd opened up some over the winter, and on the trip here from Mardani-land. While Ferrarius had never formally enrolled in the legions he'd done some travelling with forces loyal to Gaius Marius during the last round of civil wars, doing much the same thing he was doing here—forging swords, armor and missile heads and babying ballistae. Though now, at least, Ferrarius could choose his own hours at the forge, supervising and teaching younger men.

They dug into the balky ballista, carefully laying aside the parts as they did to make re-assembly easier. Finally, they found the problem: a gear that kept getting stuck. There was something familiar about it that Kevin couldn't quite place. He and Cleon lifted the problem gear out carefully. Not quite carefully enough, though; Cleon cut his finger on a small but sharp burr on one the gear teeth.

"You'll want to get that looked at," Kevin said, remembering Chlorus. "Even a small cut can fester. Besides, I overhead my uncle and Livilla talking about a new poultice they wanted to try, that's supposed to help wounds heal clean."

"I will, Flavens," Cleon said after sucking on his finger.

"You found the problem," Ferrarius rumbled. "Or at least your finger did." The ironsmith pointed out the burr to the commander. "I can file this smooth right here and that should solve the problem. If not, we'll take 'er apart again and I'll forge a new gear myself."

As Ferrarius filed away the burr on the gear tooth, it suddenly struck Kevin *why* the gear looked familiar; size aside it was almost identical to the speed governor on his victrola. "*Aissi!*" he exclaimed in Korean. Roughly, "oh damn!" in English. His companions looked at him oddly. Kevin felt himself blush. Luckily some of his time with Ferrarius over the winter included tutoring in Latin swears.

"Sorry. That was in Korean. My birth language. The Latin would be roughly '*Perduint!*'," he said. "Since most people around me didn't know Korean, I found I could swear in it and not get in trouble as a kid." Everyone laughed at that, especially the artillery officer. His Latin had the same quality as Ferrarius's. Kevin guessed that the officer had been one of those rare *plebs*, as the lower-class Romans were called, who'd risen through the legionary ranks. It was a rare thing. "No, I just had a revelation," Kevin said. "A problem I've been having with on a side project. This gear is similar, and it makes me wonder if there's a flaw in it."

"Your *loquitur laminam*? Ferrarius asked." He'd taken to calling the gramophone by that Latin phrase. It meant "talking plate." If the machine was something Kevin could manufacture—with help, of course—he hoped "victrola" would catch on instead, as it sounded Latin and definitely rolled off the tongue better. Technically "victrola" was trademarked, or used to be, but it's not like the RCA Corporation could send a cease-and-desist letter 2000-odd years back in time to a parallel universe.

"Yes. Something for a later time."

Ferrarius nodded and for a time the four of them busied themselves reassembling the ballista. Once that was done, the commander took a spear from a pile that had been rejected for one flaw or another. The iron points had been hacked off to be re-used but what was left would be more than good enough to test the weapon. The artillery officer had a crew load and fire it. The first attempt went well. A second test, and then a third, worked flawlessly. They'd fixed the problem. The commander thanked the three of them.

"If you ever want to join my ballista cohort, I'll welcome you with open arms!" he said. Kevin suspected the man was kidding a lot less than he let on and was flattered. Artillery wasn't something the Romans emphasized. Ferrarius explained his theory of why as they walked back to their tents.

"It's really only useful in limited circumstances," the blacksmith said. "And slow to reload. In situations such as the one we're in, where you can funnel soldiers to specific points of attack, they can be very formidable indeed. If only they could fire as fast as a good Mardani slinger."

"My tutor told me once there was someone in Alexandria working on a ballista that could shoot several bolts before needing to be reloaded. It was called a *polybolos*, he said. I don't know if anyone ever made one," Cleon said.

"I saw a model tested once," Kevin said, thinking of an episode of *Mythbusters* where they'd made and tested a working *polybolos*. It was possible at least. And then, he had another revelation. "I wonder..." he said. Thinking of the ballista's ability to hurl either stone balls or giant spears, he added, "I wonder if we could make a repeating *manuballista* that would shoot either arrows or lead shot like the Mardani use. It wouldn't have much of a lethal range but might be useful as a close-in weapon. If nothing else, it would be a good 'proof of concept.'" Kevin said the last phrase in English, not knowing a Latin equivalent.

"What was that?"

"'Proof of concept,'" Kevin repeated. "Where I come from, someone who thinks of a new mechanical device will often first make a smaller model meant to emulate the function of the finished product. Especially if it's a large thing like your *polybolos*, Cleon. It's a way to show the idea *will* work. A repeating *manuballista* is a great way to show that a larger repeating ballista will work. And would be useful by itself."

"Yes," Ferrarius said. "Yes, I think you could be on to something, Flavens. I have a feeling, once this siege is done, that Caesar will mop up and go to winter quarters. This will be a good project to keep us occupied."

Cleon agreed, and Kevin nodded. He didn't tell them the other picture he had in his mind, one from Korean military history, of a machine that would launch multiple rockets at an oncoming enemy. That would take a lot of time, and multiple steps but Kevin thought it would be possible with the Romans' level of technology. Kevin had lots of ideas. If he could help Cleon with a repeating ballista, it would be a start. A Roman *hwacha* would have to wait.

Caesar had been thinking a great deal about prophecy lately. Stories about the dire consequences of misinterpreting cryptic oracles abounded. He himself used to wonder why oracles couldn't be more plain-spoken. Of course, his own experiences as the Pontifex Maximus of the state religion had led him to understand that with mystery came power. The utterances of the Sibyl, or the Oracle of Delphi, or any of their famous sisters, had power precisely because they were so frustratingly enigmatic. With Davidius and Flavens, he felt he had an answer to the oracles given at the sacrifice last summer. There was Davidius's tattoo matching the ram's birth-mark and the fact that they'd arrived from the sea. Caesar knew better than most how omens and auspices could be creatively tortured to suit the needs of the moment, but it wasn't a stretch to interpret their arrival as the fulfillment of those auspices. Even Cornelius Aquila had admitted as much, if grudgingly. The lictor had taken a dislike to Davidius in particular. Caesar could under-stand why, but he did not approve. Still, he would say nothing for the moment. The two men rarely came into contact with each other. Unlike, say, Antony and Trebonius, who bickered like an old married couple.

Caesar felt rested. Action would come, most likely tonight. One could not expect the Gauls to fight in daylight like civilized men but Caesar, unlike many aristocratic Roman commanders, chose to prepare for circumstances as they were. Not what he wanted them to be. He felt rested. Those two pills David had given him had allowed him to sleep soundly, and far later than he was normally accustomed.

Without quite knowing how he got there, Caesar found his way to David's tent. He waited while Keffin Flavens announced his presence. Livilla greeted him. She was a remarkable woman, if a little too head-strong and unrefined for Caesar's tastes. She seemed to suit Davidius and his unconventional attitudes rather well, though. He actively and openly sought her counsel. It was rather unmanly really.

"David is finishing his bath, Caesar. Come, rest yourself. Would you like some wine?" she asked. As soon as the words left her lips David entered. Caesar sipped his wine, an excellent Falernian vintage that was no doubt gifted by Antony.

"Apologies, Caesar. I slept late. I was going to have lunch before seeing if Celer needed any help. Would you care to join me?"

"That is acceptable," Caesar said. "I assume you are cooking, since you still refuse to take a slave?"

"My feelings on slavery have not changed. Yes, I am cooking quesadillas, just something light."

"Quesadillas?" asked Caesar, stumbling over the unfamiliar word. "It sounds like it should have something to do with cheese."

"You are correct. They are tortillas—you remember the flatbread I've served you—with cheese on them. And I plan to add olives and onions."

That sounded good to Caesar, who preferred light meals. "If only I'd brought my dried figs."

"I'll get them," Flavens said. Caesar inclined his head in thanks.

Keffin Flavens left. Caesar watched as Davidius set an iron pan he called a "skillet" on his brazier and spread olive oil on it, waiting for it to heat up.

"Did you rest well last night?" David asked.

"Yes, thanks to that medicine. What was it?" Caesar asked.

"It's called 'valium.' It's a good relaxing medicine when used correctly."

"Valium." That sounded like it should mean something. Many of the strange words Davidius said in his native language, called "English," sounded like they should mean something in Latin but weren't quite understandable. Such as the word "quesadilla." Though just as many seemed to derive from Latin.

"Yes," Davidius said, as if reading Caesar's thoughts, "it does sound like a Latin word, doesn't it? But as far as I know it doesn't really mean anything. It's just a name, something that the people who developed it hoped would help it sell well. Perhaps they were right."

"Be that as it may, it worked wonderfully. You have my gratitude."

"Yes," Livilla said rather pointedly. "David has worked hard for you, Caesar. You'd have many more dead if it weren't for him."

Caesar ignored the breach of propriety and merely nodded.

"I can assure you, Livilla Ferraria, that his efforts are highly appreciated and will not go unrewarded." He turned back to Davidius. "As for the coming battle, I'm sure it will be tonight." Caesar then changed the subject to lighter things as Davidius finished cooking his strange lunch dish.

Caesar enjoyed the quesadillas. Like the dish David called "fajitas" the flatbread provided a sort of edible plate. It was light and filling and, David said, a nice healthy lunch. The figs were a perfect way to finish, and Davidius, Livilla and Flavens all seemed to enjoy them.

"Ah," said David. "Now, if more people where I'm from ate like this, we'd have many more healthy people.

Pleasant as the meal had been, it was time to see to preparations. "Thank you for the meal, Davidius. You will have to give my cook the recipe. I should like to serve this dish myself sometime."

"Of course, Caesar. And let me know if I can be of further help."

"You are being of great help, and I say again: it will not go unrewarded. Although if you would, please let Celer and Corvus, and those working with you, know that I appreciate their efforts. And you, Livilla Ferraria, have done an excellent job organizing the women."

Caesar walked out into the daylight. His soldiers, clearly exhausted, were working hard to prepare for the next attack. He stopped here and there to offer encouragement. He was glad to see that those he spoke to seemed re-energized. Caesar had great faith in his men. They would make him proud. They would stand victorious when all was done.

They had to. For this was only the opening act of a much larger play.

22

(ALESIA, CENTRAL GAUL, 52 BCE)

The moon was rising when Vibius Pullo heard the first scraping at the wall. The attack was not a surprise. The word had come down from Caesar, through Pullo's commander Labienus, that an attack would come. He'd heard the Gauls filling the ditches with their wicker hurdles, making their way slowly and cautiously to the contravellation wall. Pullo's orders were specific and strict: they were to give no indication they were aware of the Gauls' approach.

Pullo was ready when the first warrior's head appeared above the battlements. The Gaul's war cry became a gurgle as Pullo's sword opened his throat. He heard a soft thump as the body hit the ground.

That first warrior was replaced by three more, then another three. With a cry of his own, Pullo charged forward.

THE EXPECTED BATTLE HAD BEGUN, with the attack concentrating on the weakest point in the Romans' fortifications: the spot in the north-western corner where obstacles had prevented extending both the inner and outer walls. The Gallic relief army was hammering away at that opening and assaulting the outer wall at either side; Labienus had command of that section and for now he was holding.

Caesar had received reports that other sections of the outer wall were under attack but for the moment they seemed little more than distractions to keep the Romans from reinforcing Labienus. Quintus Tullius Cicero had sent one such report, emphasizing that he was not in trouble but was reluctant to move to help. He wasn't the only one.

The attack at the outer wall was only half of a two-pronged strategy by Vercingetorix and his allies. When one of the warriors from Alesia fell into a pit trap and cried out when he was impaled by the wooden spikes at the bottom, the men on the inner wall sprang into action and the artillery began its work. Ballistas spat iron-tipped bolts and balls of stone and iron at the enemy, hampering their efforts to fill in the ditches and advance. The ballistas couldn't stop them, not entirely, but it slowed their progress to a crawl. That was all Caesar needed. If the relief force failed to break through, Vercinge-torix's assault on the inner wall was doomed. Caesar doubted the ballistas would stop Vercigetorix altogether, but it would buy them precious time.

Caesar turned to Alexander, as always trailing in his master's wake.

"Pass the word. I want a reserve force of at least ten cohorts. More if it can be managed. I will command them personally."

"Yes, dominus," he said and hurried off.

Caesar gave the artillery crew words of encouragement before continuing on his inspection. Dawn would bring victory. It must.

THE GAULS WERE BOILING over the wall like stew left too long on the fire. Pullo cut through them as they came. He refused to give in to his exhaustion, feeling alive with every stroke of his sword. He was a storm of iron, churning through flesh. If each Roman soldier is worth ten Gauls, thought Pullo, then I am worth at least three Roman soldiers.

He was a little too good, though. Pullo soon found he'd gotten too far ahead of his comrades and was surrounded by the enemy.

No matter, he thought. I'll cut my way back out.

He began fighting his way back to where the Romans were regrouping. One Gaul fell, then another, then another. Another fell, this one not touched by Pullo's sword, followed by several more. One of the Mardani slingers had found a piece of high ground on the battlement, and was picking off the enemy one by one, helping Pullo clear the path. Suddenly instead of a half-dozen Gauls between him and the Romans there were just four. Then three. Then two and just one.

"For the Senate, and the People of Rome! For Caesar!" Pullo cried. He charged forward. And there, his luck ended as he stumbled. He swung his sword blindly at the spear thrust toward him, deflecting it but not enough. He felt pain as the spearhead penetrated, and then very soon felt nothing at all.

ANTONY WAS GROWING INCREASINGLY FRUSTRATED. He was getting reports from messengers in route to Caesar. The Gauls were on the outer wall, though not in control as yet. Other reports said that Vercingetorix had reached the inner wall. They were pressed on all sides. He did not consider himself Caesar's equal as a general, but he could put together the tactical picture easily enough. They were in trouble. Labienus was badly outnumbered, and Antony did not think he could hold much longer.

Antony's own section of the wall was quiet. Caesar had already anticipated the enemy's strategy but it hadn't helped the Romans a great deal that he could see. While the gap in the northwest of the siege works was an obvious target, it was hard to know where else the enemy might attempt to break through so the Romans had to be ready everywhere. He had orders to hold this section of the wall, but it seemed stupid to keep troops in reserve when they were badly needed elsewhere. It was time to roll the dice.

"Philip," said Antony to a messenger standing nearby.

"Sir?" Philip was young, probably barely old enough to wear the *toga virilis*, the Roman symbol of legal manhood, before he'd joined Caesar's army.

"I want you to go to Trebonius. Tell him I'm going to Labienus's aid. Tell him if his section of the wall is as quiet as mine, that he must join us. Bring me his response, and quickly."

"Yes, sir." Philip ran off toward Trebonius's post. Time seemed to crawl by while he awaited Trebonius's response. Finally, Philip returned.

"He says he is with you."

"Then sound the advance."

At Antony's order, Philip sounded the advance. At a quick march, Antony left to reinforce Labienus. He only hoped the wall still held when he got there.

CAESAR WAITED with his reserve force. Thirteen cohorts, slightly more than a legion, of mixed infantry and cavalry. The backbone had been drawn from the Tenth Legion, his personal force. They were the freshest, most effective troops he had left.

A messenger came running up to him, breathless.

"Labienus is in trouble, sir. He's not sure he can hold."

"Then we move out," Caesar said.

His plan, worked out with the centurions leading the cohorts, was a risky one. They would leave the wall, circle behind the enemy, then hit them from behind. They would be a hammer, and if the gods were good there would be an anvil left to hammer the enemy against.

Dawn was beginning to break as Caesar and his men left the walls, riding hard. The gods *were* good, and they *would* grant him the victory he sought.

ANTONY AND TREBONIUS arrived just in time to push back the surging Gauls. Antony had heard shouts from the inner wall as he rushed to help Labienus and shore up his faltering position. Vercingetorix had reached the inner wall, but apparently was being held off for now. If the Gallic king and his relief army were able to join forces, the results would be disastrous.

Antony's men were the closest thing to fresh forces the Romans had. He smashed into the Gauls, Trebonius doing the same opposite Antony, catching the enemy in a pincer movement. Slowly, but steadily they pushed the Gauls back. But for how long? He remembered the first day's battle and how the sea of Gallic warriors seemed endless. It was even worse in the dark. Dawn had to be coming soon, Antony thought as he and his men fought on. Somehow, he thought that if they could just hold out until then, everything would turn out well.

As the sky began to lighten, Antony suddenly found his small section of the wall clear. He moved to advance, then paused for a moment over the body of a fallen legionary, a spear embedded in his midsection. It was Vibius Pullo.

A pity, Antony thought. That man was a good soldier. He was about to say a quick prayer for a good afterlife when he thought he saw movement. A faint groan from Pullo removed all doubt. Somehow, he was still alive!

"Orderly! Make a litter. Take this man to the doctors! The one called Davidius will know what to do."

The breaking dawn and the spark of hope for Pullo's survival reinvigorated Antony. Forming up his men, he charged forward with a blood-curdling cry. "For Vibius Pullo! For Caesar! For Glory! FOR ROME!" With a ferocious roar that sounded like all the lions in the world, the legions followed Antony to their destiny.

David was setting a broken leg when he heard Corvus say "I'm afraid he's beyond hope. Take him to Elysium." Elysium had become the name for the area where the mortally wounded were cared for until they died.

"Antony insisted we save him! We have to save him!" said a voice David recognized. Kevin? What was he doing here? He was helping make sure the ballistas on the ramparts kept working.

"Antony's not a doctor. I tell you he's beyond what we can do!" Corvus, normally so calm, was showing signs of strain. They all were.

David finished setting the leg and left two of the junior aides to splint it. He went to look at their new patient.

"Pullo!" David said. He'd gotten to know the legionary a bit, and rather liked him. The tough soldier had a dry wit and a surprisingly perceptive view of the world, and David was touched by the way Pullo had taken Kevin under his wing. He'd also gone out of his way to befriend the Mardani men, especially Dolovix.

Pullo was in very bad shape. The multiple slashes and shallow stab wounds probably weren't fatal, but there was the small matter of the spear buried in his abdomen. He was clammy, pulse thready, deep in shock.

"They thought he was dead," said Kevin. "He's been lying outside for hours. It was only when Antony saw him move that anyone realized he was still alive."

Surprisingly, Pullo did not seem to be bleeding heavily. David guessed that the spear shaft itself was controlling the bleeding. That was what had saved him. David didn't know if he could remove it and repair the damage without killing the legionary, but he was willing to try.

"As my dad would say, Pullo is a tough old bastard," David said. "I'll do what I can. Livilla, you'll assist me. Corvus and Celer, I may call for help but otherwise keep going with other patients. God alone knows how many more wounded we're going to get in."

"Do you really think he can be saved, Davidius?" Corvus asked.

"I don't know. You were not wrong to want to send him to Elysium, Corvus, but I owe it to Pullo to try and save him."

They moved Pullo, very carefully, to a surgical table. Taking a bone saw, David cut the shaft at either end so that they could lay Pullo down flat.

"Are you going to remove the rest of the spear?" Livilla asked.

"Yes, but not yet. It's probably the only thing keeping him from bleeding to death."

After sedating his patient, David cut in. It was clear that the spearhead had damaged the intestines but otherwise Pullo had escaped damage to other major organs. The spear had shattered a rib on the way out of his body. The first order of business would be to clamp off the arteries and veins so they could remove the rest of the spear shaft.

He saw that several cauterizers heating on braziers within arm's reach. That was good; he'd certainly need them. The principle of cauterizing wounds wasn't new to the Roman doctors, but they weren't used to doing it with such precision. After seeing one of David's electric cauterizers in action, Celer had had the idea to mount thin iron points in a wooden handle, based on a rough design from Corvus. When heated in a fire, they would do the job almost as well as one of David's electrocauteries. David had brought only a few disposable cauterizers with him, and they were gone. He was about to see how good a substitute these would be.

Clamping off the major blood vessels, David carefully removed the remaining portion of the spear shaft. As expected, there were a few bleeders left. David touched the red-hot iron to them. The new-old cauterizers worked like a charm.

He ended up having to remove a small section of Pullo's small intestine. He'd never done a bowel resection before and hoped he got it right on the first try. Carefully examining all of Pullo's intestinal tract, he sewed up every bit of damage he could find. Peritonitis would be a big risk, but David thought he could control that.

Finally, he removed the fragments of shattered rib and removed the unbroken portion. Pullo would live just fine with one less rib and there was no use risking a punctured lung. At long last, he sewed him up.

The surgery must have taken hours, because by the time David finished, he could see dawn outside. Then he heard a great shout, one that could only mean victory. But whose victory? He heard another victorious shout. As he rigged an IV up for Pullo, he awaited news and wondered what he would do if the Gauls had overcome Caesar's forces.

Caesar and his thirteen cohorts smashed into the enemy's rear, taking them completely by surprise as the sun peeked over the horizon. I am just as avid a gambler as Mark Antony, Caesar thought, but I play for stakes he can barely imagine. It had been a risk to leave the walls to engage the enemy. In a heartbeat the Gallic army went from being on the verge of a great victory to being routed.

Caesar and his men cut through the Gauls like a *spatha* through soft cheese. With a roar he pressed the attack.

"Destroy them!" Caesar shouted to his men. "We end this here, today! I know you are tired, but we must pursue. Every man with me will have first pick of spoils and can sleep till the Ides of November if he wishes. For the Senate and the People of Rome!"

Tens of thousands of Gauls fled, hoping to escape the Roman pursuit. It was a vain hope. The Romans were too disciplined, and their blood too hot, to allow anyone to escape. By the time Caesar and his men overran the Gauls' camp less than a mile away, the enemy had been crushed. Only a few individuals and scattered bands had managed to escape. One of the captured was the leader of the relief army. His name was Vergasillaunus.

"I will decide your fate once the men inside Alesia had been dealt with. But I'm afraid a kind fate is not in store for you," Caesar said.

Caesar's men led Vergasillaunus away. He smiled as his men looted the enemy camp. Victory was his. Fortuna, his men and his ancestress Venus Victrix had not let him down. The only question now was how many days' thanksgiving the Senate would decree for this this great victory.

Of course, Caesar had made his own fate. And he was already

pondering what he could do to ensure no Gaul would ever think about launching another rebellion of this magnitude in the future. All of Gaul was Roman now.

PARS TERTIA

Homines quod volunt credunt
--Gaius Julius Caesar

23

———————

(ROME, ITALIA, 52 BCE)

"*By the time this reaches you, Gnaeus Pompey Magnus, the official dispatch will only be days away. Caesar has won his great victory in Gaul. The spoils and treasure he plans to distribute to the people beggars belief. I would not be surprised if the value of gold itself falls.*" Marcus Tullius Cicero watched as the reader, a drab little secretary of Pompey's named Arminius Comedentis, paused. Comedentis. "Eater." According to Tiro, this Arminius was an eater of knowledge. Especially the knowledge that came from assembling fact, gossip and distant rumor into a coherent picture. Pompey himself had a sour expression on his face and absent-mindedly scratched at a bandaged sore on the top of his left hand. Comedentis continued reading:

"*I am more convinced than ever that a strange foreign doctor is at the heart of things, the embodiment of promising omens Caesar has awaited for over a year. It is said this doctor brought the soldier Vibius Pullo back from the dead, though the doctor himself denies this and several witnesses say that Pullo was only near death and not actually dead. In any event, all accounts agree that Pullo's wounds were almost certainly mortal and yet this doctor's surgical skills saved him.*

"*Though this Davidius Medicus continues to claim he is no one special, I believe Caesar sees him as a gift from the gods. Though Caesar's courage and ability in battle cannot be denied, the heart and defiance he showed in the face of an enemy many times his numbers was extraordinary even for him. I believe Davidius was the cause of this. I do not know how or why, but something about his presence assured Caesar of victory.*

"I know you have come to view Caesar as dangerous. Davidius makes him even more dangerous. I have included some sheets of paper with his scribblings on them, discarded scraps. The man is profligate with paper, but he seems to have an unending supply—sheets all uniform in size and thinner and smoother than Egyptian papyrus. I do not know what these writings say. I believe they are in Davidius's native language. But I dare not take anything else; he keeps his private writings in a bound codex of blank pages that he would surely miss and quickly. He was quite willing to give me a copy of the records of the Mandubii camp that he'd kept for the legionary quaestors and I sent those with this letter, though I doubt they will be of great interest to you.

"I leave you with this advice, my friend and patron, though you did not solicit it: cast Caesar down now. The longer you wait, the more dangerous he becomes. Especially to you."

Pompey dismissed his secretary and looked at Cicero, awaiting his verdict. The silence between them stretched. Outside Cicero could hear the faint sounds of celebration; the twenty days' thanksgiving decreed by the Senate for Caesar's victory at Alesia were drawing to a close. Cicero nodded toward Pompey's damaged hand.

"What is that there, Gnaeus? Nothing serious I hope," Cicero said.

"It's nothing. A mole that started bleeding when I scratched it. Don't try to change the subject, Marcus. Answer my question."

"What do you want me to say, Gnaeus? That you have an excellent network of correspondents and informers? I bow before you, sir," Cicero said.

"Spare me your sarcasm," said Pompey. "I didn't bring you here to share stories of letter-writing."

"Then I'll ask you again: what do you want me to say? That civil war is inevitable? I don't believe that. I can't. You and Caesar must reconcile. For the good of the Republic. Find someone to take Crassus's place and restore your triad."

"And if Caesar feels he has the favor of the gods?"

"My brother Quintus has met this new ally of Caesar's," Cicero said. "He's a doctor, nothing more. Quintus says he is highly skilled, cultured, and insightful. Sometimes a person of insight can assemble facts in a new way. Such a man may be called a prophet or a sign from the gods, but is he? Or is he just shrewdly interpreting events?"

"You can spare me your philosophy along with your sarcasm. What else does Quintus say about him?"

"That Mark Antony hired him as his personal physician at an outrageous sum."

"That is not surprising. Money goes through Antony's hand like shit through a goose. What else?"

"That he is very friendly. That he seems to truly love his wife and is faithful to her, to the point of unmanliness. Perhaps strangest of all, to me at least, is that he refused to take a slave when offered one. Each soldier got their pick of personal slaves after the battle, according to Quintus. However, Davidius Medicus took a Mandubii woman into his service after delivering her child. He apparently specializes in pregnant women and childbirth as a doctor," Cicero added after seeing Pompey's puzzled look.

"Strange and unusual. And those are not good things when the situation is so unsettled."

"Do you want my advice, Gnaeus?"

"Now, suddenly, you have something to say Marcus?" Pompey swallowed his cup of wine in a gulp and signaled for more. Cicero had rarely seen him this angry. He decided to ignore Pompey's own sarcasm and answer.

"Get the Senate to reconsider their denial of a triumph. It's a petty slight that Caesar won't forget. And it makes you look bad to the people after such a signal victory. They're already calling him '*Malleo Galliarum.*'"

Pompey snorted. "Hammer of Gaul indeed! Cato claims Caesar exceeded his mandate as governor with his military adventures and shouldn't be rewarded for them."

"Cato needs to learn the art of compromise."

"And what will you do, Marcus Tullius Cicero?" Pompey loaded Cicero's full, formal name with scorn. "Give a speech about it? Write a letter?"

Cicero thought for a moment, then smiled. "Why yes. Yes, I will. Write a letter I mean."

"And what will that accomplish?

"It will help me get to know this Davidius Medicus personally. Quintus told me that he'd heard of me and seemed to be something of an admirer of mine from afar. Even allowing that my brother may have been exaggerating it seems worthwhile to write this man myself and take his measure. Perhaps he may ultimately help reconcile you and Caesar once more."

"I'm not sure that's possible," Pompey said. "Perhaps if Julia and the child had lived…"

"I know you still miss her, Gnaeus," Cicero said gently. His marriage to Julius Caesar's daughter, Julia, had begun as a way to cement a political alliance but true affection had grown between the two. "Her death was a tragedy in many ways. But remember, there were those who said you and Crassus were irreconcilable. Caesar managed to restore peace between you."

"It was a bit more complicated than that."

"It always is," Cicero conceded. "But civil war was averted then. As it must be now."

Cicero took his leave of Pompey and returned to his own home. He summoned Tiro, his steward and secretary.

"Take a letter for me, Tiro," said Cicero.

"Of course." Tiro produced the stylus and wax tablet he always carried on his person. He would take dictation in a shorthand script of his own devising and later transcribe it onto paper. In all their years together, Cicero had rarely seen him make a mistake. The man was invaluable.

"From Marcus Tullius Cicero, Senator, to Davidius Castellanus Medicus. Greetings. I have heard much of you and hope to learn more…"

THE ROMAN ARMY settled into its winter quarters in Bibracte short weeks after the victory at Alesia. Bibracte was an *oppidum*, albeit much bigger than Mortorgenn, and was the capital of the Aedui of central Gaul. It was there David had returned after seeing the *Stork* taken by river and portage to Massilia—the city of Marseilles in 2022—to find that Mark Antony had installed Livilla and their household in a cozy house near his own. David couldn't believe he actually had a "household." He'd taken Theda into his service after she gave birth to her daughter, and then Pullo joined their little family as their personal bodyguard. Pullo left the legions, having served in the required eight campaigns, but David was pretty sure he would have signed on as a re-enlisted veteran—an *evocatus*—if it weren't for his injuries. Though he'd recovered well, he'd never be a soldier again.

David hadn't been sure he needed or wanted a bodyguard when Pullo suggested the idea.

"Davidius, you're not in a peaceful barbarian village anymore. You don't realize how dangerous it can be. You're no fighter. You need protection. Your nephew Flavens is learning well but he would be no match for someone determined to hurt or kill you."

"My nephew, eh? Did he put you up to this?"

"He might have suggested it," Pullo said.

"What about the police?" David asked.

"Po-lice?" Pullo stumbled over the unfamiliar word.

"You know. Sworn officers, answerable to the city government. They enforce order and safety."

Pullo roared with laughter, as if David had told the funniest joke the soldier had ever heard. "Enforce order and safety?" Pullo hooted. "Your order and safety are the muscle you can hire, and you won't get better than me. Eight campaigns and decorated by Caesar himself. Not to mention anointed by your own nephew as 'too stubborn to die.'" Pullo turned more serious. "Please, Davidius. I owe you a debt. This is the best way I know to repay it."

Put like that, David couldn't refuse. Antony helped him iron out details, particularly pay. Two weeks later Pullo proved his worth when a drunken centurion tried to break into David's house. It was an innocent mistake; the officer in question thought David's house was his own. Pullo thrashed him and sent him on his way, but afterwards David admitted Pullo had been right. What if it had been a robber rather than a drunk?

He turned his thoughts to the present. Winter quarters brought an easier routine for most of the soldiers, but David found himself busier than ever. At Caesar's suggestion, David, Celer and Corvus were writing a treatise on the treatment of war wounds, with David describing his technique in removing the spear shaft from Pullo's abdomen and repairing his intestines. And then there was Soter. David had wanted to read as much of the available body of medical literature as he possibly could. The only problem was that it was almost entirely in Greek. David could not read or speak Greek and he was beginning to realize this was a grave limitation. All educated Romans were literate in Greek. Caesar used his contacts to find Soter, a Greco-Egyptian tutor living in Massilia. Soter accepted David's offer and returned with him once the *Stork* was safely dry-docked.

Soter was a relentless taskmaster. But that was all to the good. During their study time David was not allowed to speak one word of Latin or any other language. It reminded David of the Latin immersion camp he'd gone to one summer while in high school, with much begging, after Mr. Chaplin had put the idea in his head. David's father had been hard to convince but after David raised half the money he'd need to attend, Ricardo had relented. That was paying dividends, as the lessons with Soter surely would.

He was working on translating a passage of Plato's *Republic* when he felt Livilla massaging his shoulders.

"Have you forgotten what day it is?" she asked.

David turned around to look at her. She was so beautiful, truly glowing. In just a few months, she would give birth to their child. David was reminded of a short story by Harlan Ellison he'd read once, "Grail." The main character spends his life and wealth trying to find a cup that will show him his one True Love, even bargaining with dark powers; when he finally finds the cup, he finds out that his own true love lived in the distant past and they could never possibly be together. Unlike the protagonist of "Grail," David was united with his love in the distant past. His only regret was that he could never introduce Livilla to his family. They'd like her, he was sure.

"What is that look?" she asked.

"Oh, I was just thinking how beautiful you are."

"I'm getting fat," Livilla said.

"That's our baby in there. You're not fat, you're beautiful."

"You're sweet. But you need to get ready. Our guests will be arriving soon."

Poker night. Every market day, David played in one of the many floating poker tournaments going on in Bibracte. He almost regretted letting Kevin introduce Texas Hold 'Em to Mark Antony one night when Antony was bored and demanding to be entertained. Kevin had told him that it worked when Borodur said he was bored and that it would work here. Ever the gambler, Antony took an immediate liking to poker, with its multiple rounds of betting and its combination of luck and strategy. Once Antony converted It didn't take long for the game to become popular among the officers, who saw it as more civilized and cultured than throwing dice.

It also didn't take long for David's card decks to wear out, but the Romans solved that problem in a hurry. Dolovix had taken a master wood worker as a slave. Dolovix remembered the thin wooden tiles the woodworker in Mortorgenn had made for their version of David and Kevin's playing cards, and the slave quickly figured out how to do it. Dolovix ended up going into business with a Roman soldier who had a female slave who could paint. She painted the cards on the wood, changing the suits. Hearts and diamonds stayed the same, but spades became *"hastis,"* or spears, as the spades suggested spear points to the Romans. Clubs became *"fasces,"* the axe bundled in rods that was a symbol of the power of *imperium* carried by high Roman officials. Particularly consuls and proconsuls. The face cards also changed. Jack, queen, king and ace became *quaestor, praetor, consul* and *primus* respectively, and the royal flush was christened the *"cursus honorum.*" Mardani and Roman split the profits and each made out very well. Even the slaves got a small share they could use to buy things for themselves or save to buy their freedom someday. With all the plunder gained after the defeat of Vercingetorix, there had been games with pots that probably would have made even professional high rollers in Vegas sweat. The game David played in was more of a social occasion despite the occasional big rounds.

"Does Theda need help with the cooking?" David asked.

"She has everything ready. Tortilla chips and the bean dip are done, and she'll have the dormouse quesadillas ready in time," Livilla said.

"Good. She'd better make extra quesadillas. Quintus Cicero is coming, and he loves anything with dormouse."

"Already done, love."

David would have liked nothing better than to take Livilla to bed right then, but he settled for a massage. By the time his guests arrived he felt relaxed and refreshed.

It was a pleasant night, with good company and conversation. Most of the talk revolved around Caesar and his tour of Gaul with the Thirteenth Legion.

"Do you think we've seen the last of rebellion?" David asked.

"I think the sight of 5,000 warriors on crosses on the battlements at Alesia should discourage anyone else thinking they can fight Rome," Quintus Cicero said.

"You're an optimist, Quintus," said Antony. "Even with Vercingetorix in chains there will be some Gauls who think they can pull off the impossible."

"Still," said Labienus, "I should think enough tribes will stay loyal that Caesar can deal with any rebels one at a time."

"That may be," Antony said. "They'll see Caesar granted his famous mercy to the Aedui and a few other tribes. Perhaps they will be more inclined to make peace."

The conversation was punctuated with dealing and betting. By now, most of David's fellow players were learning that you didn't try to win every hand, that it was better to fold when you had no hope of winning and cut your losses on any given hand. They were also getting better at hiding their "tells," the clues of what kind of hand they were holding. That was one aspect of the game Mark Antony still hadn't quite mastered. Whenever he had a good hand, David noticed, he licked his lips the way he did when he saw a particularly attractive woman he wanted to bed.

As the game went on, David was probably making just enough to cover the costs of the wine and food he provided for his guests, but the cards were not with him this night. The last hand of the evening came along, and David quickly folded. Labienus held on through the flop and the turn but folded when the river was revealed. It was down to Quintus and Antony.

It was a true duel between them. Finally, Antony pushed all his money into the pot.

"All in," he said in thickly accented English. The phrase was becoming quite popular in Bibracte.

Quintus took one more look at his hand. From what David could see, both were convinced they had a winning hand. Whose would be better?

Two aces—*primi*, David reminded himself—showed in the community cards. Quintus revealed a pair of consuls, which with the consul turned up in the flop, made for three of a kind. Antony smiled, dramatically turning over another *primus* along with a two. Three primi beat three consuls. Antony raked in the pot. One by one, David's guests made their excuses. Quintus Cicero and Mark Antony were the last. As he was leaving, Quintus suddenly remembered something. He pulled a rolled-up, sealed letter and handed it to David.

"It's from my brother," Quintus said. "He asked that I give it to you."

Livilla watched as David turned the letter over in his hands. It was a small scroll, probably no more than a single sheet of papyrus.

"Is there something wrong?" Livilla asked.

"No," David said. "I just can't believe Marcus Tullius Cicero wrote me a letter."

Antony laughed. "My friend, you are as a comet in the heavens. Appearing out of nowhere. Strange, bright and no one is sure what you portend. By now anyone of senatorial rank who's read Caesar's dispatches knows who you are. And I imagine a fair few tales have spread beyond."

"What, like I brought Pullo back from the dead?"

"David, that is closer to the truth than you care to admit," said Livilla. "You cannot deny Pullo was mortally wounded and you saved him."

"I only did what a good doctor would. And I got lucky. I'd never done a surgery like that before."

"My father likes to say that skill creates its own luck," Livilla said.

"Your wife speaks true, as usual," Antony said. "If only I'd met you first, my dear."

"You're married," said Livilla.

"See, Davidius? You are a lucky man. Nothing gets by her. Hybrida will adore you, Livilla." Antony said. He then became more serious. "My friend, you are swimming in deep waters now, whether you intended to do so or not."

"I have a feeling there are sharks in these waters," David said.

"Then be a dolphin," Livilla said.

"A dolphin?" asked Antony.

"A dolphin," Livilla repeated. "The dolphin seems friendly and harmless but will kill the shark to protect itself and its family and friends. The Mardani revere the dolphin and view it as a protector."

"Apt indeed," said Antony.

Livilla smiled at their guest. More than a guest—Mark Antony was their benefactor. "Master Antony, you'll have to forgive us. I'm suddenly feeling very tired. David will share the letter with you in the morning."

"Yes, of course. It is easy to forget you are in a delicate condition,"

Antony said. "I'll see you tomorrow, Davidius, if Soter will let you out to play."

"Of course. Do you want me to come over or send word ahead?"

"Just come on over. If I'm in the middle of something—or someone—you'll just have to wait."

"Antony, you are a rampaging id," David said, shaking his head.

"An 'id'? What might that be?"

"It's a long story."

"So long as I'm not being insulted."

"No," David said. "I think you'll take it as a compliment."

After Antony left, David walked with Livilla back to their bedroom.

"You're not really tired, are you," he said.

"Well, I am a little. But I had a feeling that it was important you read the letter alone."

"'Alone' alone or 'with just you here' alone?" David asked.

"I will leave if you want me to," Livilla said.

"No. No, I think I want you here," David said.

He unrolled the scroll and scanned the letter. He cleared his throat and started reading it aloud:

"*From Marcus Tullius Cicero, Senator, to Davidius Castellanus Medicus,*" David read.

"Davidius Castellanus Medicus?" Livilla giggled. "I guess you've gotten a proper Roman name."

David shook his head in a way Livilla had learned meant disbelief and continued: "*My hope is that this finds you well, and you will not be offended by my writing to you, though we have not met. I have heard many things about you, particularly from my brother Quintus, with whom I believe you are well acquainted. Indeed, he writes to me of many pleasant evenings spent in the company of you and your wife. He also tells me you have heard of me and reports that I am well known in your distant home-land. I am both flattered and humbled. If it pleases you, I would be most eager to hear of your experiences with Caesar's army. I would also like to learn more about your ideas on healthy living and good government, for*

Quintus tells me you managed a camp of several thousand Mandubii with great efficiency and no corruption. Your servant, Marcus Tullius Cicero."

David put the letter down, shaking his head again.

"What?" Livilla asked.

"Getting a letter from Cicero. Marching with Caesar. It seems like something out of a story for me."

"So you've said. But you are living it. I assure you."

"Oh, I know. I just can't believe it."

"It's more than that I think," Livilla said. "You're nervous, I can tell. Partly excited, partly fearful."

David chuckled. "Woman, you know me too well. It's like you can read my mind."

"No. Though that would be interesting. Like that woman in one of Keffin's picture stories. The one with all the characters born with powers. 'Feenicks,' I think her name was. But no. Matwyn taught me to observe and think."

"She taught you well." David sighed. "I'm beginning to think that nothing will be considered 'innocent' from now on. I do know that while Caesar and Cicero aren't exactly enemies, they're not really friends either. I don't know how Caesar will react when he finds out who's sending me letters."

"Well, you don't have to worry about Caesar for now. In fact, why don't you put it aside for tonight? It may be some time before you could arrange a courier to travel back to Rome with your reply, anyway."

"True. I will leave it until then. Have I told you how much I love you?" David asked.

"Hmm. Not since sunset."

"Well, I do. You keep me grounded. I couldn't manage things without you, you know."

"I'm glad you feel that way. I don't know which of the gods brought you to me, or how, but I'm glad they did," Livilla said.

"I'm glad too," David said. "I can't imagine life without you."

They kissed and fell asleep in each other's arms.

~

Tiro handed Cicero the letter, and Cicero opened it eagerly. He'd wondered if this Davidius would respond. It was written in Latin, in a hand little better than the looping scrawl Cicero had studied on the ledgers and scraps Pompey had given him, but legible at least. The scraps and notes had been an enigma to Cicero. Though he thought he could pick out words here and there, Davidius's native language was utterly unfamiliar to him. In this letter, at least, he could tell Davidius had tried to write more neatly and his Latin, if oddly phrased in places, was understandable, even elegant.

From Davidius Castellanos Medicus to Marcus Tullius Cicero:

First, I am honored to be numbered among your correspondents. Where I am from your fame as a speaker is exceeded only by your fame as a letter-writer. I am also flattered that I have made such an impression on your brother. He is very pleasant company and well-liked by his men.

Of my experiences with Caesar's army, I'm not sure what I can tell. I fought the battles at Alesia from inside the surgeon's tent. Thanks to the experience and poise of Celer, Caesar's head doctor, and Celer's able assistant doctor Corvus I was able to save many lives, though not as many as I would have liked. I never imagined being an army doctor—it is quite outside my training—but I am pleased to have made a contribution. As to the tales of my saving the legionary Vibius Pullo, they are no doubt exaggerated. It is true Pullo was gravely wounded but with luck and Pullo's own strong will to live, he pulled through. Currently Celer, Corvus and I are preparing a treatise on combat medicine and surgical techniques which will hopefully save more lives in the future.

Please feel free to continue to write to me. I hope to see Rome someday, and if so would love to meet you in person.

.　.　.

It was a cautious letter, but Cicero respected caution. Politics could be a deadly business these days. But it left Cicero wondering what to make of this doctor. How could you gain the true measure of a man from a handful of words? And yet, it seemed that this Davidius Medicus was the sort of person he could forge a meaningful friendship with. Cicero had spent time reading the records of the Mandubii camp the doctor had set up, after convincing Caesar to let the civilians expelled from Alesia through the inner walls of the Roman defenses. Contrary to the suggestion by Pompey's spy that they would be of very little value, Cicero found them quite revealing. Every last copper *as* and crumb of food, it seemed, was meticulously accounted for. It was a shame Davidius wasn't a citizen; he'd make an excellent quaestor and no doubt an exceedingly honest one.

Something troubled Cicero about this doctor's presence. He believed—he had to believe—relations between Pompey and Caesar could still be repaired. He'd watched with alarm as Pompey drifted ever closer to Cato and his party of hard-liners in the Senate. All they seemed to care about was bringing about Caesar's downfall by any means necessary. Even civil war.

The delicate balance struck by the triumvirate of Caesar, Pompey and Crassus had been knocked askew by Crassus's death at Carrhae. Anything strange or new--including, especially, one well-meaning doctor with uncanny talents—might throw the Republic into chaos. Cicero would respond and do his best to make this man into an acquaintance if not a friend. That would be the only way to truly tell if Davidius Medicus was a threat to the Republic or a hapless bystander swept up in Caesar's wake, as so many were these days. The response to this letter would need to be weighed very carefully.

24

(BIBRACTE, CENTRAL GAUL, LATE 52 BCE)

Kevin was amused. He had come with his uncle to Mark Antony's temporary home to work with Cleon, who was still on lease and staying with Antony's household slaves. Antony's home was more of a compound, and he'd allowed Kevin and Cleon to take over a ragged outbuilding that had been the previous occupant's kitchen. Antony had built a newer kitchen building that would better suit his needs. Like the kitchen, Kevin and Cleon were carrying out experiments that at times could prove flammable. Better to lose one old outbuilding rather than the main house. At the moment, Kevin was enjoying the drama playing out in front of him. Charming, even brilliant, as Antony could be, he could also be a spoiled man-child. Especially when he was hung over. As he was now.

"My head hurts," Antony complained.

"Maybe if you wouldn't drink so much wine," David said.

"Are you going to make the drink for me or not? What is called? 'Brawndo,' I think. It's what my body craves," Antony whined.

Kevin snickered and his uncle gave him a dirty look. Kevin watched as David mixed a little bit of powdered ElectroPede along with a mixture of herbs Matwyn used for her "morning after" drink as a treatment for illnesses causing diarrhea and vomiting. The result was a green liquid and that, along with the fact it was meant to restore lost electrolytes, led Kevin to call the drink "Brawndo." The name had caught on. Giving it to Antony as a hangover cure had been a rookie mistake in Kevin's view. Uncle David had a rather large supply of ElectroPede, and hadn't had to use too much yet, but Kevin and his uncle both were all too mindful of the fact that their 21st century supplies weren't limitless. Thankfully, there'd been no large-scale outbreaks of diarrhea or vomiting among the children of Bibracte yet. That's what David was saving the ElectroPede for and that is what it was meant for. Kevin knew, from what both his uncle and Livilla had said, that Matwyn's mixture would work well on its own, but the powder gave it a big boost.

"Here," David said, handing the mixture to Antony. "But I don't have an endless supply. Once I start getting low, it's salt water for you when you're hung over."

Their benefactor grimaced, then downed the drink.

"I hope you won plenty of money, at least," David said.

"I did alright," said Antony smugly.

It was the end of the year, almost the Kalends of January. Soon it would be the year 51 BCE by Kevin's reckoning. The Romans reckoned years by who was consul, but Kevin had no idea who that might be.

"Servius Sulpicius Rufus and Marcus Claudius Marcellus," Antony told Kevin when he asked. "You really should be more informed on politics. You and your uncle both."

"I'm a doctor. I'm not interested in politics," David said.

"You are my personal physician, Davidius, and Caesar regards you both as friends and allies. You are both involved in politics whether you want to be or not. I suggest you stay informed."

"I guess we'll have to," Kevin said. "For now, I'll settle for finding Cleon."

As soon as Kevin said that the man himself entered.

"Dominus," said Cleon to Antony, "Mercurius wished me to tell you a gentleman is here to see you. Zeno of Corinth, he says his name is, and has travelled from Massilia to speak with Caesar. When told Caesar was not here, he insisted on speaking to you."

Antony groaned. "What fresh hell is this? Tell him I am not available."

"Mercurius tried. This man is very insistent. He says he has something of military value. and has letters of introduction from the Claudii. Including the brother of the consul for the coming year. Also, Davidius, Soter is here and is quite put out with you."

Antony looked at Kevin, who wanted no part of this. "Cleon and I were supposed to work in the *Vetus Culina* today." *Vetus Culina*, or "old kitchen" in Latin, was the name for Kevin and Cleon's workshop. It had become something of an informal skunkworks.

"I'm late for my lesson," David said apologetically.

"Stay here, both of you. I may want your advice. Your tutor will just have to wait, Davidius, along with all the tinkering. Cleon, tell Mercurius to show this man in and return. I want you here as well."

A few minutes later Antony's *de facto* butler, his household slave Mercurius, led Zeno in with Cleon trailing behind. Zeno of Corinth was Greek, as his name suggested, and he was chubby and florid. Kevin recognized the type instantly—he was a salesman. His mothers and grandfather had dealt with many at the Castellanos family restaurants. Uncle David, too, often complained about the pharmaceutical reps that were, for David, the least-favorite aspect of medical practice.

Zeno didn't announce himself as salesman, of course. He was, he claimed, a philosopher.

"I am very much interested in mechanical devices and what they can do," he said eagerly to Antony. "And I have a machine that will do no less than ensure military victory for the mighty Caesar."

"In case you hadn't heard, Caesar was victorious. Almost three months ago. And without any marvelous Greek machines," Antony said.

"Ah, but isn't Caesar on campaign even as we speak?" Zeno asked.

"He is visiting the people of Gaul. Assuring them that the crimes of Vercingetorix and his allies will not be held against them so long as they do not engage in future rebellions."

"There's been no fighting, then?" Zeno pressed.

"Very little," said Antony. Kevin could tell Antony was enjoying playing with this man. The salesman's mask was slipping; Kevin saw disappointment flash across Zeno's face. But only for the briefest moment. The insincere salesman's smile was back up again in an instant.

"That is good. That is good. Thank Jupiter," Zeno said, looking skyward with a piety as sincere as his smile. "But it is known that the Gauls are a stubborn people. Rebellion is in their nature. Should Caesar have to fight them again, my device will surely be of great aid."

"And what would that be?" Antony asked. Zeno better cut to the chase, Kevin thought. Antony's getting very impatient.

"The *polybolos*, good general. It is a ballista that can shoot many bolts before being reloaded. Why, one soldier can take the place of a dozen archers with my machine."

Antony rubbed his jaw. He had a sly, shrewd look that Kevin had learned meant trouble for whoever was on the receiving end of it. Kevin could almost feel sorry for Zeno. Almost. The man didn't even realize he was about to be played. Kevin decided to stay quiet and watch. Uncle David looked about to say something, then stopped.

"As it happens, good Zeno, I have heard of such things. It so happens my personal physician here, and his nephew, are quite worldly and learned."

"Ah?" Zeno sounded just the slightest bit doubtful.

"Flavens, what was it you were just telling me?"

"The repeating crossbow, ah, ballista," Kevin said, correcting his accidental use of the English word over Latin, "is an old technology. The Chinese have been using them for centuries. Even the Greeks if I remember my history correctly."

"The Chinese?" asked Zeno.

"The *Seres*, I think you call them," said Kevin, dredging up the word from a history podcast he'd listened to once. There was little, if any, direct contact between the two civilizations, he recalled, but each was aware of the other and there was at least a trickle of trade in silk, mostly through Alexandria.

"Ah yes. People far to the east. And you are correct about the Greeks, sir. You must be a very learned man."

"Flavens here is also happens to enjoy mechanical devices," Antony said with a smile every bit as fake as Zeno's. "He is a very educated man, very knowledgeable about the world."

"Ah. Perhaps he and I should talk further later," said Zeno, with an edge of irritation in his voice. Salesmen did not like to be thwarted.

"He raises a good point, however," Antony continued. "If the *polybolos* has been known for so long, I would think a man of Caesar's genius would have used it, if it were useful at all."

"Ah, but my model has many improvements. Perhaps if I could demonstrate?"

Antony smirked. "Of course. And perhaps Flavens and my man Cleon here could demonstrate something they've been working on?" After that it was all a matter of negotiation. Antony was the army's quaestor—its paymaster, essentially—and was used to people like Zeno trying to get money out of the seemingly bottomless resources of the Roman legions. After more discussion over lunch, they arranged for a demonstration in the afternoon.

It was a cold day. The wind whipped across the practice field as Zeno's slave set up the *polybolos*.

The machine looked a great deal like one Kevin had seen on the TV show *Mythbusters*. Boxy, with a crank on the side and a large hopper for arrows projecting from the top. As Kevin recalled, the *Mythbusters* repeating crossbow could fire up to 30 arrows before needing reloaded. Zeno's was not quite that efficient, with a hopper that could hold 15. Otherwise, the designs were remarkably similar, even down to extras like wheels and an angle finder to improve aim.

A chain, driven by the crank on the side, drove the complex mechanism that loaded and fired the arrows. Aside from the hopper, the other major difference was the bow. It was un-recurved and made from a wood composite.

It worked well enough...when it worked. The chain kept slipping, the hopper kept jamming, and finally the bow snapped. Zeno unleashed a string of Greek that Kevin, thanks to Ferrarius's lessons in obscenities, recognized.

"Ferrarius said knowing those words would come in handy someday," David murmured to Kevin in English. Kevin tried very hard to keep a straight face.

Kevin could tell that Antony was unimpressed, but the Roman had a shit-eating grin on his face as he nodded to Kevin and Cleon. With a flourish, Cleon whipped the rough hemp cloth covering their own prototype repeating crossbow. It was meant to be both a proof of concept for a larger multi-shot ballista as well as a weapon in its own right. The repeating manuballista could fire both lead balls about half again as big as the shot Mardani slingers typically used, or short, thick bolts with iron heads.

Kevin did the honors, firing at a dummy covered in regular clothing. The lead slugs punched through with ease. Zeno had given up on the smarmy insincerity of the salesman. He was angry.

"It doesn't have much of a range," Zeno sniffed.

"No," Antony agreed. "But this will be useful for close combat if needed. We haven't built the large version yet, but I'm assured that with routine maintenance it won't jam. Or break."

Zeno stomped off. Everyone else retired for dinner. Antony's bed slave was also a good cook, and they dined well on honeyed dormouse and pork cutlets. During dinner, Kevin's mind kept going back to China and then it came to him. The Chinese used a handheld repeating crossbow. In fact, their armies used them until nearly the end of the 19th century and ordinary people carried used them for household security even longer. In the history Kevin knew, it was the longest continually used mechanical device in human history. Caesar, by dint of his military genius and the discipline of the legions, was able to win his victories with numerically inferior forces. But what if he had a weapon that acted as a force multiplier? One that would batter oncoming forces and soften them up before they even reached Caesar's legions?

David glimpsed Cleon in the kitchen. Being a slave, Cleon had not dined with them. But instead of eating, Cleon was poring over drawings and making notes. Kevin kept thinking of the ancient Korean weapon he had been drawing speculative designs for. The essential first stage would be to create simple gunpowder. Kevin knew he could do it. He'd done it before, as a science fair project that almost got him suspended from school. How to pay for it though? Men like Caesar and Pompey, and Sulla and Marius before them, were men with the resources to raise and pay for their own armies when they had to. They were the ones who made change, for good or ill.

What resources did he have? Kevin was dependent on Mark Antony to buy things. Unlike his uncle, Kevin didn't get a regular salary. And Mark Antony practically defined the word "mercurial." He could be charming, ferocious, brilliant and dissolute, often in the turn of a single hour. When something or someone interested him, Antony gave that person or thing his whole attention. When he was bored—as he was last night—Antony drank too much wine and risked too much money at the card or dice table. Kevin knew how Antony's story ended in the timeline he'd been born in. Would this one be different? Would it change? Could Antony change?

Kevin was a tinkerer. Someone who loved old mechanical things he could build or fix, now in a world where those skills were not particularly valued. At best, he might make a living as a maker of curiosities. Time travel stories were full of travelers from the future dazzling the primitives of the past with miraculous, magical technology in order to achieve whatever ends they needed to achieve. Well, Kevin could do that. Maybe not predict an eclipse, as in Twain's *A Connecticut Yankee In King Arthur's Court*, or build a mechanical hand like Ash in *Army of Darkness*. So far, all Kevin had done was fix some balky ballistas. Though that, in Kevin's not so humble opinion, was worth more than predicting an eclipse. His knowledge made him useful to Antony, and by extension, to Caesar.

But to what end, Kevin asked himself? *I don't even know how Uncle David and I might be changing history. The best thing to do would be to go back to Pagus Mardani and live out our lives. He and Livilla could make more babies and attend to the health needs of the villagers. I would do...something.*

Kevin knew his uncle would never do that and neither, really, could he. He was too excited by seeing people and places he'd only read about. No, they had to stay with Caesar. They were too involved now to even think of leaving or switching sides.

They both had to adapt their way of thinking, of living. "When in Rome, do as the Romans do" went the old saying. Well, it was true. Kevin and his uncle had to do as the Romans did or die.

David made his apologies and left. Kevin let him know he was going to stay and work a while, and then went to the Vetus Culina to try and occupy his mind with something. He couldn't focus though. He kept looking at the rolled-up papyrus sheets. Finally, he made up his mind. Kevin would never be able to focus unless he made his own bold sales pitch to Mark Antony.

"What's this?" Antony frowned as Kevin unrolled the plans and notes.

"It's something my birth people, the Koreans, made as a war weapon. It's called a *hwacha*. It launches many arrows at an oncoming enemy."

"How?" Antony asked. "It doesn't have a string or cord like a ballista does."

"There's a certain kind of powder that, when mixed correctly, will create a fire that the arrows ride."

Antony's eyes widened. "If it was anyone else telling me this, Flavens, I would think they were mad. You can make this powder?"

"Yes. I've done it before. It will take some experimenting," Kevin cautioned. "There are varying formulas depending on your needs. Some versions explode quickly, others burn longer. We will need the latter."

"I see," said Antony. "And you will need me to procure these materials for you, I assume?"

"Yes," said Kevin. He was getting nervous now. He didn't want Antony to think he saw him as someone to be conned, to be fleeced out of money. Zeno, for instance, at least had a somewhat working product but Kevin was convinced the salesman knew his *polybolos* wouldn't live up to his sales pitch. Kevin swallowed and continued.

"I don't think the materials will be hard to find or terribly expensive. At least at first, when Cleon and I are making small batches to experiment."

"What materials are we talking about?" Antony asked. He was all business now.

"Charcoal, sulfur, and niter."

"Charcoal and sulfur should be easy to find, and cheap," Antony said after thinking a moment. "I'm not familiar with the third thing."

"I don't know its name in Latin," Kevin said. "I do know you can make crystals of it by drying out chamber pots."

"A mystery powder made from piss and shit, eh?" Antony laughed. "You have to be an honest man, Flavens. A thief would demand far more expensive materials!"

"You'll get them?" Kevin asked.

"I'll see to it. Leave a list with Mercurius before you leave."

Kevin imagined small rockets raining down on enemy lines, wreaking havoc on the tight formations generals favored in this age. Would it work? Should he do it? Kevin didn't know what the future had in store for him, aside from sleepless nights.

LIVILLA WASN'T SURPRISED that Antony kept David occupied all day. She enjoyed spending time with her husband and loved that he wanted to spend time with her. Especially as the birth of their child approached. It wouldn't be long now. A handful of days at most. Livilla was filled with restless energy; thankfully she had more than enough activity to fill her day. Today was soap day.

David required quantities of soap for cleansing before surgeries and other medical treatments. He was so fanatical about cleanliness that some of the Roman officers wondered if he might be a Jew, as Bennozha had when David and Keffin had first appeared among the Mardani. David always told her that if a doctor or midwife had clean hands while treating a patient, the patient was less likely to die of fever afterwards. As he usually was about such things, Livilla's husband was correct in this.

David's fellow doctors judged by results. They began using soap as well as acetum to clean their hands before a surgery, especially after Pullo's dire wound had healed cleanly. Demand for both was high but as acetum was made from poor-quality wine gone bad it was easier to make, unlike soap. The Romans had known of the stuff but didn't really use it. Mardani men liked to use scented soap as a pomade in their hair, as did their Gallic cousins. Matwyn also used it in certain purification rituals, so Livilla was well acquainted with how to make it. So were a number of the slaves and women in Bibracte. Livilla quickly took charge of its manufacture, organizing what her husband called a "cooperative," a type of business where a group of people worked together and shared the costs and profits. Most of Livilla's share the soap they made went right back to David or into her own household use but many of the other women sold what they made. It was a source of income for the free women; most of the slaves were able to keep at least some of the money they earned for themselves.

The first step was straining water through ashes in a wooden barrel with a hole at the bottom. The ashes had to come from hardwood like oak. Pine would not do. David called the resulting liquid "lye" and said it was very dangerous if not handled properly. He'd explained to Livilla and the other women how to avoid burns and insisted they use leather gloves and aprons too. Even the fumes could burn and damage their eyes, he'd said. Privately David had told Livilla he wished they had eye coverings but glass was nearly impossible to come by and fabulously expensive. He'd had to settle for warning them against getting any in their eyes. It will blind you, he'd said, and there won't be anything I can do to save your vision.

Apart from a few minor burns, there had been no injuries. The lye had to be just right. Livilla remembered a trick that Matwyn had taught her. If an egg barely floated in the lye, then it was good to use. A few of the women had actually heard of Matwyn and her legendary age and started using the test.

Once the lye was ready, they poured it in an iron pot and mixed in the olive oil. This step was very tedious; the mixture had to be stirred for hours. But many hands made the time pass, and the women enjoyed talking among themselves as they took turns stirring. Using olive oil made the preparation longer than Livilla remembered; Matwyn always used boar or aurochs fat in her preparation. But wherever there were Romans in abundance, there was a lot of olive oil. So, it was olive oil they used.

The result was softer than the soap Livilla was used to and it had a greenish color. But David was happy with the results, and so were her business partners. Livilla made her own batches plain but most of the other women added scented oils, and Livilla shared some scents she remembered from the village. The soap took about a month to cure but now that they were preparing it twice a week the batches were coming regularly.

On this day, Livilla found herself stirring with an old woman nearly Matwyn's age, who the people of Bibracte simply called "Old Mother." Her wits were as sharp as ever, and her one good eye gleamed with intelligence. Her other eye was milk white and had been since anybody in the oppidum could remember. It was said, however, that her blind eye could see things no ordinary eye could. The Romans regarded her as an oracle and even they treated her with respect and more than a little fear.

"Storm's coming," Old Mother said.

Livilla looked at the blue winter sky. Old Mother obviously wasn't talking about snow.

"I don't feel anything, Old Mother," Livilla said.

"Aye. It's well over the horizon. Too far away for even you to feel, daughter. Matwyn chose her apprentice well. But it is there. It is coming."

Livilla shivered. She'd spoken a little of Matwyn and Pagus Mardani, but not much. She hadn't spoken of her and Matwyn's relationship that she'd remembered. How had Old Mother known? Livilla knew better than to ask that question, instead responding, "What kind of storm?"

Old Mother motioned to two other women, who took over the stirring. She covered her good eye and stared intently at Livilla with the blind one.

"You and your man stand at the center of the storm. He merely was blown ahead of it, that is why he's here, and not the only one. Your medicus-husband alters the storm's course. The storm is coming sooner that it would have because of him."

"What kind of storm?" Livilla pressed.

"The storm of war, child. More terrible than what we've just endured. Brother against brother. Father against son. Blood and death. Betrayal. But the doctor must inflict a wound in order to bring healing, despite the efforts of one hidden in gray."

Livilla felt cold and knew it had nothing to do with the temperature. The baby inside her kicked, as if it, too, were anxious. She pressed her hands to her swollen midsection.

"Have no fear. The babe will be healthy. The doctor's seed is strong and planted in good soil."

Livilla smiled nervously at that. "Thank you, Old Mother."

"Don't thank me, daughter. People treat me as if I'm the Good Goddess walking the mortal world, but gifts can be a terrible burden. As you and your husband both know. As does his nephew. The Greeks tell a story of a she-seer who was cursed to be always correct but never believed."

Livilla was positively freezing now. She knew she'd not spoken of Kevin. It was possible word of him had gotten to Old Mother from someone else but deep down Livilla didn't think so. "I've heard that story," she said.

"A heavy burden," Old Mother repeated. "One I will lay down soon, thank the Good Goddess. As will you."

"As will I?"

Old Mother refused to say any more and was soon paying court as the other women began talking once again of womanly things and seeking her advice. Livilla was left with her own very troubled thoughts.

She dined that night with only Theda and her newborn for company. Livilla knew it wasn't strictly proper, but she didn't want to be alone after David sent word that he and Kevin would be further detained over dinner at Antony's. Anyway, she liked Theda and Theda was a free woman. Livilla had never been terribly concerned about conventions. The Mardani rarely stood on ceremony except on the most formal of occasions. She wished David were here, though. She wanted to talk to him about what Old Mother had said. What it might mean.

The sun had been down for some time when David did return, and it was clear he was troubled as well. He'd been reluctant to say anything at first, but unburdened himself as they lay in bed, in the dark.

"I don't see the problem," Livilla said after David had told her of the events of the day. "It sounds as if Antony will be polite and then send Zeno on his way."

"If that's all it was, it wouldn't be a problem," David said. "But Kevin's spending the night there and I'm convinced it has the seed of an idea that might be useful. Dangerous, but useful. He and Cleon are already working on their own version of the *polybolos.*"

"Are you worried Zeno could take his machine to an enemy?" Livilla asked.

"No. It doesn't work well, and Zeno is an insufferable jackass."

Livilla snorted with laughter.

"I just worry," David said. "I'm changing things. Kevin's changing things. But for the better? Or will we make everything worse? Anyway, enough of my worries. How was your day?"

Livilla wanted to unburden herself, pour out her own worries.

She knew David would listen. Would care, even if he felt he shouldn't offer advice. He just sounded so weighed down, Livilla kept her own worries to herself.

"It was very good. You'll really love the new batch of soap." David soon fell asleep and left Livilla to wrestle with her own troubled thoughts.

25

———

(BIBRACTE, CENTRAL GAUL, 51 BCE)

Caesar was satisfied with the way the winter had gone so far. It was the Nones of January, and he'd returned to Bibracte to check on matters with the army and wait out the worst of the winter weather before conducting provincial business further east. This day he was dining with Davidius Medicus, something he enjoyed, though he would never tell the man. For one thing, Davidius respected Caesar's preference for light meals, especially at midday. On this day, they were lunching on something the doctor called "fruit salad," a pleasing mixture of fruits sweetened with a little maple sugar. The two men dined alone. David made apologies for his wife's absence.

"No apologies needed. The child will be born soon, from the looks of her," Caesar said.

"Any day now. He's been especially active at night. I've told Livilla that means he'll be up a lot at night after he's born," David said.

"That sounds like an old wives' tale," Caesar said.

"It does, doesn't it? It's true though. So these days Livilla sleeps whenever the baby lets her."

"And you're sure it will be a boy?"

"As to that, opinion is mixed. The local woman they call Old

Mother says she's sure it's a girl, but some of the other women disagree. At least in private. I'm told you don't really openly disagree with Old Mother on much in this town. Pullo's taking odds on when the baby will be born and whether it will be a boy or a girl."

Caesar chuckled. "I shall have to place my bet then. What do his odds favor?"

"A girl, born on the Ides of January."

"And what do you think of that?"

"Babies come in their own time, Caesar. That never changes."

Caesar had more immediate concerns. After Alesia, he and Davidius had had a long discussion, over more wine than he or the doctor was accustomed to. Davidius had talked about the philosophical principle of how a world existed for every possibility. Somewhere perhaps there was a world where he had been killed by Sulla. Or where his daughter Julia had not died in childbirth. Every decision that was made could be made. Caesar knew he was well-educated enough to hold his own in any philosophical debate, but the mere concept made his head spin. Besides, phantom other worlds were a matter for true philosophers and gods. He was concerned with here and now.

"Tell me of this mad project your nephew talked Antony into backing. I'm getting complaints from the smiths."

Davidius shifted, looking uncomfortable. "Starting manufacture of the new manuballistas was Antony's idea. As far as I know he is using personal funds." Davidius knew full well that often the line between personal and state funds could be very blurry.

"And the rush on iron spear points? That is coming from legionary funds. At three times the going rate for such work," Caesar pointed out. "And with your support, or so he tells me."

"I've learned to trust Kevin's abilities. He's pursued a lot of projects I'd have thought impossible, and he's come through every time. So yes, I support this. Kevin and Cleon are confident their new weapon will be ready for a demonstration before you leave in the spring."

Caesar had looked over the plans for what Flavens and his slave assistant called the *ignidigitus.* The finger of fire. If it worked, and Flavens and Cleon were confident it *would* work, arrows would ride fingers of fire to the enemy, dozens at once. Caesar could already see the battlefield applications. Potentially, he could do to an opponent what the Parthians had done to Crassus and his army at Carrhae.

"Kevin is a perfectionist. So is Cleon. They were born to make mechanical devices in the same way you were born to lead men," Davidius said.

"Bold words, Medicus."

"True words, imperator."

Davidius poured himself some the hot brew from the flagon he called a "French press." Even the smell was strongly bitter.

"I don't know how you can drink that," Caesar said.

"My coffee is almost gone. This is about the last of it," said Davidius mournfully. The doctor made no secret of his sorrow over the loss of the strong, bitter-smelling drink he favored in the morning. "Perhaps the Egyptians could find some real coffee beans," Davidius said. "As to Kevin and Cleon's little project, I think you will have a potent weapon."

"If I need one. Pompey may yet see reason," Caesar said. His words sounded hollow even to himself. Egged on by Cato, Pompey would not concede him an inch. He'd pressed his Senate allies to allow him to stand for next year's consulship in absentia, but Caesar harbored no illusions that that would come to anything.

"Still," Davidius said, "tell me such a weapon would not come in handy."

"I will admit, it would. If it works."

"If the Seres can make them, someone like Cleon will figure it out. And once he does, he can teach your weaponsmiths how."

Caesar imagined his legionaries charging an enemy battered down by a storm of arrows raining down like lightning from the hand of Jupiter himself. Yes, this finger of fire would be...what did term did Flavens once use? "Force multiplier," that was it. Indeed. If it did come to civil war, would Pompey have the courage to fight in the shade of thousands of arrows, as Leonidas and his Spartans had?

"Davidius, what do you think? Is it possible to avoid civil war?"

"My own homeland wrestled with the same question once. Many generations before I was born. The answer proved no, but the nation rose again, albeit with scars."

"But what do you think?" Caesar pressed.

"I think the system is broken. The Republic can't continue with two sides who oppose each other as violently as your *Populares* and Cato's *Optimates* do. I know Marcus Cicero seems to think it is yet possible to fix the system, but I don't see what he can do about it. I wish I could do something to avoid war."

"As do we all, Medicus. As do we all," said Cicero. "If Julia had lived…but there is no use in dwelling with might-have-beens."

"No, there isn't."

If only. Caesar's life was full of those. He wondered, idly, if it were possible there were other Gaius Julius Caesars who'd made different choices than he had and were wondering "if only" on decisions he had made? Maybe, maybe not. There was no way to know. From where Caesar now stood, the road had narrowed to one possible course. The only question was, when to move forward down it?

Thoughts of civil war were interrupted when the Mandubii woman, Theda, who David hired rather than taking as a slave, came into the room.

"It's Livilla," she said. "Her water has broken."

THE PAINS WERE COMING CLOSER TOGETHER NOW. Livilla had gone into labor early that morning, contractions coming first at irregular intervals until David had Pullo summon Old Mother and her team of midwives. Once there, the women insisted he stay out. Livilla wanted him in the room with her, but her protests availed her nothing. The women at least washed their hands thoroughly with soap before examining her; she'd won that much of a victory. Her other arguments had left Old Mother quite unmoved.

"The birthing room is for women. The men have their world, but we rule here."

Livilla rode out another contraction. "My husband has delivered more babies than you have."

"So you say," said Old Mother.

One of the other midwives was more conciliatory. "He is right outside if we need him."

"What's he doing?"

The young woman pressed a cloth to Livilla's head.

"I believe he is at his language lessons, *domina*," she said. "Or perhaps he's with the other men."

Livilla laughed. "Of course. Soter wouldn't cancel his lessons for this."

Even Old Mother cackled at that one. "Sour as bad beer that one, but a good man nonetheless. I've seen it." The woman raised the eyebrow over her milk-white eye, leaving no doubt as to what she really meant. That eye saw things. The future, Livilla knew for a certain; others said it could also see the true nature of people. Anyone who wanted a successful match in Bibracte had their prospective bride or groom come before the Old Mother. She knew people's true natures and knew if a match would be good or ill. It was said she was never wrong.

The hours dragged on, the pains coming more closely together all the time.

"It won't be long now, Livilla," Old Mother said. No "*dominus*" or "*domina*" for her. "The babe is moving down well, and you are opened wide. I'd have not thought it to look at you, but you have good hips for birthing."

Finally, the pains came so close together that it was hard for Livilla to tell where one ended and the next one began.

"Get David," she gasped.

"It is ill luck—" Old Mother began again.

"I want my husband, you dried up old bitch! Get him in here now!"

Livilla hardly noticed the appalled looks of the other women.

Dreadful tales had been spread about those who insulted Old Mother. Those who died were the lucky ones, it was whispered. Others ended up in her barnyard and eventually her stewpot after being turned to pigs or goats.

Old Mother just laughed her high, cackling laugh.

"You've been laboring since just after sunrise and you still have fight in you yet. That's a good sign. Very well, bring her man in. Delivered more babes than me, eh? We shall see."

AFTER HIS GREEK lesson was done Kevin, Antony and Quintus Cicero kept David company. The hours dragged on. David had gone light on the wine, not wanting to be impaired should he need to go to Livilla in case of an emergency, but so far according to Theda everything was progressing well.

"Let me have another one of those...what do you call them again?" asked Antony.

"Cigarettes," David said. He hadn't smoked himself since his college days and even then only to help him get through all-night study sessions. He'd brought several cartons with him to give as gifts to the men at the refugee camp. He felt guilty about it, but he knew the men there loved their cigarettes and tea. Being able to offer hospitality would be important. Even if Antony got hooked, David told himself, once these were gone what could he do to get more? Cross the Atlantic? David gave Antony one and lit it for him.

"What is this stuff," Antony asked. Not surprisingly, Mark Antony took to them right away. He loved the relaxing buzz you'd get from smoking...at least till you built up a tolerance. Not much chance of that, though. David lit one for himself.

"It's called 'tobacco.' It's the leaf of a plant that grows very far away. The leaves are dried and ground up, and people smoke or chew them," David said.

"A pity you won't have any more," said Antony.

"A pity, yes," said David drily. "They're actually very bad for you."

"That's the problem," said Antony. "Everything that brings pleasure is bad for you, at least according to some."

Kevin and Quintus thought that was funny. They'd both stuck mostly to wine, and it showed.

"You should debate my brother on that one, Antony," Quintus said.

"Anyone who debates your brother on anything loses," Antony said sourly. David remembered well from his history classes how little love there was between Mark Antony and Marcus Tullius Cicero. Maybe this new history would be different, though David doubted it. He looked longingly toward the room where Livilla labored.

"Is he really that good?" Kevin asked.

"Flavens, it is said that my brother could talk both legs off a deaf man, then persuade him to get up and walk afterwards," Quintus said. Turning to David—a little unsteadily—he said, "I don't see why you want to be in there anyway," Quintus said. "When my children were born, I didn't want to be in the same house."

"But you don't deliver babies for a living, Quintus," David said. "What if something goes wrong? What if she or the baby dies when I could have saved them? I've delivered more babies than all of those women combined in there!" David took a drag on his cigarette and grumbled, "It would be as if there were some great battle going on, and you were forced to wait on the sidelines."

"That would be a tragedy," Antony said. "But your woman Theda said you would be summoned if need be. Try to relax."

David did try. Their conversation wandered, eventually settling on the repeating crossbows the smiths were turning out.

"The iron bow did the trick. Even Cleon smiled when we tested it. I can't wait to try it out in a battle," Antony said.

"I'm not sure how effective they would be in battle, with their limited lethal range," Quintus said. "Still, they could have uses. A city guard equipped with them, for instance, could be quite formidable."

"Time will tell, Quintus," Antony said. "For now, we're training the first men who would use them in battle. After much discussion with Caesar, we decided that the Mardani slingers would be the first."

"Slingers? Why not archers?" Quintus was surprised.

"The slingers already have trained eyes for aiming shots," Kevin said. "But they don't have bad habits from the bow we'd need to break. I'm betting they'll do much better than an experienced archer."

And so it had proven, at least in the trials. A few archers had volunteered to train on the new manuballistas and had proven themselves among the worst with them. The slingers had acquitted themselves far better.

The bows could be very temperamental. Sometimes they jammed, the bowstrings snapped or the leather belt that worked the crank broke at the worst possible moment. But once Kevin and Cleon had worked out the design flaws they became much more reliable. The manuballistae could launch ten arrows or lead slugs in less than a minute, and with orderlies to continually reload and hand the crossbowmen fresh weapons, they could keep up a nearly unending stream of projectiles.

"Once I have a fully trained cohort of these men, I will be able to break any cavalry charge sent against me. And with the iron bows, we'll shatter the enemy's shields and leave them defenseless," Antony proclaimed.

"It seems a formidable weapon," Quintus agreed. "But I'll feel better once it's proven in battle."

"True enough."

They talked more, of politics in Rome and how long the uneasy peace between Caesar and Pompey could hold.

"My brother will manage a compromise," Quintus said. He was ever loyal to his older brother and confident of his skills. With reason, as Marcus Cicero's political skills were as formidable as anyone's. "He believes he can bring harmony to the orders."

"By which he means the rich and the even richer," David replied. His first letter from Cicero had been followed by many more. David found he looked forward to them and continuing the lively debate he had going on with the great man. But he did not share Cicero's optimism that a sort of grand coalition could be built between the ultrawealthy patrician ruling class and the next layer of Roman society, the equites, commonly translated as "knights," and though they weren't the armored mounted warriors of the medieval world, they did occupy roughly the same level of society. Right below the most powerful rulers, but above the plebians, the great mass of the people. No one ever talked about them, David had noticed, and he said something to that effect.

"And what of them?" Quintus asked. "The plebs have their assembly, their tribune, their bread and their festivals. What more could they want?"

"A chance to better themselves?" David suggested. "A chance to pursue a profession, or at least a job that isn't already held by a slave? Believe me, too many idle poor in a city like Rome brings nothing good. That's why Cato's shitting bricks over Caesar."

"What was that phrase you said?" Antony asked. David blushed. Try as he might, English occasionally crept in to his ever-improving Latin. A few phrases had been adopted by Caesar's soldiers and officers. The poker players used "all in," "see" and "call," even away from the card table and "okay" was now universal. David explained the phrase to Quintus and Antony.

"Ha!" Antony laughed. "That's certainly true. Though Cato is so uptight I doubt he shits anything more than once a year."

"Still," said Quintus, "you should know that you will never eliminate slavery."

"I know," David said. "But it hurts Rome. You have tens of thousands of idle poor, but even more, there's no incentive to invent things. How many people like Kevin or Cleon are out there, able to invent fantastic devices that will never be more than toys because it's cheaper to do things with slave labor?"

"And why would we need to change?" Antony asked. "If the old way works, why do things differently?"

David was about to launch on a rant about Roman conservatism when Flora came out.

"Davidius, come with me. Livilla needs you."

Alarmed, David followed her. What could be going wrong?

IT WAS all David could do to slow himself down long enough to scrub his hands properly. The sight of Livilla, red-faced and straining, was almost more than he could bear.

"What's wrong?" David asked as he rushed to Livilla's side.

"Nothing," said Old Mother. "She wants you here for the birth. Believes it will ensure a healthy child. Though I've already assured her she will bear a healthy girl."

David knew of the Old Mother's supposed powers. Normally he'd be skeptical, but a man who'd travelled from 2022 CE to 53 BCE couldn't really be skeptical, even about supposed mystic powers.

Livilla pushed again, screaming with the effort.

"The baby's crowning," David said. He squeezed his wife's hand. "Not long now, love. A few more pushes."

"Just get it out of me," she said dully.

Old Mother cackled her witch-like laugh. "On your feet, girl. You'll find it easier to push down for this last part."

Old Mother and her assistants guided Livilla to a blanket dyed with enigmatic symbols. She braced herself against the next pain.

"Push!" David urged.

She did. The baby's head and shoulders emerged in a gout of water and blood. The doctor in David noted that the amniotic fluid was colored as it should be. No meconium, which likely meant no fetal distress.

"One more, love," David said. "One more and the baby will be out."

The baby emerged fully at the next push. David caught his child and expertly cut the cord. He laughed when he saw it was a boy. His son squalled and emphasized his displeasure at leaving the womb by peeing all over Old Mother. A boy. Even Old Mother's all-seeing eye was fallible.

"Your son has blessed me," she said, and David knew she wasn't joking. "I was sure it would be a girl, but I've been wrong before." The assistant midwives tittered nervously.

David cleaned his son and swaddled him while Livilla delivered the afterbirth. The younger women helped her back to her bed while Old Mother wrapped the placenta in the birthing blanket.

"We will plant a tree over it," the old woman explained. "It will be a strong, healthy tree for a strong healthy boy."

David took the child to Livilla and laid him on her stomach. A quick examination showed that the birth had gone very well, with no complications so far.

"You're doing fine," he told his wife. "And we have a beautiful boy."

"A boy?" Livilla said. "I was sure it would be a girl."

"The future can cast deceiving shadows," Old Mother said. "But some are clearer than others."

Livilla nodded as if she understood the cryptic remark. David didn't think about it. He merely looked at his new family, feeling a love and completeness he never knew was possible.

26

(BIBRACTE, CENTRAL GAUL, 51 BCE)

On the Kalends of March, David acknowledged his son. Ferrarius, Kevin and Pullo stood behind him as family; Caesar, Antony, Quintus Cicero and Dolovix—standing in for his father Borodur as representative of the Mardani—acted as witnesses. With pride and dignity, Livilla laid their son at David's feet. David lifted the squalling, naked newborn up, then handed him back to his mother.

It was a solemn ceremony, and David was of two minds about it. On the one hand, he had no doubt about his child's paternity and felt no personal need to proclaim it. On the other hand, as Livilla convinced him, it was a vital public statement. This child—Gaius Castellanus Moussa Ferrarius—was David's son and heir, and it was important that the world know it. And with three powerful men among the witnesses, there would never be any doubt as to his position in life and society.

"Gaius Castellanus Moussa Ferrarius. A formidable name for a formidable child," Caesar said, raising his cup in toast when the ceremony was done.

"We thought it fitting to honor his ancestors," Livilla said. "So he carries the names of his grandfather and great-grandfather."

"It is good to honor your ancestors. May your son have many years of health and life," Caesar said.

"Thank you, Caesar," Livilla said, the very picture of the demure Roman matron.

They made small talk as Livilla nursed, afterwards applying an ointment of David's devising on her nipple. It was lanolin, or as close to lanolin ointment as he could make. Seeing sheep sheared gave him the idea; he remembered that lanolin was made with grease from raw wool. It seemed to be working so far and had even won him grudging praise from Old Mother, who allowed that it proved that David knew something after all.

Livilla retired soon after nursing Moussa and the talk turned to developments in Gaul. David was surprised at how glad he was to see Caesar again after he'd left for a time to see to provincial administrative business, chiefly hearing legal appeals. However, the proconsul's return heralded the end of his domestic interlude. Several bands of German raiders had crossed the Rhine and were ravaging Aedui territory. Normally the Aedui could handle raids like these, but Caesar was determined to intervene.

"I want to cement their loyalty and show them Rome will always be here to protect them. And there's the matter of testing these new weapons of yours, Antony. These *repeteballistae* and the one you're calling the *ignidigitus*. Best to try these in a few small engagements before we rely on them completely."

Ah, thought David. That is the real reason. That stuff about the Aedui is probably just window-dressing.

"I agree, Caesar. We've been drilling with the new ballistas, both the hand-held and larger ones, and we're ready for battle. We only have a few of the full-sized models, but I think they'll be particularly devastating against horse, with their lighter shields and armor."

"We'll see," Caesar said. "Davidius, Flavens, I will want you to accompany me for the demonstration. Possibly on campaign as well, though we can discuss that further. Celer will have to stay behind but I know Corvus is quite capable."

"Celer isn't sick, is he?" David hadn't heard anything was wrong with the tough old doctor.

"A case of gout," said Caesar. "Nothing terribly serious. Even if you go, don't worry. I won't keep you from your wife and son long."

"I've told Livilla you might be taking me away for a time, and she assures me she has all the help she needs."

"Good," Caesar said. "You and Corvus can organize the medical staff and we'll make a final decision about you later. However, Flavens, you will have to come with me."

"Me?" David couldn't help but laugh a little as his nephew's voice practically squeaked.

"Excellent," Caesar said. "I will leave you to organize the surgeons." Since the dedication ceremony had become an informal staff meeting, Caesar then doled out other assignments; aside from Antony commanding the crossbow cohort, Quintus Cicero was assigned a prestigious command of his own. There would no doubt be others at the next full, formal staff meeting.

Things were beginning to move fast after a quiet winter. David thought back to his last series of letters with Cicero. He was still trying, and still failing, to build his grand coalition. Nothing the orator could do would moderate Cato's hardline attitude toward Caesar and his supporters. Not for the first time, David sent a silent prayer to whatever higher power might be paying attention. There was always another choice, a different path, another way things could go. Maybe that was true here. But if it was, the people who needed to travel down it couldn't—wouldn't—see it.

Since his arrival in the ancient world, David found himself with hours to fill. He was busy, by the standards of this time at least, but in his time first in Pagus Mardani and now in Bibracte showed him that the world of the first century BCE moved at a different and altogether slower pace. He found he had time to see patients, attend Antony when Antony required treatment or entertaining, take lessons with Soter and see his family, and he still had time left over to pursue projects of his own, such as his report of his surgery on Pullo and learning herb lore from local healers. Habits of a lifetime left David a night owl, and he stayed up hours after sundown on all but the longest summer days. Even with the relentless preparations for Caesar's campaign against these as yet unnamed Germans, David was finding it far easier to achieve a work-life balance than in Manhattan.

Caesar was taking only taking one legion plus his cohort of cross-bowmen. That left David with more surgeons than he needed. He picked what he considered the best team and but made sure he left some experienced men to tend to the legions staying behind in Bibracte. The choice of one doctor in particular raised Antony's eyebrows.

"Hipparchus? You and he fought at Alesia," Antony said.

"Yes," replied David, "but when he controls his attitude and his arrogance, he's a pretty good doctor. Plenty of potential there."

"And you think he'll control his attitude?"

David laughed. "A little humiliation did wonders."

"I went easy on him," Antony said.

"At any rate, I don't think he'll be a problem. What about the silver?"

"You're lucky you're honest and had accounted for all your other supplies and expenditures down to the last *as*. I don't think Caesar would have given a pound of powdered silver to anyone else." An *as* was the smallest Roman coin, held in about the same esteem as the American penny, even if its purchasing power was greater. Antony continued, "I still don't know why you need it. Can't you balance humors with less expensive medicine? What about those pills you gave me and Pullo to prevent wound infection?"

David sighed. "Those won't last, and as I've said many times, I can't make more. I'm finding other substitutes, but silver helps to prevent infection and isn't harmful to the body." He would make these people understand germ theory, but that was a project for a different day. It was probably the project of a lifetime. And frankly, David didn't care whether his patients thought balanced humors were what made them well, so long as they got well.

THRUM! THRUM! THRUM! The last three bolts from the new model manuballista slammed into the target, a straw dummy dressed as a cavalryman. Dolovix grinned proudly. He should be proud of himself, thought Kevin. He's barely practiced with this weapon at all, yet he handles it as if it were given to him at his mother's breast. Kevin allowed himself a small sigh of relief that the repeating manuballista had fired 15 times—ten slugs and 5 bolts—without jamming.

Still nervous, Kevin looked at Caesar. As usual, the man's face gave nothing away. Caesar wasn't much of a gambler but occasionally joined David's weekly poker game when not travelling and always did supremely well. Every man's face might betray his thoughts, his uncle claimed. Everyone had a tell. Caesar surely had one too, but as yet no one had discovered it.

Kevin surveyed the results of the ballista demonstrations. Numerous targets had been set up. The human dummy was a tattered mess. Other targets, simulating walls and shields, had taken their own damage. Both the manuballista and the full-sized model worked on the same principle: a leather belt drove the mechanisms which drew, loaded, and fired the weapon. The bow itself was iron, reinforced at the point of stress thanks to Ferrarius's experience and ingenuity. A magazine held either lead shot or arrows which could be fired in rapid succession, as Dolovix had just demonstrated.

Caesar nodded thoughtfully. Kevin took that as a hopeful sign. Antony flashed Kevin an encouraging grin. As always, Cleon trailed behind them, muttering to himself and making notes.

"The cavalryman, at least, would have been thrice killed," Caesar said. "The full-sized model did more damage than I would have expected."

"Excellent work with the manuballista, Dolovix. You have my thanks. See my cook for a good skin of Falernian and have some fun tonight." Antony clapped the Mardani warrior on the shoulder.

"Thank you, chief," said Dolovix in his barbarous Latin.

"What do you think, Caesar?" Kevin asked.

"It shows promise," Caesar said. "I expected no less. These new weapons will have limited use at first, until they're truly tested in battle. But at least I know these new ballistae will work. Now, Flavens. What is this new weapon you wish to show me?"

Kevin nodded to Dolovix, who in turn bellowed in Mardani. Four of the biggest slingers wheeled out a cart and set it at a specified point. It carried a rack of 16 hollow iron tubes tipped with heavy, pointed heads. Ferrarius had designed the tubes, along with an ingenious cap to hold in the powder. Caesar looked at it all with interest and Kevin was relieved when Cleon stepped up next to him.

"Explain to me how this works," Caesar said.

"Each of these iron tubes are filled with gunpowder—" Kevin said the last word in English and Caesar already looked lost.

"I call it *ardenti pulveris*," Cleon said helpfully.

"A burning powder, eh? Intriguing. And what's this?" Caesar asked, pointing a network of copper wires. One end of each wire went into a small hole in the cap of the tubes, and the wiring led to a box with wooden-handled rod sticking out of the top.

"This box is called a 'plunger,'" Kevin said. "Pushing down on the handle with some force creates a spark that travels along the wires and ignites the burning powder."

"What happens then?" asked Caesar. "Judging from the smirk on Antony's face it's something good."

"I think so. Stand back, if you please, Caesar."

Caesar did. Kevin checked the cart, making sure it was aimed at its target—shields arrayed in the formation the Romans called the *testudo*, or turtle. An instant mini-fortress meant to protect against flights of arrows. Satisfied, Kevin walked to the plunger and pushed it down. Hopefully his take on a medieval Korean *hwacha* rocket launcher would work.

To Kevin, it seemed like an eternity but work it did. A magneto inside the plunger box sent a charge along the copper wiring. The end of each wire was coated in a flammable lacquer Cleon and Kevin had developed together that caught fire from the electrical charge and in turn lit the powder in the rockets. An electric match, Kevin called it. Sixteen iron projectiles, riding on fingers of flame, rained down on the simulated turtle formation. Not all of them hit, but enough did to batter the shields. Roman shields were tough, but if there had been men under those shields, they would not have fared well.

Caesar looked both awestruck and frightened out of his wits. "Venus Victrix," he said, invoking the divine supposed ancestor of the Julii. "What is that…thing?"

"The Koreans call it the *hwacha*," Kevin said. "But Cleon has come up with a good Latin name."

"I call it the *ignidigitus*," the young slave said.

"Finger of fire, eh? Yes. I like it. What about that horrible shrieking sound?" Caesar asked

"An accident, a small flaw in one of the early versions of the arrows. It made a shrieking sound," Kevin said.

Antony, who'd been silent until now, spoke up. "I thought it might be useful to terrify an enemy if it did not hamper the flight of the arrows."

"Well, it worked. You have more of these ready?" Caesar asked. Kevin could practically see the wheels turning in the great Roman's head. He was already developing a doctrine for everything he's seen today, Kevin thought.

"Yes. We have enough ready to be useful in a battle, if you wish to try," Cleon said.

"And they will catch fire, even if the weather is damp, like today?"

"Yes," Kevin said. "So long as the powder itself stays dry."

"Very good." Kevin had to suppress a shiver at the expression on Caesar's face. He looked like a predator in search of prey.

27

(AEDUI TERRITORY, EASTERN GAUL, 51 BCE)

Caesar nodded as he rode up and down his assembled legion, ready to move out. In truth, even one legion was probably overkill against what by all accounts was a rag-tag foe; in other times Caesar probably would have let the Aedui deal with the threat themselves. But having crushed one barbarian army, he was reluctant to allow another one to assemble so soon afterwards. He also wanted to send the Aedui a message with a show of force, to remind them—if they needed reminding—of Rome's power. Power that could just as easily be brought to bear against them if the need arose.

Among his men, slaves helped adjust armor, arrange packs, and generally help their masters prepare for the order to move out. As he did in many things, Davidius Medicus was an exception. As their free servant looked on holding their baby, Livilla Ferraria straightened her husband's cloak.

She was formidable, that one. It was a pity she was low-born half-barbarian and the daughter of an exile. Livilla would have made an excellent political wife. She might still, Caesar mused. He lacked the means currently to offer Davidius citizenship but that was something Caesar hoped to remedy. His preparations for the current campaign had been meticulous, something that had rubbed off on Antony, who'd attacked his own duties as camp quaestor with far more diligence than was normal for him.

As always in idle moments, Caesar's thoughts went to the future. Great glory awaited him, of that Caesar was certain. The question was, should he seek sole glory or try to form a new triumvirate? He was inclined to be the only power guiding the Republic. Caesar would not go so far as to say the First Triumvirate had been a mistake; at the time it had made perfect sense. But with Crassus dead there was no credible balancing force between himself and Pompey. Crassus had been the bridge, and thanks to the Parthians that bridge was gone.

If Crassus were still alive, a grand coalition of the orders that Cicero dreamed of might be possible. Now, though, all that existed was stalemate between two powerful men. It was Marius and Sulla all over again. Caesar was determined that he would not be brought down the way Marius had been. He would be triumphant.

It was that need for triumph that had Caesar so nervous about this campaign. He was not uncertain about victory. Against a band of what by all accounts were scavenging opportunists, victory was assured. Caesar felt in his bones that a key to victory in any civil war would be the repeating crossbows Flavens and Antony helped shepherd into existence, along with the insights and ideas of Davidius. Flavens had called these new weapons "force multipliers," and Caesar had seen at once that he was correct. That Flavens and Cleon had made the manuballista a useful weapon was an impressive enough innovation. One which spat arrows at a rate only the best archers could match was a gift from the gods. And because the weapon relied on mechanical force rather than strength the way a bow did, one did not have to be an experienced archer to use the manuballista effectively. The Mardani, for starters, had really taken to the weapon and provided the core of the new archery and field artillery cohort. Because as wondrous as the new repeating ballistae were, it was nothing compared to the ignidigitus.

Success of the new weapons would mean Caesar had something

which might nullify Pompey's recruiting advantage on the Italian peninsula. Caesar's battle-hardened legions might do that. The ballistae and ignidigitus—if they worked—would ensure it.

Caesar suddenly realized his officers were looking expectantly at him. With a gesture, he started down the road, not even looking back as his army followed him. Some things, Caesar did not question.

～

Mark Antony was an angry man. These Germans were supposed to be easy meat, but they proved maddeningly elusive. The Tenth Legion and its auxiliaries had been tramping all over the countryside after these sons of mangy forest cows, but aside from a few skirmishes the Romans had been unable to force a battle.

They made camp next to some Aedui town whose name Antony hadn't cared to learn. He reclined in his tent while he, Davidius and Flavens shared wine. A slave refilled their cups.

"I'm not saying that I want to treat battle wounds, but it would be a change from broken bones and injuries caused by drunken brawls," Davidius said.

Antony lifted his wine in a mocking salute. "I never thought I'd see the day when my soft-hearted physician craved battle."

"I just know what soldiers with too much time on their hands get up to."

"Well," Antony said, "Caesar thinks he can trap the raiders against a lake hereabouts. These Germans can only run so far for so long. If they were smart, they would have made a quick raid then dashed for the Rhenus. Caesar never would have bothered chasing them so far or crossed that river. Not for something like that."

"Of course, if they were really smart, they never would have come here in the first place," Flavens observed.

Antony laughed at that one. "Who ever said barbarians were smart, eh? And they'll find out how stupid they were once they meet those new weapons of yours."

"I hope they work," Flavens said. "I wish Cleon were here."

"And if the worst happened, Caesar would lose both the men who know about these gifts from Mars. Not that anyone thinks we'd get wiped out but Dis is filled with generals who refused to consider the worst possible outcome."

The next few days proved Antony knew Caesar's mind. Roman scouts found the German camp strung along the lakeshore. Now that they were within his grasp, Antony knew that Caesar would not let them go. With troops stationed to prevent the barbarians from retreating yet again, the rest of the Tenth Legion throwing up a crescent-shaped system of hastily built earthworks and palisades. They were flimsy and sloppy compared to the siege works around Alesia, but they didn't need to be as strong as those. Whoever this barbarian chief was, he had a certain cunning. It was clear, though, that he was no Vercingetorix.

The call came to form up for battle. The new cohort looked smart indeed, as they should. Antony had seen to that. He'd been the champion of these new-generation ballistae as well as the new ignidigitus. Even though it was Flavens and the slave Cleon who'd done the physical and mental work, neither was a soldier, and neither had a military reputation to lose. Even with Caesar as his patron, Antony didn't want a failure of men or machine blighting his career. So he'd relentlessly drilled this new cohort who—at Davidius's suggestion—had adopted the name "Dracones Sagittarii" for themselves. As far as Mark Antony knew, the mythical archer Sagittarius had never had any dragons, but it was a suitably formidable name.

The Romans arrayed for battle. At Caesar's direction, Antony divided his cohort into two groups, flanking the main body of troops, with the manuballista archers intermixed with the ignidigitus carts. They'd been drilled to fire and reload quickly and smoothly, and when the infantry advanced, half the archers would move forward with them to provide cover while the rest protected the carts. Antony hoped with more experience the soldiers working the ignidigitus carts would be more mobile. For now, Caesar treated them as fixed points. Antony had agreed.

Battle plans, though, frequently evaporated as soon battle was joined, and this one certainly did. The barbarians charged. The legionaries set to receive the charge, but the barbarians never got there. Antony, commanding the left wing and Quintus Tullius Cicero, commanding the right, each gave the command to shoot.

The barbarians were met with an unrelenting storm of arrows, followed by iron spear points riding on fire and shrieking like a flight of harpies. Antony recalled the Persians' boast to Leonidas before the battle of Thermopylae: "Our arrows will blot out the sun." These barbarians were not cut from the same cloth as the Spartans, and they did not care to fight in the shade. Faced with the combined fire of the repeating manuballistas and the ignidigiti the front ranks went down as if they were mowed by scythes.

The first line of crossbowmen moved back to reload, and the second line stepped forward, unleashing death with each crank of their ballistas. The ignidigiti belched another volley of their own. That broke the barbarians, and they ran. Caesar, commanding the foot soldiers in the center, ordered the pursuit. Antony signaled Quintus and they both signaled their men to follow, firing as they went. By nightfall, all that remained of this rag-tag band of barbarians were even more tattered remnants starting to spread stories that Caesar fought with weapons gifted by the gods.

THRUM. Thrum. SHRIEK!

This is what I live for! The exultant thought filled Caesar's brain. There was something about battle that sharpened his senses in a way nothing else could. Colors were more vivid, sounds louder, smells sharper. Especially the new smell, the acrid odor of burnt burning powder.

Caesar had thought to lure the barbarians into charging his lines with a series of false charges of his own. But his enemy had even less discipline than barbarians usually do and charged without provocation. Being like animals themselves, Caesar thought, perhaps they were determined to fight like animals now that they were cornered.

In the end it gained them nothing but death and, for the few survivors, enslavement.

Thrum. Thrum. SHRIEK!

The sound of the manuballistae and ignidigiti were like the rhythmic strumming of a lyre punctuated by the screaming of the damned. No, not a lyre, Caesar realized; it was like a heartbeat. The new heart of his order of battle. These were weapons to bring victory.

And if it was to be civil war with Pompey, he could afford nothing less. It would be win or die, and he did not intend to die, at least not at Pompey's hands. He would not go the way of Gaius Marius. The question then became who wanted victory the most? He or Pompey?

Thrum. Thrum. THRUM!

No shriek this time. The ignidigiti were done for the day. A cheer after the third volley from the manuballistae snapped Caesar out of his reverie. The barbarians broke and his commanders ordered the pursuit. He noticed with no small satisfaction that the crossbowmen joined, firing away at the fleeing enemy. Antony had drilled his troops well. The Germans had gotten nowhere near the Roman lines. From his vantage point atop his horse, Caesar saw one Roman go down. He rode up to the fallen soldier. He recognized the man, a grizzled evocatus named Saturninus. The man clutched his leg. Caesar couldn't tell if it was broken or not.

"I'm sorry, Caesar," he gasped.

Caesar signaled two stretcher-bearers starting to move wounded Germans to the surgeon's tent. Treating the enemy wounded was more of Davidius's soft-hearted nonsense but the man had made a compelling case that he and the other surgeons needed practice treating battle wounds. As Davidius never tired of reminding him, the strange doctor was more at home delivering babies than treating sword and arrow wounds.

"Don't worry, Saturninus. Davidius will see to you. You'll be healed in time for the next campaigning season."

"Thank you, Caesar," Saturninus said as the orderlies took him away.

Could Pompey command such loyalty from men like Saturninus? Caesar doubted it. And that, thought Caesar, is why I will win.

DAVID HADN'T KNOWN what to expect, marching on campaign with Julius Caesar, but he hadn't expected boredom. As they chased these nameless Germans all over Gaul, he hadn't really had a lot to do except treat pulled muscles and blistered feet. The worst injury he'd treated was a torn rotator cuff one of the older centurions got from a spear-throwing contest with one of the younger recruits. And there wasn't much David could do about that except prescribe exercises and tell him to drink a decoction of willow bark for the pain and inflammation. He wasn't about to attempt shoulder surgery while on the march.

That had pretty much been his glorious march so far, as a newly minted Surgeons' Tribune, a rank equivalent to that of military tribune and giving him charge over the other doctors and medical orderlies in the camp. The tribune outranked the centurion but was below a legatus. Probably about the equivalent of being a major in the United States Army. Military tribune was a coveted post, appointed by the Senate and given to young men of prominent families to start them on their political and military careers. At need, military tribunes could also be created in the field by commanders, which is the precedent Caesar cited for David's appointment. As far as David knew, surgeons' tribune was an office Caesar invented to reflect David's current administrative responsibilities, and his first act in his new office was to name Corvus an *evocatus medicus*, a title that, with Caesar's approval would be given to medical staff who distinguished themselves in some way. Celer would be given the same rank, once they returned to Bibracte.

The days tended to drag when he couldn't busy himself with household matters. David was glad he brought projects with him. There was the monograph on the surgery on Pullo. Poor gout stricken

Celer had sent a draft back with Caesar, and David was polishing the work. Cicero had promised to make sure it was circulated in Rome. Another project was a guide to the properties of medicinal herbs. He'd spent a lot of time in Bibracte talking to Old Mother and the local healing women and tribal priests, building on training he'd begun with Matwyn in Pagus Mardani. David figured he had a good start on a work which would include exhaustive notes on effective use and possible side effects of any and all herbs for which he could find legitimate medical uses. That, David knew, would be the work of years, maybe a lifetime.

He still had time to think, though, and he was thinking a lot. Unlike most people, he knew what was coming. Not just civil war. Most of the Romans on down to the common soldiers in Caesar's legion reckoned that military conflict between Caesar and Pompey was inevitable. David alone knew how bloody and protracted the war would be, though events were already changing from the history he knew. They wouldn't change enough to make Julius Caesar and Gnaeus Pompey Magnus kiss and make up, but what would it change? He'd read all about the butterfly effect but to see it happening was unsettling.

An orderly poked his head into David's tent. "Davidius Medicus, the wounded are starting to arrive."

"Ours or theirs?" asked David to the orderly's retreating back. He got his answer in the surgical tent. There was one Roman soldier and dozens of barbarians, many of them bristling with crossbow bolts. David noticed Hipparchus and some orderlies moving among them, using the colored wooden tokens David had had made for triage. David nodded with satisfaction. He then saw Caesar standing by the legionary, motioning for David to come over. David examined him; the man's injury seemed straightforward—his knee was grotesquely swollen.

"I'll have an orderly give him some wine mixed with poppy juice for the pain. For now the best thing we can do for him is keep his knee from moving. I'll drain it when I've seen to the most seriously wounded. And then I'll talk to Kevin about designing a brace to hold his knee still while he walks," David said.

That satisfied Caesar, who nodded and then left the tent without a word. The rest of the day was spent in surgery after surgery. David had made a study of the Romans' medical instruments since falling in with Caesar and Antony, and one device he hadn't recognized was coming in handy now. It was an arrowhead extractor. By the time the sun set and it was too dark to do any more operations, David estimated he'd taken out more arrowheads than every surgeon in New York City combined.

He then saw to the luckless legionary with the injured knee, whose name, David learned, was Saturninus. David's expertise in such things was minimal but he wouldn't have been surprised to learn that Saturninus had a torn anterior or mediate cruciate ligament. David drained the knee and made sure his patient wasn't in too much pain.

"Will I be able to walk again?" Saturninus asked, clearly worried at the answer.

"Yes, definitely. I will have my nephew design a brace for your knee. You may not be able to march double-time, but you should be able to walk without any problem. The brace will hold your knee in place so it can heal."

"Your nephew? The one who built the ignidigitus?"

David hadn't had time to get full details on the battle, but he'd gathered Kevin's Romanized hwacha had scared the Romans almost as much as it had the Germans. Kevin—"Flavens" as the Romans called him—was a hero.

"Thank you, doctor," said the veteran, with almost pathetic gratitude. Or was it really that pathetic? David may have just saved Saturninus from being a cripple. Even if his military days were over, the veteran could find an honorable trade and not have to worry about being a beggar.

It made David think about what he took for granted that he couldn't count on now. There was no worker's compensation or disability insurance or Social Security. Your support system was as good or bad as your connections with your family or patron, and the help those people could give you. Maybe that was something he could change, but David wasn't going to hold his breath. He would do what he'd been doing for the past year and a half—concentrate on the present and let everything else play out as it would.

28

(BIBRACTE, CENTRAL GAUL, 51 BCE)

The house felt lonely with David away. Livilla was managing, though; Moussa was keeping her busy. He was a good baby, very sweet-natured and already smiling (how David would hate that he missed that), but he ate as if he had a bottomless pit in place of a stomach. During the day, it wasn't so bad. Feeding her son gave Livilla time to relax and she usually had a nice chat with Theda or, if Livilla were out of the house, with the other women she'd gotten to know in Bibracte.

Night feedings, though, left Livilla with a lot of time to think. One of the things she kept thinking about was how big her world had gotten since she'd met David. She may have been half-Roman by blood, but Livilla thought of herself as Mardani, and until about a year ago never thought about leaving her village...unless it was to go to Mortorgenn, or the coast, or a neighboring village. Her father's tales of life with Marius's army, when he chose to share them, had interested her as a girl but it hadn't instilled in her any great desire to experience the wider world.

What a father's tales couldn't do, love did. When David asked her to marry him, Livilla realized that she would go wherever he went, even if that meant leaving Pagus Mardani. Somehow, she'd known it would come to that, even though David claimed to be perfectly happy being, as he put it, a "country doctor." On that same level, Livilla also knew that when she and David left the village with the Mardani warriors to join Caesar's army that they weren't coming back.

She wasn't sure how she felt about the prospect of moving to Rome, for that was where she and David would end up now that David had cast his lot with Antony and Caesar. David's knowledge was too important to Caesar, too necessary, for the Roman leader to give her husband leave to return to the back country of Gaul.

They'd talked about that before David left on this latest campaign. He seemed excited at the prospect of seeing Rome, even living there. Though Livilla would never admit it, the very idea terrified her. It was said that Rome had a million people living in it, a number beyond imagining. That seemed like more people that could possibly live in the entire world. That didn't bother David. He'd spent many of their hours alone telling Livilla about the city where he'd lived, the place called New York. According to David, in the time he'd lived, New York was bigger and more important than Rome. David said that this city had eight million people living in it, probably more than lived in all of Gaul. If a million was unimaginable, eight million was inconceivable.

"What do you think?" Livilla asked the curly-haired baby at her breast. "Are you ready to be a big city Roman?" Moussa's only response was to continue suckling.

Sometimes, at night, even darker thoughts came. They usually revolved around Old Mother's cryptic words to Livilla not long before Moussa's birth. Would she even see Rome? Would she see her son grow up? Only the gods knew.

With David away Livilla lived for soap-making days. Oh, market days were fun too; she enjoyed a good haggle as much as anyone. But soap days were just the women together, losing themselves in work and fellowship and not worrying about household matters for a time.

"He's a beautiful boy," said Trixia, a mousy-haired Gallic woman. Trixia was a native of Bibracte and a free woman; her husband and family had either not taken up arms against Caesar or hadn't been caught at it.

"Thank you, Trixia," said Livilla as she mixed soap. She spared a moment to look at her son, cooing happily at Theda. Already Moussa and Theda's slightly older daughter were inseparable.

"Any word from your husband?" Trixia asked Livilla.

"Not recently. You know how it is when they're out on a campaign. Last word I had he was chasing Germans around Gaul with the rest of the Tenth Legion."

"Next word you have will probably be when he comes home," Trixia said.

"Oh he'll come alright," said Theda, bringing laughter. "You will too, I wager."

Livilla felt her ears heating. The only way to beat Theda was to give as good as you got. "You need to get laid, Theda. Little Davidia is old enough and you have your body back. What are you waiting for?"

"A real man!" one of the other women said, bringing more coarse laughter.

The rest of the afternoon continued in much the same vein. Bawdy banter punctuated by gossip and more serious talk.

When she and Theda returned to the house, Livilla found Pullo standing by the door. He seemed half-asleep but Livilla knew better. In fact, for all Livilla knew, Pullo hadn't moved a muscle. She remembered when David had questioned the need for a bodyguard at all. Where he came from, the government paid people to protect its citizens and enforce the law. She had a feeling David still didn't truly understand that all too often, you received justice only when you were powerful enough to make the state take notice of your cause, or you had the resources to mete out your own justice. In any event, thanks to Pullo's looks and fearsome reputation, Livilla figured she was one of the safest people in Bibracte.

"Any trouble, Pullo?" she asked.

"None, mistress. You did have a caller, though. Trebonius came while you were away."

"Trebonius?" Caesar had left his legatus in charge of the

remaining garrison in and around Bibracte. What did he want with her, Livilla wondered?

As if reading her mind, Pullo added, "He didn't say what he wanted, but he would be back tomorrow." By Pullo's tone, he found Trebonius's visit as odd as Livilla herself did. He opened the door and stepped in ahead of her and Theda.

They'd arrived just in time; Moussa was starting to fuss. She sat down to feed him while Theda put together a light evening meal. As Moussa nursed, Livilla forgot all about Trebonius.

Marcus Tullius Cicero would say this much about Gnaeus Pompey: the man laid on a respectable luncheon spread. An excellent *prandium*, midday meal. The food and wine had been up to the usual standards of Pompey's household, but his host and the other guest, Cato—sometimes called Cato the Younger to distinguish him from his legendary great-grandfather—both looked to be suffering a severe case of indigestion. The cause, of course, was not lunch. It was the fact that Caesar was sharing the spoils of his campaigns in Gaul with the Roman people. As some had predicted, the value of gold was indeed dropping.

"He'll want to run for consul again," Cato said. "And he'll want to run *in absentia* again as well. I won't have it."

"Yes, and your gambit last time worked so well," Cicero replied. "Caesar returned to Rome and won his consulship. Your making him choose between office and a Triumph was a slight he won't forget, Cato. You mark my words."

"You leave us plenty of words to mark," Pompey said sourly. "In the meantime, I've learned very little about this doctor that seems to be constantly at Caesar's side."

"You mean your little spymaster hasn't been able to find anything out? That's your first problem, Gnaeus," Cicero said. "If you knew anything at all about Davidius Medicus, you'd know he's more constantly at Antony's side than Caesar's. He is in Antony's pay as a personal physician, after all."

"Enough, Cicero," said Cato. "If you have anything useful to add, I suggest you add it."

"You might try writing to the man, Cato. You'd likely learn a lot."

"And I suppose he'd just write back?" asked Pompey sarcastically.

"He might," Cicero said. "He wrote me back. We've been keeping up a lively correspondence, in fact."

"And what have you learned?"

"Any number of things," Cicero replied. "I'm learning more about anatomy and herbology than I ever thought possible, for starters. But he seems to share my hope that you and Caesar may yet avoid civil war. He says that the government of his own land at the time he left was hopelessly polarized. He also says that all sides must be willing to bend a little but that the result could be glory for all." He also, Cicero thought, strongly advocated the abolition of slavery and any number of other impractical proposals, but he didn't need to share those with Pompey and Cato. On the more practical side, Davidius did have some interesting proposals for public health policy and works projects to make the city less prone to the diseases filth could breed. On those, he'd asked Cicero's advice on making them palatable to the Senate. Those Cicero did share with Cato and Pompey, not that the other two men were greatly interested in public health. A pity, that.

Post-prandial conversation continued in a vein of useless anger at Caesar and events in Gaul and pointless speculation about Antony's new doctor. The former didn't worry Cicero much; so long as he kept one plebeian tribune firmly in his grip, Cicero could count on a veto of any rash bills to strip Caesar of his *imperium*, the authority that gave him license for his Gallic campaigns. The tribunes of the plebs were officers whose authority checked those of quaestor, praetor, or consul. In short, any office which granted imperium to the person holding it. The tribune could veto any act or bill in the name of the people. Long ago it was a means to keep the patrician class from abusing the plebeian masses and served that purpose for a long time.

But it could be manipulated by those who how to play the game of Republican politics and in his own humble opinion Marcus Tullius Cicero played that game as well as anyone. It was this tribunician power that Cicero was using indirectly to prevent an open break between Caesar and Pompey and the civil war that would inevitably follow such a split.

As the litter bore him through the streets of Rome from Pompey's house to his own, Cicero took time to read reports from his sources. He loved collecting gossip; you never knew when it might come in handy. One piece he read was that Caesar's great-niece Octavia was eligible for marriage once again. Pompey was a widower as well, having not remarried since his former wife, Caesar's daughter Julia, had died in childbirth. Julia had been the last real tie between the two men. Perhaps that could be forged anew. But how could he encourage such a thing?

Cicero found his faithful secretary Tiro waiting for him. Some new correspondence had come in while he was lunching at Pompey's. Most of the letters were from Rome. One had come from Gaul. An answer to the problem of renewing the marriage alliance between Caesar and Pompey might just lie in the long-distance letter. It was from Davidius.

To my friend Marcus Tullius Cicero, warmest greetings from Davidius Castellanus. I hope this letter finds you well. Since Caesar's victory at Alesia things have been pretty quiet here, Cicero read. *Though they may be about to heat up again with reports of a previously unknown band of Germans crossing the Rhine into Aedui lands. That's probably the biggest news in Bibracte right now. The rest is merely small-town gossip that would not interest you.*

There Davidius was wrong, Cicero thought. He didn't share any of the gossip. A pity. Cicero skipped ahead:

Enclosed is a treatise written by myself and my fellow army surgeons Celer and Corvus on the methods we used to remove the spear from Vibius Pullo and save his life. Please critique it and do not spare my feelings. Latin is not my native language and I'm still finding my way as a writer of it. You don't even want to know how my Greek is coming. All the best, David. His name was written was in a loopy scrawl Cicero could scarcely read, contrasting with the meticulously printed words in the body of the letter.

Yes, Cicero's doctor friend would do nicely as an intermediary in the matter of a marriage between Octavia and Pompey. Davidius had Caesar's ear. And Cicero had Davidius ear. What could be more perfect?

ARMINIUS COMEDENTIS HAD HEARD Cicero's snide remark about him and his role with Pompey. He tried to tell himself it didn't matter and started to even believe it. Looking at Delfina's smooth brown back as she shrugged a dress back on, he wished she didn't have to go back to the kitchens. She'd been very good at helping him forget.

He said nothing as she left, staring at the ceiling and running matters over in his head. The more he thought about it, the more he felt that this mysterious doctor and his equally mysterious nephew were the key to whether his own plans succeeded or failed. Pompey had told Comedentis to spread the rumor that the young man called "Flavens," supposedly from Serica, was the doctor's lover. He'd done so, if half-heartedly. Maybe that's why the rumor didn't really catch on. No matter. Pompey had no clue about the true threat these two men represented. His source inside Caesar's winter quarters in Bibracte had described, very clearly, a number of projects that told Comedentis that Davidius and Flavens had knowledge that did not belong in this world. Knowledge that threatened his own ambition of seeing Pompey as sole ruler of Rome and himself as the invisible guiding hand. He would enjoy all the benefits of power with few of its responsibility. Let Pompey deal with those. Comedentis had spent his professional life doing the work while powerful men like Pompey reaped the benefits. No longer.

Arminius Comedentis finally rose and dressed. He sat down at his desk, dipped his quill in ink, and began writing.

THE SPY CONSIDERED the letter in his hands, and then burned it as its writer had instructed. Getting the materials requested might be tricky. Davidius was sure to miss some of them and raise an alarm. Retaining his own usefulness as a spy in Caesar's camp would be difficult, maybe even impossible once that happened. But his master in this matter was a man of immense power, and it was good to earn the gratitude of men of power.

The spy considered his options. He could arrange for Davidius's house to be robbed. But there was almost never a time when it wasn't guarded by either the veteran Pullo, or by Mardani barbarians. Either would give any ordinary run of thief a lesson to remember—if the thief survived the experience. An alternative would be to overwhelm the guards with numbers but that was hardly discreet.

He could use his slave, Titus. The rabbity little man from Ostia had a certain flair for not being noticed. But again, the risk was unacceptable. If caught, Titus would lead directly back to him. If it was good to earn the gratitude of men in power, it was just as bad to earn their wrath. Getting caught would earn the wrath of both the spy's patron and Caesar.

That left the spy a third option: suborning someone in Davidius's household. It seemed more promising and was his only real option. The question was who. Not the wife, certainly. By all accounts and the spy's own personal observations, Davidius and Livilla were madly in love. Neither had any lovers that might be bought or coerced. Pullo and Theda were both intensely loyal, having been on the receiving end of Davidius's extraordinary medical skill. They could not be bought, either. Besides, Pullo would probably kill him, and the spy wouldn't have bet against Theda doing the same.

That, however, did leave one possibility. Namely, a certain tutor of Greek. He didn't seem to have any unnatural animus or loyalty toward Davidius. Such a man would be ideal for the spy's purposes. The question was, what was his price?

At this hour of the night, the temple of Asclepius was all but deserted. The shrouded figure left his bodyguards on the temple steps. He stood in front of the altar, as if undecided on a course of action.

In truth, Gnaeus Pompey Magnus considered the rolled copper sheet in his hands. Deep in his heart, he sometimes wondered if the gods even existed, if the prayers and petitions of men had any point. Or if their curses brought the disaster desired. Caesar's new protégé was a doctor, so if Pompey was to call down a curse on him, he would have to petition Asclepius. Whether Asclepius would answer— whether Asclepius existed to answer—was a question beyond Pompey's ability to know.

But what if? What if this person really was Asclepius in mortal guise, as some said, choosing to aid Caesar in his hour of need? Calling down a curse on a god wouldn't end well. But didn't Cicero persist in saying this Davidius was a mere mortal of great skill? Pompey would have risk it.

The curse he set on the altar of the god of medicine was elegant in its simplicity, as befit one who had been called *adulescentulus carnifex*—the teenage butcher. Caesar had been acclaimed for his military prowess in Gaul, but would he have had the tactical sense and subtlety Pompey had shown in crushing the pirates who plagued the Middle Sea, or that upstart king, Mithridates?

This curse, then, was another aspect of that same subtlety of tactics. Most curses were detailed and explicit, calling calamity down on every aspect of the target's life and (if they were male) that their pricks wither for good measure. Pompey had written one thing on the copper sheet, just one simple thing: *Gloria eius in cinerem*. It was, Pompey thought bitterly, the worst fate that could befall a man.

29

(BIBRACTE, CENTRAL GAUL, 51 BCE)

David panted hard as Livilla flopped to the mattress beside him. He was drained in every possible sense of the word. Livilla looked immensely pleased with herself.

"I haven't managed that since...well, I don't even remember the last time," he said when he'd gotten his breath back.

"Three times. Not bad for an old man," Livilla teased. "Here, give me that thing. What do you call it?"

"Condom."

"Condom. I'll throw it in the chamber pot. Though why you insist on using the silly little things is beyond me."

David propped himself up on one elbow. "Dearest, you know I love you and want to have many more children with you. Just not too close together. For your sake especially. It's not good for your body."

"That's why I'm nursing. You can't get pregnant again if you nurse. At least that's what the women say."

"There's some truth to that," David said, "but it's no guarantee. So in the meantime, we use the 'silly little things' to make sure."

It was good to be home, David thought. Moussa was already smiling and bestowed several big grins on his father, who couldn't believe how much the baby had grown.

David was glad of the comforts of home after two months on the march with Caesar. Life settled back into a comfortable routine: seeing patients, curing Mark Antony's hangovers, and taking lessons with Soter. And he was getting more correspondence. Many letters were from Caesar's allies in Rome, curious about this new person in the great man's circle. But the letters David looked forward to most were from Cicero. His initial awe at being pen pals with one of history's most renowned statesmen had given way to a healthy respect and honest liking for the man. They didn't agree on everything but had had stimulating debates on a range of policies. Additionally, Cicero had been encouraging about David's ideas on public health and had promised to help circulate his paper on Pullo's surgery once it was polished.

As if thinking of Cicero was enough to conjure him, or at least, conjure a letter from him, Pullo announced the arrival of a courier who did, indeed, bear a missive from the man himself. As soon as David read past the greeting, he could tell this letter would be different. It lacked the light, breezy style that had marked their recent letters to each other. This was much more serious. Marcus Tullius Cicero needed to talk business.

Livilla knew something was different as soon as she looked at David.

"What's wrong?"

"Nothing's wrong, not exactly," David said. "It seems that while I was busy trying to avoid Roman politics, it was busy not avoiding me."

Livilla quirked an eyebrow.

"Cicero. He wants me to be an intermediary with Caesar." David explained Cicero's proposal. "I don't think I'm the man for this! Hell, his own brother is one of Caesar's generals, why not ask him?" Even as he said it, David knew why; Quintus Tullius Cicero was competent, even good, as a commander but otherwise he was at best an amiable non-entity.

Exasperated, David turned to his bodyguard. "What do you think Pullo?"

Pullo looked startled to be asked. "Honestly, *dominus*? I'm glad it's you and not me."

David laughed at that. "I wish it wasn't me. And what have I told you about calling me *dominus*?"

Livilla was holding Moussa, who was having a great time trying to crumple the papyrus David was holding. Anything that crinkled or rattled was the best thing ever. As she shifted the baby out of reach of the paper, she said, "I don't know why you should be surprised. You are trusted by men of influence. That gives you influence that people will want you to use on their behalf."

"I suppose. I'm not sure how Caesar will react," David said.

"There's only one way to find out," Livilla said.

WHEN CAESAR WAS a child at his lessons, he learned about snakes which survived by looking as if they were poisonous when they really were not. It was important to know the difference, his tutor insisted, because snakes ate vermin and benefitted men and besides, snakes were sometimes powerful messengers of the gods. Killing one might bring dire consequences, but a truly poisonous viper must be dealt with. For Caesar, this raised an interesting philosophical question: do you kill a snake which may or may not be poisonous to take no chances, or do you risk being killed by the venomous snake you spare?

Caesar looked at the letter before him as if it were a snake which may or may not be venomous.

"Cicero certainly does not believe in modest proposals," Caesar said.

"How will your grandniece feel about such an arrangement?" David asked.

"Octavia will do what is required of her, for the good of the Julii and for the good of Rome. The question is, is this the right move to make?"

"Cicero certainly seems to think so."

"He would," Caesar said. "He would avoid civil war at any cost."

"Surely that is worthwhile?" David pressed.

"Perhaps. But what if it merely delays the inevitable? I would rather fight now rather than give Pompey time to marshal his resources to wage war against me at a time of his own choosing."

"Well," David said, "there is that."

"You're helpful," Caesar said sourly.

"Look, this is all new to me," David said. "I catch babies, not advise statesmen on marrying off their nieces. But no. I suppose if you view civil war as inevitable, it would be foolish to give him breathing room. Still..." David trailed off, as if he was thinking of something.

"Speak, *medicus*."

"I was just thinking of public perception, Caesar. It might make sense if you make the proposal. If Pompey refuses, you look like the reasonable man."

"Yes," said Caesar. "Yes, you may just have something there. Davidius, I want you to write back to Cicero. Tell him I will write my niece Attia and speak with her regarding Octavia and a possible union with Pompey. I will mention it in a letter to a few people in Rome I know are particularly bad at keeping a secret. We will see how Pompey reacts. What do you think of that, *medicus*?"

"I think politics is very much the same, no matter where one finds themself."

～

To Mark Antony, Caesar's course of action seemed clear.

"Screw the Senate," Antony said. "Screw Pompey and screw Cato twice."

"No thank you," Caesar said. "Not if you paid me."

Antony had always heard rumors that Caesar had had a few men while working his way through three wives and a string of lovers. Caesar's wife may need to be above reproach, but the man himself wasn't exactly pure as the driven snow. Antony said none of this, however.

"Honestly, though, who in their right mind would think Pompey would accept such a proposal? I have a hard time believing even Cicero would be that naïve," Antony said. He poured himself another glass of wine. "That being said, I think Davidius is right. The perception of the people matters. If they see you as the reasonable one and Pompey as unwilling to compromise, they will be more likely to support your cause. It certainly won't hurt your popularity."

"True," Caesar said. "But do you think it will help me with the Senate? Their next logical move will be to revoke my imperium."

Imperium was the authority Caesar enjoyed as a provincial governor and military commander. Most importantly, Antony knew, imperium provided Caesar with immunity from prosecution. To enter Rome without it would be suicide, perhaps even in the literal sense. Though it was hard to imagine someone with Caesar's ego committing suicide of any kind.

"I don't think this will help you with Cato and his faction, but then, you wouldn't expect it to. Let Davidius give a positive answer to Cicero. If nothing else, Cicero and his faction may stay neutral. They may even support you. Gods know I don't have much use for the man, but you have to take what you can get I suppose."

"Yes. Yes, I suppose that is the obvious course. I thank you for helping me clear my mind in this matter, Antony. And don't worry. I have some plans for you in this matter as well."

Caesar looked pleased with himself. Antony didn't know whether to be thrilled or frightened.

"This is unacceptable!" Pompey shouted. Cicero said nothing and merely looked on. Pompey was in a high temper, flushed in a way not even too much wine could bring on. "I will not be made a fool of!"

"No one's making a fool of you, Pompey," Cicero said, with what he hoped was not exaggerated patience. "It's a perfectly reasonable proposal, Gnaeus. Why not consider it?"

"Because I will not be seen crawling back to Caesar! If anything, he should be crawling to me."

"You know that will never happen," Cicero said. "Any more than he would agree to enter Rome without his army and trust your good graces to protect him. Why not restore the family bonds which once united you? Octavia is a perfectly good girl who will make you a fine wife. Rumor has it she is willing to divorce Marcellus Minor to marry you."

"Rumor," Pompey sneered. "Yes, Caesar played me like a golden lyre with that one. Wrote to the biggest blabbermouths in the Republic and begged them to keep this proposal a secret, on the pretext he was seeking their counsel."

That was remarkably well-played, thought Cicero to himself. Ever the tactical genius, Gaius Julius Caesar, whether the field of battle is war or politics. Not that the two were likely to remain separate for long at this rate.

The more Cicero thought about it, the more out of proportion Pompey's reaction seemed to be. He'd expected the man to be annoyed, certainly, even angry. But Pompey was in a towering rage, as if he would drop dead of apoplexy at any moment. If that happened, Cicero wondered if civil war could yet be avoided. Lacking a leader of proven military ability, Cato and his faction of Senators might back down. He knew that if Caesar caught an arrow in Gaul there was no question that Pompey would be the Republic's supreme power. Pompey was calming down, though, so the consequences of his temper would have to wait for another day. No, something else was going on. What could it be?

Like a stroke of lightning, it came to Cicero. Pompey was enraged at the offer of Octavia's hand because he'd already accepted another offer.

"Who is she, Gnaeus?" Cicero asked.

"What do you mean?"

"Who is your betrothed? It's the only thing that makes sense.

Caesar's maneuver enrages you because you have already accepted someone else's marriage offer. So, I repeat: who is she?"

Pompey's eyes widened. He looked like a child caught raiding the kitchens for sweets.

He sighed. "Cornelia Metella."

"Cornelia Metella," Cicero repeated. "Cornelia Metella the daughter of Caecilius Metellus Scipio? *That* Cornelia Metella?"

"Don't play games, Marcus," Pompey growled. "You know it is."

"I hope she is worth war, Gnaeus, I truly do."

"And what will you do?" Pompey asked.

That was an excellent question. Right now, the gods themselves only knew.

30

(BIBRACTE, CENTRAL GAUL, 51 BCE)

There were many wonderful things about being David Castellanos's wife, Livilla thought. He was a man like no other, from a place like no other. Of course only she, her father and her grandfather knew the true story of David and Kevin's origin. Most people chalked their eccentricities up to being foreigners, and it was easier to let them go on thinking that. David, for one, truly respected her and her opinions. He wasn't intimidated by her outspokenness. He seemed to enjoy it and said so.

And David was a far more involved father than she'd ever expected her husband to be. At first, she wasn't sure how she felt about that. Any Roman man would have left the child rearing mostly to the mother. But David enjoyed spending time with Moussa, reveling in the child meeting what he called "developmental milestones." And there was the prosperous lifestyle they were already enjoying thanks to David's medical skills. The life her first husband said she deserved but could never provide for her.

There were drawbacks. By and large David and his nephew seemed to have adjusted to their new lives. Some of their attitudes were utterly strange, though. Such as David's adamant refusal to own slaves, for the simple reason that he believed it to be wrong.

And there was his insistent punctuality. David kept his many strange devices largely out of view, except when he needed one of his medical instruments and could not make do with anything else. One of the items he kept hidden, yet consulted as frequently as possible, was something he called a "watch." It looked like a sundial, but it had moving hands and so did not rely on light and shadow in order to tell time. It was most ingenious, but it seemed to make David annoyed as often as not; when other people did not show up at the appointed time as marked by the "watch," he found it irritating.

Today it was David who was late. Usually, he was waiting for Soter when it was time for their lessons, but David had been summoned by Caesar before lunch and still hadn't returned.

"Come in, Soter," Livilla said to the tutor. She was never quite sure how to handle the tutor; he was one of the prickliest men she'd ever met.

"I suppose Davidius isn't here yet?" the tutor asked.

"No."

Soter let out a martyred sigh. "I suppose I shall wait." He sounded very put out.

"You can wait, or you can take it up with Caesar," said Livilla. She allowed herself a small moment of triumph at the look Soter gave at that. "If you'd rather not take it up with him, you can wait for David here. You can go to the kitchens and have Theda make something for you if you'd like."

"As you say," Soter said, and left for the kitchens.

Moussa fussed, wanting to be fed, and Livilla gave it no more thought.

David walked into his study to find Soter bent over his desk, as if he were looking for something. Probably checking up on me, David thought. Make sure I'm keeping up between lessons. Soter was a strict taskmaster and David wouldn't put it past the man to check up on him. He was bound to be disappointed, though; David's Greek was coming along; using Greek in his letters to Cicero was good practice. He had a long way to go, though. Cicero had sent him some medical texts in Greek and it was all David could do to puzzle out the words and follow the writing.

David cleared his throat. Soter jumped like he'd been touched by a live wire. His hand went to a small knife at his side. David could have sworn Soter looked guilty about something, but the expression of guilt—or whatever it was—was gone so quickly David couldn't be sure it was ever there.

"So. You're here at last. Shall we begin?"

"When did you start carrying a knife, Soter?"

"Ah-ah," Soter said. "Greek, please."

Soter believed in total immersion. During their lessons, David was allowed to speak, read or write nothing but Greek for the next two hours or so. On this day, David found paying attention a struggle. He was tired, after having attended an early morning birth and then going to a particularly draining skull session with Caesar. Kevin was still there. It was on days like today that he really missed coffee.

David still didn't know what he thought of Caesar's plans. On the one hand, it made sense to have a staunch ally in Rome. On the other, it would be a dangerous proposition. In the 21st century, people joked about politics being a blood sport. In first century BCE, in Rome at least, that metaphor was quite literally true. And allies of Caesar's had ended up dead. But if anyone could take care of himself, it was Mark Antony, and David knew from the history he was familiar with that Antony would acquit himself well.

David still didn't know how much he and Kevin were changing things, but that he was couldn't be denied. Kevin had insisted that the Battle of Alesia had gone differently than it had in their own timeline. Whether his nephew was right or not David couldn't say. History was not his strong suit unless it involved science or medicine. This victory had been even more decisive and had pacified Gaul at a stroke. The only campaign of note since had been undertaken mostly to test the new crossbows and Kevin's hwacha. History may be one of the gaps in

David's education, but even he knew that Caesar never had a multiple rocket launcher originally made in medieval Korea.

Events were gaining a momentum all their own. From some oblique statements by Cicero, David gathered the Senate was on the verge of recalling Caesar to Rome and revoking his imperium. Was that supposed to happen yet? Even Kevin, with is steel-trap memory, hadn't been able to say for certain.

David sighed. Just think about this timeline. That other one is gone. Gone forever. This is your home now, and you have to make the best of it.

Feeling oddly dispirited, David wrote a token entry in his journal. He always wrote that in English. He was starting to dream in Latin now, over a year since he was thrown into the past. There were only three English speakers in the world, and it was kind of nice to have a language he understood and almost no one else did. Secrets were a valuable commodity in this day and age, and if no one else could read his except Kevin—who was family and who he trusted with his life—David felt safe.

He looked over some of his other notes. Among the books he'd brought with him, on paper and loaded on his laptop, David had some showing obstetric equipment from the days before high tech had computerized just about everything. David had copied the sketches and given some to Cleon to see if he could reproduce them. An old-fashioned fetoscope—a tube flared on both ends used to listen to the fetal heartbeat—wasn't a patch on an ultrasound, but David wanted to be prepared for the time when his technology inevitably failed. He couldn't find what he was looking for, though. Maybe he'd thrown the papers away? They were just rough drafts anyway; Cleon had the clean copies.

David felt arms encircle his chest. He looked up and smiled at Livilla. She really did make this time and place bearable.

"Moussa finally go to sleep?" he asked her.

"At long last. I'm not sure he feels well," she said.

"I'll take a look at him in the morning."

For a few moments they said nothing at all. Livilla broke the silence.

"You seem very far away tonight."

"I suppose I am. I just miss...the place where I come from," David said.

"Tell me more about it. This great city, many times bigger than Rome."

David did. He talked about the Metropolitan Museum of Art, going to Yankees games, and where to find the best hot dogs. What a hot dog even was. He wouldn't be going home again, but sharing his former life made his present one more bearable.

ONE DAY more or less bled into another in Bibracte for Kevin. Over the months that followed, a few minor revolts flared up and were promptly put down. Far from satisfied, Caesar had been tense, a tension that did not ease when he departed to attend to provincial business in Cisalpine Gaul in Mutina. Mark Antony said once it was as if the world were holding its breath. Caesar's return was a violent exhalation if there ever was one.

"Two legions, Marcus. I had to give two legions to Pompey! They are pulling my teeth a molar at a time." Caesar took a deep gulp of wine. He must be upset, Kevin thought. Caesar was a sipper, not a gulper. And he did not even seem to notice that Kevin was even there.

"Better a molar at a time than all your teeth," Antony pointed out.

"If Pompey were smart, he would have pulled all my teeth at once," Caesar said.

"Pompey's problem is that he's not as smart as he thinks he is," Antony said. "From what I've been hearing he's been acting more and more erratic."

"As have I. A ruse, probably. Gnaeus Pompey is a canny and dangerous enemy. Never forget that." Rounding on Kevin, Caesar said, "Where's that uncle of yours? I want him here too."

"Delivering a baby," Kevin said. "Lucius Vorenus managed to

knock up one of his slaves and she went into labor. You know he won't leave till the baby is born and he's sure everyone is healthy."

Caesar grumbled but did nothing more. Neither did Mark Antony. Antony had made the mistake of trying to pull David away from a delivery and it was one of the few times Kevin had seen his uncle truly angry. Kevin found it amusing that even Caesar knew the limits of his power here but given the man's current mood he kept his amusement strictly to himself.

"No matter," Caesar said after downing more wine. "This affects you both directly in any event and I can tell Davidius what he needs to know later."

"I'm not sure I like the sound of that," Antony said. Neither did Kevin but in his case silence seemed the best course.

"You are going to be a tribune of the plebeians for the coming year, Antony. Your candidacy has been announced and I've made sure you will be elected. You will need to go to Rome to take office."

Antony looked like he needed a drink himself now.

"What is the 'tribune of the plebs?'" Kevin stumbled. His Latin was fluent now, but some of the formal words still gave him trouble.

"It's a great honor, of course, but why me?" Antony asked.

Caesar answered Kevin's question. "The tribune's primary power is the tribune's veto, his ability to block measures from the Senate. I need someone I trust on hand to veto any attempt to revoke my powers as a provincial governor and strip me of my military power."

That was all well and good. But more than one of Caesar's allies had ended up dead, Kevin knew. And while Kevin also knew Mark Antony was no coward, Antony was very much attached to his healthy, living person. In theory, a tribune was sacrosanct and safe from attack. In practice, who knew what would happen? Kevin remembered the Gracchi from high school Latin. Being Tribune of the Plebs hadn't saved either of the Gracchus brothers.

In the end, though, no one had a choice. Antony, Kevin, Uncle David. No one. They were Caesar's men, their fates bound to his. Where Caesar pointed, they would go. In Mark Antony's case, that meant Rome.

"You do me a great honor, Caesar. I shall start making preparations to return to Rome immediately.

"Should I tell Uncle David and Livilla?" Kevin asked.

"I will handle your uncle. He shall have his role to play, same as you."

Kevin wasn't sure he liked the sound of that, either. He knew Uncle David would like it even less.

THE SPY OPENED the small scroll. It was tiny, almost small enough to arrive by pigeon. A small scroll for a small message. By now, the spy was used to the strange, looping scrawl his contact used in his letters. It was one word, and to the point.

"*Fiat.*"

The spy straightened in his seat. It was time to set things in motion. His mole inside Davidius Medicus's household would do what needed to be done.

SOTER FOUND himself dreading today's lesson. It's not that Davidius was a poor student. Quite the opposite, in fact. No, Soter's other employer had told him in no uncertain terms that today was the day he was to take all of Davidius's papers he could lay his hand on and turn them over. From there, they would be sent to Rome to parties unknown to Soter, though he had a few guesses as to who those parties were.

Soter took a look at the pouch of coins, half his promised payment. The other half would come when he turned over the documents at the rendezvous point. With the rest of his reward, he could buy Berenice out of slavery in Massilia and have enough left over to start their life together.

The longer he looked at the money, though, the more uneasy Soter became. The son of a Greek father and Egyptian mother, fear of the gods ran deep in his blood. And there was no sin greater than that of betrayal. He only hoped his love for Berenice would make up for what he was about to do in the gods' eyes. Putting those thoughts firmly out of his mind, he set out across Bibracte toward Davidius house.

ONE OF THE things Caesar liked best about Davidius was his punctuality. The man did not believe in wasting time, an attitude Caesar very much approved of. Better to waste money than time, Caesar had always thought. Money could be earned back if one was sufficiently clever; time, once lost, could never be recovered. Which was why it was strange the man was late. If he was attending a patient, Caesar was sure he would have sent a messenger. His nephew perhaps, or that slave Cleon that Antony was borrowing, Or Pullo.

Despite it being summer, the late afternoon had grown cool, and one of the slaves had lit a brazier. Caesar stared into the glowing coals and tried not to worry. If it were anyone else he would be angry but Davidius had a knack for timeliness that would shame Janus himself.

Caesar's body slave, Alexander, came in. Looking very distressed. Caesar knew at once something was wrong; Alexander had been told not to interrupt.

"Caesar, you need to come at once. It's Davidius."

LIVILLA WAS ENJOYING a quiet family day, something that was far rarer than these days than she would have liked. Especially days that allowed her to lounge in bed with her husband. Theda had even nursed Moussa before leaving for the market and buying food for the next few days. From down the hallway, Livilla heard her son start to fuss. She threw on the dress on the floor next to the bed. David stirred and mumbled something about her staying asleep.

"No, I'll get him. He's probably hungry."

"OK love," he said.

She walked down the hall toward the room where Moussa slept. David called it the "nursery." She thought the practice of children having their own room was strange, but she'd never lived in a house with this much space before and wondered if the custom she was used to came from necessity. In Pagus Mardani, no one's home except Matwyn's had more than two rooms.

A room David used for his studying and writing was in between her and David's room and the baby's. Motion inside caught her eye. She stepped inside to see Soter. He was bent over the desk, studying papers and putting most of them into a leather bag.

"Soter, what—"

Soter whirled around. Livilla caught a brief glimpse of something metal in his hand before she felt it drive deep into her stomach, ripping upward. She opened her mouth to scream but nothing came out. She slid off the blade and onto the floor. Her last coherent thought was surprise at feeling no pain, only a sensation of her life draining out of her.

GAIUS JULIUS CAESAR was used to taking charge and bringing order from chaos. But he was utterly uncertain about what to do here and it burned him. There was nothing worse than feeling helpless. It was not a feeling he was used to.

Caesar had insisted on coming into the room at Davidius's home. He could see at once the wound was mortal. Of that he was certain. He'd seen any number of grievous battlefield wounds that had seemed fatal and yet the wounded had survived, Pullo included. An indomitable will to live could carry someone far. But only so far. Seeing the gaping tear in Livilla's midsection, the huge amount of blood soaking her clothes and the rug underneath her, the strongest will in the world would not hold life in the body. That she'd lived even this long was miraculous.

Davidius was a man possessed, doing what he could to revive her, despite serious wounds of his own. He, too, had been stabbed and was bleeding heavily from his side. Finally, though, he gave up.

"There's nothing I can do," he screamed to heaven. How Davidius was still conscious Caesar could not even guess. The doctor began raving in a strange, growling language that sounded like a refined version of some barbarian Germanic tongue. Caesar didn't need to know Davidius's native language to know that he was cursing the limits of his extraordinary skill.

Davidius leaned down next to Livilla, who struggled to say something. He nodded, and then screamed before at last lapsing into unconsciousness. Livilla was dead.

A tear slid down Caesar's face. He was unashamed.

31

(BIBRACTE, CENTRAL GAUL, 51 BCE)

Kevin barely remembered the funeral and the days that followed. Livilla's burial was one of the only times he'd left his uncle's side. Theda was wet-nursing Moussa and Uncle David was hovering between life and death, wavering in and out of consciousness. Kevin spent his time reading aloud to his uncle and drowning himself in strong wine and the last of the cigarettes. The smokes made his chest hurt but at least he felt something. The sensations kept him grounded, kept him in the physical world. That and the works of George Orwell. Kevin had finished *Nineteen Eighty-Four* and was now reading *Homage to Catalonia*. Uncle David had never had much time to read for pleasure, at least in the 21st century, but the man loved his Orwell.

Kevin put the book down. Carefully, he lifted the sheet covering his uncle and then lifted the thin tunic. Gingerly, he then removed the linen bandages covering his uncle's side. Celer and Corvus had done a good job stitching the stab wounds but despite their best efforts, using methods David himself had taught them, infection had set in. As a last resort, Kevin had intervened and raided his uncle's dwindling stock of antibiotics. The stitched knife wounds still looked red and angry but weren't weeping pus like they had been, and his uncle's fever had broken.

After the breakup with Sandy, Kevin knew, his Uncle David had been in a bad place. David had confessed one night, during their Atlantic crossing, that he'd also been relieved. Even so, his uncle had felt the need to sail an ocean to a remote island refugee camp in order to get over his split. Kevin had decided he had to come along for the ride to make sure David didn't do anything stupid, as well as to hopefully give him a sense of purpose his own life had been lacking. They'd sailed the Atlantic and ended up two millennia back in time with no hope of ever going back to the modern age.

"Kevin?" Kevin Rhee-Castellanos—who'd picked up the Roman name of Keffin Castellanus Flavens—startled when he heard his uncle's weak voice.

"I'm sorry I woke you up, Uncle David. How do you feel?"

"Please tell me everything was a dream?" Kevin's heart broke when he saw the look on David's face. His uncle was pleading with him, begging Kevin to tell him his wife's death was just a bad dream. That it wasn't true. Kevin didn't need a mirror to tell him the expression on his own face. His uncle's reaction said it all. David Castellanos broke down and wept. Harder than anyone Kevin had ever seen.

"Uncle, be careful. You don't want to rip out your stitches."

"She was my rock, Kevin. My soulmate!"

"I thought you didn't believe in soulmates," Kevin said, wiping the tears escaping his own eyes.

"I held back at first, remember? She was half my age but she was an old soul. As old as Matwyn. But she helped me, Kevin. Livilla helped me cope. Cope with life here. When she was with me, I could deal with the smell, the cruelty, the darkness of this world. You're a science fiction buff, aren't you Kevin?"

"Yes."

"Did you ever think—that we're in an alien world? Just as if we'd gotten on a ship and crossed the stars? I remembered a conversation I had with a girl in college. It was a marathon bull session, we were high as kites, and I was probably trying to get in her pants. Can't remember if I succeeded. Somehow, she got onto the subject of the merits of Roman civilization versus medieval. She called the Romans 'morally obtuse.' She probably read it in some book she was reading for a class. I remember arguing with her, probably just to argue. I'm sure I was taking out my ass. Now I can see she was right." David sank back into bed. His brief time of consciousness had taken every bit of his energy and he was lapsing back into sleep.

One piece of news Kevin hadn't revealed was the revelation of who Soter had been working for. Caesar said he'd long suspected a traitor in their midst, ultimately reporting back to Pompey. Trebonius had disappeared the very night Soter was returned to Bibracte. The Mardani men and Pullo, eager to see justice for Livilla, searched for Trebonius, but he was long gone.

Kevin lit a cigarette from the butt of his old one. He looked out the window He didn't see the stars tonight, only the dark.

THE DREARY WEATHER matched Caesar's mood. Despite the pronouncements of his own priests and the ancient woman the people of Bibracte called "Old Mother" that his path was clear, Livilla's death had cast a pall over everything. Unlike almost everyone else, Caesar didn't feel guilt over Livilla's death. For one thing, he was not a sentimental man. For another, it was clear from Soter's testimony—under expert torture, no less—that she and Davidius had simply been in the wrong place at the wrong time. Panicking upon being discovered, Soter had impulsively reached for his knife.

But the Tenth Legion, which had spent most of the last two years since the Battle of Alesia based in Bibracte, was taking Livilla's death hard. Hardened veterans were even less inclined than Caesar to be sentimental, yet they'd adopted the young woman as a camp mother or a little sister. Many of the men regarded Davidius as Asclepius in mortal guise and so were inclined to view Livilla as the consort of a god at the very least. When Soter was captured and brought back they had to draw lots to see who would put the tutor to the question. Quintus Tullius Cicero had said it was only the supreme discipline of the evocati, the most experienced veterans of the legion, that kept the rest of the soldiers from either tearing Soter limb from limb or riding out into the night to bring Trebonius back to face their own brand of justice.

Trebonius was another reason Caesar felt so sour despite good omens. That had taken him by surprise, and he was not a man who liked surprises. It was the basest betrayal by a young man he'd given a good position and every opportunity to succeed. I may be famous for my mercy, thought Caesar, but Trebonius made sure he would never receive it. And Jupiter help him if Davidius ever catches up to him.

Caesar cast his mind back once again to the strange conversation he'd had with Davidius on that wine fueled night many months ago. The one where Davidius had put forth the notion that a new world was created when a choice was made. As their conversation wandered, they somehow came back to the philosophy of history. Caesar was inclined to agree with the notion that the course of events were restrained or unleashed by the actions of great men. Davidius had put forth the notion that the mere action of an insect flapping its wings in Serica could cause a great storm in Rome. Caesar had laughed at the thought then. He wasn't laughing now. One half-Roman village girl had been killed and now an entire legion was had their blood up.

The tall African doctor, Corvus, had come while Caesar was lost in his thoughts and stood patiently waiting to be acknowledged. A good man, this one. Worthy of the newly created rank of *medicus evocatus*.

"Yes, Corvus?"

"Flavens asked me to come to you. Davidius is strong enough for visitors."

Pompey was beyond fury. Arminius Comedentis tried to hide his fear. Gnaeus Pompey Magnus either didn't notice or didn't care. After a while, Comedentis stopped hearing words. Pompey's rant became a meaningless drone.

"—said this would happen smoothly. That we would gain useful information we could use to bring down Caesar. Instead, we get a conquering hero wielding the sword of avenging justice with a battle-hardened legion at his back. And Rome is ready to explode! Already there have been fights between my gangs and Caesar's and do you know what his people have been shouting as their battle cry? '*Memento Livilla!*' So tell me, Comedentis," Pompey loaded Arminius's cognomen with scorn, "how are we going to salvage this mess?"

Comedentis tried to think. He thought he'd gamed out all the possibilities in his head, a thousand times. But Trebonius had managed to bungle this operation about as badly as it could have been bungled. On top of that, word had raced out of Bibracte well ahead of the turncoat legate. That latter was no doubt thanks to Caesar and his loyalists, and it was brilliantly played. Trebonius was (presumably) still enroute but stories of the innocent and beloved young woman killed at Pompey's direction, with her upstanding husband badly wounded coming to her defense, was all over Rome. Caesar's partisans, both in the Senate and on the streets, were predictably outraged but many people who had not been on either side were joining the wave of revulsion sweeping the city. Up to and including Marcus Tullius Cicero. Up till now Pompey and Cato had counted Cicero as at least a soft supporter of their cause but no longer. Cicero had not declared for Caesar but had given a scorching speech at the Senate that would have flayed Pompey alive had Pompey been in the chamber that day. He was not, luckily. Some were whispering that Cicero's speech was even better than the ones he gave attacking Cataline so many years ago.

Arminius Comedentis had been taught, in his own youth, that when you couldn't explain away an inconvenient fact, that you did what you must to turn it into an advantage. So that's what he did here.

"Pompey, this mess will surely blow over. How sustained can outrage be over the death of one barbarian woman from nearly the end of the world be? By next week the mob will have something new to distract them and the Senate will be obsessing over some other matter."

"I had it, Comedentis. In the palm of my hand, I had it. Caesar would have been stripped of his imperium. Helpless."

Comedentis seriously doubted Caesar would have allowed himself to be helpless in any situation. He'd long ago realized that Gnaeus Pompey was prone to flights of what some might call "magical thinking" because like many powerful men Pompey rarely had to deal with setbacks. Comedentis had it on good authority, for starters, that Mark Antony would have been named Tribune of the Plebs with or without Trebonius's bungling in Bibracte, effectively giving Caesar a veto over Senate business. Especially on matters such as extending or terminating Caesar's imperium.

"Perhaps, Pompey, this course of action will force Caesar's hand. Perhaps he will be provoked into doing something rash. You know as well as I do how fickle passions run in this city. If Caesar, for instance, entered Italy with an armed force who knows what the reaction would be, especially on the street? People want stability. If they see Caesar as starting a new civil war they will flock to you."

"Yes," Pompey said, taking Comedentis's words in. "Yes, you could be right. You are always able to look at things, Arminius, without emotion. That's why you're so valuable."

Arminius Comedentis allowed himself a small smile. Pompey would think he was smiling at the praise he'd just served up. Let him think that. Let him also think Comedentis actually believed what he'd just said. If Pompey were thinking rationally he, of all men, would know Caesar would never be forced into rash action, least of all by a hot-blooded legion. No matter how strong a bond the Tenth had with him.

No, Arminius Comedentis smiled because he'd made Pompey believe he himself believed those words. Perhaps the situation could be salvaged and Comedentis could make Gnaeus Pompey Magnus the master of the Roman Republic. If nothing else, it would buy him time. Arminius Comedentis was very good at what he did. He was sure there would be someone, someone very wealthy, who could benefit from his talents. Even if that someone were outside Rome's borders. Because ultimately, Arminius Comedentis's loyalty was to himself only. He would do what he must.

DAVID LOOKED up to see Corvus enter the room, and his eyes widened a little when he saw Caesar enter behind him. He hadn't had many visitors. Kevin was a constant presence, of course. Ferrarius had come a few times, but never stayed long. David sensed that it hurt his father-in-law too much. Even Antony had come by once, but on the whole David just didn't want to be around people.

Caesar took the empty stool at David's bedside, then took David's hands in his own. It was all he could do to not break down all over again when he saw the mixture of grief, anger and sympathy in Gaius Julius Caesar's face. There had been many times, in the almost two years David had known Caesar, when David had wondered whether Caesar felt genuine emotion at all. Pullo had said that even when announcing his own daughter Julia's death, he'd been emotionless. David wondered if emotions were just more tools for Caesar to use and put aside when needed.

Now, though, David saw it differently. Caesar wasn't unfeeling; rather than no emotions, he felt things so strongly that he had no choice but to put up barriers. Barriers so strong they made the siege works at Alesia seem flimsy by comparison. Kevin had squirreled away countless hours of his favorite movies and TV series to bring with him, back when their adventure involved sailing first to France and then to an island refugee camp in the Atlantic off the coast of Spain. David had never been much of a *Star Trek* fan himself, but they watched an episode of *Star Trek: The Next Generation* where Captain Picard mind-melded with Spock's father, Sarek, because Sarek could no longer blockade his raging Vulcan emotions with cold logic. Maybe Julius Caesar was secretly a Vulcan. What David was sure of was that he was getting a very rare look behind a mask that almost never came off.

"I am so sorry, my friend," he said.

David teared up, and he cursed himself. He didn't want to lose again, especially not in front of this man.

"I couldn't even go to her funeral, Gaius," David said. He'd never used Caesar's praenomen before, but it felt right here. "Trebonius even took away my last chance to say goodbye."

"She died in your arms at least. I think that is what she would have wanted."

"No," David said, not even trying to hide the bitterness he felt. "What she wanted was to grow old with me. Have more children. Work by my side to make peoples' lives better. That is what she wanted. Not an untimely death because of some political squabble."

Caesar looked almost offended at that. "Political squabble?"

David looked up at Corvus. "Corvus, may I ask for privacy with Caesar please? Normally—"

Corvus cut him off with a gesture. "This is your house, Davidius," the African said in his soothing voice. "Your wishes are paramount. I will be nearby, should you need me."

Once Corvus was gone, David fixed Caesar with a stare. He couldn't believe what he was about to say, or who he was about to say it to, but he didn't care anymore. If he were put to death as a lunatic, so be it. A big part of him didn't want to be alive anymore anyway. Kevin would be fine; he had made himself too valuable to lose. And Kevin would see to it that Moussa would be well cared for.

David took a deep breath and blurted it out. "Caesar, I'm from the future."

Caesar just shook his head, as if he wasn't sure he was hearing what he heard. David started to repeat himself, but Caesar cut him off.

"You've been lying to me?"

David actually laughed. He'd just said the most outrageous thing he could ever imagine saying, and Caesar was upset at being lied to? It was absurd.

"No. Not really. I was—will be—born about 2000 years from now, in a nation that is the Rome of its time, located across the *Mare Atlanticus*. My nephew and I were sailing for the coast of Gaul, though in the world and time I was born in, it was known as France. We went through a strange mist and found ourselves...here. So the story about Kevin and I being lost travelers is true. We just said that and didn't correct everyone's assumptions."

Caesar's initial anger mutated into grudging respect. "Did Livilla know?"

"She knew. So does Ferrarius and two others back at Pagus Mardani. Dolovix does not know, nor does his father."

"The Mardani chieftain?"

"Borodur, yes."

Caesar said nothing. Instead, he looked at one of the books on the table next to David's bed.

"I could kill you outright for such an outlandish story," Caesar said. "No one would question it, either. Not really."

"Why don't you then?"

"Two reasons. The first is that you have been loyal to me, and I have seen the loyalty you inspire. Without even trying. Though I don't know Ferrarius personally terribly well, I do know his type supremely well. I know he wouldn't have approved of his daughter marrying you if he thought you were some madman claiming to be from days the forward face of Janus can barely perceive."

"You said there were two reasons. What's the second?" asked David.

"The second reason is quite simple. I believe you."

"You...believe me?" David was stunned. "How? Why?"

Caesar picked up the book he'd been looking at, a copy of Orwell's *Nineteen Eighty-Four*, though this particular edition used numerals rather than spelling out the title.

"This codex. The paper seems quite cheap compared to good

papyrus. But the printing is so small. So uniform. It can't possibly be hand-copied and yet how else do you print such a thing?"

"Believe it or not, it is printed by a machine. A machine that can make many copies, so the book is inexpensive. Less than an hour's pay for most workers where I'm from."

"What is this work called? I presume the symbols on the outside are its title?"

David almost laughed again. Of course. Romans used, well, Roman numerals for their numbers. Caesar didn't recognize the Arabic numerals on the cover of the book.

"The title would be translated, literally, as 'one thousand, nine hundred and eighty-four.' In the case of this story, the title comes from the year the story takes place in."

"What is the story about?"

David summarized the bleak world of the story's hero, Winston Smith, and his doomed struggle against the all-powerful Big Brother. Caesar was fascinated.

"You'll have to translate it. I would love to read it."

"I will, when there's time. Most of the books I have are medical textbooks and I would like to translate those as well." He showed Caesar the book that had been underneath *Nineteen Eighty-Four*— Orwell's memoir *Homage to Catalonia*. "You'd really like this one. It's the same writer. He fought in a civil war in what you would call Hispania.

"Hmh. Yes. Very apt, given the current situation." Caesar sighed. "Physician, we need to talk business. Are you with me? Or do you still believe, as Cicero does, that civil war can be avoided?"

David looked to his left. Where Livilla should have been but wasn't, and never again would be.

"Where I come from, we have an expression: 'ride or die.'" David said the phrase in English. He didn't have the mental energy to try translating the expression into Latin. "A 'ride or die' is the person you are loyal with even to death. I'm ready to be your ride or die, Gaius Julius Caesar, so long as you promise me one thing."

"What is that, Davidius Castellanus Medicus?"

"Justice. Pompey and everyone working for him whose actions contributed to Livilla's death must be held accountable."

"That is a condition I have no problem agreeing to, Davidius."

"Then you are my ride or die."

Caesar laughed a genuine laugh. "Ride or die," he said in English with such a thick accent he could barely be understood. "I like that."

He reached out, and David and Caesar clasped forearms in the Roman version of a handshake. Once, David had thoughts of staying out of what he knew must come. But if he was honest with himself that had become impossible long ago. Maybe as long ago as when he agreed to travel to Alesia with Pullo. Maybe it was never possible. No matter. *Alea nunc mittitur.* The die was now cast.

EPILOGUE
(BIBRACTE, CENTRAL GAUL, 51 BCE)

Memento Livilla.

Remember Livilla. Dr. David Castellanos, OB/GYN, stared numbly at his wife's tomb. The outside world had ceased to exist. He had only a vague sense of his almost one-year-old son squirming in his arms. Nothing else mattered. Was this whole life he'd lived for the last three years just a dream? A beautiful dream turned nightmare? Would he wake up in Manhattan, in the late spring of 2022, having overslept? Would the physical pain in his side, where he'd been stabbed, be gone? Would the far greater pain over the loss of the person he felt closest to in the world—closer, even, than his nephew—also be gone?

Memento Livilla.

"It's beautiful, don't you think?" Gaius Ferrarius, Livilla's father, spoke. That's right, David thought. He's here. With me. With us. David took a moment to look at the monument taking shape over the place where Livilla was buried. The place David had not chosen for her because at the time of her burial he'd been hovering between life and death himself, doubly endangered by two stab wounds and the infection that had set in.

"Yes," said David in a voice that seemed like it was spoken by someone else. And it was beautiful, if incomplete. Livilla had become beloved of the Roman soldiers here. She was a stand-in for all the mothers, sisters, lovers and wives the men had left behind to march with Gaius Julius Caesar. On their own, the men of the Tenth Legion started building a rough stone obelisk over the grave. Antony, on his own authority as Legate, organized the efforts and was besieged by volunteers. Caesar himself finally stepped in, chose a work crew consisting of the men he felt most deserving of the honor, and secured marble with which to clad the monument. A sculpture of Venus Victrix, the legendary ancestress of Caesar, would top the obelisk. That was still in the works.

Memento Livilla.

The Tenth Legion had already adopted it as a battle cry. According to reports already filtering back from Rome, pro-Caesarian street gangs were swarming the streets, chanting it. She'd become a martyr to people she barely knew or never met.

Memento Livilla.

The words were carved in stone, at the base. David had no choice of course. There was a part of him—a tiny part—that wished he *could* forget. Wipe his brain, like the characters in the movie *The Eternal Sunshine of the Spotless Mind* and erase all the pain. Though even that didn't really work, did it? That was kind of the point of the movie. David had no choice. He had to remember Livilla. He had to remember her for their son, who would never have memories of his own of her. And he had to remember because he had to make sure that Gnaeus Pompey Magnus and everyone working for him would not forget her.

Memento Livilla.

David could understand, now, why some people in the claws of grief just wanted the whole world to burn. It was a trope that seemed ridiculous, he thought. Until it was you. Trapped in your own grief. David still had only a vague understanding of the fight that had all but paralyzed Roman politics for nearly a decade. Despite Cicero's best efforts to educate him in their letters, David still didn't know the finer points of the dispute between Caesar's *Populares* and the *Opti-*

mates led by Cato and Scipio, and of late embraced by Pompey. David didn't want to burn the whole world down. Just the part of it represented by Pompey. David Castellanos would gleefully light that world ablaze.

Memento Livilla.

"Come," Ferrarius said. "We should get Moussa indoors before he gets a chill. And we should all get a good night's sleep before we leave for Mutina in the morning."

David said nothing. He just followed Ferrarius, one leaden step after the other.

Memento Livilla.

CHARACTER LIST
(IN ORDER OF APPEARANCE)

(H=historical figure)

Gaius Julius Caesar (H)—Triumvir of the Roman Republic; proconsul of the provinces of Gallia Transalpina and Illyricum.

Gnaeus Pompey Magnus (H)—Triumvir and rival of Julius Caesar.

Marcus Licinius Crassus (H)—Triumvir and would-be conqueror of Rome's eastern rival, Parthia.

Arminius Comedentis—One of Pompey's secretaries; also Pompey's spymaster.

Delfina—One of Pompey's household/kitchen slaves; lover of Comedentis.

Wyatt Carver—Multi-billionaire entrepreneur; funder and director of the Mohole 2 project.

Taggart "Tagg" Schmitz—Old money politician and would-be dinosaur slayer.

Herman Grayson—Carver's executive assistant (mentioned, non-appearing).

Dr. Nicole Kapoor—Molecular geneticist attached to Mohole 2.

Dr. David Castellanos—Obstetrician; traveling to a refugee camp on an island near Spain as a volunteer doctor.

Kevin Rhee-Castellanos—David's nephew, adopted by David's sister when she married Kevin's mother, Anne. Anne and Kevin Rhee fled North Korea when Kevin was 7.

Matwyn—Medicine woman/priestess of the Mardani tribe of Northern Gaul.

Livilla Ferraria—Acolyte of Matwyn's, daughter of the blacksmith Gaius Ferrarius.

Gaius Ferrarius—Blacksmith and exile; fled Rome during the reign of Cornelius Sulla.

Sevel—Mardani mystic; father-in-law of Ferrarius, grandfather of Livilla. Later revealed to be Steadfast Cooper, an Anglican vicar who went missing near the Cornish port town of Torbay in 1688.

Borodur—Headman of the Mardani.

Kellax—Deceased husband of Livilla (mentioned, non-appearing).

Bennozha—Friend of Livilla's. Bennozha was found in a canoe with her dying mother that washed ashore near Pagus Mardani. She was adopted by the Mardani and later becomes the lover of a young Roman officer named Gaius Cornelius Chlorus and gets pregnant by him. Much later, David will realize that she came from North America after the canoe she and her biological parents were in was swept out to sea.

Ramira—Friend of Livilla's, wife of Jobix. Very pregnant when the story opens.

Gaius Cornelius Chlorus—Young man of the aristocratic Cornelii family, serving under Caesar to gain military experience. Junior to one of the legionary quaestors.

Publius Cornelius Aquila—Uncle of Chlorus; priest and lictor to Julius Caesar.

Paisley Goodwin—Childhood friend of David's (mentioned, non-appearing).

Ralph Chaplin—David's high-school Latin teacher, and later Kevin's (non-appearing).

Hipparchus—A Greek doctor originally accompanying Chlorus. Later turns up with Caesar at Alesia.

Jobix—Husband of Ramira.

Galwyn—Mother of Ramira.

Chloe—Younger sister of Ramira.

Allodur—Oldest son and heir presumptive of Borodur.

Vibius Pullo (H)—Legionary veteran, assigned to Chlorus's command to help season Chlorus. Later hired by David as a bodyguard.

Surena (H)—Parthian Great General and victor over Crassus at the Battle of Carrhae.

Auldur—Newborn son of Jobix and Ramira.

Aethelwynn—Adoptive mother of Bennozha

"The Archdeacon"—Operative seeking to drive James II off the English throne and replace him with his Protestant daughter, Mary, and her husband, William of Orange.

Livia Elizabeth Cooper—Young daughter of Rev. Steadfast Cooper. Later, she marries Gaius Ferrarius and gives birth to Livilla Ferraria. Later dies in childbirth.

Vercingetorix (H)—War-leader "king" of the united tribes of Gaul; surrenders to Caesar at Alesia (mentioned, non-appearing).

Mark Antony (H)--Protégé of Caesar, legionary legate, and Caesar's cavalry commander.

Postumus Agnus—An especially tough *evocatus*, or elite veteran, of Caesar's forces

Lucius Celer—Medic and member of the Remi tribe of Gaul who has adopted a Roman name and manners.

Corvus Numidicus—Former hostage trained in Roman medicine, from a North African tribe inhabiting the fringes of the Sahara. Exile became permanent when his tribe was wiped out. Claims his birth name is unpronounceable by anyone who can't speak his native language. Fellow medic and chief assistant of Celer.

Gaius Trebonius—One of Caesar's legionary legates.

Dolovix—Younger son of Borodur and leader of the Mardani slingers joining Caesar at the siege of Alesia. Later becomes a leader of the auxiliaries who name themselves the "Dracones Sagitarii," or

"Dragon Archers" after the Roman version of the hwa-cha Kevin develops.

Vorenus—A centurion serving under Caesar.

Alexander—Caesar's body slave.

Theda—Mandubii woman, one of the refugees expelled from Alesia during the siege. David hires her to help Livilla. Theda gives birth to a daughter she names Davidia.

Cleon—Young Greek slave leased by Antony to help with engineering. Fascinated with machines. He and Kevin quickly become friends.

Quintus Claudius—One of Caesar's officers. David removes his appendix when it becomes inflamed.

Labienus (h)—One of Caesar's commanders.

Phillip—Young legionary; messenger during the Battle of Alesia.

Quintus Tullius Cicero (H)—One of Caesar's commanders and brother of Marcus Tullius Cicero, senator and legendary orator.

Marcus Tullius Cicero (H)—*That* Cicero. Strikes up a correspondence with David.

Marcus Porcius Cato (H)—Aka Cato the Younger. Leader of the Senate party known as the Optimates. Rabid opponent of Julius Caesar.

Soter—Hired by David as a Greek tutor.

Zeno of Corinth—Would-be salesman of a *polybolos*

Old Mother—Aedui seer and midwife who lives in Bibracte.

Moussa—Gaius Castellanus Moussa Ferrarius, son of David and Livilla.

Saturninus—Legionary; injures his knee in a battle against Germanic raiders.

Trixia—Gallic woman who lives in Bibracte.

GLOSSARY

Acetum: Concentrated vinegar, made from bad wine.

Ad Urbe Conditum: "From the founding of the city." Though Romans typically used the names of the elected consuls to identify years, they had a system of numbered years they used to hold certain infrequent sacred games and festivals at the correct time. Year zero was reckoned as the founding of the city of Rome.

As: Lowest Roman coin in circulation, analogous to a penny, though its purchasing power was greater.

Ballista: A crossbow-like artillery weapon used by the Roman legions, capable of throwing large spears or stone or iron balls as needed. Smaller versions were the *arcuballista*, mounted on walls; the *carroballista*, mounted on a cart or chariot; and the *manuballista*, a hand-held version.

Caduceus: Winged staff with two twined snakes. Symbol of the god Mercury.

Codex/codices: The forerunner of the modern book, as opposed to the scrolls favored by many ancient civilizations.

Cornicens: Roman brass instrument resembling a skinny tuba or sousaphone.

Cursus honorum: Literally, "track of honor." The ladder of political offices of the Roman Republic starting with quaestor and culminating in consul.

Denarius: Roman silver coin, equal to 10 *asses*.

Dominus/domina: Honorific given to a superior. Depending on context, it may be translated as "lord/lady" or "master/mistress."

Evocatus: Elite veteran of a Roman legion, one who is asked to re-enlist.

"Fiat": "Let it be" or "make it so."

"Gloria eius in cinerem": May his glory become ashes.

Hwacha: A primitive multiple rocket launcher used in medieval Korea.

Imperium: Absolute authority granted consuls and certain provincial governors in the Roman Republic. This authority could be granted or revoked by the Roman Senate.

Kalends, Nones, Ides: The fixed points of the months of the Roman calendar. The Kalends was the first day of the month; the Nones the ninth day; the Ides either the 13th, 14th, or 15th day depending on how long the particular month was. All other days are referred to in relation to the Kalends, Nones or Ides.

Libra: Roman pound, equal to approximately three-quarters of a modern pound.

Lictor: One of an honor guard assigned to certain high officials of the Roman Republic. Lictors carried axes bundled in rods called *fasces*.

Medicus: A doctor or physician.

Mile (Roman): Equal to approximately .97 modern mile.

Oppidum: Roman term for the fortified villages and towns of the Celtic tribes of Gaul. Frequently built on hills, which made them easy to defend and very hard to capture.

Pes/pedes: Roman foot, slightly less than a modern foot (1 pes=.97 foot).

Pilum: Javelin carried by Roman legionaries.

Plebs/Plebeians: The common people of the Roman Republic. They had their own assembly, led by elected tribunes, that theoretically acted as a check on the Roman Senate.

Polybolos: A repeating crossbow or ballista developed in Alexandria in the third century BCE.

Pontifex Maximus: Chief priest of the Roman state religion.

Populares and Optimates: The two opposing factions of Roman politics in the Late Republic. The Populares claimed to champion the interests of the plebeians; the Optimates were the party of the Patrician elite.

Praenomen, nomen, cognomen: The three parts of a Roman man's name. The praenomen would come from a limited list of male names, such as Marcus, or Gaius. The nomen denotes the *gens,* or clan, the person comes from. The cognomen could be an inherited or acquired nickname, usually denoting a physical trait, such as Chlorus (pale) or Calvinus (bald). A person could gain a cognomen as an honorific. Gnaeus Pompey earned the cognomen Magnus (the great) due to his military victories. Women typically were given a feminized version of their fathers nomen, such as Gaius Julius Caesar's daughter, Julia.

Quaestor: One of the junior political offices in the Roman Republic, charged with overseeing the public treasury. In the military, a legions quaestor functions as paymaster and releases funds to pay for supplies.

Solidus: Roman silver coin.

Spahbod: "Great General." Military leader of the Parthian Empire in present-day Iran, answerable only to the Parthian emperor himself.

Spatha: Short sword carried by Roman legionaries.

Testudo: Literally, "turtle." A defensive formation in which legionaries form a shield wall on four sides and overhead, meant to protect from arrows and other projectiles.

Toga virilis: The formal toga; wearing it signifies a boy has become a legally adult Roman man.

Other fine books available from Histria SciFi & Fantasy:

For these and many other great books visit

HistriaBooks.com